Profile: Isaac Cone

Rosey Sparks was found dead on July 2nd, 1982. She died from blood loss caused by an injury to her neck. Her trachea–and all the surrounding skin, muscle, and cartilage–had been eaten off; from her chin to her collar was bare spine.

Apparently Rosey had a fear of spending the night alone, so she invited close friends for sleepovers quite often. All the time, her neighbors saw men and women pulling up at sundown and leaving by the next morning. It never struck them as odd. Most of the time, it went completely unnoticed, except for one odd fellow who the neighbors couldn't help but gawk at. He was a tall, portly man–a gargantuan really–with a large beige bandage under his glasses that covered his right eye. But stranger than all that combined, his skin was greyish-purple.

The cops immediately investigated the personnel at Colbean Chemicals. They manufactured silver nitrate which gave several of the employees severe abdominal pain, respiratory illness, and, in rare cases, a noticeable case of argyria. Only one man, however, was missing an eye: Isaac Cone, the line manager.

Safety equipment was not being properly enforced at Colbean, and so when Isaac lost his goggles they allowed him to keep working as long as he wore his reading glasses. These glasses did not offer proper protection, and when a bolt blew off the side of a vacuum pan, a shard of its thread flew right under Isaac's lenses and shredded his iris.

Isaac Cone was arrested outside Northeast Iowa Regional Airport. Isaac had a license to pilot, and once he caught word he was a suspect, he attempted to avoid authorities by hopping onto the Comanche he leased. They got him in handcuffs just as he opened the cockpit.

Isaac was brought down to the police station for questioning. But before they could get anything out of him, Cone's lawyer, Shelby Frederick, arrived on scene. She demanded to know why they went after Isaac in the first place. They had no evidence. It just seemed that of numerous men and women who visited Rosey, Isaac seemed to be the most distinguishable, but the color of your skin is not an admission of guilt.

The police kept their mouths shut and let Isaac free. After all, they had what they wanted. Before Cone arrived, maintenance installed "dream catchers" in their police station bathrooms; removable filters placed at the bottom of toilets that allow water to pass through, while capturing the fecal matter. Cone had been given plenty of coffee while waiting for his lawyer and produced a mess in the stall that was immediately taken to forensics. Human muscle protein was found in Isaac's stool.

Shelby Frederick was still unsatisfied with the question of why Cone was targeted in this investigation to begin with. There was no witness testimony that had placed this man at Rosey's on the specific night of her murder. This whole case was caused by his appearance. "Unless..." suggested Shelby to the officers. "Unless of course, you were entirely aware that silver-exposure, the same kind that could lead to purple-pigmentation, could also lead to psychotic episodes..."

Erethism argyria. Silver could theoretically affect the central nervous system, but whether that affect is harmful or beneficial is very much still up in the air. But the courts agreed to acknowledge the existence of such a disease if it kept the arresting cops out of trouble and Cone behind bars.

Reporters, unconvinced that silver deviated Cone's thoughts and feelings that day, would often interview the cannibal in an attempt to expose the lie. But Cone, faking it or not, would always reply with such creative answers that it's still uncertain as to the legitimacy of his illness.

"Why the neck, Isaac?" asked one reporter. "Why devour the neck and nothing else?"

"She sucked out my soul," he answered, straight-faced, "I needed to get it back before it left her esophagus."

"Were you two entangled in a romantic relationship?" asked another.

"It was romantic for me, but she was purely predatory," explained Isaac. "She'd been tracking down salt-of-the-earth types like myself. Easy souls doing hard work."

"Do you regret it or do you still think she deserved it?"

"I currently feel lots of remorse for what I've done, but in that instant all the moral fiber had been sucked from my body. I didn't care if she died till I got my soul back in place. By then, it was far too late."

Five years ago, I decided to sign up for a prisoner pen-pal program in hopes of conquering my carcerophobia, an irrational fear of prison. My therapist suggested that communicating with a prisoner could change my perspective on a couple different matters.

First, I get to know what a real criminal is like; what they say, what they think, and what they do. My therapist thought this would help me recognize the difference between criminals and myself. I've done bad things and I've had bad thoughts, but she assures me, it's nothing like the real bad guys behind bars.

Second of all, she wanted me to learn what it was actually like in the prison system; so I could see that if—worst-case-scenario—I did end up in jail, I wouldn't be immediately shanked, raped, and forced into the servitude of a hate group.

The pen-pal program matched me up with Isaac Cone and I almost immediately felt better when he explained how he got to jail. Murder and cannibalism were certainly more extreme than my crimes against humanity: drug use and some light verbal abuse against an ex. Isaac also explained that, despite refusing to join the Aryan Brotherhood after numerous offers, he never experienced anything sharp and metal in his chest or up his butt.

A year into our letters and our conversation veered away from the things I needed to hear to things Isaac wanted to say. He listened to music a lot; they gave him his own MP3 player to keep him calm. It was an old SanDisk stuffed with popular songs, mainly classic rock. Isaac liked to talk about the strange ideas these songs gave him. He made up dark twisted stories from otherwise benign lyrics. His head was like a filter; the lyrics went in one side and came out the other with this tinge of middle-aged depression and psychosis. I eventually convinced him to start writing out his interpretations, and that's when I got "Margaritaville", the popular Jimmy Buffet song reinterpreted as a southern gothic. By the time I read the closing paragraph, I knew I'd stumbled across a great idea.

The minds of cannibals were well worth milking for their artistic talent. People constantly choose their next read based on the author's ethos. Wellness advice should come from a doctor; true crime from law enforcement; and science fiction should come from an engineer. So shouldn't dark fantasy come from the mind of a cannibal?

The cannibal subculture has been long disenfranchised due to the horrible prejudice that one loses their right to be heard when they ingest the cells of another human being. I counter that unique experiences build unique voices. These authors have tasted forbidden knowledge, and so their minds are chemically and cosmically separated from our own.

Starting with Isaac, I began to seek them out and add their written word to my growing collection.

Margaritaville

Destin Dune was married to his wife Kimmy since they dropped out of high school in '74 to start a family at 17. Destin worked as a ball boy at the local country club; Kimmy worked as a park ranger. They saved up, and with support from all their parents, they bought a house in Black Hammock, a tiny suburb right outside of Orlando.

Living near Orlando, people often asked Destin if he liked to frequent Disney World. He didn't. It's a place for kids. Adults need their own getaway, and Destin's was Key West, an eccentric island off the southern coast of Florida. He didn't visit regularly, just when it was necessary. It was usually towards the end of summer. Tennis season was at its peak and Destin would be off at work more than usual. This gave his wife plenty of time to move fat-cats and barflies in and out of their bedroom without notice.

Destin would eventually find stray clothes or a misplaced watch, and he'd know his wife was at it again. He'd never file for divorce however, not with a three-year-old in need of a structured home. So in order to forgive her, he had to complete the ritual. It starts with a seven hour drive to the Key West Firehouse.

"Is Rey around to chat?" asked Destin, walking up to a probie cleaning out the wheels of the fire engine. Rey Roja was the town's distinguished fire chief. He was also a prolific dealer.

"What for?" he replied, with a look of suspicion.

"I'm here to... patch up the fire hoses," said Destin with a wink.

The man looked Destin up and down. "Only conchs see Rey."

"It didn't used to be like that," said Destin with a grimace. Conchs were locals to Key West; direct descendants of white immigrants from the Bahamas. Rey Roja grew up around conchs; he trusted conchs. Tourists, on the other hand, could be snitches or undercovers.

"I take care of the tourists," the probie reached out and shook Destin's hand. "I'm Javon."

Javon dropped his sponge into his bucket and stood up tall. He towered a foot over Destin and was in peak physical shape. Javon motioned for Destin to follow him. He led Destin to the changing room, where he pulled open a locker marked 17. He reached up to the top shelf and pulled out a tiny glass bottle with a cork in it; the kind you find filled with colorful sand in a souvenir shop. Destin's name was printed on the side. The little white crystals inside looked innocent enough, but they were really bath salts smuggled onto the island from a cartel in France.

"Did you pay already?" asked Javon. He handed Destin the bottle.

"Shouldn't you know that?" asked Destin, snidely. "And shouldn't you have asked before you handed me the drugs?"

Javon gave Destin a threatening glare.

Destin sighed. "No. I didn't." He pulled out a roll of cash, held together by a thick orange rubber band. "Does Rey know you rely on an honor system?"

"Everyone just knows not to lie to us," growled Javon, "we talk to the Chickcharnie." Javon widened his eyes and stood up out of his chair slowly. As he walked away he pursed his lips and made a bird call; a series of sharp little whistles as he wandered off. Destin shook his head and pocketed his drugs.

Destin then got back in his car and drove to a local dive just down the street. It was Sloppy Joe's, a bar most famous for tending to Hemingway's needs during his 30s. Ever since, it's been a hub for postmodernists looking to capture the late author's essence and subvert the Hemingway hero.

Destin's host for the weekend, Gregg, would be working behind the bar at Sloppy Joe's, catering to these artists. When Destin arrived, Gregg was serving gin & tonics to minimalists and Zombies to the maximalists. "Come behind the bar and help me for a bit," said Gregg, seeing his friend walk in. "Milly's heel got chewed by a coral snake, so we're short staffed."

Destin was staying for free at Gregg's, so he used this opportunity as a way of paying him back. Destin quickly flung up the bridge and hopped into the backbar, where he immediately dropped himself in front of the nearest customer without a drink. She was a young ironist wearing a mini-dress covered in silver sequins. It was impossible to tell whether she actually found it fashionable or not. She had tense lips, and eyes hidden behind a pair of square sunglasses.

"I'm new here," said Destin, "so please don't ask for anything too complicated."

"Alright then," said the girl with a delicate laugh. She squinted at the specials written in chalk on the wall. "How about the frozen margarita?"

"Frozen?" Destin turned around and faced the chalkboard. "Like on the rocks?"

"Let me show you," called out Gregg. He got Destin's attention, then pulled out a curvaceous chalice from the cabinets underneath the bar. He then cut a lime into pieces and used one of the quarters to wet the edge of the glass. Then he rubbed the rim in a tray of salt. Finally, he sat the glass under a large machine with a revolving drum in its center; it perpetually sloshed around a bright green slushie. Gregg pulled a lever under the drum and ejected the frozen mixture. *Brrrrrr.* Gregg

10

handed the drink over to Destin, and Destin served it to the customer.

"Transcendent," purred the girl. She took a snapshot of her drink with a Polaroid in her purse.

"I think you can handle the next one yourself," called Gregg. Destin nodded. It seemed like a simple recipe. He'd make one for himself just to practice. Of course, his would be a little special.

Destin pulled out another margarita glass from under the bar and cleaned it out in the sink. Destin loved Gregg, but he didn't love his hygiene. Destin took one of the remaining quarters of lime and rubbed it around the edge of the glass. He then poured some of his bath salts into an empty ashtray and rubbed the rim against the particulate. Then, he shoved the glass under the machine. *Brrrrrr.*

Destin toasted his glass with the girl at the bar then took a sip of his creation. His drugs mixed well with the flavor of the booze. The bitterness in the bath salts combined with the citrus in the margarita mix and made something like grapefruit. Thinking about grapefruit made Destin suddenly hungry for breakfast foods.

"Do you have any cereal?" asked Destin to Gregg.

Gregg shook his head. "Why would we have cereal behind the bar?"

"How 'bout some eggs?" asked Destin. "Like for fizzes and flips..."

Gregg cracked a smile. "There's no fryer, Destin. Here." Gregg tossed his house keys to Destin. "Go home and get yourself something to eat. Wash up while you're at it, you sweat like crazy when you take that stuff. Meet me back here when you're done."

Destin nodded. He slipped out the door when Gregg wasn't looking. He didn't want Gregg to see that he took his drink with him.

As Destin traversed the back alleys between the shops downtown, he could feel the effects of the drugs kicking in. It was the most incredible euphoria. The sensations of the island were spine-tingling. The traveler's palms looked like peacocks and the banana trees smelled like candy. The crashing waves were just down the street and the clear blue sky was slowly fading into orange. Everything was going dark, and so were all the bad thoughts in Destin's head. His wife's infidelity suddenly seemed like a drop in the ocean.

Abruptly, Destin's tripping was interrupted by the obnoxious polychromatic flashes indicating a police presence. Destin checked his surroundings. He'd wandered into the back parking lot of a crab shack. The cops were all circled around a body lying next to a glaucous Gremlin parked illegally between two spots.

Hearing his sloven footsteps, an officer sensed Destin's presence. Destin saw one of the officers turning to face him. He wasn't too afraid of open container laws, but the drugs in his pocket had him paranoid. He quickly tossed them in the hedge of frangipani growing to his right. He then just kept walking forward as though nothing happened.

"I'm gonna have to ask you to pour that out, sir, and dispose of the glass!" shouted the cop as he came within Destin's proximity. "I can't see you drinking that."

"Oh... I'm so sorry Officer," said Destin with a sincere disposition. "It's such a nice night out, I just wanted to enjoy my drink outside."

Destin tossed his drink out onto the asphalt, then set the empty glass on the ground.

"Well there's outdoor seating at Louie's and Two Friends," groaned the officer. "It's not just a silly rule, it's dangerous to be intoxicated out here all by yourself."

"My apologies," said Destin, sinking the corners of his mouth. "Is that boy okay?" From where they were standing, Destin couldn't see any blood on or around the body. The only strange thing was that the boy's shirt appeared to be on backwards.

"No, no," frowned the officer, "he had a run in with the Chickcharnie."

"I keep hearing that word," muttered Destin.

"He's an enforcer. There's a lot of drug trafficking in the area. This kid was only sixteen, but we found nine bags of coke under his shirt. Somebody put a hit out on a rival mule. The Chickcharnie delivered."

The cop dropped his head with a look of disgust. A street lamp reflected off the oil on his forehead, making Destin wince. The officer's heavy Coppertone suggested he may be from out of town. Possibly out of state. Out-of-town cops meant these crimes were something serious.

Saying all he needed to, the cop turned around and walked back to the crime scene. This gave Destin an opportunity to grab his drugs out of the bushes and take a different path to Gregg's trailer park. However, when Destin went to retrieve his bottle, it wasn't where he'd left it.

That's when Destin heard a low buzz. He stuck his head deeper into the bushes and saw a cat purring happily with his drug bottle clenched in its jaw. Destin sneered. He looked the cat up and down, noting its features in case it ran. Its fur was clean and white. Its nose was black. It had an extra finger on each of its paws.

13

The cat suddenly took off. Destin charged through the bushes, and followed closely behind its tail. He wanted to call out for it to stop, but he needed to wait till the cops weren't within hearing distance. Destin looked around the street and could see he was heading back the way he came, but before they reached Sloppy Joe's the cat turned the opposite corner and led him down Whitehead Street.

Suddenly, the cat clawed its way up the side of a brick wall. The drugs in Destin's heart made him feel like he could ascend it himself, but he realized how suspicious he'd look. He decided to walk around the border until he could find a legitimate entrance. He wound up in front of a gateway leading into a beautiful limestone estate.

"Gates unlocked," called out a voice behind Destin. "We can just head inside."

Destin turned around and saw two young men dressed for a high-class occasion. The boy on the left was wearing a mint blazer with matching pants over a pink shirt. The man on the right was wearing an argyle three-piece and a black cabbie hat. Both of them had their top three buttons undone, letting the breeze reach their chests on this hot summer day.

"Uhm..." Destin's mind churned. "Do you live here?"

"No... this is Hemingway's old house," said the boy on the left. "Aren't you here for the séance?"

"I'm actually looking for a cat," replied Destin, "he took my souvenir."

The boys looked at each other and snickered. Then they looked back at Destin.

"Did he take your drugs, man?" asked the boy on the right.

14

"What?"

"The cat took your drugs, right?" asked the boy on the left. "Look, it's no big deal. These cats were bred to steal drugs. Hemingway taught them to do that."

"Why?"

"Free drugs..."

"Right."

The boys walked past Destin and opened the gate. They encouraged him to follow them onto the yard.

"I think I see your stash, man," said the boy with the hat. "Psspsspss." The boy's noises attracted the kitty, who came up close to receive some pets. The boy nabbed the bottle out of the cat's mouth. He eyed the substance inside with a look of curiosity. "What on Earth are you smoking?"

"I don't smoke it," said Destin, taking the bottle from the young man's hand. "I eat it. I snort it. Or I put a little up my ass."

"Is it crank?"

Destin shook his head. "It's white lightning."

"Far out," laughed the boy with the hat. "You shouldn't miss this then, man." The boy pointed towards the front door. "We're making contact with the spirit of Ernest Hemingway. Sounds like your stuff might help you see into that other world."

"I don't know if I'll fit in," grimaced Destin. "Look how I'm dressed." Destin pointed down towards his old satin shirt, complete with a torn chest pocket and sweat stains under his arms.

"You'll be fine." The boy with the hat grabbed Destin's arm and yanked him through the front door. Before he knew it he was in the dining room of Hemingway's old home, at a long table surrounded by hippies. There were civil rights poets, freelance journalists, and even a nudist. Destin recognized one of the writers. It was the woman in the silver sequins he served at Sloppy Joe's. She talked to neither person sitting beside her. It seems she came alone.

"Please, I want everybody comfortable," said a woman in a Miami Dolphins t-shirt and a white dhuku. She was this evening's spiritualist, a zine, the common word for a Bahamian medium. "Help yourself to Hors d'oeuvres and refreshments."

Destin never got his breakfast food, so he made due with limeade and a little piece of sponge cake.

"Surrounded by his personal possessions I will be able to conjure his spirit before us," said the zine. "Once he's present, I will be busy keeping the connection clear. Feel free to ask him any questions."

The zine placed her palms flat on the table and shut her eyes. White noise blew through the air as her powers took over and filled the room with a shadowy aura. Suddenly, the darkness was illuminated by a bright ball of turquoise light in the center of the table. It rose from the tablecloth up into the air, then began to bubble. Its volume expanded and it took the shape of a skull. Slowly, sinew and skin overlaid the bone and the head of Ernest Hemingway became clear.

The glow from the face lit up the room. Everyone stared in disbelief. For most of the gathering, this was their first interaction with a soul from beyond the grave. Destin himself had seen ghosts numerous times when under the influence; mainly unresolved victims of vintage hurricanes wailing about the sirens hurting their ears. They may or may not have been hallucinations.

16

"Ask him something," murmured the zine.

"Is it possible you were a homosexual?" asked the nudist, standing up onto his feet in excitement. His exposed groin was caught in the glow of the spectre. Everyone looked away.

"I'll only be answering questions concerning art..." replied Hemingway, sternly.

"But it could explain all the failed marriages..."

"Do as he says!" shouted the zine. "If he becomes distraught, I will lose the connection!"

"What was the single greatest inspiration of your life?" called out the man in the mint suit.

The floating head turned to face him. "Defeat. My characters suffer defeat as much as I have. Some writers gravitate towards authoring miraculous victories to give the reader the sense of winning a ballgame, but tenured readers crave the opposite. They want to know they're not alone. They want to see men and women handling disappointment in wonderfully unhealthy ways. It makes us feel normal."

"If I read you something I've been working on, will you offer your wisdom?" called out the girl in the silver dress.

Everyone around the table groaned.

"It's short!" she shouted. She licked her lips, then pulled out and unfolded a piece of notebook paper. "Carne agua celulosa. Ají... maltodextrina! Sal avena ... "

"Uh, pause, I can't understand Spanish," excused Hemingway.

"You don't have to!" argued sequins girl. "Lecitina de soja... especias! Tomate en polvo... azúcar... cebolla en polvo-ácido cítrico…" The words kept flowing and they were lost on most of the audience. One Spanish-speaking poet could tell the lady was listing ingredients, but she didn't quite get what it was hinting at.

When it seemed sequins girl had finally finished, she folded the paper up and placed it back in her pocket. The room fell into an awkward silence.

"Clap. Don't be rude," scolded the zine. Everyone did as she instructed.

"Uh, I think it was… abstract… in a good way." Hemingway feigned a smile and looked sequins girl in the face. "Maybe add some context first." He then turned away. "Anyone else?"

Suddenly all the poets and authors around the table wanted to hear Hemingway's thoughts on their work. Hemingway obliged, but as the pieces went on, his comments only grew more and more belittling. His final words on a poet's sonnet left them wondering if they should depart from the field altogether.

"No more critiques!" snarled the head. "Does anyone have an actual question?"

The room fell silent. Suddenly, Destin, who was sitting quiet till now, felt an urge to speak. He knew very little about literature, reading it or writing it, but Hemingway wasn't just books; he was an interesting take on the human condition. The drugs inside of Destin wouldn't let him pass up such an opportunity to explore the world of philosophy.

"I'm not sure if this pertains to art, or on all things really," stuttered Destin, "but how do you persist when you've lost all your purpose?"

The crowd around the table all turned to face Destin. Being the most under-dressed, Destin certainly looked the type of person who lost his motivation.

The ghost nodded, then contemplated the question deeply. "I find hunting and fishing to be quite reinvigorating, especially during periods of debilitating writer's block," explained Hemingway with a look of delight. He liked this question. "In fact, I once had a religious epiphany after shooting a marlin with my Thompson. It was like finding a hidden passage in the back of a Bible. When taking the life of a beast, you feel like a Roman myth. You cannot kill a monster without leaving a legacy. Thus, returning your sense of purpose..."

"Transcendent..." A flash startled the room, as silver sequins took another shot with her camera.

"Please. No photos," groaned the zine. "It makes the spirits shy."

"No, no, it's quite fine. It's now or never anyways. I'll be departing..." explained Hemingway. "I fear such a fine question will be the best I get from this crowd, I bid you all a good night."

Hemingway's head suddenly melted back into a skull, which then bent and contorted into a lumpy ball. The ball inflated, then popped like a bubble. The shadows vanished and the room's fluorescent lighting took over.

"That concludes today's séance."

Most of the artists left tips for the zine, but Destin had nothing left to give. His drugs weren't cheap, and what little he had left needed to go towards paying for gas. Destin dipped out of the estate before anyone could see he didn't pay up, leaving the other hippies far behind him.

Destin decided to continue his original journey back to Gregg's mobile home, a double-wide with bamboo walls, parked in a trailer park along the waterfront. It was a whimsical scene. By the time he got there, Gregg's shift had ended and he was standing outside with his shirt undone and his pants unzipped. Under his right arm was a short woman with long blonde hair and a black tank top. Her pants were old military fatigues; she tore off the legs to make them into shorts.

"Well it's about time you got to the party!" shouted Gregg with a drunken gleam. "You want to tell me why you never showed up for work..."

Destin shook his head. "The island had other plans for me."

Gregg shrugged and patted his girl on the back. "Treasure, this is Destin. Destin... Treasure." Treasure smiled and reached out her hand. Destin stared at it with a crooked expression. "Well don't be rude," growled Gregg. "We've got to show these ladies a good time."

"Ladies," enunciated Destin. "There's more?"

"Of course there's more," laughed Gregg. "Check the trailer, bud! She's been waiting for you."

Destin shook his head. "I thought it'd just be you and me tonight. I didn't know there'd be any women."

"Isn't that the whole point of this?" asked Gregg.

"Of what?"

"The drugs... this weekend!" shouted Gregg. "It all seems to be pointing towards you having the courage to... shag somebody else."

"It's not revenge I want, Gregg," said Destin. "It's the healing power of the island. The night I met you I was going to hang myself by a coconut tree. But then I got high and the island led me to your bar. You talked me up and nursed me back to health. When I repeat the process, I always end up hearing the one thing I need to keep on living."

20

"You sound like such a tourist," laughed Treasure. "It's nothing special out here, honey."

"Neither are you," sneered Destin. The comedown from his last hit was making him all edgy. "Who knows? Maybe the island led you too, but maybe this is just the best you can be."

"Fuck you!" snarled Treasure. "Bones!"

"Hey now, let's all calm down!" called out Gregg.

"Bones, we got a fucking brat out here. I could use your claws!" shouted Treasure. She turned around and faced the trailer. "Bones, get out here!"

There was no response.

Everyone looked towards the trailer. There seemed to be a thin layer of smoke rising out of the top of the door frame and one of the open windows.

"She was supposed to be monitoring the shrimp!" snarled Gregg. "I hope she didn't fucking burn them."

Gregg led the charge and everyone came running inside the trailer all at once. Bones was lying on the couch, passed out. Her hair was in an awkward position, flipped down in front of her face.

"She fucking fell asleep!" yelled out Gregg. He went to go check on his shrimp. They weren't burning, but the water in the pot was boiling over sending steam towards the ceiling.

"Bones, you look kind of funny... are you okay?" Treasure lifted her locks. "Ack!" she screeched. "She ain't got no face!"

"Oh God," exclaimed Gregg. He came up beside Treasure and took a closer look at Bones. He pulled Bones' hair upwards, peeling her head off the pillow. "That's because her head's on backwards..."

Destin felt the mood suddenly shift from fighty to scared shitless. Trying to calm himself down, he gave himself another hit, pulling a rock from his bottle and sticking it between his cheeks. He cowboy-walked up to the body and stared with disbelief. Immediately, his mind went back to the crime scene he walked through earlier.

"Where the fuck were you two?" shouted Destin.

"I took Treasure to the bushes so you could have the camper," said Gregg, looking dumbfounded. "I like doing it in the open. It reminds me of summer camp."

"So someone snuck in?" exclaimed Destin. "Maybe it's the killer..."

"What killer?"

"The cops told me 'bout it... the Chickcharnie," said Destin. His eyes went wide. "He's a hitman."

"I thought that was just a story..." said Treasure softly.

"What do you mean?"

"When I grew up in Nassau, we used the Chickcharnie to scare children," continued Treasure. "It's a little sprite with the face of an owl. If it doesn't like you, it'll put a curse on you where your head gets flipped around so you can only see behind your back. The working witches supposedly brought them over as familiars; I guess one got free..."

Destin nodded and scratched at the back of his head. His drugs were kicking-in and his exhilaration was returning.

"Call your madame, Treasure. She'll need to take care of the body," suggested Gregg. "Till then, let's all hole up inside."

"No!" hollered Destin. "I need to find out who did this."

"That's not our job, man."

"But it is!" countered Destin. "I'm supposed to catch this Chickcharnie."

"What's entitled you with that?"

"The island gave me a sign tonight. I was told by an ancient spirit that the hunt could restore my vigor," recalled Destin. "I just needed a monster."

"It's too dangerous."

"This town is always dangerous!" replied Destin. "Every time I take my drugs, it's dangerous! But the risk is always great when the reward is so precious."

The zing of his drugs stung at Destin's face. He quickly ran up to Bones' body and searched her dress for pockets. He couldn't find any. "Did she bring a purse?"

"No."

"I want to see if she was a mule," explained Destin. "Is she carrying any merchandise for anyone?"

"No... we are the merchandise!" replied Treasure. "The pimps and the dealers are all the same people. If they're taking out each other's mules, they're taking out each other's girls. It's stiff competition."

Destin's mind was going a zillion miles per hour. "The killer knew she was here. He must have followed her here from wherever Gregg picked you up," deduced Destin. "So where were you?"

"The Garden of Eden," answered Treasure.

"Where's that?"

"Top floor of Ed's Isle."

"How come I've never heard of it?"

"They don't talk about it," explained Treasure. "It's clothing optional, a good place for girls like me to advertise."

Ed's Isle was like Sloppy Joe's without the history, or the friends behind the bar, so Destin never felt compelled to go before. But the added gimmick, a rooftop nudey bar, definitely intrigued him. It wasn't the perversion or voyeurism, or even the freedom, it was simply the novelty. The way it contrasted the very clothed, very secure life in the suburbs back home.

As soon as Destin walked in, he spotted the only stairwell open to the public. He walked two flights of stairs to the second floor. There was only one room, a changing room at the midpoint between the clothed world and the world of the bare. Being clothing-optional, Destin skipped past the checkpoint and climbed up two more flights of stairs to the main event.

When he got to the top, he walked into a wide open space. It wasn't as packed as he thought it would be. Most of the patrons were dispersed amongst several small blotches surrounding the tiki bar in the center. These groups were either homogeneously clothed or homogeneously naked. There was no in-between.

The edges of the roof were lined with special panels that kept things blurry from the outside, but were completely see-through from the inside. There was a bulky woman trying to get atop her husband's shoulders so that she could reach her breasts over the glass; she was trying to flash the passerbys below. A burly bouncer quickly tore the women off of her man's shoulders. He warned them not to do it again or they'd be removed.

24

Destin sat at the bar. He didn't have enough money for a full margarita, so he just ordered the tequila. He squirted a lime in his mouth, licked some of his drugs off the back of his hand, and downed the shot in a single gulp. He spun his barstool around and turned towards the crowd. He tried to let the magic of the island guide him towards his perpetrator. He let his eyes drift around wherever they felt best, which just so happened to be a six foot five female towering over her friends in the corner of the rooftop. She was butt naked, showing off a bony frame that reminded him of his wife but in much more exaggerated proportions. It was trippy. The woman turned to face Destin and saw him staring. She smiled. She approached.

"$200," she said, taking a seat beside Destin. "I'll let you call me mommy."

"Uh, no."

"Big sister? Baby-sitter?"

Destin winced and shook his head.

"Surely you don't think me old enough to play grandmother?"

"Certainly not."

"You stare like that at a tall girl and she assumes you're thinking dirty things."

"I was," snickered Destin. "You look as though my wife got shot with gamma rays."

The tall girl looked at Destin strangely.

"Does anyone just come here and watch you?" he followed up.

"You..."

"No I mean... like all the time. Maybe he disappears for a bit, but he always comes back."

The girl nodded. "Yeah I guess so." She pointed towards the staircase where Destin had entered. There was a man leaning against the wall beside the doorway. He was watching people come and go. His face looked sullen. Destin immediately recognized him. He was the nudist from the séance. Seeing him in public, he appeared to be far smaller than he was around the dining room table.

"I don't think he's built enough to turn somebody's head around," replied Destin. "Let me phrase it like this... has anyone ever looked at you like they were trying to kill you?"

"Are you saying there's a killer on the loose?" she asked with a look of concern.

"Oh don't fret!" assured Destin. "You're probably fine, sweetheart. You could just step on him if he tries to fuck with you."

The hooker gasped. She looked offended. She slapped Destin's cheek and walked off.

Destin felt confused. He really meant no harm by the comment.

"Unhand me! Unhand me!" shouted a familiar voice across the bar. The bouncer from earlier was now shoving a lady towards the exit. She was wearing silver sequins. "Do not touch my purse!"

"Lady, we just need to make sure anything you took was destroyed."

"I didn't take anything!" she snarled. She got her arm free and quickly dashed down the stairs.

26

Curious, Destin followed after. He squeezed between a nude couple coming up the stairs. He cringed as their body hair brushed against his shorts. He made it through and saw the sequins girl make it to the bottom floor.

"Wait up!" He shouted from above her.

She stopped and looked up at him.

"Do you remember me?" He called out to her as he continued down the stairs.

"Of course I recognize you," sneered the woman. "It's abundantly clear the island's been planning for us to conversate. We don't just run into each other all the time by coincidence."

Destin was impressed. Another believer in the magic of the island. "I'm Destin," he said.

"I'm Fe," said the girl in the silver sequins. She motioned for Destin to follow her. She sat down at the bar. Destin did the same.

"Why were they throwing you out?" he asked.

"I tried capturing a few of their physiques on camera," explained Fe. "It seems that goes against club policy."

"They can't have you shooting unauthorized pornography."

"Pornography?" Fe bit her lip and held in her laugh. "My photos aren't meant to be enticing." She pulled out the photo she took at Sloppy Joe's. "It's funny how things crossover onto American soil and they suddenly grow ugly. Margaritas turn into ice cream. Tacos turn into Taco Bell. This whole place is America's ugly version of beach culture."

"And you're an expert on what beach culture is supposed to be?"

"I'm from Acapulco," she said with a sly smile, "but don't sound so offended. I'm not looking to ridicule your home."

"It's not my home."

"Then why do you look so hurt?" She squeezed tightly on Destin's shoulder. "If this place has special meaning to you, that's valid. I'm just looking to capture the difference between our worlds. Beauty is in the eye of the beholder. And if it makes you feel any better; I consider myself very ugly on the inside."

She reached into her purse and pulled out an ornate compact mirror with a cliff diver painted on the back. Then she pulled out a short plastic straw. "All this audacity. My heart rate is flying... I need to calm down." She crushed up a pill in the makeup compartment and stuck her straw to the powder. She sniffed.

"What's that?" questioned Destin.

"Valium," she answered. "You want some?"

Destin nodded. When you're on drugs, more drugs always sounds like a good idea.

Fe pulled her drugs in towards her chest. "What are you on right now?"

"White lightning."

"That's an upper. This is a downer."

"I mix my drugs with booze all the time. It mellows out the high."

"This is far stronger than alcohol," frowned Fe. "You don't want to pull yourself too hard in both directions. You'll tear, dear."

"But tears are ugly... don't you like ugly?"

28

Fe thought for a second. He had a good point. She nodded, then handed him her compact. He sniffed, then handed back the mirror.

"How much does your wife know?" questioned Fe. She noticed the ring on Destin's finger when he held up her mirror. "Be honest."

"She knows I'm here. And she doesn't care if I do drugs."

"A wife who doesn't care if you snort lines in paradise without her?" Fe rubbed at her chin. "She must feel she owes you?"

Destin nodded reluctantly. "Spot on." He looked uncomfortable with the subject at hand.

Fe deduced further. She thought for a minute, then snapped her fingers. "And that's because... she's wronged you, hasn't she?"

"Well yes," sighed Destin, "but only because I wronged her first."

"You cheated?"

"She cheated, because I lied." Destin shook his head. He cringed and scratched hard at the center of his shirt. The drug cocktail was burning his chest. "I promised her way more than I possibly could provide her with. Some people say I was just young and stupid, but I fear I was selfish and manipulative. I convinced Kimmy that a family with me would make her happier than Bryn Mawr. I painted this perfect picture of a happy suburban life, like we had growing up. But all I've managed to make for her is this... ugly version of it."

"And so... she can cheat?"

"She doesn't want to!" cried out Destin. "She has to..." Destin's head dropped. A warm bubble floating around his skull rested in his frontal lobe. He leaned back and let it slide into his brain stem. He heaved deeply and let his eyes close.

Reality suddenly began to blip in and out. Destin was awake and moving, but the sights went by too fast to process. Little clips of sound entered his mind, then disappeared before he could respond. Everything was just a blur, until someone sat him down in what looked to be some kind of salon. There he waited for a while, drooling into his lap, just trying to keep alive.

"I can't do this with you, Fe..." murmured Destin through the dizzying haze. "I've made it clear... I can't have sex with you..."

"Don't worry, we aren't," assured Fe, pulling off her stockings.

"Then stop... undressing."

"Darling, no. It's for the artist." She undid a thin strap around her waist and lifted up her shirt. She wasn't wearing anything underneath. Destin got lost in her beauty and focused between her legs. He could see everything. He felt his body perspire. Then he shut his eyes and held his breath. Everything went dark and mute.

The next thing he remembered was being on the grass of a townhouse two blocks from the shore. He was lying on somebody's front lawn. There was grass on the inside of his mouth. He spit it out and stood up.

"No encontraré otra mujer, que a mí me quiera como tú..." Destin heard singing. "A nadie más podre querer, oh no... Pues tú te llevas mi amor, todo mi amor." He turned to his right, towards the porch swing in front of the house. Fe was there, strumming a tune on the guitar.

"You let me fall asleep outside?" sneered Destin.

Fe stopped her playing and looked down at Destin from the porch. "I have one bed inside. You refused to share it with me."

Destin tried recalling the memory, but ended up wincing in pain. His head was throbbing. To add to the discomfort, his back stung like crazy. "I've got wicked sunburn. Why'd I take off my shirt?"

"To sleep." Fe went back to playing her song. "Nos dijimos adiós, tú me dijiste adiós a mí... Y yo te dije adiós, queriéndonos así..."

Destin walked up to the splintery white post holding up the canopy above the porch. The comedown from the drugs had him mad. As he woke up out of his slumber, the searing anger boiled over. He began banging his head furiously against the post.

"Stop that!" shouted Fe. "What is the matter with you?"

"I wasted the fucking night away."

"Of course you didn't..."

"I'm supposed to be catching a criminal..."

"Your Chickcharnie is right here!" She sneered and held out a polaroid.

"What?" exclaimed Destin. He peeled his head off the pole and looked at the picture.

"This is the photo that got me kicked out of the bar," she explained. "When I showed it to you last night everything clicked, but I couldn't understand your gibberish."

Destin ripped the photo out of her hand and held it up close to his eye. The camera was focused on a three-hundred pound tourist with a pina colada spilled in his lap. Behind him, however, was somebody much more fit. Somebody Destin recognized. "Javon," said Destin, softly. "My dealer."

31

"It's him?"

"It makes sense. The island led me to him from the very beginning. He's at the bar. He's involved with the trade. He's built like a monster. It's him."

"So what? Now you kill him?"

Destin nodded. "Now I kill him."

"How?"

"In his element," replied Destin with a confident gaze. "Tell me, what's the ugliest place you've captured here?"

After a long walk, Fe had Destin in front of an old dilapidated storefront near Boca Chica Field. The letters had fallen off the sign out front, but the silhouette said Lenny's Loggerhead Jerky. This was a reminder of Key West's dark past as a giant in the turtling industry. Hunters would harpoon the loggerhead sea turtles and scoop the meat out of their shells. The business was retired years ago when conservation efforts put a stop to the madness.

"It's time to put it out of its misery." Destin lit a liquor-soaked towel stuffed into a fifth of Sauza. He chucked it through an open window, then asked Fe to leave. "I'll come find you when it's over."

Destin called 911 from a payphone and reported the fire anonymously. He then snuck inside the building and waited for the fire truck to arrive. He waited at a safe distance from the fire on the second floor of the shop. This floor used to be the attached slaughterhouse; with hooks still hanging from the ceiling. Destin hid under a steel butcher's block. He could feel the fire burning slowly beneath him. The heat was rising up and turning the room into a kiln; Destin's clothes were soon soaking wet from the sweat. He took off his shirt and held it to his chin to filter the soot in the air before it reached his lungs.

It took ten minutes before the fire crew showed up. Being abandoned, they only sent two men to take care of the job. When they got out of their vehicle, Destin let out a scream. "Help!" he shouted. The crew responded immediately by sending the most fit of their team: the newbie, Javon.

Javon busted through the front door with his axe and began searching for the civilian, toppling over old tables and furniture.

"Help!" Destin let out another scream, signaling for the fireman to search upstairs. While the flames hadn't touched the second floor, the smoke had begun to fill-in. This made Destin practically invisible, crouched down underneath the table. He remained quiet and waited for Javon to turn his back to him. At this point, Destin grabbed two of the meat hooks hanging above him and jabbed them into Javon's calves.

Javon screamed in pain, but his respirator mask muffled his shouts. Javon swung his axe around trying to hit his attacker, but he was blinded by the smoke. Destin tried scurrying away, but the blade caught the bottom of his foot. He almost cried out in terror, but he managed to hold his tongue and pull his heel off of the blade.

Injured, Destin could barely stand. He hobbled around until he reached the edge of the room. Destin felt around the walls till he found where the chains were wrapped around their giant reels. He reeled in the chains, pulling the hooks up towards the pulley systems on the ceiling.

Javon went up into the air. He wriggled furiously, trying to reach the hooks dug into his legs. Every time he bent his knees to shorten the distance, the hole in his muscle tore wider and the pain drove him wild. He began flailing at random, hoping that with enough force the chains would simply tear all the way through and he'd fall to the floor. Destin couldn't allow that.

Destin picked up Javon's axe off the floor and swung it down into Javon's neck. He suddenly stopped struggling.

With the other fireman waiting patiently below, Destin couldn't be seen leaving the building. He limped back down to the first floor, and found an open window in the back. He crawled through it and escaped into a grassy ditch behind the house. He kept low and traversed this ditch all the way back to the roadway. When he was far enough away to avoid any association with the fire, he climbed back onto the shoulder of the road and threw out his thumb. His adrenaline was fading and it was becoming impossible for him to continue along the route with his foot torn apart.

Within just a few moments, a black Mustang with tinted windows pulled-up. Destin heard a pop; the doors were unlocked. He took that as an invitation and pulled open the door. Sitting inside was a familiar face attached to an even more familiar body. It was the nudist from the seance.

"Boy you look ragged," said the nudist with a look of worry. "You're leaving a trail of blood behind you..." The nudist looked down at Destin's soaking, red sock, then started his engine. "Jesus Christ, what's wrong with your foot?"

"Cut it on a soda can," replied Destin, keeping his eyes forward and his voice low.

"Must have been a Foster's to leave a wound that deep."

"Yep..."

The nudist pushed on the gas pedal and the two of them drove off. "I'd say that might need stitches."

"Yeah. Probably does."

"Should I drop you off at the hospital?"

Destin shook his head. "I'd prefer Sloppy Joe's downtown."

"If you say so..." The nudist cleared his throat and turned his head towards Destin. He leaned a little and looked behind Destin's bare back. "You know I don't normally pick-up strangers, but I really admire your tattoo. I love nudity, so it's right up my alley."

Destin took his eyes off the road and stared at the nudist with confusion. "What are you talking about?"

"When I drove up from behind you, I could see your tattoo perfectly."

"What tattoo?"

The nudist gave Destin a strange look. "The one on your back, man."

"What is it?" Destin looked panicked, he kept trying to force his neck to twist around unnaturally, but he couldn't possibly look behind his own back. "What does it say? Describe it to me!"

"It just says 'You're Welcome'," explained the nudist, "and above is a big portrait of a Mexican lady. Butt naked. Legs spread."

Destin began to shiver. He was stuck in disbelief. "You're pulling my leg!"

"Why would I lie about this, man?"

"I can't go home," whimpered Destin. "My wife can't see this!" Tears started rolling down Destin's cheeks. His heart was racing; he was having a panic attack. "How much longer till we're there?"

When Destin got to Sloppy Joe's, he charged out of the car and bashed through the front door. Fe looked up from her drink and smiled. She flashed her camera. "Trans-" Before she could finish her words, Destin ran up to her and decked her in the nose. He then picked her camera up off the floor and started smashing it to pieces.

"Destin, stop! Stop!" shouted Gregg. He ran out from behind the bar and tried to pull his friend away from Fe. Fe kept a straight face and tried to distance herself from the attacker. "You can't do that, you psycho!"

"She ruined my marriage!" snarled Destin.

"I saved you from it," sighed Fe, wiping the blood from her nose. "I take it you found my gift to you?"

"You're disgusting!"

"This is the most important thing I've done this whole trip. More important than any photographs or poetry." Fe nodded. "This is the will of the island working through me. This is why we were put together. I'm supposed to trap you here. Now, you can't go home."

Destin broke down into more tears. He pulled himself free of Gregg and collapsed on the ground.

"The island is claiming you," said Fe, crouching down beside Destin. "You're a conch now. It's official. You're a small, ugly part of this big, ugly thing." Fe stood up and looked at Gregg. She shook her head and walked towards the exit. "I won't be pressing any charges." She grabbed her broken nose and snapped it back into place, then stepped outside.

Destin balled up on the floor and pulled his drugs from his pocket. He swallowed what remained and shut his eyes tightly, allowing whatever should come to come. His heart beat faster

36

and faster. He heard Gregg's screams, "Get up! Get the fuck up!" An icy cold feeling engulfed his lungs, it felt like he was choking on snow. His body rattled uncontrollably. His mouth was filled with sweetness and bitter. He heard the sounds of sirens sounding off in the distance, followed by the screams of children and young women. He saw his own body lying on the floor as his spirit lifted from his frame. Gregg was kicking him in the ribs, trying to resuscitate through sheer force of anger.

Suddenly, three sharp fingers laid on Destin's incorporeal shoulder. He turned around and made eye contact with the face of an owl. Its fingers ran up his neck, then reached the back of his head. They held on tightly.

Profile: Matthew Hoga

People Serving People of Cincinnati, Ohio should not be confused with the philanthropic organization People Serving People of Minneapolis, Minnesota. The former of which has been on the FBI watchlist for the last decade, but due to their secrecy their crimes have gone completely unpunished. That is, until one former member, Matthew Hoga, betrayed the rest of his club out of desperation and revenge.

Matthew had been an official member of the PSP for the last three years of its ten year activity. All twelve members would meet bimonthly, each time at a different member's house. They would then be served dinner by the host. The dinner being some human victim that the host personally traps, kills, and cooks all by himself. The rest of the members judge the meal on its flavor, presentation, and creative risk.

It was December of 2016 when it came time for Matthew to serve his first meal to the society. He was admittedly nervous, but had some clever ideas on how to earn top marks. Matthew decided on serving his victim in croquettes fried in peanut oil and served on a bed of bibb lettuce. His efforts were universally praised in all three categories, a difficult achievement for a member's first time hosting. But all this glory was immediately tarnished, when he was asked to explain his method of victim selection and he revealed he'd chosen his own son, Thomas Hoga.

The other members cringed in disgust, embarrassed they'd lauded such an amateur mistake. "You don't kill family," they griped. "It's distasteful. It's disrespectful."

"But most importantly, it makes it too easy to get caught," proclaimed the leader of the group, now identified as senatorial candidate Suze Filo. "When someone disappears, the family is the first people they investigate. Your actions could lead the authorities right to our organization. You've endangered us all." Suze tossed her remaining food in the garbage.

Matthew quickly apologized for the shock and tried his best to assure them there was nothing to worry about. Matthew had just won full-custody of Thomas after a nine-month court battle. In the eyes of the court, Thomas's mother was an emotionally abusive drunk. When Thomas turns up missing, they'll think it was her who harmed him in an act of payback.

"Stunts like this can't go unpunished." Suze grabbed her coat and gestured for the rest of the club to follow her lead. They fled Matthew's home in a matter of seconds, leaving no trace of their presence behind.

From that day onward, Matthew stopped receiving the coded messages containing the addresses to the bimonthly meetings. They'd usually come in the mail disguised as a fake electric bill, where the numbers in the various charges could be deciphered into letters. Matthew assumed this banishment from the dinners was the "punishment" Suze was referring to. And, for the most part, Matthew was understanding and accepted responsibility for his mistake.

Although his usual meal plan was canceled, Matthew still held interest in eating other humans. He actually found it difficult to work and live otherwise without the joy his secret meals used to bring him periodically. Matthew realized, in order to feel happy, he would have to continue hunting down bodies all by himself.

Matthew had three targets in mind. He planned on killing them all in the same week in order to get a massive amount of protein he could gradually eat over the span of a year. There was a young intern at his office, Sarah Donovan, who worked late and walked to her car by herself in the middle of the night. Then, there was Jeffrey Wright, an elderly neighbor who would get mind-numbingly stoned on the weekend, causing him to leave the door to his home unlocked throughout the evening. And finally, there was Carissa Comay, a little girl who biked to a nearby playground and drew on the asphalt all by herself every Sunday afternoon.

He bought some rope and chloroform and practiced his approach every day for an entire month till he felt he was confident for the real thing. But the week of his planned attacks things began to mysteriously fall apart, all at the same time. Sarah Donovan stopped working late and began walking to her car with a friend by her side. Jeffrey Wright bought a padlock for his door and started locking it all up before touching his bong. And little Carissa Comay just stopped showing up to the park altogether.

Matthew knew this couldn't have been just a coincidence. Someone had purposely sabotaged his three assaults. He decided to experiment just to be sure. He started stalking a potential fourth target he'd ruled out earlier on. A single mother who lived in a trailer parked outside the local Walmart. Soon as he started to track her, unmarked police cars began to conveniently appear parked next to her van.

Things were looking quite grim for Matthew's meal prospects, and he was convinced his suspicions were completely confirmed. The old club was ratting him out. They hadn't just stopped inviting him to dinner, they were seeing to it that he'd never get the taste of flesh ever again, dropping anonymous tips to whichever victims he had planned.

Matthew already had contacts with the FBI due to his son's disappearance, so when he decided to come clean, it was an easy transition. He offered to admit to his son's murder to show his willingness to comply, but in order for him to give the names of the rest of the PSP, he had a demand that the FBI found difficult to fulfill.

40

Matthew wanted his rightful meal. He wanted human protein and he didn't care how it was acquired. This left the authorities with some interesting options to consider. They could, of course, refuse and risk leaving a small militia of cannibals at large, or they could somehow oblige Matthew without breaking any laws. For the latter, they decided all they really needed was a willing donor; and that could be found in any medical center in the country.

"We tried to keep the idea hush-hush, but ultimately we needed the word out, so we ended up making international news. FBI looking for a leg," explained Special Agent Byrd. "Leg amputations are common practice, all we were waiting for was the perfect candidate, somebody who wouldn't mind forking over their severed limb for the greater good. Fate landed on a firefighter crushed from the waist-down in the line of duty, Carl Summ. Remember that name. His injury ended up saving countless lives."

For assisting the FBI, Matthew Hoga only spent ten years in prison and nine months on parole. He is currently working for Parolee Perogies, a felony friendly Polish restaurant in Cleveland, Ohio.

Matthew doesn't express remorse for any of his crimes, but he's certainly uninterested in returning to jail. That's good enough for the American penal system, but not satisfactory for me. I neglected to meet Matthew in person despite his numerous offerings. I kept everything over email.

I eventually was sent his story "Comorbidity" along with a handful of other horror fictions where the main character is always a zombie. He openly admits these creatures all seem to be avatars for his repressed cannibalism.

41

"It's like a eunuch writing porno," types Matthew. "My primary function safely reduced into words on a page."

Comorbidity

All the nukes, guns, tanks, and jets were taken away and picked apart by 2050. This was step three of a ten step plan established by the United Nations in order to usher in an era of world peace. Things were looking optimistic until 2068 when step six demanded an alternative resource permanently replace dwindling oil supplies. One country reached 100% solar efficiency faster than the rest of the world, then refused to share its secret with anyone but old economic allies. Tensions quickly grew, sides were taken, and the world devolved back into fighting. Old feuds made a resurgence, and it seemed like everybody had an enemy they wanted gone. But with all the weapons taken apart, the only thing left to hurl at each other were germs.

Six countries were involved in the exchange; by no coincidence they were the world superpowers at the time. China released parasitic eggs into the water supplies of the US and Russia. Russia hid B-033 virus in their kasha exports to China and Mexico. The US fired perlmann prions at China and Japan. Mexico infected a rugby match in Australia with drug-resistant bacteria. Australia infected a soccer match in Mexico with drug-resistant fungus. And Japan released the chekkuauto onto itself.

Russia's B-033 attack targeted Beijing specifically, creating a race of infected called the Pekingese. They were mainly named after the old word for Beijing, Peking, but it also stems from the fact that the Pekingese share certain features with the titular dog breed. The virus causes mutations in the infected's face where the gums tend to enlarge and the teeth splay. The eyes then turn outward as the tear ducts swell with necrosis.

Being one of the Pekingese, Hsin Li had two objectives on his mind; a greater and a lesser goal. The greater goal was to spread the B-033 to the uninfected. The lesser goal was to sync-up with several other Pekingese in order to create a horde. The horde would then help make the greater goal more possible.

Hsin Li lost his last horde when crossing a river. The Pekingese cannot swim, so when the water got too deep most of them were simply carried away by the flow. By the time Hsin's feet touched the ground again he'd been displaced miles away. Rather than try to reassemble with his former cohorts, he figured he could easily find new partners by heading towards the metropolis in the distance. He found himself lumbering all alone into the big city of Zhengzhou.

Upon entering the city limits, Hsin immediately sensed the presence of uninfected. Vagabond children ran from their trash fire down a back alley. An armed survivor cocked his gun behind a boarded up window. A manhole cover clanged closed.

Hsin made a soft gurgling noise to show his growing frustration; there were so many possible targets, but a Pekingese can very rarely catch somebody on their own. Pekingese bodies are cold, stiff, and brittle. As they move, their arms are stuck reaching outwards, and their heads are perpetually slumped to one side. Their legs move very gradually, taking short stomps forward. They cannot outrun their prey, so instead their best bet is to surround them.

Hsin called out to his fellow infected through the use of a low guttural yawn. There was no immediate response. Despite having relatively simplistic life goals, Pekingese can feel powerful emotions when these ambitions are obstructed, which shouldn't come as too shocking as these infected are generated from humans who are naturally inclined to feel scorned when rejected from offerings of companionship or reproduction.

Hsin was feeling the emotional equivalent of a mother of five with a recently emptied nest calling each of her old college roommates trying to rekindle their friendships after twenty-five years of mothering. As each call goes to voicemail and her texts go unread, a feeling of dread looms over her; the strange feeling when you're in-between social groups, unsure if you're capable of finding a new one. Maybe you're unlikable now. Maybe you've lost what used to draw others to you.

Then suddenly, "Brooooooooooorgh!" Phoebe Alpha Phi texts you back.

Hsin's heart accelerated with excitement. The noise was coming from a KFC two blocks down the street. Hsin waddled over to the front doors. The sliding glass wouldn't move out of his way. The power was out. It wasn't like that in the last city. Hsin realized he'd have to burst through.

Thud. Thud. Thud. Moving rigidly, it was difficult to gain the momentum he needed to crack the glass. He raised his arms over his head and pressed his face against the door. His puffy lips left a trail of drool as he smeared his face in sorrowful circles.

Thud. An infected on the other side of the glass copied his moves and started rubbing his face in the exact same pattern. They were so close to connection. Their skin was separated by a mere half-inch of glass.

They both pulled back and stared at each other. Hsin examined the other infected up and down. They did not look healthy. Their teeth were falling out and their eyes were bloodshot. Pekingese feed off of sunlight with their snow white skin. This Pekingese must have got caught inside the KFC right as the power went out. Trapped indoors, he's been starving for days.

Hsin realized there wouldn't be any way they could penetrate this obstacle on their own. This would require a special tool.

Hsin figured a bullet could make short work of it, he just needed one of the survivors to fire upon him, but he wasn't all that intimidating all by his lonesome.

Instead, Hsin realized he might stand a better chance at disgusting them. A zombified anus might garner their attention. Hsin shoved his ass against the glass wall and wriggled until he shimmied out of his pants and underwear. Once they'd fallen down, he turned his butt away from the door and bent over.

"Tiān nǎ, bù!" cried out a muffled voice in the distance. "Wǒ de yǎnjīng!" Somebody was screaming about the horrific sight outside their window.

"Yǒurén pāi nàgè dōngxī!" screamed another voice. They were begging somebody to put the monster down. Hsin's rotting hole was scaring their children.

"Jiānchí, shāo děng. Nüèdài zhàogù tā," came a third voice, more calm than the previous two. The sound of a gun cocking filled the air. Then came the shot.

Kapow! The bullet shot Hsin right between the cheeks. It traveled through his intestines, then his stomach. It traveled down his esophagus. He opened wide. The bullet flew out his mouth with a trail of blood. It struck the door. Crash! The glass fell into pieces.

Hsin grabbed his pants and stood back upright. He felt an achy feeling all throughout the center of his body. It was like acid reflux. It wouldn't kill him though. Not as long as nothing hit his brain.

The infected on the other side of the door didn't waste any time. He needed to sync up their brains. He grabbed hold of Hsin's hands and stared at his vacant face. He then applied pressure behind his eyes, ejecting a thin stream of blood from his tear ducts. The blood shot Hsin in his own eyes and absorbed into his tattered ducts. Almost instantly, Hsin could hear the other infected's thoughts.

The other infected was named Lu Chen. He was infected by the kasha and onions he had for breakfast a month ago. Hsin was overjoyed to hear that; he too had been poisoned by his breakfast, and he too liked his kasha with onions. This commonality filled them both with endorphins. They were both so thrilled they realized the only thing that could make them happier was to add a third from which they could find more commonalities. This would be far easier now that there were two of them.

Lu and Hsin knew where there were survivors based on the angle at which they struck Hsin's behind. They were hiding in the apartment above a Luckin Coffee. Lu and Hsin walked over to the front door aligned between the storefront and the neighboring alley. It was locked, but there was a mail slot near the bottom that they could easily reach through. Hsin slid his arm through but he couldn't touch the locks inside; they were too far upwards. He needed a longer arm. Or perhaps two moderately sized arms.

Hsin turned to Lu and grabbed hold of his forearm with both hands. He pulled downwards with all his might. A slight tear formed in Lu's skin. Hsin repeated the tugging over and over until Lu's depreciated flesh and bone gave way. Hsin pulled Lu's left arm straight off. Lu felt mild discomfort, but it wasn't anything crippling. Hsin held onto the arm's exposed humerus and slid it completely through the mail slot, followed by the length of his own arm. Detached from Lu's body the limb could still move using the same telepathy that connected Hsin and Lu. Together, they controlled the arm to reach up to the bolt lock, then the smaller lock on the doorknob.

47

Click. Click. The door was free. Hsin slammed it open, revealing a staircase up to the apartment's living room. A woman stood at the top of the stairs with a shotgun pointed at them. Hsin and Lu hobbled backward before she could fire.

Hsin and Lu used the combined capacity of their minds to formulate their next plan. Lu got on his knees. Hsin came up behind him and grabbed onto his head. Hsin tore upwards till Lu's neck tore and the head popped right off. Lu's head was his weak point. Hsin laid it down behind the counter of the coffee shop, where it would be safe while Hsin borrowed Lu's body for protection.

Using Hsin's eyes, Lu directed his headless body up the stairs. Immediately the woman at the top started blasting. Lu's body acted as a shield, absorbing all the pellets. Hsin followed behind Lu's body, climbing the stairs completely unharmed. When Lu's body reached the top, Hsin waited for the woman to fire all her ammo. Then he stuck his head over Lu's severed neck and squirted his blood. It shot up the woman's nose. She gasped in horror as it penetrated the thin membrane in her nostrils. Quickly, she was accepted into Hsin's horde. Safe from fire, Hsin took a moment to place Lu's arm back in place and press his head back onto his shoulders.

Usually, it takes a full hour for the effects of the B-033 virus to turn the infected white and stiff. In the meantime, the limber body of the new recruit is still fully assimilated and usable by the horde. Lu and Hsin introduced themselves to their newest cohort, Hua. Together they turned Hua's body against her fellow survivors, Bing and An, her husband and son respectively. Hua pulled the trigger twice. Once while aiming at her son's legs, then again while aiming at her husband's legs.

Now that they were both crippled, Hsin waddled up to their bodies on the floor and leaned the top of his face over each of their mouths. He released a burst of blood from his eyes over

48

their tongues. Soon Bing and An were added to their crew as well.

An army of five Pekingese was officially a major threat to the citizens of Zhengzhou. They no longer needed clever tactics to open doors. The five shoving at once had enough force to push them down. Hsin's forces were now a terrifying swarm that was quickly growing in numbers. Six. Seven. Eight. Hsin never wanted to quit. He always wanted more and he pumped these wants and needs into his followers' brains.

They eventually found their way to the hospital attached to Zhengzhou University. There were bound to be tons of easy targets inside. Survivors bound to their life support systems and medicine supplies. Their only protectors were nurses and doctors armed with mere scalpels and needles; neither of which posed any serious threat.

Hsin's herd crowded around the steel doors out front. They all shoved forward in sync, applying enough pressure to actually crush some of the bones of the Pekingese up against the door. They didn't mind. They were helping. Ping. There was a lock on the chain tethering the doors closed. It was slowly starting to break. They all leaned back like a wave, then stumbled forward. Crack. The doors swung open to reveal a waiting room.

Hsin's group scattered inside. Three went to the left. Three went right. Two went forward. Their telepathy worked through walls, so they could all hear and see each other's perspectives. Pekingese can remain mentally grouped within 100 meters of each other, roughly the size of a football field.

Hsin went with the young boy, An. The wing they explored was the elderly services department. They expected to see cowering seniors as they trudged down the hall, but the rooms were mostly empty. They did witness strange markings on the wall; streaks of blood. Hsin wondered if they'd arrived too late, perhaps another pack of Pekingese had already invaded. This wasn't necessarily a bad thing; they could always combine forces. Hsin liked the idea of blended families.

Suddenly, something caught An's eye and everyone connected froze. Hsin moved beside An and helped him scan the grim scene. It was an old woman. Her arms had been torn off and discarded to the sides of her bed. Her head was cracked open like an ostrich egg, a polygon of skin and bone stolen from the front of her skull. Upon closer inspection, the cavity had been completely emptied of its brain tissue.

Moments later, Bing, Lu, and Hua discovered two more similarly dismembered bodies. It was a doctor and a nurse sprawled out on the floor of an operating room. The right half of the nurse's head was caved in and her lobes had been scooped out from the side.

The remaining three – newcomers Chung, Jun, and Deshi – fully expected to find their own body or bodies somewhere in the emergency department. But as they reached the last room in the wing, the only thing they found was completely alive.

Bang. A little girl lept from a counter and struck Chung in the head with a bed pan as he entered the doctor's office. The force knocked him over. The girl ran over Chung's body, just barely avoiding a blast of blood from his eyes. She dashed between Jun and Deshi, and dodged their fire as well. She tore down the hallway back towards the waiting room. She was far too fast for any of the Pekingese to catch. It looked as though she might just escape. Then, something large and quivering dropped from the ceiling tiles and blocked her way. The little girl skidded to a halt only a few feet away from what looked like a man in a suit, but he had bright red skin and he walked on all fours.

The girl turned to look at the Pekingese behind her. She looked nervously at the new threat in front of her. She took too long to think. The red man jumped on her.

Five minutes of shrieking and crying, and the little girl's head was reduced to rubble thrown along the floor. The red man made a wide enough gap in her skull to sink his jaw into. He ate directly from the wound like it was a bowl of Manhattan clam chowder.

Compared to the light-hearted, crustiness of the Pekingese, this other fellow was a true monster. It was carnivorous and aposematic. It was like a creature from myth, but the reality of the situation was its origins were all too similar to the Pekingese themselves.

Tony Ng was on a tram traveling to Theatre Lane, where he polished shoes. That's when the Americans dropped their aerosol bombs over the city. The one that struck City Hall had a blast radius of four miles. The chartreuse mist looked like a cartoon stench. It traveled through the windows of the bus and layered the passengers' lungs.

America had struck Hong Kong with perlmann prions. It was a fast and savage attack that made fast and savage infected. Hongkongers, they were called.

Tony Ng's skin turned red from a consistently high-fever. His new brain chemistry demanded he gallop around all fours to show dominance. His sinew thickened and he grew stronger and faster. Externally, Tony was physically better than ever. But internally, Tony's brain had mutated to feel an overwhelming sense of mental inferiority.

Tony was feeling the emotional equivalent of a recent graduate with a precise degree: computer science with a minor in psychology. He's found the holy grail of job listings, a UX designer position at Alibaba that not only fits his unique qualifications but pays well. The only problem is Tony's grades are just shy of all the other applicants. In Tony's eyes, the prions make him see every other living thing around him as the other applicants. He has a strong urge to consume their brains; the source of their usurping brilliance.

Crunch. Tony bit into the little girl's tough, rubbery pons, signaling he'd picked the brain down to the core. Tony felt a sudden rush of confidence; like he was the smartest person in the room again. Then he saw the Pekingese staring at him from the end of the hall. Judging by all their friends, Tony felt his emotional intelligence was clearly inferior. Their hiring potential was incredible.

Tony charged forward down the hall. He growled as he galloped, spewing flecks of brains from the corners of his mouth. Chung, Jun, and Deshi all stared at the beast's tongue and shot loads of blood down its throat. Tony gagged, but he wouldn't stop running. The B-033 had entered into his body but instantaneously dissolved. His body temperature was far too high to support the virus's growth.

Tony was now jealous and disgusted. He leapt into the air and rammed his hands into Chung's head. He then palmed Chung's face and started lifting and dropping his skull against the hard floor of the hospital. Blood began to trickle from the growing breach in the occipital bone. It made little red trails along the borders of the sheet vinyl tiles.

Once the back of the skull was pulverized, Tony turned Chung's head around and dug his hand inside the wound. He shoved his hand between the brain and the bone, cutting the soft meninx with his fingertips. He wrapped his hand around the brain and pulled out the top two thirds of the organ. He dropped the brain on the floor and picked it apart with his large, exaggerated chomps.

Jun and Deshi ran away while Tony finished eating. They hobbled faster than they've ever hobbled before. They crossed back into the waiting room where they met up with the rest of the subgroups. Once they were recombined they escaped through the doors they came in through.

Hsin's army tried their best to distance themselves from the hospital and the monster inside; but little did they know when one finds a Hongkonger, it's only a matter of time before there are more. Perlmann prions are contagious by air.

As Hsin led his herd back down the street towards the KFC where it all began, two Hongkongers emerged from opposite alleyways and began fighting each other in the middle of the road. One was a portly man in police clothes. The other was a teenage girl in a school uniform. The police officer got his hand on the back of the girl's head and smashed her nose into the concrete. The girl squirmed away and swatted at the officer's face; her nails clawed off the skin beneath his right eye.

Hsin's crew backed away slowly and subtly, making sure not to draw the ravagers' attention. They retreated backwards up into Hua's old apartment where they could all converse telepathically and try to come up with a plan to escape.

Hsin shared his memory of the river outside the city. It took him far and fast before and it could do it again. Lu countered with the memory of Hsin rescuing him from his fast-food imprisonment. Lu reminded Hsin of the main objectives and how heading back to the river would mean separating the herd.

Hsin argued that neither of their goals would be possible if they were all dead.

Lu begged him to consider the possibility of fighting back. They still had power in numbers.

53

Jun and Deshi sullenly pointed out that their ranks might not be as high as it seems. They might soon be down two more members.

Everyone in the crew suddenly realized there was an uncomfortable heat growing in their hive mind. It was coming from Jun and Deshi's perspectives. Their bodies were burning up. The crew turned to face the two. Their pale skin was starting to blush. The swelling in their faces was shrinking. Their muscles were pressing tightly against their skin.

Jun and Deshi had contracted the Hongkonger's disease when they came in close proximity back at the hospital. There was no telling how long until Jun and Deshi would become infectious themselves. Everyone in the group seemed to be in agreement, except for Lu. They wanted Jun and Deshi to hobble far, far away before they spread it to the rest of them.

Lu continued to fight for togetherness, unable to handle the deep emotional pain that occurs when a Pekingese counteracts the secondary objective. Hsin placed his cold hands on Lu's shoulders to comfort him. Bing, Lu, and Hua joined in on the hug, while Jun and Deshi quietly slipped away.

Jun and Deshi hobbled down the stairs and into the street. The police officer from earlier was lying on the sidewalk; his vacant head showed through a hole torn straight through his uniform's cap. Jun and Deshi chose a direction at random and kept walking forward until the connection to the horde approached the limits of its range.

Deshi looked off at the mountains in the distance, gracing the other Pekingese with the glorious sight of the sun set before disconnecting. As the sun went down, strange blue lights began twinkling in the forests. It's like there were stars in the mountains. They were bright enough to be visible from so far

54

away. They were more dispersed at the top of the mountain and grew denser as they reached the midsection, then they just stopped.

Deshi took a few more steps forward. The sight he broadcasted to the others went fuzzy as he left the transmittable distance. A few more lunges and the connection went completely blank.

The idea of fighting back became more ominous with less and less people in the herd. Hsin suggested that, instead, they simply go on the defense. If they could wait patiently, the Hongkongers would slowly start killing each other off. They could finish off what remained at the end of a month.

Lu was skeptical. He knew the Hongkongers would sniff them out eventually; and if they stayed in the apartment, they were fish in a barrel. Hsin assured his brethren their defense would be more sophisticated than just standing around indoors.

First of all, they needed to not contract the airborne illness themselves. This wasn't difficult, as they didn't necessarily need to breathe anyways. They only did so to help keep their bodies cool, and occasionally moan and scream. As long as they kept their mouths closed and their diaphragms still, they would be fine.

The next step in the plan was then to take off all their heads except for Hsin, who would be the sole eyes and ears for the team. The heads would be stored safely on the roof, with Hsin standing close-by.

Hsin went to the roof of the apartment complex and controlled the headless bodies from his perch. He led them out onto the street in order to collect the dead Hongkonger in the officer's uniform. Pulling all at once, they were able to move the body all the way up the stairs and onto the roof with Hsin. They positioned the hulking corpse at the very edge, hanging halfway over the gutter. The bodies were then sent back downstairs and into the street. They were told to wait.

The first Hongkonger didn't take long to appear. It was a man in a blue morph suit. The hands were covered in black stains and so was a perforated patch of fabric over the mouth. Little threads kept the mouth hole from splitting completely in two.

The Hongkonger stared at the headless bodies just hanging inside the Luckin Cafe on the bottom floor. Hsin had the bodies wave to the creature in order to confuse it. The creature was maddened by the existence of the bodies, but could not figure out where they were hiding their brains so he could kill them. It came up closer for a more detailed investigation.

Hsin activated his trap and nudged the dead cop hanging off the side of the roof. It fell down three stories, then smashed all its weight on top of the Hongkonger. Hsin had the bodies pull the cop off the shriveled creature so that they could get a look at the injuries.

The creature's spine was clearly broken, somewhere between the ribs and the hips. Everything under the split went motionless, everything above it still flailed about and growled. The bodies all stayed a safe distance from its slashing arms.

Hsin withdrew the bodies back up stairs with the officer's corpse. They tossed it down a few more times until the Hongkonger finally laid motionless. Then, they took both their dead Hongkongers back up the stairs, increasing their ammo from one to two.

The rest of the day there were no more Hongkongers. The disease had only just begun to spread, so their numbers were still relatively sparse.

As the night came again, Hsin found himself staring off into the distance from atop the roof. He graced his hardworking friends with another shot of the sunset. Once again, he could see the blue stars dotting the mountains in the distance, only they'd reached the bottom. He could see them spreading forward through the trees on the outskirts of the city. They reminded him of glow worms on the roof of a cave.

Crack. Crack. Crack. The sounds of feet running over debris caught Hsin's attention. He quickly turned around and looked over the front of the building. Surprisingly, it wasn't Hongkongers. They were survivors.

It was a team of scientists sneaking stealthily through the streets. They were wearing N95 masks to protect them from the prions in the air. The two up front checked to see if the coast was clear. The remaining four waited close behind, weighed down by large white coolers on their backs.

The two up front pointed at the headless bodies. They pulled out hack saws from inside of their coats. The four in the back did the same. The scientist up front gave a signal outstretching his pointer and his middle finger. The whole team charged forward.

Hsin panicked. Without their heads, the bodies downstairs were relatively useless against survivors. He couldn't assimilate them when they reached close range. He tried to scramble the bodies, but the scientists were too quick. They dug the teeth of the saws into the flesh of the bodies and started to yank hard back and forth.

This wasn't good. Hsin's defensive strategy only worked for Hongkongers because they didn't attack in groups. He quickly tossed the two bodies he had over the ledge and took out as many scientists as he could. The officer struck one on the head, killing him on impact. The other one missed by a few inches. The scientists all looked up and saw Hsin staring down at them.

They pointed up and started talking amongst themselves. Then, they got back to work, sawing twice as fast as before.

Hsin's body started to shake nervously. He was the only one left that could squirt them, but he was all the way up stairs. He ran for the door and hobbled as fast as he could down the steps. He tripped and ended up descending the long flight of stairs on his stomach. Several ribs rattled around in his chest. His chin nearly broke off; it dangled by a thin hair of flesh on the end of his face. He got back up and, more carefully, descended the second set of stairs. He barged through the door at the bottom and began spraying like crazy, but it was all for nothing.

He stopped squirting and let his eyes regain focus. The scientists were long gone. They took everything apart and stuffed it in their coolers. All they left behind were the feet and a lone thumb. Hsin could feel the stolen parts pressed together tightly, surrounded by cold plastic walls.

Hsin wanted to call out in rage, but he couldn't risk breathing the prions. He vented his rage and kicked at the feet left behind. He crushed the stupid thumb under the weight of his heel.

The other heads demanded that he stop. They took control of his body and made him sit on the ground.

Hsin took a moment to collect himself. He immediately started formulating his next plan. He was going to pick up the remaining heads and set them up like turrets down the street so when more survivors came through, he could tag them from afar.

Hsin tried to stand up to gather the heads, but his brethren wouldn't let him. They sullenly shared their new hopes and dreams; to be left on the roof, alone. Bing, Hua, and An all felt like they stood a better chance there than being carried around by Hsin. Connected brain to brain, they couldn't hide the fact that they no longer had any trust for Hsin and his plans. There was one exception, however.

Lu controlled Hsin's body and had him pick up his head. Lu's dedication to hoarding was stronger than the rest of the pack. Despite Hsin's failures, Lu honored their connection.

Hsin walked out into the streets holding Lu's head beneath his shoulder. They followed the will of the group and kept walking until the rest of the party was disconnected. By the time they reached Jinshui District, only Hsin and Lu remained.

It was suddenly quiet inside of their heads; far less conversation; far less calculation. Every move they made was a simple choice with only two people voting. Hsin led their party of two to the Henan Museum, where they caught sight of the Hongkonger they met in the hospital.

Tony Ng was lapping at the scum building on top of the undrained water feature in front of the museum. His raised body temperature made him constantly thirsty. He was so fixated on rehydration, he did not notice the Pekingnese sneaking up behind him.

Hsin had a new plan. It was practically suicidal, but desperate times called for desperate measures. He and Lu agreed that there was always another means of adding somebody to their herd. They didn't have to be "blood brothers" so to speak. They simply needed to recall the lost art of domestication.

Hsin kept his mouth closed and hopped onto the Hongkonger's back like a horse. Immediately, Tony felt the weight climbing on top of him and began to buck. He bounced around, kicking his legs backwards with every leap. He was trying to knock the intruders off, but Hsin's stiff body stayed firm, his legs wrapped around Tony's flanks.

Tony's inferiority complex took up most of his brain power, leaving very little left over to intelligent thought. Tony could not formulate a clever plan to pull Hsin off his back, all he could do was panic. He flailed and snarled. Then snarled and flailed. He shook his body around, splashing around in the shallow waters in front of the museum.

The sound of splashing echoed throughout the city attracting more Hongkongers out of the dark, all of which craved water as much as they craved violence. The school girl from earlier crawled onto the scene from their left. To their right, the rouged body of Deshi appeared, carrying a half-eaten brain in its teeth. Three more Hongkongers not yet seen joined in and helped form a circle around the jeux d'eau.

Tony stopped his raging as his insecurities changed focus to the ranks of Hongkongers surrounding him from all sides. Suddenly, Deshi charged forward. Tony braced for impact, as did Hsin; but before the Hongkonger could touch them, the school girl cut off Deshi's path and tackled him instead. The two of them wrestled in the pond, each trying to get a hand on the other's head. It looked like two catty drag queens reaching for each other's wigs.

Tony crouched down and seemed prepared to pounce into the center of their brawl. Hsin couldn't allow Tony to take that risk. It was time for Hsin to really tame this beast. Hsin held Lu's head with the top of his skull in one hand and the stump of his neck in the other. Lu's mouth opened wide; Hsin slammed it down onto Tony's neck. Tony howled at the pain. Hsin handled Lu's head like the reigns on a horse, pulling in the direction he wanted Tony to go.

Hsin spun Tony around away from the duel and faced the other Hongkongers closing in. Of the three, one looked weaker than the rest. It was wearing a sun helmet and dressed in a mail carrier's uniform. Its right arm was missing from an earlier fight.

Normally, Pekingnese would run from such a perilous situation, but Hsin wanted to see the full capabilities of his new stallion.

Hsin kicked Tony's ribs, sending him into a mad dash forward. When within range, Hsin pressed down on Tony's crest, commanding him to lower his head. Tony's shoulder rammed under the mail carrier's neck; that's when Hsin reared his beast, flipping the mail carrier up into the air. He arced, then landed with a snap. He sprawled out on the ground writhing in pain. Hsin then let Tony take back full control and allowed him to do what he did best; bashing open the mail carrier's skull and feasting on his cortices.

The remaining two Hongkongers, a boy in bathing shorts and a girl in a bright yellow pinny, stared from a safe distance. Their instincts were overwhelmed by the sight of Hsin and Tony working together. They were programmed to fight other Hongkongers one on one, but Tony was breaking all the rules; he had a teammate, even if it was against his will. A Pekingese riding atop a Hongkonger offered the best of both worlds. The Pekingese mind leading Hongkonger brawn.

Hsin clenched Lu's jaw, signaling for Tony to halt his feast. Hsin then turned Tony towards the two gawkers that were hesitating to assault. Hsin would not be so indecisive. He sent Tony rocketing forward at the nearer of the two; the young man in the shorts.

The boy tried to dodge, but Hsin predicted his adjustment. Hsin veered Tony slightly to the right. Tony caught the boy's leg in his mouth. Tony pulled the boy to the ground, then tore at his leg till it fell out of its socket. The boy tried his hardest to escape but Tony just kept pulling him back in. The boy decided to reach his mouth down to his hip and chew off his own calf. Only then did he have the opportunity to limp his way to safety, leaving a trail of blood behind him. The girl in the pinny screeched, then followed after the boy to finish him off.

Hsin redirected Tony towards the last remaining Hongkonger, the school girl who just made short work of Deshi. She picked her face up from Deshi's shattered skull, then hissed. Brain matter sprayed from between her teeth. Hsin had seen this girl fight a few times now and he realized she always reached for the head of her enemy with her left arm. Hsin made sure when they charged, Tony swept under her right arm that remained on the ground. With both her front limbs up in the air, the school girl fell down and landed on her chin. Hsin let Tony go wild. He curled his fingers together and made a ball out of his hands. He raised them up over his head, then hammered downwards on the school girl's temple.

Both Hsin and Lu were feeling a rush of power. Never before had they bonded with a creature outside of their disease, but the Hongkonger was the ultimate ally. Hsin and Lu knew they had to go back for the other heads. They may not have trusted Hsin in the past, but once they saw his new ride, they were sure to return to their previous ranks in the horde.

When Hsin got to the apartment he rode Tony up the stairs, but had him halt when they reached the top. There was somebody looming over the heads of their friends. It was the body of one of the scientists from earlier. Hsin recognized him by the special mask on his face.

Hsin rode over to the man and nudged him with the front of Tony's face. The body teetered a bit, but didn't move. It's eyes were open, but it seemed unconscious. Despite all their special jackets and filters, it seemed some unknown pathogen still got through to the man. There were holes bored through all his layers of clothes. Through these holes, Hsin could make out what looked like blue veins undulating under the man's skin. Upon further inspection, they were worms.

Hsin walked past the motionless corpse and looked at the heads of his former teammates. They were writing in pain as the same worms now crawled under their skin. The worms' flicking tails protruded from their friends' eyes and lips. For some reason, these worms weren't glowing as they did with the scientist; and, when Hsin drew too close to them, the worms reached out and tried to touch him.

Hsin quickly backed away to a safe distance, then he shot blood into Hua's mouth so that he could access their recent memories. He saw the scientist barge in and creep up the stairs very slowly with his arms outstretched like he was offering a hug. He looked more like the heads do now: the worms weren't glowing, but they were hanging out of their host, trying to bridge the gap to the nearest living thing. Once the scientist wrapped his arms around the three heads, they crossed over into their new hosts. The worms remaining inside the scientist lit-up. The scientist dropped his arms and grew stiff.

These parasites were the results of the eggs China seeded into Russia's drinking water. China's original plan called for a wall to be built around their borders before they released such a plague on their neighbors, but when they got struck by Russia and America first, they realized there was no point in waiting. Over the past few months the parasites, clonorchis lux, traveled all the way from Moscow back to their homeland.

The parasites have two phases. When they first invade a body, they burrow into the tissues and change the host's mind to seek out physical contact with an uninfected. Once contact has been made stage two develops, where the worms glow while continuing to reproduce inside the now motionless body; both a nest and food source for at least twenty generations of the parasite.

Hsin felt the pain and anguish of his old teammates as the flukes slowly nibbled through their brains. Having destroyed their

63

bodies, Hsin felt some responsibility for this pain. He wished there was something he could do to stop it. Maybe he could put them out of their misery without touching them.

Hsin looked down at his steed. He had an idea, but it would bring him back to a significant disadvantage. Lu begged him not to do it. He tried to override it. They had a good thing going for them finally, and he wouldn't let Hsin ruin it. Hsin's body convulsed as two opposing wills tried to take command. Hsin was always the dominant one, however, and his stamina lasted far longer than Lu's. He yanked Lu's jaw open and detached him from Tony's neck. Tony was free. Hsin and Lu jumped off.

Tony immediately jumped at the opportunity to devour the heads just laying there in front of him. He grabbed the two on the ends and slammed them into the sides of the middle one. He squeezed them together like a sandwich until the brains popped through the top. Tony lapped up the loose gray matter and all the little worms marbled throughout it. Soon, these worms would spread throughout Tony's body and start releasing the proper hormones to change him from vicious and bitey, to sweet and huggy.

Hsin and Lu waddled out into the street. Hsin took full control as Lu went completely silent. Losing Tony was like giving up an armored tank in the middle of an apocalypse. It hurt seeing it go just because Hsin felt some sort of burden.

Hsin couldn't help it. The whole pathology of their virus relied on building connections; this of course came with an incredible amount of empathy. Lu felt Hsin showed more empathy for the heads he's not connected to, than the one that shares his most intimate thoughts.

Hsin set Lu's head on the ground. He stepped away and took his hands off the steering wheel, so to speak. He left control up to Lu. If he really wanted their relationship over with, he was free to walk Hsin's body out of distance. If not, he could tell Hsin's body to pick back up his head.

For the next couple minutes, neither Pekingese made any noise inside their shared headspace. They both kept their mental stillness going in revolt against the other. Hsin just stood hunched over the top of Lu's head.

Hours passed. Night fell. The strange blue stars once in the mountains had reached the city. Pekingnese, Hongkongers, and survivors were all frozen in the street, reduced to equals, with the same worms excavating their diverse bodies. As the parasite spread across the city, the light pollution filled the streets. Soon the whole city was glowing blue.

Back at the apartment, Tony's parasitic infection had grown to the stage of complete control over his body. However, the worms had their own brains to work from, they didn't do anything with Tony's. It just sat in its prison, feeling its nerve endings get pecked apart. Tony had chewed apart so many nervous systems himself, it was odd to be on the other end of things. It wasn't as humbling an experience as it should have been, however. In fact, it only made Tony's ego worse. Supplying the food and shelter for an entire colony of worms made him feel like the center of their universe. And no one's better than the center of the universe.

Tony's body came creeping out of the apartment with its arms outstretched. It approached Hsin as he stood there motionless. It wrapped its arms around Hsin and held him close. The worms pierced Hsin's flesh. Tony's body lit up blue.

Soon, a vast network of tunnels was assembled throughout Hsin's body. The hormones bid him to do the same as Tony just had. Hsin picked up Lu's head and let the worms crawl from his palms into Lu's ears. Hsin lit up blue and froze in place.

With Hsin frozen and Lu missing his body, the two were stuck within range of each other's thoughts. Neither could leave the other and break the connection. Despite their animosity, they were hoarded forever; or at least until the worms sapped Hsin's nutrients down to the bone.

To Hsin, life was ideal. Although he couldn't read their thoughts, he felt connected to the hundreds of individuals now crawling around his body. On the other hand, Lu never felt more alone. He couldn't control his own arms and legs; let alone those of others. The change in his locus of control was debilitating. The two outlooks combined together to form a melancholy middle ground; which seemed like a pretty appropriate reaction for the end of the world.

Profile: John Doe

John Doe's real name can't be revealed. He's entrusted me with
the details of several assaults for which he hasn't been held
liable. All I can tell you is that, through word of mouth, my
"cannibal project" reached his eyes and ears, and he approached
me anonymously.

John brought my attention to a Polish YouTube personality
named Dobry Nowak, who specializes in reviewing vegan food
options at popular food chains. Dobry originally gained his
following making insightful recommendations to the growing
vegan world community; but then he began to expand his clout
selling a line of nickel-free kitchen utensils. He gained a
significant amount of wealth, gaining international news
attention for his approach to modern entrepreneurship.

Dobry was only sixteen, and so it's understandable that excess
and fame would inflate his vulnerable ego. During an interview
with Cezch news source CT24, he made the sudden leap from
trendy health advocate to religious fanatical. "I've been selected
by God," he explained to interviewer Zuzana Tvarůžková, "I'm
destined to deliver the panacea."

"So I take it religion has had a long influence over your life?"
probed Zuzanna.

"I should hope so," replied Dobry. "I believe I am the
reincarnation of his one beloved Son."

Six months of media controversy followed. Dobry eventually
found himself invited onto BBC's Celebrity Mastermind. He
keeps his conversation short and friendly; keeping his chin up as
they give him a few knocks for his earlier claims. Overall, the

dialogue is unimportant and uneventful. What really matters is his choice in clothing: a tank top that exposes the lower portion of his neck where it meets with his shoulder. You can see a ring of flesh with some faded discoloration. According to John Doe, this is no hickey.

"It's my bite mark," explained John. "His address was leaked online and so I waited outside of his home in Zamosc. When he went to hop on his Vectrix, I ran up to him and caught him by surprise."

This is not the first time Joe has attacked someone claiming to be Jesus. Ian "Blonde Leader" Johnson led a small cult, the Arkansawyer Apostles, in the Boston Mountains in the early 1990s. They avoided media attention by being a mostly benign religion; abstaining from sex and drugs and preaching for peace and love. Their only controversial tenant was that "Blonde Leader" was their redneck Messiah.

John Doe actually spent a six week vacation exploring the rural towns hiding deep within the Ozarks in an attempt to learn the Apostles' location. Eventually, he was led to a practicing Apostle who worked at the Walmart in Japser. He agreed to take John to their campgrounds. Here, John requested to meet with their leader under the false pretense that he was seeking enlightenment. Ian agreed to see the stranger, having recently opened their doors to new members. John was told to kneel before Ian so that he may anoint him with a blackberry ointment. Ian reached down to touch John's head, John turned his face upwards and chewed off the tip of his pointer finger.

"I almost didn't make it out of that one," explained John Doe. "I was surrounded. Not my brightest idea, but it was my only opportunity to get him. They were a peace loving community so they had no weapons. They grabbed hold of my shoulders and tried to shove my chest to the ground. I let myself fall then wriggled backwards between their feet. When I sensed nobody overhead, I managed to pick myself up. At this point, I took a second to actually swallow the flesh still hanging in my mouth. It tasted delicious with the blackberry jam. After that I booked it down the only road back to civilization. I hid in the bushes every time I heard a car approaching. I was paranoid they would come after me… or send a cop after me. I'd come to find out that the cops never investigated my attacks."

It's hard for these Messiah-claimants to get the police on their side. Most of these men are deeply despised by the world's major religious communities. Claiming to be God or his son is considered an extreme form of arrogance, and anyone agreeing with the blasphemer would be worshiping a false-idol. And so, when these attacks occurred in vastly Christian parts of the world, the investigative forces were far from enthusiastic about finding the attacker.

"I've tasted six different people in my life, all of them having claimed to be Jesus," continued John Doe. "I'm not looking to punish these people. I'm just looking to test them. The real Jesus should taste like warm bread and fine wine."

I inquired as to what will happen when John finally chooses correctly.

"Well, first and foremost, he'll forgive me," said John with certainty and a smile, "and then I think naturally I'd become one of his new Apostles. After all, tasting his body and his blood seems to be the qualification for such a role."

John Doe is publishing his own book, the Eucharist Trials, under a yet-to-be-determined pen name. Outside of his non-fiction, John Doe has a lot of unpublished short stories from his time spent alone at an all-boys boarding school. John had no interest making friends with boys at that age, and so he spent his free time writing religious fiction.

John's inspiration for "Jesus Christ Meets the Chupacabra" stems from his own relationship with God, which was especially strained during his youth. Battles with childhood obesity fueled John Doe's self-destructive tendencies. John believes this particular story captures best the battle between good and evil playing out in his young heart.

Jesus Christ Meets the Chupacabra

As the new millennium drew closer, Ímuris, a small village in Northern Mexico, began to experience unusual phenomena attributed to bicentennial anxieties. The people of Ímuris have a wide range of beliefs stemming from different sects of Christianity, and some of these tenants suggested that the end of the world might approach with the coming of 2000 AD. One loving mother of six suddenly disowned all of her children, fearing her sins would hold back her offspring from attaining rapture. Several businesses lowered their prices to almost nothing in order to empty stock before their stores were reduced to ashes. A Presbytarian elder converted to Baptist. A Baptist bishop converted to Methodist. And a Methodist minister lost his faith entirely. But the strangest of them all was certainly the Black Bestialist. Although his actions couldn't be easily explained by the apocalypse, everyone in town knew it was no coincidence that his assaults popped up at the turn of the century.

The Black Bestialist dressed in dark suits in the middle of the night, only to hop the fences of local goatherds. Once inside, he'd pin down the nearest nanny onto her back. As the goat bleated for mercy, the Bestialist would undo his pants and have his way with her. He wouldn't stop until the chivero heard his flock screaming for help and would come rushing out with his rifle.

"¡Pervertido!" shouted the chivero. He fired his carbine at the man's feet and grazed the rapist's ankle. The Bestialist howled in pain, pulled himself off the nanny, then began to gallop away towards the fence. The chivero sent his xolo, Mariana, to finish the man off, but the dog was too slow and the attacker managed to hop the fence and hobble to safety.

"Esta bien chica…" called out the chivero. "No es tu culpa." The farmer wasn't mad about his dog's loss; she was only lethargic because of the puppies growing in her stomach. Otherwise, she would have torn off the man's legs.

Mariana was impregnated by a stray Chinese Crested roaming the country-side. An older mother, she only had three in her coming litter. When the puppies finally came out, the chivero's son, a bubbly ten-year-old, was excited to have fun with the offspring. He named the three Mango, Chico, and Hambriento.

Hambriento was the little boy's favorite, at least at first. Hambriento would snort and shove his brothers away when he went to feed on his mother's teat. His aggression was adorable at that age; a chubby grey blob hell-bent on getting his milk. The little boy played games with Hambriento all day, placing him in his lap and tickling his bulbous belly. Everywhere the little boy went, Hambriento traveled in the pocket of his jeans.

But then, Hambriento got older and problems began to develop. The whole litter had gotten demodex mites from their mother. It happens to dogs all the time and is usually asymptomatic, but poor Hambriento was the only brother to inherit SCID from his father. His immune system was shot, and so the mites quickly turned the puppy's skin puffy, pink, and raw.

"Está enfermo…" said the father. He warned his son that the puppy's illness would surely spread to all the other animals on their farm if he did not get rid of him immediately. The child frowned and put the puppy in his pocket one last time.

The little boy was too young and innocent to put the dog down, so he took Hambriento on their trip to the farmer's market out in Nogales. Before they packed up and went home, the little boy dropped Hambriento in a back street behind a prominent taqueria. The boy hoped the puppy could feed on their disposal, but poor Hambriento would not be so lucky.

A pack of stray bulldogs quickly descended upon the puppy as soon as the boy left with his father. They had to protect their main source of food from outsiders; there wasn't enough to go around. Even though he was such a small threat, the bulldogs treated him like any other intruder. A one-eyed bitch grabbed Hambriento by the throat and violently shook him about. Her jaws cut into Hambriento's skin, irritating his mange even further. Blood flew from his freshly opened lesions. He was tossed out into the street where he quickly ran off into a less populated alley.

Hambriento would soon learn the hard way that most of the garbage in Nogales was like this; guarded by unruly packs of strays. As Hambriento grew up, these difficulties would only add to his list of malformations. His malnutrition would lead to shrunken stature and prominent bones. Having to fight for scraps left scars on his face and legs. His mange added scabs and scales to his back. The infection left yellow crust built up on his eyes, nose, and ears. His soul had calloused all the same.

"¡Perrito malo, déjame en paz!" Desperate for food, Hambriento turned away from the alleys and began a new strategy: stealing from the humans. Because of his small size he had to target the small and weak, so his targets were mainly children. "Déjame solo…" cried out a little boy, holding his pambazo over his head.

Hambriento growled. The boy looked scared but he wouldn't drop his treat. Hambriento snapped his teeth at the air. The boy took a few steps backwards; it looked as though he was going to bolt. Hambriento feared he'd lose his meal if he let the boy run. He panicked.

Hambriento leapt up in the air and tried to bite the snack right out the boy's fingers. But instead of the taste of spicy sausage, greasy potatoes, and warm bread, his mouth was filled with wet and bitter. It was the taste of blood. Hambriento immediately let go and backed away. The boy was in tears rubbing the cuts dug into his wrist. Hambriento's heart broke at the sight. He looked at his victim and he imagined the little boy that used to tickle his belly. The memories tore him apart.

Hambriento sprinted away, ashamed of himself. He charged through the streets of Nogales with tears rolling off his cheeks. He tried to find a place for solace. He passed by a burned-down pawn shop he used to sleep in before the monstrous rats drove him out. He figured the infestation wouldn't bother him till after sunset. He jumped through the open window and curled up into a ball beside a blackened wall.

As he whimpered, Hambriento spotted several necklaces and earrings that had survived the fire hiding under the charred sales desk. The sunlight that glowed through the window kept bouncing off a particularly expensive-looking piece that had the crucifixion in gold at the end of its chain. There were diamonds encrusted around Jesus' waist coating the area where the loin cloth would be.

As Hambriento cowered, his perspective shifted with his shivers and the light played tricks on his eyes. It seemed as though the little gold Jesus was struggling to get his hands free from the cross. Then suddenly… ting, ting... the figurine fell to the floor. Its arms pushed forward and its knees clenched inwards. It stood up off of the ground. It grinned. "I'm gonna call you Ham." The little Jesus spoke a language that Hambriento could perfectly understand. It wasn't Spanish or English, or anything he's heard the humans speak. "I hope you don't mind if I take this off," said the little Jesus, peeling off the diamonds around his groin. "When they stuck me on the cross, I was no more clothed than you are, friend."

Hambriento nodded. He wasn't panicked by the sight of the animated jewelry. Many human things appeared to be magical from his perspective. Cars and TVs were no less miraculous than this Jesus sprung to life. Humans had tons of shit that just didn't make sense. He accepted it for what it was.

The little Jesus walked up to Hambriento's nose and climbed all the way to the top of his head. Here, he straddled the top of the dog's neck between his ears. Jesus reached between the matted fur and rubbed as hard as he could. The sensation soothed poor Hambriento and he began to pant.

"You're an interesting breed, aren't you," said Jesus, picking dead bugs out of the dog's fur as he brushed. "There's a million dogs out there, all different shapes and sizes. But I've been looking for you."

Hambriento cocked his head and raised his ears.

"Hardened. Determined. Local," Jesus stopped his grooming. "Maybe a bit penitent?"

Hambriento thought about the child he bit and lowered his chin. He whined.

Jesus shook his head. "It's a shame how far you've strayed, sweet Ham, but we're all at fault. There's moments like that to teach us when to stop. And there's moments like this to offer redemption."

Hambriento nodded. He was curious what Jesus had in mind.

"There are dark forces in this world, Ham. They're seeking to shift the paradigm with the bicentennial. And it could be your job to stop them."

Hambriento picked himself off the floor. His tail began to wag. He begged to know more.

"A man possessed by the demon Baphomet has impregnated the wombs of numerous she-goats along the Mexican-American border. He is building an army of enchanted offspring."

Hambriento barked. His heart began to race.

"These kids are not much older than you. They must be put down."

Hambriento began pacing back and forth. He began snapping his teeth at the air.

"Your excitement's appreciated," said Jesus with a smile. "Now this will require a little legwork, so I hope you spared some energy to travel."

Hambriento nodded.

"There's a farm just East of here along the Santa Cruz river. This is where our first target thrives. Her name: Capricorn. She must be killed."

Hambriento growled. He wasn't comfortable breaking into a farm. That's how you get shot at. If killing livestock was easy, he would have resorted to that years ago.

"Don't worry. I'll come up with something to distract the farmer," assured the little Jesus. "I can be quite clever when need be."

The farmer was Yolanda Pérez, a smallholder raising Angora goats in order to harvest and sell their lustrous mohair. Yolanda built her fences on the north and southern borders of her pasture. The western section was capped by the back wall of her hacienda, and the east was blocked off by the depths of the river; this gave the livestock a natural source of drinking water to which they had infinite access.

Yolanda often allowed her goats to go unsupervised as she spent her time indoors knitting sarapes with her overstock. Yolanda, a devout Catholic, often wove religious symbolism into her shawls. She was working on a nativity scene placed on a royal blue backdrop when Hambriento arrived at her property. Jesus quickly left his little gold body and entered into the baby stitched in the sarape. "¡Este es un hermoso diseño, Yolanda," spoke the baby Jesus with a smile. "¡Trabajo excelente!"

Yolanda was a very innocent old lady. Hearing her artwork speak immediately sent her head into a spiral. She immediately passed out in her chair. Not dead, but fully unconscious. Her needles fell to the floor. This was part of the reason why Jesus only delegated holy work to dogs. Humans witness a miracle and they either pass out from shock or try to start a new religion with themselves as grand-leader.

With Yolanda dispatched, Hambriento was free to work. He dug beneath the cable wire fence and immediately began to scope out his prey. It was obvious which one was Capricorn. All the goats were brownish white, accept for one doe slurping out of the river's shallows. She was jet black.

Capricorn had deep blue eyes and short black horns that grew outwards 45° from her neck; each horn had a subtle curve directed downward. At the sight of Hambriento's approach, Capricorn raised her lips and chattered her teeth.

"Be careful, Ham!" called out Jesus, returning his presence to the charm on the dog's back. "She's not going to go without a fight."

Hambriento felt confident this frail specimen could be easily reduced to tiny scraps of carpetto. Hambriento pounced. He charged forward at the speed of a vicious wolf.

"Maaaah!" The goat screamed with a wide confident stare. Suddenly, the river water began to rise rapidly around her legs. It looked as though the tides were changing. Hambriento felt his paws getting drenched as he splashed through the flood. Quickly, the surface of the waves rose up to his chest. Moments before he could reach Capricorn, he found himself paddling. The force of the water became too strong and he was carried away.

Hambriento's head went under the water. He could see Capricorn, standing calmly under the surface as though nothing had changed. He tried to swim to her, but the current kept pulling him back. Hambriento swallowed some water and gagged. He winced in pain and let the river carry him to dry land.

The little Jesus hung on for dear life. "Thank God I don't have actual lungs," shouted out Jesus. "You're going to need a different approach."

Hambriento nodded, then vomited a torrent of river water and grass out of his throat. He barked twice, then shook the water from his skin.

Hambriento broke into the hacienda through a backdoor and began looking for something he could possibly use as a flotation device. There was nothing that looked like it would work, but then he came across Yolanda's spools of thread and he had another idea.

Hambriento took the thread and ran down the length of the river till he came across a nearby bridge. Once he was on the other side, he ran back towards the farm. Across the river from Capricorn, Hambriento asked Jesus to help him tie the yarn around a cypress tree. He then took the other end of the string and pulled it all the way back to the pasture at the hacienda. He pulled the strand paw over paw so it stretched over the river and through the pasture.

Hambriento made a second charge. This time he kept his eyes fixed on Capricorn's lips. As soon as she cried out for her rushing water, Hambriento bit down as hard as he could onto the yarn. As the water passed over him, it wasn't able to pull him with it. He was held nicely in place by the make-shift rope clinging to the tree.

Eventually, the water passed completely over him and he could see Capricorn standing with a dry riverbed behind her. Hambriento smiled. He let go of the yarn and pounced on the goat. He got a mouthful of her wet locks. He knocked her backward into the barren ravine.

As soon as Capricorn felt that searing in her neck, she lost her concentration. The river started rushing out of the pasture back into place. As it gushed over the two of them, they were launched forward across the width of the riverbed. They washed ashore on the other side.

Hambriento bit down hard on Capricorn's windpipe so she couldn't utter another spell. Once her breathing came to a halt, her eyes closed. Hambriento dropped her body beside the cypress tree wrapped with yarn. He dried off, then began sniffing her body. He hadn't had mutton his entire life. He felt he'd earned it.

"Wait no!" cried out the Lord. "You mustn't eat her."

Hambriento hesitated. He backed away and cocked his head to the side.

"Come on, you'll be fine," said Jesus. "You've already had plenty to drink…"

Hambriento stuck his head down and licked his lips. He began to whimper. It had been so long since he had a good meal. It was something he'd hunted down all by himself.

"It's unclean," explained Jesus. "See how it doesn't bleed…" Jesus pointed to gashes in Capricorn's neck; the tissue inside was dry and grey. "This creature lived off of a strange dark aura that fuels its body. You mustn't allow that into your system."

Sharp whistles continued to blow from Hambriento's nose. His stomach was growling incessantly.

"No! You mustn't go back to your old ways either. Leave the children alone, Ham," scolded Jesus. "You must be patient. I will promise you a meal when we're through here. But till then… you must abstain."

Hambriento reluctantly agreed. Eager to get his food, he asked Jesus to lead them to the next fight immediately. Jesus was happy to oblige.

"This one's a buck. His name is Pan," explained Jesus. "There's no farmer to worry about this time. Pan was pegged to be slaughtered, so he planned a daring escape along with the rest of the farmer's trip. They lie farther east."

Jesus pointed them forward out of the grasslands and into the harsh heat of the Chihuahuan desert. It took a full night and a full day of travel. On their trek, Hambriento had plenty of time to talk with Jesus about all sorts of things. He knew very little about him and he wanted to get to know him. He asked Jesus if he had a dog when he was a kid.

80

Jesus shook his head. "No. Joseph was a carpenter. So was I. Only herders had dogs."

Hambriento wondered if there were any dogs in Heaven.

Jesus nodded. "The good ones."

He asked if these dogs were like him, selected for God's holy work.

"Not always, but some," explained Jesus. "God picked Hachiko to protect the soul of his master while he was stuck in limbo. He chose Balto to save a small town in Alaska from a plague of leather throat. He used Rin-Tin-Tin to teach the world to love again after WWI. And he would have prevented WWII if it wasn't for a mean case of parvo. God only has so much control."

Hambriento wondered if his name would go down in history like they did.

Jesus sighed. "You know, I won't answer that," said Jesus shaking his head. "Cause that's really not the point."

By this time, Jesus had led them into the dead center of the desert, where the dunes rose and fell like the tops of ancient temples. Pan and his army were positioned just over the hill, taking a break to fornicate in a large undulating mass.

This was how Pan acquired leadership over his herd. It wasn't mind-control; it was a trade. In exchange for their undying loyalty, Pan offered the goats something even a simple animal could desire. Pure sexual energy. Pan's dark powers emitted supernatural pheromones that whipped up his followers into exciting orgies full of ultimate pleasure.

"Ew," cringed Jesus. "Let's try to wrap this one up fast. I'm a bit timid when it comes to relations. Especially those involving livestock."

Hambriento stepped forward so that he was in clear view of Pan's trip. Most of them stopped their humping and stared with concern. Pan, making love to a billy's over-sized rear, kept pumping. He was in the zone. "Bah, bah, bah, bah, bah, bah…" he moaned with each thrust.

Jesus hid his eyes behind his hand. Hambriento loudly cleared his throat. Pan opened his eyes and realized the orgy had come to a screeching halt. He held in his orgasm and pulled out from his lover. He walked to the front of his herd and sneered at the sight of Jesus hiding his eyes like a child. "Bah, bah, bah, bah, bah, bah!" he mocked.

Hambriento snarled and white foam leapt from his lips. He got a good look at Pan as he slowly approached. Pan was a different breed than Capricorn. His hair was straight and short. His beard reached down to his knees. His horns were longer and made two spirals along their extension. This was a TexMaster; a chubby breed with an exaggerated amount of meat on their bones.

Pan shivered as Hambriento came in close proximity. A red mist expelled from his coat and entered into the nostrils of the other goats. They all suddenly felt a charge of excitement. The whole herd entered into a frenzy and began to circle Hambriento. They kicked up dust that twisted upwards into a spiral. Pan disappeared into the stampede.

"Careful, careful," warned Jesus.

Hambriento hesitated. The circle of goats began to contract.

"You don't want to rush this, or you might get trampled."

Hambriento squinted his eyes and tried to make out Pan from the rest. He was, once again, the only one with a black coat. He could barely see the dark blur amongst the rest of the whites and ambers. He couldn't rely on his eyesight alone. Hambriento sniffed the air. He could smell the strong musk passing by his nose every other second.

Hambriento counted. One. Three. Five. Hambriento leapt forward on six and had Pan in his teeth by seven. He held on tight as Pan kept rushing around the circumference of the stampede, carrying Hambriento on his neck. The weight was exhausting and after three more laps, Pan finally began to slow down. The rest of the trip followed his lead and the spiral of goats suddenly came to a halt.

Pan fell to the ground. Hambriento put in work, flailing Pan's tired body around in the air. He could feel the goat's neck bones snapping out of place. Soon, Pan's breathing came to an end.

"He's dead… stop," said Jesus.

Hambriento shook the body more and more. He felt the flesh beginning to detach from the neck.

"Spit him out, Ham! This is not your reward!"

Hambriento couldn't stop. He was so hungry. He hadn't eaten in days.

Jesus panicked. He couldn't let Ham devour the tainted flesh. "Just think of the little boy you bit!" shouted Jesus.

A flashback quickly entered Hambriento's mind. His eyes suddenly snapped open. He shuttered.

"…think of the blood."

Hambriento's jaw popped open. He imagined the child's limb gushing into his mouth. He gagged and quickly ran away from Pan's fallen form. Aggravated and starving, Hambriento curled up into a ball.

"I will not warn you again," said Jesus sternly. "Do not fall for temptation or it will turn around and consume you."

Hambriento was growing frustrated with these rules. Surely his hard work deserved some immediate gratification.

"Well of course it does!" said Jesus with a smile. He crawled up the side of Ham's head and began scratching the dry skin flaking off behind his ears. "Who's a good boy?"

Hambriento was not amused.

"Who's a good boy?"

Hambriento reached his leg up to his head and knocked Jesus off. Jesus fell face first into the sand. He pulled himself up and spit sediment out of his mouth. Being the Lord, he forgave Hambriento's act of anger and brushed himself off.

A night of rest was needed so that Hambriento could cool his temper. When the morning came, the two continued their trek east to their next destination; a small tourist town along the Rio Grande called Boquillas. Here, a small gift shop attracted customers with an adorable pet: A pygmy goat they bought for cheap at a local fair. Kids would come in and give the wether pets between its stubby little horns. The owners named him Frijole, but his real name was Azazel.

"I'm going to pull the same trick on the shopkeeper as we did on the old lady. Once they're passed out, you know what to do…" Jesus leapt out of his body and entered into a cartoon of himself printed on the side of a novelty mug. Jesus read out loud the text

84

on the side of the cup. "Todo lo que necesito es a Jesús y al café," Jesus winked and snapped his finger. "Suena como un perfecto domingo por la mañana."

The owner's jaw dropped at the sight of the animated cartoon. "Soy rico," said the owner quietly. Then he burst out in excitement, "¡Soy rico! ¡Soy rico! ¡Soy rico!" The owner was overwhelmed with joy as he thought about all the money he'd make from his miracle mug. He leapt over the counter and went to reign in some customers with his new pitch. It would blow the goat idea out of the water.

This wasn't exactly the reaction Jesus was going for, but it could work all the same. "He's still gonna be gone for awhile. He may sound like a crazy person, then get arrested if we're lucky."

Hambriento wouldn't take that chance. He decided to take out Azazel as fast as possible. Without skipping a beat, he galloped through the front door and charged the little wether.

Hambriento was actually surprised Azazel didn't seem to be doing anything to fight back. He just stood there and looked up. He was by far the meekest looking of Hambriento's targets and yet he had no fear, even as Hambriento towered over him.

"I do not fear you because I am like you." A strange monotone voice popped into Hambriento's head. It was speaking the same magical language Jesus used to talk to him. "The world is a grueling experience for minds like ours. I too was born into a loving home, only to have it stripped away. These salesmen castrated me and turned me into a walking billboard."

Hambriento turned his head and looked at Jesus. He stared back at him confused. "What are you waiting for?"

Hambriento turned back to face the goat. The beast winced devilishly. "He can't hear us," said Azazel. "You know, I possess greater powers far beyond that of the God Bastard."

Hambriento took a step forward. He clenched his jaw and growled.

"In a past life, I have fed the loyal hounds of Hell. I will bring you the bowl of Cerberus if you allow me to live."

Hambriento's stomach roared at just the thought of dinner. It churned so loudly it echoed over the sounds of his snarl. He shook his head and tried to snap out of it.

"You can't hide gluttony…"

Hambriento snapped his teeth. He barked angrily.

"Right, right," agreed Azazel. "It isn't gluttony if you're starving."

Suddenly the world behind Azazel dipped into darkness, as though the back of the store was cast in a large shadow. In this black void appeared a table fit for a throne room, with three steel saucers atop it the size of car wheels. Stacked across these plates were cemitas, pabamos, and empanadas respectively.

"Behold, a feast fit for three heads."

Hambriento's heart almost beat out of his chest. The assortment of snacks was something of legend. Street dogs have killed each other for an iota of this amount.

Hambriento walked past the goat and kneeled at the towers of consumption. He began to drool. Then, Hambriento snapped.

When the dog came to, he felt cold steel resting against the side of his head. He'd passed out on the ornate table; his body sprawling across the emptied platters. His stomach sat on the middle plate like a loaf of bread, warm and swollen.

Hambriento looked around. The shadow that engulfed one corner of the shop now encompassed everything. And the spot between his shoulders was missing a rider.

Hambriento began to cry out. He shrieked and he shrieked, begging for someone to find him in the dark. But he was alone. Even the table he awoke on had magically disappeared.

Then suddenly, he heard voices. "Monstruo. Monstruo. Mata al monstruo." Hambriento got what he wished for. He was no longer alone as a large angry crowd holding torches and pitchforks came stomping slowly out of the darkness. The faces looked familiar somehow. It took him a moment before he realized they were all the people he'd ever stolen from; innocent lives he'd terrorized in the pursuit of sustenance, but their features were warped. Their clothes and hair were all jet black. And their pupils were replaced with goat-like slits.

A little boy with a bandaged arm led the pack. He pointed at Hambriento with his tattered fingers and unhinged his jaw. "Maaaaa!" he bleated. The whole crowd began chasing Hambriento through the dark.

Hambriento called out for Jesus, but the little man was nowhere to be found. Black walls made of solid coal began to rise up from the blackness, forming tight alleyways that led Hambriento deeper and deeper into a never-ending maze.

Hambriento eventually found himself in a long hallway with the angry mob chasing him from behind. In front of him, a pack of black dogs with long curling horns extruding from their heads blocked the exit. They gnawed at the air and took small steps forward, trying to back Hambriento into the arms of the mob.

Hambriento shrieked for help. He spun around and panted nervously, looking at the crowd of angry people. Then he spun around again and stared into the eyes of the horned dogs. He shivered, boxed into the center of the hallway. He tucked his paws under his body and laid down, surrendering himself. He shoved his front paws forward and tucked his nose between them. He thought about something happy to numb the coming pain.

Suddenly, a creaking noise sounded to Hambriento's left. He cracked an eye and stared in its direction. There, on the wall of rock, a white border was drawn, the size and shape of a door. When it opened, a bright light shimmered into Hambriento's face. He wanted to enter into the glow, but he was scared it was just another wrong turn.

"Hola mi niño hambriento…" whispered a young voice from the white light. "¿Acariciar el estómago?"

Hambriento saw a small, golden silhouette materialize in the light beam. The voice suddenly became familiar. The silhouette stepped forward and the boy's face became clear. It was the little boy from Hambriento's old life on the farm.

Hambriento's heart froze. He looked around. The mob and the dogs had disappeared. He turned back. The little boy and the white door seemed to be growing taller. He looked down at his body; he was shrinking; changing back into a baby. His scabs healed and his scars vanished. He was a little grey blob once again.

The little boy reached down and scooped Hambriento into his hands. He pursed his lips and planted a kiss on Hambriento's head. The little boy turned around and carried Hambriento into the shining white void.

Hambriento felt a tickle on his stomach. At first it felt like fingers running along the exterior, but then the sensation grew stronger and stronger. He could feel it along his insides. It was like worms wriggling around in his chest, then suddenly, blek.

Hambriento vomited onto the floor of the gift shop. He was back in reality. He stared at the fresh up-chuck shot out of his mouth. It looked like a knot of grey nerves tangled together and wriggling madly.

Hambriento stood up onto his legs and looked around the room. Azazel was staring at him from afar. He was perched atop a playhouse built into the corner of the gift shop. There was a slide in front of Azazel's hooves; a prop for him to play with to attract customers with the cute-factor.

Hambriento snarled. He beat the squirming ball of bizzarity with his paw, crushing it into lifeless goo. Then he rushed up the plastic slide and snatched Azazel up into the air. The bottom of Azazel's jaw was gripped into Hambriento's mouth. Azazel hung in the air, lifted up high by the strain in Hambriento's neck.

"You are stepping in the way of magnificent change," said Azazel in Hambriento's head. "The kind that makes beasts like you into kings."

Hambriento shook his head. He swung Azazel over to one side, then launched him over his opposite shoulder. Azazel came hurtling down off of his playground and slammed onto the floor of the shop with incredible force. He landed on his face and severed his vertebrae. The shard pierced his spinal cord and paralyzed him.

"I thought you'd abandoned your mission," came a familiar voice. It was Jesus; he'd reappeared between Hambriento's shoulders. "I was worried you wouldn't return."

Hambriento begged Jesus for forgiveness. He couldn't help himself.

"There's no need to grovel. Your time in Hell was punishment enough."

Hambriento thanked the Lord for guiding him out.

"I did nothing," said Jesus. "If something pulled you out of the darkness, it wasn't me. It was something inside of you."

Slam! Suddenly, the door to the gift shop swung open and the shop owner returned. "¿Que es esto?" The owner saw his poor little mascot lying motionless on the ground. "¿Que pasó?"

"We should leave," suggested Jesus.

Hambriento looked around for a second exit. The windows were all shut and there was no backdoor.

"Si quieres mi alma," said the shopkeeper with a blank expression, "tendrás que hacerlo mejor que eso."

"What's going on? Who's he talking to?" asked Jesus.

Hambriento's eyes went wide. He looked over at Azazel. He wasn't dead yet. He was using his telepathy on the store owner.

"Tendrás que mostrarme el dinero primero," said the man. Suddenly, gold coins began spilling from his sleeves. The store owner flexed a wide grin under his thick mustache. "Bueno. Soy todo tuyo." The store owner had just sold his soul to Azazel for a prodigious treasure.

90

The owner's face twisted in pain. His eyes turned completely black and a pair of rusty steel horns pierced through the skin above his brow. They were the same shape and size as Azazel's.

"Duck!" screamed Jesus.

The shop owner's mouth opened wide and a torrent of fire came billowing out. The flames missed Hambriento and landed on a wooden shelf full of tiny mariachi caricatures. One after another, the figurines exploded as the water in their cheap ceramic boiled. The shards flew through the air like shrapnel and struck poor Hambriento in the hip.

"Ham! Are you alright?" called out Jesus.

Hambriento shook his head. His left leg stung like crazy; he couldn't move it without wincing in pain.

"You need to burn Azazel's body, it's the source of the shopkeeper's powers!" shouted Jesus. "I'll distract him!" Jesus climbed off of Hambriento's back and landed on the check-out counter. He ran across the top, then leapt with all his strength onto the shopkeeper's face. He grabbed the man's mustache with his arms, then shoved his knees under his bottom lip. He clenched his body together and shut the man's lips tightly.

Meanwhile, Hambriento limped to Azazel's fallen form and grabbed the billy by the horns. He yanked him foot by foot to the flaming shelves.

"Will he protect you from the streets when all this is over?" sneered Azazel in Hambriento's head. "Once you've served your purpose, he will throw you back in the gutter!"

Tears welled up in Hambriento's eyes. The ashes were irritating him.

"There's no amount of food he can give you that will change your life." Azazel laughed. "You'll die a mongrel and when you do, I'll see you in Hell… because no one will ever forgive you…"

Hambriento wheezed as the smoke entered his lungs. With the remainder of his strength, he lifted Azazel's little body and chucked it into the inferno burning at his back. Suddenly, the shopkeeper, too, went up in flames. He ran out the doorway into the street and began rolling his body around in the sand, to no avail.

Hambriento slowly crawled over to Jesus and shoveled him up onto his head with his nose. He then crawled out the front and hid in a nearby alley. The streets quickly became crowded with curious tourists filming the burning shop and shop keep with the cameras on their phones. Hambriento would rest until they disappeared.

"There's still work that needs to be done," said Jesus while they hid. "But it's the final two. An inseparable pair. Tanngrisnir and Tanngnjóstr."

Hambriento nodded weakly.

"Your strength is gone," said Jesus, sensing his companion's pain. "Perhaps we should rest for a few days first.

Hambriento shook his head. Something had changed in his demeanor. Pain nor weariness didn't seem to bother him. He was filled with some new energy. A bright light emanating from his heart.

He felt a responsibility for the happiness of all of humanity. And he wouldn't rest till he was sure no one would interfere.

92

Once the coast was clear and the fires were out, Hambriento left Boquillas around nightfall. Their final stop was in Piedras Negras. It took them two days to reach the city, travel through its heart, then come out the other side. The twin goats would be waiting for them on the outskirts to the East. Tanngrisnir and Tanngnjóstr were on a path to Texas, and brought a horrifying storm cloud with them that would cause mass destruction in the American South.

Hambriento would intercept them only feet from the border fence. By the time he reached the twins, Hambriento had been reduced to skin and bones. By this point, he hadn't eaten in over a week. If it wasn't for the power of the Lord coursing through his veins, he would have died days ago.

Tanngrisnir and Tanngnjóstr laughed hysterically at the frail specimen that had come to block their path. The downdraft alone was almost enough to topple Hambriento. He was swaying in the breeze. Tanngrisnir winked at his brother. He wouldn't need any special powers to kill this "savior".

Tanngrisnir charged and headbutted Hambriento right in his face. Hambriento's incisors all snapped off and flew down his throat. Hambriento coiled up into a pile and slid across the dirt. He got back up, spit out some blood, and showed his remaining teeth. He snarled, spraying amber foam onto the ground in front of him.

Tanngnjóstr shook his head and continued to laugh. He repeated as his brother did and charged forward, but this time he lowered his skull so it rammed right into Hambriento's elbow. Immediately, his left arm shattered.

"Come on! Get up Ham!" shouted Jesus.

With his left arm folded up towards his chest, Hambriento put all his weight on his right arm and pulled himself up. He

93

hobbled forward; this time he would be the one charging. The brothers stared with expressions of pity on their faces. They were almost disgusted by the dog's mangled form coming near them.

Tanngrisnir considered ending the miserable creature with a lightning bolt. He looked up at the sky and could see a charge brewing in the cloud above them. Tanngrisnir smiled and concentrated on his target.

Then suddenly, pow... zoot. A sharp whistling noise sounded, and Tanngrisnir's head was turned inside out. Tanngnjóstr stared in disbelief. For a second he thought that somehow the dog had done it; but then he saw the gentlemen sitting in their lawn chairs on the other side of the border fence, and he realized no miracle of God was at work here. It was just an act of boredom by some boring, old men.

Liam Williams and Aiden Smith thought of themselves as "patriots". They would drive to the border from La Pryor on Sundays when they had the day off from working at the local Valero. These two brought their rifles and a couple of lawn chairs. They'd sit at a deserted spot in front of the border fence and threaten any Mexicans getting too close to the crossing. They carried a sign with them "TRUSPASSERS SHOT ONSIGHT".

Ironically, there weren't many immigrants crossing near Piedras Negras due to the nearby border patrol station. So, Liam and Aiden would often find themselves drunk and bored. To pass the time on these dry days, they would take shots at the local fauna. They made a game out of it. Big lizards were one point each. Prairie dogs and squirrels were two points each. Escaped livestock were four points. And plain ol' weird shit could win you the whole game automatically.

94

"Let's see if you can tie things up," said Liam to his friend. He'd just pulled ahead by four points by taking out a stray goat. He wanted to give Aiden a fair chance to catch up, so he let Aiden take the next shot.

Aiden licked the corner of his mouth, then put Tanngnjóstr in the scope of his rifle. The crosshairs lined up right between the horns.

Tanngnjóstr saw his attacker and laughed. Pow... zoot. The bullet passed through the goat's head and carried its brains out onto the sand.

"Tied," said Aiden with a snicker. "Your move."

"Betcha' I can take out that, uh... well jeez... what the fuck even is that?" asked Liam, squinting at the last living thing in their vicinity. He pulled the lens of his scope over his eye. Even with the image clear he still couldn't figure out what Hambriento was.

Aiden took a look too. "It's a coyote!" he shouted.

"Nah, it's too small," replied Liam. "I think it's a racoon. With mange."

The gunmen put Hambriento in his sights.

"Kill it in one shot," said Aiden, "and I'll buy you a Zima."

Hambriento looked down at the two goats. His fractured body was shaking uncontrollably. He couldn't run from his coming fate if he wanted to. Instead, Hambriento lied down on the ground and found that happy thought he used before.

Jesus crawled up the side of Hambriento's head and placed his lips inside the dog's sunken ear. "Your dinner's being prepared as we speak," whispered Jesus. "Tell me, Ham. What's your favorite food?"

Hambriento didn't know many in his time on Earth. He took a guess based on what the other dogs fought for most viciously.

"Really?" said Jesus with a smile. He leaned away from Hambriento's ear and stared off into the distance. "Consider it done."

When the bullet passed through Hambriento's head, it exited behind his ear. Here, the bullet struck the soft gold body of Jesus and split him in two. The golden crumbles piled on top of Hambriento's dead body and left a trail of glitter over his cold, lifeless torso.

When Hambriento woke up, he was standing over a water dish in a house he didn't recognize. He looked into the metal bowl and could see his own reflection. His mange was cured, his scars had faded, and he was standing six inches taller.

Hambriento took a step back and raised his head. He looked around the room with a bewildered expression. He saw a young man staring at him from the kitchen table. "¿No vas a comer?" said the man before lowering his head and taking a bite out of his Choco Krispis.

Hambriento walked up to his new owner and sat down at his feet. He looked up into his eyes. This face was familiar; it was just older than when they'd last met.

Two dogs suddenly joined Hambriento at his sides. It was Chico and Mango. They led Hambriento over to their food, a single bowl they all shared filled to the brim with cornbread and al pastor. Hambriento shoved his brothers aside and went face first into the dish. He ate and he ate, and it seemed the pile of food was endless. In Heaven, the bowl wouldn't be empty until Ham decided it was done.

Profile: The Spokane Spleen Spitter

The Spokane Spleen Spitter, a ghoulish legend of eastern Washington, got his name for the means in which he left his victims. The abdomen was cut open with a lancet and emptied of all the internal organs. The only thing left inside would be a lonesome spleen, displaced from its connective tissue and lying half-masticated on the back of the rib cage.

Arsenio Aloso is not the Spokane Spleen Spitter, but he is, nonetheless, an important origin point in this story. The Spokane Spleen Spitter started as a small tick encased in Arsenio's locus of control. Due to sexual abuse by his uncle in his preteen years, Arsenio suffered random blackouts where he'd enter into a dissociative state. In this state, witnesses would describe his face like a child about to take the hardest test of his life. He would remain silent, then obsessively chew through his fingernails, biting deeper and deeper all the way down to the lunula, where the pain would finally snap him out of it.

For the first twenty years of his life, Arsenio allowed these episodes to come and go freely. But in Fall 2011, Arsenio started his journey to becoming an RN. He entered into the nursing program at Gonzaga University where he quickly realized how dangerous it would be to enter his dissociative states while on the job. He decided it would be best to curb this habit that could distract him while he's potentially saving someone's life.

Arsenio added a new step to his morning routine. Next to his toothpaste, behind his mirror, he began keeping a jar full of sliced jalapenos. Before finishing up in the bathroom, he'd take one out and rub it on the tips of his fingers. This treatment would work like magic. Whenever Arsenio would black out, it would take less than a minute for him to come back. All it took was for his finger to reach his mouth, then blam, the flavor would sting his lips and immediately wake him up.

Arsenio's success in nursing school would go unhindered by his tick, and by the end of the first semester he felt confident in his future. However, as finals rolled around Arsenio noticed a change in his dissociative states. He wasn't entering them. It seemed, at first, that somehow his habit had died. He figured that the peppers had either pulled off some sort of miracle or that the stress from finals was somehow suppressing his ticks.

Then there came the night of his first and hardest final, Basic Nutrition. Half-way into the exam he noticed his teeth chattering, then he suddenly found it hard to remember anything he studied. Then his thoughts went blank and his sight went black.

The next thing he'd remember is a harsh, bitter taste snapping him out of his trance. But it wasn't from the brittle texture of a fingernail. His mouth was filled with something tender and wet. Arsenio dropped his jaw and let the source of the flavor fall out of his mouth. He wiped at his tongue with his sleeve and stared down at the ground.

There was the first victim of the Spokane Spleen Spitter: Jonathan Mash. A fellow nursing student in his final year. Arsenio barely knew the guy. They'd worked together on a partner quiz at the end of class just one time. Somehow, Arsenio was in this guy's apartment, hovering over his dead body.

Arsenio is not to blame for this first murder. Arsenio could never have predicted it. He only took a small step to mitigate what was, at the time, a minor tick. Little did he know, this tick was actually a split personality. A completely benign one, at first. But once Arsenio took away his favorite chew toy, the personality took greater actions to achieve oral satisfaction.

Arsenio is, undoubtedly, responsible for the next two murders. He could have, and he should have, reported his first crime; whether conscious for it or not. He's been open about this decision and admits he made an immoral choice. He just thought he could live a normal life again if he restarted biting his nails. But his change came too late. Once the Spokane Spleen Spitter got a taste for cannibalism, it trumped onychophagy in all possible ways.

Arsenio took the lives of Mary Yetts and Tabitha Ho. Only then, did he lose all hope of a future in the outside world. He turned himself in and admitted to all wrongdoing.

Arsenio has willfully accepted his occupancy at a psychiatric facility, where he and the Spokane Spleen Spitter can be kept under close surveillance. As professionals have come to understand Arsenio's condition, they have tried to absolve Arsenio of any guilt. He shares his body with a psychopath over which he has no control. He's done all he can to prevent further murders, and for that, he's a good person.

The ward's staff have tried to keep Arsenio entertained over the years by introducing him to numerous activities taught on their grounds. Admittedly, Arsenio prefers outdoor leisures, soccer specifically, but he still commits a short time each week to creative writing. There's an excellent instructor at his facility who believes that writing can be therapeutic, especially if the patient puts a piece of themselves into their work.

I've selected Arsenio's "A Vacancy in Staffordshire" for this collection because it's clearly inspired by the perils of his own split personality. The story reflects his hopes for a cure one day, all while placing the characters in a setting Arsenio can only hope to imagine. From what I understand, if Arsenio was ever

100

freed from the killer inside, his first trip would be to a tea house in London.

A Vacancy in Staffordshire

Victoria departed from Birmingham Airport in a black taxi. They traveled an hour out, then curled onto an unmarked road layered with loose stones and white soil. It led them into a region of dense forest where the grey tones of England's sky were further dimmed by a canopy of bracken and birch. They came to a halt in front of an old, dilapidated inn at the center of the woods.

Victoria paid her driver, then grabbed her luggage out of the trunk. She carried her bags and marched through the strong breeze acting against her. It coated her otherwise pristine work clothes in dried leaves and petals. She reached the front porch and wiped a layer of crisp heather out of her eyes. She looked up at the bronze lettering over the double doors of the entrance: Lassjoyce Tavern.

Victoria twisted the little copper door knob, mixing brown rust with the sweat in her palm. The door was tough to move, but with a hard enough shove it finally unstuck. Victoria came tumbling inside and almost tripped in her high-heels. She kept herself from falling by catching the edge of the front desk.

"Well hello!" gleed a short grandlady behind the counter. "I am so sorry about that door, miss. It gets stiff when the wind gets cold."

"I- I almost face planted..." huffed Victoria with a tinge of annoyance.

"It won't happen again! I'll be sure to throw some oil on those hinges just as soon as it's done frying the potatoes." The lady pointed over her shoulder at a cloud of smoke emanating behind her. It poured out from under the kitchen door and left a black streak across the lobby's rug.

"Oh!" exclaimed Victoria. "I think something's burning back there…"

"Oh no no… it's just very good oil," assured the old lady. She then picked up a small booklet chained to her desk and began tearing through the little pages. "So then let's see… today's Tuesday, so then you must be… Elliot Mo?"

"That's correct." replied Victoria. Elliot Mo was an alias selected by her employer.

"And you're sharing the big suite with Oscar Groux and Burton Ernie?"

"err… yes," cringed Victoria. She just realized that her employer had made all their aliases based off Sesame Street. That was definitely not the best way to go unnoticed.

The old woman reached into a drawer, then handed Victoria a key to her room. "You're gonna wanna look for 2B."

"And which way's that?"

The old woman shrugged.

"You don't know… where my room is?"

"I'm so sorry, dear, but my husband decided the naming system before he died and I just can't figure it out myself."

"Well if it's 2B, then maybe it's the second room on the second floor?"

The old woman nodded with uncertainty. "Sure. Sounds like you know what you're talking about."

Victoria smiled nervously and thanked the old woman. She found the staircase and began to ascend. She stopped at a window where the stairs changed direction and stared out into the forest below.

Lassjoyce Tavern was such an eyesore in and out that it was lucky to be curtained by the tall trees of southern Staffordshire. If anyone saw it coming from far away, they'd turn around and bolt. From what she understood, Lassjoyce was normally only used by cheap college students gone abroad. Victoria and her associates were probably the first adults to stay in this hostel for the last five decades.

Victoria found the door to 2B right where she thought it'd be. She knocked twice and was immediately answered by whom she assumed to be David, her employer. They'd never met before, but he described himself as 'taller than you're expecting'. Victoria herself was tall amongst her usual posse, but even she had to tip her head back to peer eye to eye with the colossus before her. David's face was perched atop an impressive six-foot-six stature. His thin face had a handsome, bronze glow. When combined with his delicate eyes, his Japanese background was apparent.

"Elliot!" exclaimed David, welcoming Victoria by her alias.

Victoria hurried inside and threw her heavy luggage onto the nearest bed. She then turned to face David and sneered. "Why on earth did you name us all after Muppets?"

David rolled his eyes. "I've already had this argument once today so let's keep it short. First, the apology: I'm really sorry. Second, the explanation: I was high when I booked it. And lastly, the fix: none needed, the manager is a fucking moron and suspects nothing."

Despite his briefing, Victoria still looked worried. "I mean do you get high often, then? Is this a problem I need to be aware of?"

"No! Of course not. I'd never jeopardize our expedition like that," exclaimed David. "I did one Jim Jones and it was the last time I ever will. It was an experiment to see if it could enhance the effects of the Psychopomp."

"Well... did it work?" asked Victoria.

"Yes, but the cocktail was superfluous. The weed and PCP did nothing to help. The acting ingredient was all the cocaine. And so... voila," David pulled a tube of white powder from his pocket. "Me and Markie drove south of the river and picked this up last night."

Victoria glanced at the vial with a morbid expression. "Oh... that's a felony."

"It's necessary," argued David. "It helps to control the effects of the Psychopomp to our advantage."

"But is Markie really okay with snorting blow? I thought he was a good little Christian."

"I am!" came the voice of Markie. It was shouting from the adjacent bathroom. "But I won't be the one partaking." Markie washed his hands and came out into the bedroom to join the others. He appeared just as in his online profile. A long black ponytail, bloodshot eyes, and a Babymetal t-shirt.

"Will it be Mikey, then? I'm sure he's less reserved."

Markie shook his head. "Neither of us have to. The child will take the dosage. Which I won't have any part of. Giving kids drugs is mighty unholy. Mikey's creepy, he'll take care of it."

"Does Mikey know I've arrived?" asked Victoria.

Markie shook his head. "We only share long term memories. Perhaps it would be best then that I bring him out so you two can meet in person."

Victoria looked nervous. "I mean… his nihilism is a little grating… can you promise you'll tuck him back in after we're done with introductions? I don't want to deal with him all night."

Markie nodded. "We've set boundaries. He knows if he doesn't follow directions, I shave off the ponytail and throw out the cool t-shirt. And if he really gets out of hand, just tell him to roll up his sleeves…"

Markie began to take audibly loud inhales. He began respirating faster and stronger, increasing his pace till his lungs were sore and his face turned blue. Once he felt a light-headedness coming on, he shut his eyes and cleared his thoughts. This was equivalent to stepping out of his mind and leaving the door open. Mikey filled the emptied void.

"H-hello…" It was still Markie's body, but a new voice had taken control. It was made from the same vocal chords and regional accent, but controlled completely differently. Mikey spoke sporadically and louder than Markie. Like he was always buzzed on too much caffeine. The added shouting strained his throat and made his voice sound raspier and higher-pitched as well.

Mikey pointed to Vicky. "Smart girl's actually arrived. I thought she'd make us do all the hard work ourselves."

106

Vicky rolled her eyes. "I only invented an alloy with psychoactive properties..."

"Yeah well I heard you found it by accident," griped Mikey. "I also heard there was a very good chance you wouldn't be showing up tonight. You must have very little respect for David's work."

"That's already too far, Mikey. You're just picking fights," interjected David. "We've accomplished introductions, so switch back to Markie, now."

"Not before we have a chance to talk!" exclaimed Mikey. "It's our first time meeting in person. Allow us an opportunity to bond..."

"I was given twenty-four hours' notice that this was happening," explained Vicky. "I couldn't guarantee my part in this evening. Not when I have classes to teach. I was lucky to get this time off."

"I thought universities wanted their staff communicating with top collaborators!" replied Mikey with a twisted smile. He pointed over to David. "Clearly they don't have any respect for poor Dr. Matthews here."

"They let me off, didn't they?" rebutted Vicky.

"But it was for a personal vacation, wasn't it?" sneered Mikey. "They won't cover the travel expenses for you to see a crackpot."

"Back in your cage, you fucking troll!" shouted David. Mikey has a habit of turning everybody against each other. It's due in part to an underdeveloped mind. Mikey only emerges in small bursts and in those large periods of downtime it's equivalent to entering a temporary coma. When Mikey is inactive, the neurons making up his personality go unfed and unmaintained. They essentially 'rust' from unuse.

"Regardless of my employer's opinion, I don't think it's appropriate you call him crackpot," replied Victoria, with a look of disdain. "He's the one curing you."

Mikey scoffed with a short burst of laughter. "Curing me? Please… we all know he's curing Markie of me."

"That's enough!" shouted David. He grabbed Mikey's hand and held it up to his face. David undid the first button at the top of the sleeve and revealed a black cross drawn in marker on his wrist. "Fuck!" yelled Mikey. He cringed at the drawing on his skin. This "tattoo" was fake now, but Mikey knew what Markie was implying. It would become a permanent fixture on their shared flesh if Mikey didn't follow orders.

"Fine," huffed Mikey. "But you'll hear from me, later…" Mikey puffed out his cheeks and took in big gulps of air. He began to hyperventilate. Within the next minute he forced himself out of consciousness, allowing Markie back in control of their body.

"…and we're back," smiled Markie, his softer mannerisms returned to his voice. His smile faded as he realized David had a firm grip around his arm. "…was there an issue?"

David shook his head. "No issue. It just took a little pushing. Nothing you didn't prepare us for." David let go of Markie's wrist and allowed him to button it back up. Markie liked to look professional at all times.

"With all the introductions carried out, I think we should make note of the hour…" said Markie; he'd caught sight of the time on his opposite wrist. Everyone else checked the time posted on their cell phones. It was 6:30PM. They were due to begin

108

searching at 7. Luckily, their hotel was already located in the woods, so they could begin as soon as they left the front steps.

All that was left to do before heading out was to change into hiking gear and distribute the Psychopomps. These Psychopomps took the form of what may look like joy buzzers at first glimpse. Their main body was a flat circle that gets pressed into the palm of your hand. This flat circle is 'clipped' onto the hand with a bobby-pin welded to the back. This clip is slid onto the skin between the middle and ring fingers, holding the contraption in the proper place.

Each Psychopomp handed out was created in Victoria's Materials Science Lab at Georgia Tech. Victoria clipped the latest version to her hand, a model with a blue outer layer that she's dubbed "Vanth". This latest addition is more effective than the previous models. David got the alpha-version, a white metal clip called "Hermes", and Markie got the first prototype ever created, a dark-grey clip referred to as "Charon". Once they were all suited up, they immediately ventured off into the woods.

Lassjoyce was only a mile south of the sighting they were following. The exact point of the encounter can only be reached by foot. The original witnesses were three campers with open food left out while they slept. One of the three heard noises in the middle of the night and awoke the other two to investigate. All three reported the same scene. Two black-eyed children rummaging through their food supplies, stealing their canned steak.

"They got away clean," read David to the others. He'd brought a copy of the newspaper that had printed the story. He held a lighter up to the page and read it as they walked. He tried to estimate the exact point of contact based on tiny little hints in the details. "The newspaper specified that the sighting was in the middle of Cannock Chase. But when the kids disappeared they were heading west."

"Is that which way we're going?" asked Victoria.

David nodded. "Along with their dark eyes, the kids were described as having black markings on their arms and legs. I think the latter might just be soot from the coal mines at Brindley Heath. I think they use it as a hiding spot. We may want to make some loud noise to scare them and trick them into heading there."

Markie took his backpack off his shoulders and reached inside. He came out with a dark blue air horn. Markie held it towards the stars and let off a loud honk, applying the necessary sound to get the children running.

"Jesus fucking Christ!" shouted Victoria, protecting her ears from the blare.

Markie shuttered. "David, you said you'd make it clear to her she can't say that around me..."

"I'm gonna keep screaming His name in vain as long as there's a maniac firing off sound effects!" snarled Victoria. "Why the hell do you have one of those? That sounds like a terrible idea around Mikey."

"I bought it last night to scare off any nocturnal animals. We're in the wilderness after all. But don't worry about Mikey, it won't enter my long term memory for 24-hours. In other words, Mikey has no idea what we have here and he won't till 2AM tomorrow morning. And by then, there won't be any gas left in the canister."

"What makes you think you'll use it all?" asked Victoria.

"Cause we're not alone out here." Markie pointed to a bush rattling in the distance. There was a creature hurrying under its branches, closing in on their search party.

Markie aimed the nozzle of his canister at an opening in the foliage. He was prepared to fire off when David held out his arm and motioned for Markie to lower his instrument. "Wait. Don't freak it out. It's only a dog."

David turned around and got on one knee. He accepted the dog's head into the palm of his hand as it emerged from the bushes. The dog immediately froze its pursuit as David began patting the dog between its ears. Markie and Victoria gathered around to examine the canine. It was a black otterhound with blonde patches on its hands, feet, and nose. There was a beaded necklace in place of a traditional collar. There was a dog tag hardened in amber and placed as an emblem in the center of the string.

MY NAME IS SHUCK
RETURN ME TO: DUDEL RANCH, ARMITAGE, RUGELEY, STAFFORDSHIRE, WS15 4AJ
I'M ALLERGIC TO SHELLFISH!

Victoria looked up from the dog and stared at the patch of trees from which it came. There was now a human shape following the beaten path towards them. "I thought you said we'd be alone out here."

David sighed. "I guess I'm not so alone in this world…"

The sighting they were following had only made local news due to it being misinterpreted as a cryptozoological story. It was buried in obscurity with all the other Bigfoot sightings and goat-man encounters. David only found the story because he was monitoring such niche outlets religiously. He knew local news would be the only resource desperate enough to report on a black-eyed kid sighting. But apparently, his interests weren't as niche as he once believed.

David stopped scratching under Shuck's chin and stood up tall. He could make out the features on the stranger approaching. It was a woman, mid-forties, with numerous animals draped over her outstretched arms.

"I'm sorry miss," called out Victoria, "but I believe our partner's recklessness might have spooked your dog."

"Oh, no! He's not scared. I sent him over to yah'," smiled the woman. She stopped when she reached just behind her dog's tail. In the moonlight, they could see thin purple robes coiled around her body. It also became easier to tell the various pets hanging on her arms. A flying fox dangled from her left hand, a hedgehog sprawled out atop her head, a polecat was wrapped around her neck, and a shorthair kitten perched itself on her right elbow.

David stepped forward and reached out his hand. "I'm Dr. Oscar Groux."

The animal woman looked down at David's hand and shook her head. "No. I don't think you are."

David's face turned to concern. He withdrew his hand and stepped back away from the woman.

"Don't worry," she laughed. "Shuck here says you're putting out good vibes. I'm sure you have an excellent reason to lie to strangers. But don't mind me, I'd really like to know who you really are for my own good reasons."

The animal woman shut her eyes. The cat on her arm did the same and began to purr. When the animal woman opened up again, she smiled. "You're Dr. David Matthews. You're the parapsychologist."

"No. I'm a neurologist," sneered David. He didn't like getting upset, but he had a raw nerve surrounding the legitimacy of his research. His thesis at UCL was a product of eight years of sleepless nights and hard labor, yet it's constantly attacked, having been called pseudoscience by his fellow professionals. A single citation linking his work to anthroposophy has made it impossible to get any of his current research published in top journals. "How'd you know my name?"

"I can sense the good and evil in people through Shuck. On the other hand..." The lady pointed to the cat on her arm. "Pard here can see your names plain as day hovering over top of your heads."

"And the cat shared this information with you, how?" asked David.

The animal woman nodded and tapped her skull. "We have a link. Same goes for all my pets. They each have a different flavor of ESP and are able to communicate what they learn directly to me. Now normally when they give me a person's name it's just a funny way to catch them off guard, but I recognize your name from Astralcast."

David cringed. His difficulties with getting published had messed with his sleep and irritated his bipolar. His frustration built until it needed release. In a hypomanic episode, he gave into his label as pseudoscience and submitted his work with disreputable sources, spiritualist bloggers, herbalist forums, and Facebook groups for curing cancer with CBD. Astralcast was most certainly one of these dumps.

"Are you out catching lost souls for experimentation?" asked the animal woman with a look of suspicion.

113

"Uh, no…" David shook his head. "I don't suspect there's any souls out here."

"Oh I'm sure there is!" guaranteed the animal woman. "I've already found them. Twenty minutes back. A little boy and a little girl. Both aged around ten. And with big black eyes, like a pair of Funko dolls, just as the paper said."

"You found them?" exclaimed Victoria, excitedly. "What did you do with them?"

The animal woman pointed over her shoulder at a black streak rising from the trees in the distance. It was barely visible against the black background of the night sky.

"Holy shit," said David with an expression of horror. "Did you light them on fire?'

"Oh my god, no!" laughed the animal woman. "I just left them some burning sage. I live around these parts and children get lost in these woods all the time. I believe these black-eyed kids are the spirits of the dead. Poor kids are trapped here, and a hot bucket of sage can help get them unstuck."

"So then where are you headed now?" questioned David.

The animal woman's expression turned bleak. She knelt down beside her pooch and rubbed under his ear. "Shuck sensed something dark closing in on us as we lit the sage. We're trying to lose it. I think it's an evil spirit. Whatever demon is keeping these kids bound here to feed off their energy."

Markie grabbed at the cross on the necklace around his neck. He didn't take the word 'demon' lightly. "I've had chills the whole time we've been out here," said Markie, looking fearful. "Maybe we should be leaving."

114

"Then just follow after me!" exclaimed the animal woman. She patted her dog on the back, instructing him to lead the way again. He ran off in the direction of Lassjoyce. The animal woman began following after. She stopped before disappearing completely and motioned for Markie to follow.

Markie turned to his friends. They returned his gaze with a judging glance. "Weren't you just scolding me for chickening out not too long ago?" scolded Victoria.

Markie shook his head.

"Oh right, that was Mikey… sorry I still get you two confused sometimes."

"Understandable," admitted Markie. "We only look exactly the same." Markie turned back towards the animal woman and motioned for her to go on without him. He then looked back down at the cross around his neck. He began rubbing his thumb over the sides of the 't' nervously.

While Victoria began following the smoke in the distance, David tried to get Markie going again. "That woman back there is the type of quack I try to distance myself from. I think it's in our best interest to oppose any of her advice."

Markie couldn't be convinced. "She said there's pure evil closing in."

David sighed. He was losing his patience. He walked up to Markie, grabbed his shirt and pulled him along. "I'm an expert in this field and I'm asking you to respect my opinion. Souls need a container. So there's no loose spirits hovering around causing havoc. And that's all the same for demons."

Markie pulled his nice button down out of David's grasp. He took a moment to fix the wrinkles he'd caused and then started following along with the rest of the herd. He was silent for the rest of the trek.

The gang followed the smoke signal in the sky, catching good glimpses of the streak when it passed over the white stars. It led them along the path of a shallow creek, sourced by a flooded coal shaft. At the entrance to this mine, the explorers found the animal woman's sage, burning brightly in a steel bucket.

"The kids must be living in here," said David, pointing to tracks in the wet soil outside the cave. They were child-sized footprints. David then knelt down and overturned the steel bucket, trapping the smoke beneath the seal. "We don't want anyone else finding this place."

"I think somebody may have already," warned Victoria. She pointed at a separate trail of footprints; they were much larger than the childrens', but they didn't look like the type of print left by the sandals the animal woman was wearing. There were two sections to each print, a toe and a heel. They were spaced close together and were both relatively large and homogeneously flat. "These are men's dress shoes."

"It's that 'pure evil' we were warned about," scoffed David. "A man in a pair of Church's." He turned to Markie and snickered.

Markie turned away and rolled his eyes. "He could still be dangerous."

"Well let's get a closer look before we form such rash opinions," cautioned David. "He could just be another hippie."

"I'm afraid not," replied Victoria, walking deep into the cave and peering around the first corner. "He's too nicely dressed." She quickly hid behind the rocky corner and motioned for David

116

and Markie to join her in cover. Once hidden, they each took a turn staring down a path in the cave where a dim light illuminated the body of a stern-looking man. The light was coming from the man's sunglasses; the lenses glowed a flickering blue light as though they were scanning the area.

"Does he have a gun?" whispered Markie.

Victoria snuck another glance, then shook her head. The man was dressed in a three-piece suit. Every article was the same shade of middle grey. Around the man's waist was a bronze badge, a clunky black phone, a fully loaded pen case, and a bright yellow flashlight that made up the only spot of color on his person.

"...we should knock him out," suggested David.

Markie shuttered in shock. "What's the need for that?"

"He looks legit. A government agent probably. Not sure which country, but they might have a project similar to ours," explained David. "He's not going to let us take those kids if he wants them for himself. We're gonna need a little force."

"I'm a pacifist," replied Markie.

"But Mikey isn't," suggested David.

Markie sneered. "By simply letting him out, I'd be complacent in a murder."

"Not a murder. We're just gonna incapacitate him." David pointed to the Psychopomp in Markie's hand."This can get him out of our way."

Markie was aggravated, but after a long fit of tension he gave in and started inhaling deeply. A couple of breaths later and he promptly flipped places with Mikey. David kept a hand to Mikey's mouth just in case he yelled something snarky upon emerging. Mikey seemed to get the message that he should keep quiet. David removed his palm.

"I've been summoned for something dirty, haven't I?" whispered Mikey; he stared at the nicely dressed man they were hiding from. "Holy shit, do I get to kill a cop?"

David shook his head and pointed to Mikey's Psychopomp. "Just mame him."

Mikey nodded with an eerie smile. "All it takes is a touch?"

David nodded.

Mikey snuck up on the agent, taking his steps slowly. He held out his hand and reached his palm for the back of the agent's neck. He got within inches of touching him when the agent yawned and moved one step forward.

"Oh fuck it!" shouted Mikey. The agent quickly spun around, but before he could draw his weapon, Mikey slammed the Psychopomp's surface onto the front of the agent's throat.

The Psychopomp was made from a special alloy of plutonium and mercury that could conduct souls like electricity. Once the connection between Mikey and the agent was made, their souls began looping through each other's bodies like a current. Their memories were traded as their consciousnesses rapidly whipped back and forth between heads. This constant movement caused both bodies to regurgitate then collapse onto the floor.

Mikey woke up sometime later with his body laid down on the hard ground beside a campfire. He wasn't alone. There were three other bodies also laying around the flame. Two of them

118

were small and wriggling. The other was still, easily recognized as the agent Mikey had knocked out.

Mikey got up onto his butt.

"Who goes there?" came the voice of David. He was curious as to which personality had risen to the top of the Mikey/Markie body.

"I was wondering why you had me touch the agent… you didn't say this shit would glitch us both. You hairy cunt."

"It's just Mikey," sighed David.

"Hell yeah it's Mikey," sneered Mikey. "I'm done coming out if this is the treatment I'm going to get. I've got a whole head full of nonsense now."

"What do you mean?"

"That dude's name is Johnathan Poole," said Mikey, pointing at the agent. "Some of his memories got left in my head. Some really strange shit. Little green men. Flying saucers."

"That information is highly classified," droned the tired voice of Agent Poole, still lying motionless on the ground. "Speak any further and you'll be hunted indefinitely by the highest forms of government."

"Yes, yes. I can see that…" snarked Mikey. He could access a memory where a traitorous agent was apathetically vaporized for leaking a few hints about the Martians to his wife. The vaporization was done with a wand cleverly disguised as a flashlight. Mikey wondered if Agent Poole's gear was similarly clandestine.

Mikey grabbed the flashlight off of Poole's belt loop. He held it out towards a wall and flicked the switch on its side. A beige pillar of light suddenly shot forward and blasted a small hole in the rock. The loud explosion was followed by the sounds of tiny high-pitched screeches.

"Put that down!" scolded Victoria. "You're scaring the children…" Victoria knelt down beside one of the two small wriggling bodies next to the campfire and ran her fingers through the little boy's long locks. "We found them while you two were sleeping," explained Victoria. "Poor things were living in the back of this cave. They're feral. We had to tie them up to keep them from scratching at us."

Mikey kept silent. He walked up beside Victoria and knelt down with her. Both children were dressed in old tattered clothes, and their hair looked wild and untamed. Mikey shook his head. "British intelligence doesn't think these are kids at all…"

"Keep quiet, you parasite!" shouted Agent Poole.

"They match their current description of Saturnian forces," explained Mikey. He turned to face David. "How sure are you they're not wrong?"

"Now you've done it!" screeched Poole. "You've crossed the line. Expect a black Wildcat to land in your backyard…"

"I don't think there's any reason to worry," said Mikey with a shrug. "They don't have our names. And they don't know what we look like."

Poole shook his head. "Well I'll tell them what you look li-"

Mikey flicked the switch on the flashlight. Victoria covered the children's eyes. David watched intently, curious as to the beam's effect on live tissue.

120

As the beige laser beam passed over the agent's body, it was like erasing with the back of a pencil. Every swipe wiped away a layer of the agent. First were his clothes, to which the agent responded with cringes. Then his skin, to which the agent responded with screams. Victoria covered the childrens' ears at this point. Then went the agent's innards, to which he responded with a gurgling buzz that slowly faded into a quiet whining sound. Once his chest had been fully erased, Poole went silent. Mikey finished the head last.

"You know, you could have at least tried bribing him?" sneered Victoria.

"Don't shame me. That was practically selfless," sneered Mikey. "I won't even be in this body come tomorrow. What do I care if they know its description? I did this for all of you. None of you deserve MI5 tracking you down for the rest of your lives. I sufficiently suppressed the evidence and I'm the only one who has to deal with the guilt of it all."

Victoria released her grip on the children and restored their senses. The children looked down in terror at the pile of ash laying where the agent used to be. Raised like wild animals, they couldn't understand the difference between friends and enemies. All they knew was that Mikey had the power to eradicate a body in an instant.

The children cuddled up to the sides of Victoria, as though she was their mother.

"Could there be any truth to Poole's intelligence?" asked Mikey, kicking the black sand left behind by the agent. "Are you sure you're not about to slip my soul inside a dead-eyed space creature?"

"No. That's just ignorance," sighed David. "They assume the human phenotype can't take miraculous forms without outside interference, but being born without a soul is no more extraterrestrial than being born with arms and legs. It's a simple birth defect. A congenital disorder caused by heavy drug consumption while the mother was pregnant."

"Then should we perform the transfer, now?" said Mikey, excitedly. He reached out his hand for the forehead of the boy restlessly waiting in Victoria's arms.

Victoria huffed. She reached up and swatted Mikey's hand out of the way. "Now is not a good time," she said angrily. "Do you know how long you were passed out last time you used that thing?"

"Ten minutes?"

"An hour!" exclaimed Victoria. "We can't wait that long again. And, no offense, you're too heavy to lift all the way back to the Tavern. It took both our strength just to get you to the back of this cave."

"Well what are we in such a rush for?" griped Mikey. "Just wait for me to recover. No need to carry me…"

"You're the one that needs to be patient, Mikey," commanded David. "There's a strong possibility now that high powers are after these kids. The MI5 is just one of them. I have no doubt we are no longer safe in these woods. We must escape immediately." David reached down and picked up one of the two black-eyed children. It was the girl of the two. He threw her over his shoulder, then pointed to the boy. "Don't be rude. Pick up the boy for Victoria."

Mikey snickered. He wouldn't be doing any heavy lifting, but he had someone to fill-in.

122

Markie was suddenly thrust into control of his body. "Oh God..." he said with a woozy look. "Why do I feel like I marathoned the X-files?"

"Probably best you just ignore those thoughts," scoffed Victoria. "New World Order shit's just gonna drive that little Christian Science brain of yours insane."

Markie frowned. "Don't be hurtful..."

"Oh, sorry again," snickered Victoria. "I'm just used to being catty while looking at that face. It's just a reflex at this point."

David instructed Markie to grab the other kid, and once he did, the group departed from the cave, trying their best to hurry. They were about fifty minutes from the entrance to the forest as long as they kept to the shortest path possible. But the temptation to steer away from this course became enticing as strange sights began to appear in the canopy above them. Something was fluttering over their heads, leaping from branch to branch. Every so often, it swooped down and left little trails of blood splatter along the dirt path.

When the blood sprayed on Markie's ear, he winced and called out, "What the fuck is it?"

"It's just a bat," replied Victoria. Without a child on her shoulder, she could lift her head and make out the animal. "It's missing the tip of its wing."

Suddenly, the bat made a sharp dive and face planted hard into a nearby tree. The thud was audibly clear and followed by high-pitched mammalian weeping. Like a puppy.

"The theriomancer," said David. "That was one of her pets."

"Why's it injured?" questioned Victoria. "...and why's it not with the old lady?"

The bat was psychic, like most of the old woman's pets. It shut its eyes and tried its best to reach into the minds of the three travelers. Instead of sensing their names or their intentions, it instead left a gift. A flashback of how it lost the end of its wing.

David was the first to receive the vision. "Oh. Oh we're fucked." He froze in his steps and replayed the memory again and again. The old woman was following the same path as them in order to leave the forest. A whistling noise catches her attention. Suddenly, Shuck's front legs are cut at the elbow, he falls onto his chin while howling in pain.

"No!" cried out Markie. He could see the old woman looking left and right trying to spot the intruder. Then she saw a shimmering blade, the type that belongs to a circular saw, floating in the night air and glowing under the moonlight. It hovered as it spun rapidly, blood flicking off its circumference. The floating blade made a pass at the old woman; she ducked out the way, but her hedgehog was vivisected. In its final moment, the hedgehog let out a pyrokinetic blast at some unseen intruder. This fiend walked forward, marked clearly by the tiny flame burning on his shoulder. He licked his palm then squeezed it tightly onto the fire. The fire hissed and disappeared.

The man was dressed as a priest, except for an extravagant color scheme. The robes were indigo and the clergy collar was neon green. Whenever this priest stuck his two fingers to the side of his head, the circle saw blade seemed to spin and levitate wherever he commanded it internally.

He brought the blade high up into the sky, then nosedived it down onto the back of the old lady's neck.

124

"Poor thing," exclaimed Victoria. She walked over to the bat to comfort the creature as it bled to its untimely death. "It was so brave of the little guy to show us that. Now we might have a chance against that… priest? We just need to find another way out of the woods, he's probably waiting for us if we follow as we are."

"He's no priest," said Markie. "He mowed down an old woman."

"She was a pagan," said David. "A radical priest might take that as an offense."

"What branch of Catholicism baptizes with a telekinetic buzzsaw?"

"The type waging war on ghosts and goblins," replied David. "Those hippie websites weren't wrong about British intelligence messing with UFOs. They might be right about other things. They say every organized religion that crosses continents has enough money to fund a paramilitary. Someone's sent their soldiers after these kids. Did you happen to notice the symbol on the priest's necklace?"

"It's the Seal of Solomon. He's a demon-hunter," explained David. "They think the kids are demons… or possessed by demons. Either way, they want them washed away before they reach the public eye."

"The Pope's scrubbing out kids?"

David shook his head. "Given our locale, I'd guess it's more likely Justin Welby."

Whrrrrr. The sound of a saw slicing into the bark of a tree suddenly caused their conversation to drop.

125

"We've gotta get out of here," said Victoria, staring into the childrens' eyes. Even while shaded completely black, they were able to easily express fear by growing wide and quivering. "Let's head east for fifteen minutes before we start heading south again. That should lose him."

Thud! The sound of a tree crashing to the forest floor sent them all scrambling in the same direction.

"Why's he knocking down the forest?" called out Markie. His anxiety was peaking. He didn't like the thrills of running for his life.

"He's trying to block our path out of the woods," called out Victoria as she darted forward. "But that shouldn't stop us now."

"No," whispered David. He stopped dead in his tracks. "Everybody wait! Stop!"

It was too late. The priest stepped out from behind a tree and grabbed onto Victoria's neck. He'd sent his blade far off into a separate part of the woods. He was hoping to scare the explorers off the fastest trail and right into his direction with the bang of a falling tree.

Markie shoved his heels into the ground and managed to halt. He spotted a strange red button on the side of the priest's head. It looked shiny and plastic, like the type you'd find on an arcade machine. The priest pressed two fingers to the button, shut his eyes to concentrate, then tossed Victoria upwards at an arc. The saw blade came whistling out of the woods and cut through Victoria's stomach while she hung in mid-air.

"No!" shouted Markie.

126

The blade then took a hard left and aimed straight for David. He leapt out the way, but the serrated edge caught the little boy on his shoulder. The child's neck was cut clean open.

"Markie, you have to blind him!" shouted David. "Markie, use the flashlight in your pocket. Aim for the face."

Markie, panicking, followed whatever orders David gave him. He picked up the flashlight in his pocket and directed it at the attacker's head. He flicked the switch on its side.

The beam of beige light struck the priest right in the center of his face. Vapors rose into the air at the point of contact, as his nose immediately crumbled to the ground. The priest let out no sounds as the beam bored further and further into his skull, eventually piercing through the brain stem. At this point, the priest's knees buckled. He fell to the forest floor. His saw blade followed soon after. It made a shimmering clang, like a brass cymbal, as it bounced off a rock pointing out of the earth.

"Did you know that would happen?!" screamed Markie. His shaking hand lost grip of the flashlight. It fell to the grass at his feet. Markie turned to face David, his eyes filled with tears and cheeks turned pale white. "David, did you know I'd kill him?"

David sighed. The little boy in his arms had stopped his growling and went cold and lifeless. David dropped the body and turned to Markie. He slowly nodded.

Markie's head dropped. "You've no respect for me."

David shivered. The temperature was dropping as midnight rolled around. "Markie, I'm sorry. I bypassed your pacifism out of desperation. I meant no offense. I do have a great deal of respect for you. I mean, this whole expedition is for you after all. We want to give your annoying roommate a new home."

127

"Change of plans," sighed Markie. "You've ruined this body. Blackened its record. Forget Mikey. I'm the one starting fresh…" Markie grabbed the child hanging over his shoulder.

"Help me!" The voice of Victoria suddenly shrieked through the night air. It caused both Markie and David to jump. They thought she'd died from her injury.

Vicky held one arm over the gaping hole in her chest. She managed to stand up and began slowly creeping forward towards Markie. Victoria slid her Psychopomp between her fingers. "Please…" she hissed. "…the kid."

Markie cringed. He cradled the little girl in his arms and pulled her away from Victoria's reach.

"Markie, for God sake, I'm dying," whimpered Victoria. "Let me have her body."

Markie shook his head. He looked offended. "You were never a part of this step," he growled. "I need a new temple and she was always mine to begin with."

"The boy was yours!" snarled Victoria. "The girl was to come with me and David for testing… we decide what's done with her."

Markie smiled. "There's no need arguing with you…" He clipped on his Psychopomp and lowered his palm toward the child's filthy forehead. That's when David called out.

"Don't knock yourself out just yet," shouted David. "That won't do anything without this." David said, pulling out his vial of coke. "Without giving this to the child first, your soul will just circle between your bodies, just like with the agent. The cocaine makes the switch polarized in one direction."

128

"Well then hand it here!" shouted Markie. "You promised…"

David shuttered. "You're not getting this so easily. Not while Victoria's dying."

"Oh is that what it takes? A mortal wound?" Markie picked up the flashlight off the ground and stuck the face to his chest. He pulled the trigger and let out a wheezing noise like the wind had been knocked out of him. The beam of brown light shined through his back.

"Dammit Markie, I expect this from your other half!" scowled David. He ran up to his fallen friend. "We could have just found another child."

"After another six years and another death defying mission, I don't feel like waiting through all that again," grimaced Markie. "My body's done for. Now give me the drugs."

David rolled his eyes. He grabbed the black-eyed girl off of Markie's back, unscrewed the lid to his coke, and poured the bump down the little girl's sinus. She struggled the whole way through. David had to cup her mouth with his hand to get her to breathe it in through her nose. Once the drugs hit, the little girl began to spasm. Any soul passing through her now would be stuck in her brain like a magnet.

"There's only one fair decision," said David, grabbing Markie's hand. He stuck it to the little girl's head. Then he grabbed Victoria's and did the same.

"What did you do to me?" cried out Mikey. He was the only one left now in his dying vessel. He looked down at the wound in his chest and cried out. "I don't, I didn't."

Mikey gasped for air as his lungs collapsed. He was shaking and confused. He kept pushing pressure on the hole, but blood kept seeping through the cracks in his fingers. He felt dizzy. He felt scared. "The only good that comes from sharing a body..." said Mikey as he shut his eyes. " I didn't think I'd have to die alone." Mikey's breathing stopped.

David grabbed the flashlight from Mikey's pocket and directed it down at him. He couldn't leave behind any bodies as evidence. He flicked the switch.

With only a child to carry back, David made the trek back to the Lassjoyce Tavern with ease. When he got to 2B, he laid the child under the covers to rest. He then crawled under his own sheets and tried to recover from the night's ordeals. But of course it wouldn't be that simple.

Right before he faded into sleep, the child cried out and stood up in the center of her bed. "What in the fuck are you doing in here?!" screamed the child, angrily.

"Just... trying to rest," huffed David.

"Not... you!" growled the little girl. She put her palms onto the sides of her head and screamed.

A knock came at the door. "Hey now, what's going on in there?" came the old lady manning the Tavern. "You might wake the other guests..."

"There are other guests?" the little girl shouted out.

"No... good point." The old lady walked away.

"David you... I can't swear... Victoria you say it!" called out the little girl's voice. It kept switching between Markie's soft draw and Victoria's stern utterances. "David, you fucking shithead!... Why are we like this?"

130

"I maximized the lives saved," said David with an exhausted sigh. "All but Mikey survived the night. I'd say that's a success for many reasons."

The little girl called out as her two souls spun around her head, rapidly taking turns maneuvering her lip muscles. "I... er... Dav... er... Vicky stop!... No!... er... aaaaaaaaa!"

"Like I said," shrugged David. "This can all get fixed if you're just patient. The next kids will show up before you know it."

Profile: Greige Wagner

Men are more likely to be cannibals than women, or perhaps more men just get caught.

While living in a trailer park in Sun Valley, Nevada, Greige Wagner and her wife were trying to conceive. They tried ICI four times, but had no conception. The chances of pregnancy are about 25 percent per cycle, so it's likely they were just having some bad luck.

Greige vented her worries to her neighbor, 32-year-old Dannie Acra. Despite passing fertility testing, Greige feared her early years of hard drugs had made her organs incapable of supporting life. Dannie consoled her, and assured her that with the proper medicine, anyone can get knocked up.

Dannie herself had three kids. Two of which were perfectly healthy, but her youngest, Jeremy, had a genetic condition that caused severe anemia. It was remedied with frequent blood transfusions donated from his older siblings.

Dannie grabbed a blood bag coming from her eldest son, a nine-year-old. She squeezed a small amount of blood out of the bag and into a shot glass. She held the glass up to Greige's lips. "Ce qui entre, sort," said Dannie. "What comes in, comes out." The tradition, Dannie explained, was to consume a little child to make a little child. She'd seen it work a dozen times before with much worse cases than Greige. "Old women way past the age to conceive…"

A week later, Greige found out her latest attempt at ICI was a success. She was pregnant and she believed she had Dannie's medicine to thank.

132

Nine months later and Adder Wagner was born. He was 7lb 5oz and perfectly healthy. He was a well-behaved baby and even better toddler. He was sharp, he was loving, and he even liked to clean up after himself. Greige couldn't have asked for a better birth, so when Adder wanted to have a little brother, she knew there was something she'd have to do first.

Dannie had moved away long ago, however, so she needed child blood from someplace else. She considered taking some from her own son, but she was worried he'd spill the beans to her wife. If Greige's wife saw the puncture mark, there was no way she'd be cool with all this. Her wife was a strict conservative.

Greige decided to, instead, take blood from a kid at random. She disguised herself with some of her mother's clothes, a pair of gardening gloves, and a tote bag over her head. She waited in the bushes three blocks away from their local elementary school. She nabbed the first kid to pass by, traveling alone, age under ten. She gagged him with her glove, then stuck the needle under their armpit. She drew as much blood as she could before the child could squirm away. Once free, they'd go running and crying down the street trying to find an adult; in that time, Greige would slip away and set up for her next victim.

It took three attacks in total to get a full shot of blood. The string of attacks made local news. "Somebody is out there injecting our kids with AIDS!" sneered the sensationalist reporters. The childrens' testimony clearly led to some confusion, but it worked in Greige's favor. The police's suspects were limited to locals infected with HIV.

Greige poured the blood she collected into the only shot glass she kept in her kitchen, a souvenir from their trip to the Grand Canyon. She used the blood to wash down three pills of Xanax. Her anxiety was peaking, having just attacked children for the first time in her life. She vowed to never do it again, but this only proved true through her first marriage.

Her second spouse, a man named Tyler Brine, wanted kids of his own and wanted Greige to be their mother. Greige knew how important this wish was to her new husband, and decided to fulfill the request through any means necessary. She just had to dip into that dark side of her personality one last time. She dug up the old gardening gloves.

Greige is hardly the worst cannibal in this collection. Nobody actually died from her crimes, so it's hard to say what kind of punishment she should have deserved; had she lived long enough to see justice. There was no way she could have seen her demise coming that day. It's rare when a child under the age of ten carries a pocket knife, and even rarer that they use it when faced with actual danger. Eight year old Kevin Walker, however, really held his own when Greige's hand wrapped around his face, plunging his knife deep into her neck.

Greige's children have used their mother's diary to better understand her dip into madness. They explained that she was having wild thoughts far before she first accepted that shot of blood from Dannie.

"She had a hit list of Scorpios that deserved wiping from the face of the Earth," her son Adder said. "There's also detailed conversations described with Dr. Walter Witkin about 'suspicious moles', but we can't find any record of his existence."

Adder noted her thoughts just kept getting darker and darker, with a steep decline after the first time she attacked a child. Her deep depression manifested as a series of short stories she wrote in small segments throughout the margins of her notebook. The

134

story had no name, but Adder has called it "The Life & Times of a Rockefeller Pregnancy Zombie".

The Life & Times of a Rockefeller Pregnancy Zombie

The New World Order (NWO) is a cabal founded by the Rockefellers at the turn of the 20th century. It's a powerful network of billionaires and mad scientists that allows the Rockefellers to assert their dominance over the United States, and make waves in the world beyond.

The largest misconception about the NWO is the popular theory that their aim is depopulation, but really they want the exact opposite. The NWO is powered by extreme wealth, and there is a strong positive correlation between urbanization and the national average income. More people means more cities, which means more hubs for innovation. Each city is an economic milestone which contributes directly towards technological advancement; which means cooler toys, scarier weapons, and longer lifespans. It all makes it sound like the NWO might just be the good guys.

In order to influence population growth, the NWO became heavily involved in the music industry. Their goal was to seamlessly insert Meek beats into the backgrounds of America's Top 40. Meek beats are subaudible tones discovered in the 50's that can alter human behavior without them realizing it. At first, it was difficult to mask the artificial sound of the beats; but once the 80's embraced synthesized melodies, the NWO dug up the project and began to experiment.

The NWO began their experimentation in San Francisco, where they had several facilities already built from when they were testing the AIDS virus as a means of minimizing non-reproductive sexual activities. One of their greatest assets was San Francisco's fog, a product of the Rockefellers' weather tampering technology hidden in the Farallon Islands. It's a shroud keeping the public eye from seeing the kidnappings occurring right in front of them. Last time it was gay men in their twenties and thirties, this time it was little girls, ten to thirteen. They're snatched up off the street into black Chevy Suburbans and driven to a secret bunker underneath the Seven Sisters.

Dawn Sullivan was twelve years old when they came for her. Her mother, Margaret Sullivan, left for work three hours before her daughter woke for school. At this hour, the fog hadn't settled over Bay View, otherwise she would have arranged for someone to drive her daughter to school. By the time Dawn left her front door, the air was thick and silver. She made it to Oakdale Avenue when a station wagon crept up behind her. The man inside pulled her in through the window and held a pocket square coated in halothane over her lips. She was placed in the back unconscious with six other victims.

Dawn woke up inside a battery cage. The room outside the cage had cream-colored walls with strawberry trim. She looked around at all the different compartments in the cage system. Most of the girls were still asleep. Dawn looked down at the row beneath her and saw a girl in a hickory-brown school uniform staring up at her. She had long blonde hair, with three black hair clips lined up above her right ear.

"Hello," said Dawn through the thin bars between them. "Did you see the man that took us?"

The girl below shook her head. "I did, but I don't remember anymore… I think they gave us something to forget."

"Has anyone come in here to check on us?"

She shook her head again. "But I've only been up a few minutes before you."

"Where are you from?"

"San Francisco."

"Yeah, but what part?"

"Hunter's Bay."

"That's right near me."

Suddenly the door opened. A man stepped inside in a baggy, rubber hazmat suit the same cream color as the walls. The man's helmet had a black window that disguised his face. This man walked up to the top row of cages and undid Dawn's lock. He reached in and pulled her out.

"What are you doing?" called out the girl on the bottom row. "Fight him!"

Dawn tried to lift her fists up, but the man in the suit squeezed her arms to her sides. He was extremely strong, and she was just a child. He carried her out of the room holding her outstretched in his arms.

The next room looked exactly like the last, except instead of cages there was a chair in the center. The man in the suit dropped Dawn into the seat. As soon as her arms hit the rests, braces clamped onto her wrists.

The man in the suit walked over to a desk in front of them and pulled a gun out of its drawer. He walked back over to Dawn, then grabbed her jaw. He forced her mouth open, then shoved the pistol inside of her cheeks. Dawn's eyes went wide with panic. The man pulled the trigger. A metallic click sounded off as the spring inside the gun extended, launching a pill down the barrel. It flew from the muzzle and rammed itself down Dawn's throat. The man pulled the gun from her lips, then cleaned off the tip with a rag and ethanol. He then walked behind Dawn's chair and pulled the headphones off the hook attached to the rear of the backrest. He raised them up, then pulled the speakers apart. He lowered them down onto Dawn's head. Her little ears were small enough to fit completely inside the crevice of each cushion.

There was absolute quiet inside of those headphones for the first couple of minutes. During this time, the man in the suit waited patiently in the corner. Every couple of seconds, he'd check the watch on his wrist. After checking for the fourth time, he grabbed a pen and notebook on the desk behind him and focused his attention on Dawn.

Sound suddenly emanated from within the headphones. A fast beat began to play with electronic snares rolling and snapping. Strings came in next, then low synth tones. It all sounded catchy and infectious, like the backtrack to a pop-song. The only thing missing was lyrics.

As the music played, Dawn couldn't complain. If this was meant to be torture, it wasn't doing a very good job. It went on and on with significant changes where the chorus and bridge would be. Then it stopped and the man in the suit set down his notepad. He walked over to Dawn, removed the headphones, and caught her by surprise with a needle in the arm. Her heart beat twice, squeezing the drug injection up into her brain. Dawn passed out.

When Dawn woke up again, she was back in her bed at home. She felt seriously ill. She looked at the clock; school had started two hours ago. She tried to get out of bed, but she was too weak. Her mother, hearing the rustling, came in to check on her.

"No no no!" called out her mother. "You're much too sick to stand. What is it that you need?"

"I need nice clothes. I'm late for school."

139

"You've already called in sick, sweetie."

"I did?"

"Yes, then you called me and asked if I could come home and take care of you."

"I can't even remember that."

"It's no wonder, sweetie. You've got a horrible fever."

The fever was a parting present from the NWO combined into the sleeping agent. It was made to last thirteen days. Long enough for the fever to affect memory; distorting it to the point where one might confuse it with a dream.

When Dawn recovered, she found herself rushing to catch-up on homework. She noticed her concentration was a little off. At first she thought it was fatigue from her virus, but as the shakes and chills disappeared her mind only grew worse. It was vague at first, generalized anxiety, but then it became oddly specific. Her period. She was worried about getting her period.

Dawn had only experienced menstruation twelve times in her young life, and never before had she given such bodily normalcy two thoughts. She's long settled on tampons over pads, and overall she's felt blessed with no cramps, unnoticeable bloating, and a light to mild flow.

But now it was like there was a ticking bomb in her uterus. She developed this overwhelming feeling that something horrific would happen to her if her period came. Something akin to having her guts spoil and spill out between her legs. As it got closer and closer to that time of the month, she somehow convinced herself she was going to die if this period happened. So she made it so it didn't.

140

The process wasn't like how the older girls described. She wasn't nervous. Her mind was too preoccupied to be nervous. She felt like she was being operated on. Like they were reaching inside her to take out the bomb. The process was painful, but medicinal.

Dawn didn't show any signs for the first six months. This wasn't too much of a surprise considering adolescent pregnancies tend to carry underweight offspring. The timing of the pregnancy was also convenient. The first six months were in the fall and winter, she was able to mask her shape with puffy jackets and windbreakers.

Dawn's mother only came to realize her daughter's ailment when the torrents of vomit ran from her mouth all day and night. One trip to the doctor and the truth came out.

"You never told your daughter about safe sex?"

"I didn't think it was relevant," said Dawn's mother. She wasn't angry, just confused. "What boys do you even know?"

Dawn shook her head. "I only met him once before."

"Who was it?"

Dawn wouldn't say. She didn't want to get the boy in trouble. It was her idea anyways. Not that she seduced anyone; not at such a young age. All she had to do was tell a fourteen year old boy what she wanted and they submitted like their prayers had been answered by God.

"Did somebody hurt you?" Dawn's mom wasn't worried about punishing some small child. She was worried her child was being abused. "Dawn doesn't know any boys, but she knows plenty of men."

Dawn shook her head.

"Was it Mr. Brandon?"

"No!"

"I forbid you to see him anymore!" Mr. Brandon was her guitar teacher. He was a decrepit old man; an easy target for molestation accusations. Dawn was disappointed he'd been banished from her life. He had just begun teaching her some valuable aural skills.

"Ms. Sullivan... what options are you seeking for your daughter?" asked the doctor. "Something like maternity care... or something more along the lines of termination."

"The latter."

"No mother!" cried out Dawn. "I'm worried God won't forgive me."

Dawn had been exposed to the NWOs influence on more than one occasion. Every Sunday, Dawn was exposed to their brainwashing through their vice on the Catholic Church. They made her young mind firmly pro-life without needing any Meek beats or magicry.

"God doesn't want girls your age to have babies," sneered her mother. "It's unnatural."

Dawn's face wouldn't change. It was frozen in this mode between fear and sadness.

"You're not keeping it!" shouted her mother.

"You can't force her," warned the doctor. "Coercion is illegal. Please don't put me in a difficult position."

"You can't be serious. That can't be correct!"

"I'd have no choice but to involve authorities."

Dawn's mother glared at her daughter with a look of pure hatred. "Fine. You have your baby! But prepare yourself for the worst pain a woman can have in her life."

Her mother's threats couldn't persuade her like her own fears did. She would have the baby or die trying, and she almost did. Her blood pressure spiked during the last trimester and she had what they called a "pre-stroke" three weeks before giving birth. She lived, but that was the extent of her good luck. The baby was born severely underweight. He did not make it past the second day.

The hypnosis Dawn carried with her was very specific. It only made her care about the baby up until birth. Then, it cut off. During its two days on Earth, Dawn never once visited her baby in the NICU. It was like when the baby left her body, she went back to feeling like a child herself. She didn't want the baby, she just wanted it out of her.

Dawn's mother wouldn't let her daughter go back to public school. She had lots of good reasons. First and foremost, Dawn now had a sign on her back that read "easy". The boys in her class would certainly start giving her unwanted attention.

Dawn's mother sent Dawn away to a Catholic school in Hunter's Bay. It was girls only, including the teachers, just to be safe. Dawn's access to boys turned to an absolute zero, as the process for taking her to and from school became strictly monitored by the nuns in charge. Her bus would arrive at exactly 3:03PM; that's only three minutes after her last class. She was asked to be packed before the end of the day, so that she did not miss her ride. If she did miss her ride, she was threatened with corporal punishment.

Dawn had enjoyed the break from her period during her pregnancy. As the day approached yet again, all the same fears and anxieties from before began to haunt her, but now it was almost impossible to make them go away. She'd been cut off completely from the male chromosome. She figured the other girls might know a way to meet boys, but it was difficult to start any friendships. Her "pre-stoke" gave her palilalia. It made her conversations awkward and turned her into an easy target for bullying.

"I was wondering if you were part of any interesting clubs... clubs... clubs."

"You talk like my grandmother," sneered Jessie, an older girl. Dawn noticed Jessie had a hickey on her stomach while they were changing for gym class.

"It looks like you fit in well," continued Dawn. "I'd think you'd know where I could make some friends... friends... friends."

"I'm sorry but I don't, don't, dont," laughed Jessie as she walked away.

Dawn stomped her foot and gritted her teeth. She couldn't help herself from crying just a little. All the stress she felt was constantly overwhelming. Being isolated by the rest of her class, that was just salt in the wound.

Dawn stopped halfway down the central staircase to wipe her eyes and blow her nose. As she crumpled up her tissue, she got the feeling somebody was watching her. She felt like another barrage of insults was coming; this time they'd target her for getting upset. She looked around for the stranger. She looked

144

over the railing and stared down at the first floor. A girl was looking back up at her; they met eye to eye. She had long blonde hair and three dark black hair clips. Immediately, something about the whole sight seemed eerily familiar. The face she'd seen before, but the body looked different.

"Do you remember me?" asked the girl down the steps.

Dawn shook her head.

"I'm not surprised," sighed the girl. "We weren't meant to…"

"What's your name?" asked Dawn.

"Trillium," said the girl, "but call me Lium."

"I'm Dawn… Dawn…"

"Well Dawn. Are you a virgin?"

Such a personal question, but the way she asked wasn't like a bully lining up their target. It was concerned, like all those doctors and the nurses concerned she was being abused. "No," answered Dawn, "no… no…"

"Do you want to know why?"

Lium brought Dawn's darkest dreams to life. Lium described in detail what the men had done to her in the cream-colored lab and, as she did, Dawn could see the exact same incidence happening to her. It was a lost part of her consciousness that had reattached to the mainland.

"They made it so we'll die," said Lium with a vacant stare. "We keep finding boys or we die."

"Why?" asked Dawn.

145

"I think they're Satanists. I heard about them in the news. They just do fucked up shit to kids. It's how they worship."

"Well then what do we do… do…?" asked Dawn. She felt like the dread inside her was validated, but it made no difference to the harsh reality she had to face. She either stopped her period or faced whatever dastardly illness they put inside of her. "We've got to find boys."

"I've done it once before," replied Lium.

"And they let you stay here?"

"No one knows I had my baby. Everyone just thought I got fat. I did get fat. I can't stop eating, I'm just stressed all the time. I keep thinking they'll come for us again. It was so easy for them last time."

"What did you do with your baby?"

"It wasn't breathing… so I threw it away."

Dawn wanted to say 'I'm sorry' but it just didn't seem appropriate. It might have been worse if it lived. Dawn certainly felt better now that hers was gone.

"How'd you find a boy… boy… boy…?"

"Tech Bowl," said Lium, quietly. "All the sports are separated by gender, but that doesn't happen with a thinking competition. Our team is all girls… but just wait for regional qualifiers."

While athletes are notorious for their rambunctious personalities, the mathletes were stereotypes for their meekness and domicility. As such, Dawn's middle school assigned a single

146

nun, Sister Tabitha, the advanced math teacher, to look after their Tech Bowl.

Sister Tabitha found the girls to be delightful and quite clever, so she often let her guard down during competitive events. The events were usually held at a centralized high school in the region. Classrooms were converted to host different events. Multiple events happened in parallel, so Sister Tabitha couldn't possibly monitor them all.

Lium and Dawn signed up for the Problem Solving: Design competition. They had two hours to build a functioning pulley system using only the household materials provided to them in a cardboard box. The machine had to lift an egg two feet off the ground and keep it there for sixty seconds.

Lium and Dawn finished their project in thirty minutes, giving what looked like an honest attempt at the challenge; but ultimately let the egg crack on their first attempt. This automatically disqualified them.

Lium and Dawn snuck out of the room unseen by Sister Tabitha. They made their way into the school's gymnasium where the Poster Board competition was taking place. The girls went exhibit to exhibit and chose their boys based on who seemed to half-ass their project. If they had a good chance of winning, there was less of a chance they'd ditch their poster and follow the girls into the bathrooms.

"Mitigating Rhizopus in Store-Bought Bread using All-Natural Preservatives from Olive Trees." It was too noble. The authors clearly cared.

"The Effects of Indirect Sunlight on the Functional Stability of Multi-Phase Electrolytes." It sounded mildly techy if not a tad bit rudimentary. They clearly care; they just might not be that smart.

147

"What Color Food Bowl do Cats Prefer?" That was it. That was the one.

A few months later and Dawn was experiencing the worst pain of her life.

"Mom stop! Ouch, my hair!" Her mom lifted her off the ground. "My hair... my hair..." She yanked Dawn's curls upward, then tossed her against the door to their pantry. The rusty handle scratched her wrist.

Because of the school uniforms, there was no way Dawn could conceal her bump. Her mom found out far sooner this time and she didn't take it well.

Her mom couldn't stop herself from exploding with violence. The disappointment she felt was overwhelming. It was like nothing she'd ever felt before. Her daughter was so smart at school; it was difficult to accept that socially she was dangerously naive. "I can't let you keep doing this to yourself!" she cried. "You only get so many chances before it actually kills you!"

Dawn was more concerned her mother would kill her first.

Eight months later, Dawn gave birth to her second child. Her high blood pressure struck again and led to post-partum hemorrhaging. It took two blood transfusions to stabilize her. It was a miracle that she and the child both survived. The child was immediately placed in foster care, while Dawn was not allowed to leave the hospital.

"We want to keep her in our psych ward," said her obstetrician.

"We can't hold her against her will," replied her mother.

"We can though, as long as we can prove she's a threat to herself or others."

"You think her promiscuity could be construed as suicidal?"

The doctor nodded. "First she has a stroke. Then she almost bleeds out." The doctor paused and stared up from their clipboard. "When a child runs out into the middle of the street the first time, it's naivety; but when they do it again and again, it could be a cry for help. We should at least keep her until we figure out why she's acting this way."

Dawn began receiving daily visits from a psychiatrist at her bedside. Dr. Santos was a tall, slender man with a long grey beard and a shaved head. He talked slowly and sweetly, well-trained in therapeutic conversation with minors. He slowly tried to dissect the cause of Dawn's hypersexuality.

"Have you ever felt pressured into acting this way by other girls? Girls much older than you, perhaps?"

Dawn shook her head. "I don't talk to many other girls."

"Well then what about the boys?" probed Santos. "Have they ever made you feel bad for not wanting to have sex with them?"

Dawn nodded. "Sort of. At least, I think they're men."

"Is this more than one?"

"A group, yes… yes…"

"Have they threatened you if you don't perform?"

Dawn's eyes filled with moisture. She started to cry.

Santos reached out to her and hugged her tightly. "No, no, baby! It's okay, they can't hurt you! You're safe now!"

"No I'm... I'm," Dawn sniffled, "I'm not."

"What did they say they'd do to you?"

Dawn shook her head while wiping at her eyes. "They didn't say anything. They... put a spell on me... on me..."

"...a spell?"

"They picked me up on the way to school and put me in a cage."

"Who?!"

"The men!" cried Dawn. "They chained me to a chair and made me listen to music. Somehow that song made it that I... need to get pregnant or... or... or..." Dawn paused. "...or" Her eyes went wide.

"Or what?" egged on Santos.

"I'll die."

"Confabulation caused by vascular dementia." Dr. Santos immediately reported his findings to Dawn's mother. "In other words, her stroke has caused more damage than we first thought. It's leaving holes in her memory that she's filling in with wild improvisation."

"But how does that explain her behavior?"

"I believe she had a mini-stroke long before her first pregnancy. It went completely unnoticed as it didn't affect her motor function. Instead it's affected her impulse control. Has she had other behavioral problems in the past?"

150

Dawn's mother nodded. "She had this phase when she was ten. She'd come home with candies and little toys, but I hadn't given her any money. I confronted her and asked 'who's buying you these nice things?' She tells me they're free, but I think she's been shoplifting since she was a pre-teen."

Santos agreed. "It seems likely. She needs our help."

Dawn's mother was on board with whatever they suggested.

"No! No! No! Nooo!" screamed Dawn. "You can't. Nooo!" For the second time in her life, Dawn's wrists were being shackled. This time tight belts were mending her to her hospital bed.

"It's just till the end of the month," explained Dr. Santos. "Your period should arrive any day now."

"You're sick! You're sick!" shouted Dawn. "Do you want me to die… die…?"

"I promise you, you will be unharmed."

"You don't believe me!" cried Dawn. "I'm not lying. Just ask my classmate, Trillium. It happened to her too!"

"Trillium," repeated Santos. "You don't mean Trillium Woodsworth, do you?"

"Yes… yes!" shrieked Dawn.

"How exactly are you two connected?"

"What do you mean?"

"She checked-in after an alleged suicide attempt. She's been under my care for the last week," explained Santos with a look of concern. "What did you say to her? Did you tell her your story?"

"No!" shouted Dawn. "She told me!"

Santos jotted something in his notebook.

"Just ask her! Ask her about the men at the lab!"

"I can't ask her anything," sighed Santos. "Not unless she wakes up."

Three days later, the tissue in Dawn's uterus started to crumble and she found herself trapped in a waking nightmare. She felt it trickle down her leg. She saw it soak into her johnny gown. Her body started showing symptoms similar to withdrawal. The muscles in her abdomen ached and seized. Her skin was pouring out sweat; the droplets made her want to scratch but she couldn't move her hands.

Dawn's mind brought up images she saw in her Social Studies class; graphic images of the ebola outbreak in Zaire. She saw men, women, and children shooting blood from every orifice, curled up in dirty rooms in over-crowded hospitals. She could feel her own body dying. The flesh passing through her thighs contained pieces of her heart and lungs. She felt her blood thinning; she could feel it pulsing less and less. She felt her lungs turning cold and stiff. She had periods of blacking out entirely.

This all went on cyclically for six days straight. Then, things started to change for her. The pains in her stomach went away. The cold sweats stopped coming. Her head stopped assaulting her with gore and pestilence. Everything sort of calmed down.

On day eight, the nurses found that her period had completely stopped. They undid her cuffs and encouraged her to get some exercise. She asked the doctors if she could go see Trillium. Lium

152

had awakened three days prior. Dr. Santos was immediately hesitant sending Dawn into the room with a girl on suicide watch. Dawn hadn't exactly been a ray of hope leading up to her treatment, but she did seem different now that it was over. They allowed it on the condition that they be monitored by a nurse.

When Dawn stepped into the room, she lit up with a smile when she saw her friend. She ran to her and squeezed her in her arms. "My god, Lium, you're so thin now."

"Well I haven't been eating."

"Lium, why… why…?"

"Why what?" Lium sounded aggravated.

"Why are you here?"

"Because I took all my mom's fen-phen."

"But why are you trying to kill yourself… kill yourself… kill-"

"Because the pregnancy didn't take…" grimaced Lium. "I thought I'd take my own life before finding out what they had in store for me."

"Nothing," said Dawn. "Nothing happened to us."

"Nothing that we know of yet…" said Lium, bleakly.

"No, Lium. Nothing's going to happen to us… to us…"

"How can you be so sure?" sneered Lium. "Strange men performed strange experiments on us."

"I'm not sure about that either."

"But you remember now, don't you?"

"I remembered what you told me to remember."

"Dawn, no!" shrieked Lium. "You can't let them convince you that."

"I'm not... there's no convincing me of anything," sighed Dawn. "I convinced myself. There's nothing to fear. It was all mental... mental..."

"No!" cried out Lium. She scrunched her fists and struggled against her bindings. "You believed me! You're the only other one who can believe me! You were there!"

"I had a stroke, Lium," said Dawn, sullenly. "I had brain damage; I was highly susceptible to anything you said."

"They'll call me crazy," hissed Lium. "If you don't back me up, they're gonna lock me away. Don't let them lock me away."

"No one's locking her away," interrupted the nurse standing guard.

"She's lying! She could be working for them!"

"Dawn, sweetie, I think I've got to break up this reunion," explained the nurse. She grabbed Dawn's shoulder and shoved Dawn behind her. She put together a syringe and prepared Trillium for an injection to calm her.

"No! No!" called out Lium as Dawn left the room. "Don't let them shut me up!"

Dawn received another month of further intensive therapy. Dr. Santos wanted to make sure they truly got all those wretched thoughts out of her young mind. Once they were sure she was ready, they sent her back to public school where she could continue to be the clever girl she used to be.

Over the next few months there were still some residual effects from her psychosis. She couldn't help but overheat and cramp up whenever her period showed; but for many women that's already the norm. What was more important, was that her thoughts were crystal clear when her time of the month came; no more apocalyptic threats from her subconscious.

Dawn found herself climbing back to the top of her class. She put her past behind her and saw a wonderful future with a boy who caught her eye. A handsome young new waver named Arnold Webber. The two had been partners in Tech Bowl for the last three years. After winning States at the end of their junior year, the two admitted their love for each other and began a passionate relationship.

As they reached the end of high school, Arnold and Dawn were excited to spend their last prom night together. Arnold had made it a special occasion, renting a VMAX to drive to the event in style. He also snuck a little bit of acapulco gold to smoke in the bathroom. It made for a wildly romantic experience.

On the dance floor, Arnold and Dawn head-banged to "I Ran" and slow-danced to "Lovesong". They were constantly gazing into each other's eyes. Dawn saw a wonderful future staring back at her. She smiled wide, then leaned in for a kiss.

"Lovesong" came to an end and the DJ hyped up the next song. He would be playing a new big hit on the radio. All the girls knew exactly what it was; they cheered. Some of the boys knew too; they groaned.

"You got the right stuff, baby, love the way you turn me on. You got the right stuff, baby, you're the reason why I sing this song!" It was the latest pop-jam by New Kids on the Block. Dawn

155

hadn't heard it before, and yet it was oddly familiar. The lyrics were new, but she could recall the beat. It was from forever ago. Was this a sample? Was this a cover?

"No." Before Dawn could safely cover her ears, she realized too late how she knew the chords. "No!"

The NWO had formed New Kids on the Block as a means of clandestinely distributing Meek beats into the ear canals of unsuspecting youths. The frequencies they used on Dawn in her childhood had been severely nerfed to create a more subtle reaction. In the case of most listeners, a slight urge to procreate was planted in their mind; But because she was exposed before, Dawn's reaction to hearing the beat again was far more severe.

All the blocks that surrounded her prior brainwashing vanished in an instant. Old fear crept back into place, but mutated into a more resilient form. She pictured Trillium at the mental ward all those years ago spouting her mean ramblings. "Nothing that we know of yet... yet... yet..."

Dawn saw her body rotting. She saw holes forming in her guts, fleshy pink sinuses burrowed through her internal organs. One for every egg she let pass through her over the last five years. A psychosomatic response loomed over her mind. She was falling apart, growing weak from the perforations. It was hard to breathe. It was hard to stand.

"I know," said Arnold, staring at Dawn's look of dismay. "It's not my type of music either."

Suddenly, Dawn broke out of her trance. She immediately attacked Arnold's face, harder than before. These weren't soft, playful kisses. This was serious necking with a goal in mind. Tonight, Dawn would get Arnold into bed; and, together, they'd start that beautiful future she had in mind.

156

Three weeks later, Dawn confirmed her pregnancy with a Clearblue stick. When she showed Arnold the test, his first reaction was to get down on one knee and make the easiest decision of his life.

Angel Webber was the first baby Dawn had ever named. It was supposed to symbolize that things would be different with this one; she would love her and take care of her. But the attachment for Angel just never came, no matter how much she bathed her daughter, changed her daughter, fed her daughter, and rocked her daughter to sleep. Something in her past had truly diminished the bond she could feel with a child. She was trained at a young age to want to see her babies disappear as soon as they left her body. She couldn't help but still feel this same way.

Dawn had no better luck with either of Angel's two sisters or three brothers. They all came about in a measly four years. With each passing baby, Arnold felt more experienced than the previous. He was a good dad, but he still grew overwhelmed by the sheer volume of work raising six children entails. Not to mention, his financial situation was being stretched pretty thin to cover eight mouths that need feeding, including his own. Arnold was merely a piano teacher; a skill he had left over from his synth-pop band in high school, Burgundy Boys.

"Why haven't you been in the mood lately?" questioned Dawn one night as the two lied back-to-back in bed. "Is there something I did?"

Arnold licked his teeth nervously. He rolled over to face Dawn. She did the same.

"I suppose I've been tired lately."

"Not too tired to jerk off."

"...what?"

157

"I heard you in the bathroom. I found your porn mag," griped Dawn. "You hang it on the towel bar under the towel."

"So?"

"Save some for me, please!"

"...no."

"What do you mean, no?" sneered Dawn. "Don't you find me attractive anymore? I think I look pretty good for pressing out six kids... kids... kids..."

"Going on seven?"

"Pardon...?"

"Are you having a seventh?"

Dawn's mouth hung open and her eyes squinted. "I guess we'll see."

"We won't have to see if you just let me pull out."

"It goes to waste if you do that."

"Not if you don't want a seventh ."

"Is that what you're saying?" asked Dawn, sharply. "You're trying to stop."

"I'm happy with what we have now."

"Why haven't you told me to stop before... before... before..."

158

"Well to be honest, I just thought you were being Irish," said Arnold.

Dawn stared hotly at her husband.

"Irish Catholics have big families. It's a thing," he explained. "Now we're twice the size of a nuclear family, and that's where I draw the line."

"If you can't afford it, we'll just put it up for adoption."

"No! I'm not going to willfully bring a child into this world just to throw them into the foster care system."

"Then I'll get my baby somewhere else…"

"What does that mean?"

Dawn crossed her arms and looked off into the corner of the room. "I'll get what I want… want."

"You'd do that?" said Arnold, as the life left his face. "You're saying you'll cheat on me?"

Dawn hesitated to respond. Then she lifted her chin slowly and let it fall.

Arnold looked heartbroken. "Don't, don't do that." Arnold's eyes went wide; he grabbed his wife's shoulder firmly. "You'd end our family for this?"

Dawn leaned over and kissed Arnold on the lips. She widened her mouth and did it again. She climbed on top of him, then started to grind.

Arnold kissed her back at first. Then he got mad and shoved her off.

159

Nine hours later, Dawn found herself in a bar, three hundred miles East of San Francisco. She sat at a bar in Sparks, Nevada. She just sat and waited. She was 22. She was pretty. The men would come all by themselves.

This lackadaisical strategy would last well into her forties, but that's when things would get tricky.

"Will you fuck me for thirty dollars... dollars...?" Dawn pleaded with the man sitting next to her. "...dollars."

The man she was speaking to was wearing an oversized flannel with the sleeves rolled up above his elbows. He had dirt brown teeth, yellow eyes, and a thin wisp of hair covering the bare skin on top of his head. "You're drunk," laughed the man.

"No. I just talk like this... this..."

"You're serious?"

Dawn nodded. The man looked her up and down. He hadn't had a lay in months, but the sight of Dawn was repulsive. Her parade of pregnancies had her battling acne for the last thirty years. The scars on her face had built up over time, giving her cheeks the texture of a cheese grater. Her weight fluctuations placed cellulose deposits in odd amounts around her chin, breasts, and thighs.

"I'll do things," said Dawn. "I'll do things other girls won't let you do." She leaned in close to the man's ear. He could smell pickles and ice cream on her breath. Her weird pregnancy cravings had become the norm for her; she never switched back to regular foods. "I'll let you cum inside me."

The man slid backwards out of his seat. He dropped onto his feet and stumbled. "Joseph, keep my tab open. I'll be back later." The man turned around and walked hurriedly out the front door.

"You know, if I didn't pity you I'd have you arrested," sneered the bartender. "You can't pay people to fuck you, here. That's soliciting prostitution."

"I'm having a rough night. I'm trying everything I can."

"A rough night? You've been trying for the last week…" griped the bartender. "This place clearly isn't working for you. Why not try somewhere else?"

Dawn's shoulders dropped. Her face crinkled up. Tears welled up and stirred into her foundation. "This is supposed to be the 'ugly guy' bar."

The bartender looked offended at first, but then he nodded. "I guess it kind of is, isn't it?"

Dawn's period would start any day now. She had exhausted all of her options and there wasn't much time. She had a backup plan just in case something like this happened. She pulled out a yellow, lambskin wallet. She'd gotten some supplies three pregnancies earlier during a similarly desperate situation. She was lucky enough to have not ended up needing them, but this time was worse. She always moved somewhere new after getting knocked-up, as to never run into the father again. But this time she accidentally chose a town where even the lowest people's standards were set way too high: fucking Dewey Beach, Delaware. She thought all east coast coastal towns were full of beach bums and divorce dads. She found the one exception.

Dawn unzipped her yellow pouch and pulled out a pair of pills: viagra and rohypnol. She felt a sudden surge of guilt, staring at them. She made them disappear from sight, clutching them tightly in her hand. "Oh god... oh god... oh god..." she whimpered. She threw the drugs onto the floor and crushed them under her flip-flop. "I can't."

Later that night, Dawn laid in the crusty bathtub stuffed into the bathroom of her efficiency apartment. It was all she could afford; jumping from town to town, she lived off of part-time positions working mostly in diners and car washes. On the side of the tub was an open bottle of beta-blockers; she's gotten prescriptions for it on and off for years to help with her blood pressure during pregnancy. All she had to do was pour them all down her throat, and the running could all finally come to an end.

"Aaaah!" Dawn cried out. She thrashed around in the water like crazy. Her fists banged at the floor of the tub, knocking chips of paint loose that then floated towards the surface. She screeched louder and grabbed the pills in her hand. She flopped her torso over the side of the tub and flipped up the toilet seat. She spilled the pills down into the bowl and flushed. Then, she screamed some more.

Dawn exhausted herself and woke up in the morning still lying in the water. She looked down at her wet, lumpy form, uncovered by the half-drained suds. She cringed. She looked down between her legs; she was surprised not to see any blood yet. She thought her period would have come by now.

Over the next few days, Dawn would keep checking her underwear, once an hour, sometimes twice, but her period still wouldn't come. Dawn took a pregnancy test just in case, but it turned out negative. It was tough for her to accept the fact that her period wouldn't be coming ever again, but as she reached seven days after her cycle was due, she finally came out of denial.

She got herself a hot cup of coffee at a local diner. She smiled. She breathed a sigh of relief.

162

After menopause, Dawn decided to settle down. She found a nice affordable townhouse in Delmar where she could watch the sunset from a rickety little porch. There was a nice old man that lived next door to her. He often read the paper on his patio chair.

Dawn would often stare at the man lustfully, but she ultimately decided not to make a move. She already had so many experiences with men over the years; she wanted this time to be different. No men, just relaxation.

Dawn lived in Delmar for two years without anyone bothering her. She made a few friends who she liked to bike with, but no one ever visited, so she was surprised when she finally received a wrapping on her door.

"Uh, hello," said the girl, brushing her shoes on her mat.

"Oh. Hello," said Dawn back with a little wave.

"Do you… can you recognize me?"

Dawn took off her sunglasses and scanned the girl up and down. "Did I sleep with your husband a few years ago?"

"No…" The girl's eyes rolled back. She shook her head frustratingly. "No, Dawn, that's not why I'm here." She sighed. She pulled out a picture from her purse. It was her as a baby. "I'm Angel Webber."

Dawn stared at the photo with surprise. There she was, a much younger version of herself holding the baby beside her ex-husband Arnold.

"Oh god, you?" Dawn stepped backwards. "Do you want to kill me?"

"No! God no! You see I knew you'd be fucking weird," griped Angel. "May I please come inside?"

Dawn's whole body was shaking. She looked down at her feet and listened to her own heart pounding. She figured there was a slight chance her daughter could want some sort of financial reparations for her abandonment. Dawn figured she did owe her something like that. She invited Angel inside.

Angel took a seat in her kitchen. "I represent a group consisting of your offspring from 1982 to 2021. The party formally known as The Spawn of Dawn. I take it you're not aware of our existence?"

"No... no... no..." Dawn tried to sip her morning tea, but it dribbled over her lips. "I don't follow what happens to my offspring."

"My father, your ex-husband, started the group. After you disappeared, he tried to piece together a map of where you were heading. He's tracked your progress across the country."

"Why?" snarled Dawn. She felt spied on.

"You were leaving a path of motherless children in your wake..."

"That was none of his business to follow me."

"He was scared you'd lost your mind," explained Angel. "He wanted to help you, or at least those kids. When I got older, I used my father's work to connect with my half-siblings."

"Uh... how are they?"

"A lot of your later children were born with disabilities. It's not recommended women have children that late in life and with that little time between pregnancies."

"You turned out normal though…"

Angel pressed her palm against her cheek. She widened her eyes and sighed. "I'm sorry, I'm actually not here to guilt you; kind of the opposite actually. I'm hoping I can get you to feel comfortable enough to come back to California with me."

"Absolutely not."

"It'd be just for a week," begged Angel. "I was going to make a big conference out of it. Invite all your kids. No one wants to hurt you; but we just have all these questions…"

"Questions can be answered remotely," replied Dawn. "I refuse to leave this county."

Angel's brow crinkled. She had a feeling Dawn would be this stubborn. She pulled a notepad and a pen out of her purse. "Fine, then we do it now…"

Dawn stared at the pad. She shrugged. She nodded. "Whatever you want to know…"

"Have you been officially diagnosed with sociopathy?"

"What? No!"

"Don't act so offended. You abandoned thirty-nine children in total, it would make sense that you, to some degree, lack empathy," explained Angel. "What about schizophrenia?"

Dawn's eyes dropped down to the table. She looked dour. "I was diagnosed with vascular dementia. I have a history of stroke which affected my brain."

"Interesting," said Angel, jotting that down, "but is that what you really believe you went through?"

"Pardon?"

Angel pulled out a print-out of a website copied onto a plain sheet of paper. It was an amateur blog built on WordPress. The homepage was titled "Project Vodou".

Angel was not the first person to track down Dawn. Trillium had found her too, about six months prior. Trillium had started a website to discuss her thoughts on her brainwashing freely, hoping to connect with girls who experienced the same things growing up. Trillium called up Dawn hoping for an interview for her blog.

"It says here you believe you were kidnapped in '82 and exposed to mental programming by a secret society operating under the Reagan administration."

Dawn nodded. "I'm positive on what they did to me, and I can guess who, but the why remains completely baffling."

"You talk about starting a private collection of evidence in the interview. Did that ever come to fruition?"

"Yes well, I haven't really assembled what I had in mind, but I can show you the main piece of the attraction." Dawn ran away from the table and fetched something in her bedroom that rattled and clanked as she brought it in the kitchen. She held it out excitedly. "I was having gastrointestinal bleeding," explained Dawn, "They blamed it on pica. They found little

166

pieces of metal in my stool. I started to collect them myself, so they couldn't dispose of them."

"Dawn, that's disgusting."

"It's evidence!" exclaimed Dawn; she sat back down. "It's parts from a sensor they stuck inside me. It self-destructed once I ran out of eggs." Dawn held up the jar in front of Angel's eyes. She shook the shards inside. "There's no need to monitor me anymore. Experiment complete."

"Have you asked a professional to look at this?"

"No. They have the same reaction you did," sighed Dawn. "Honey, I'm not going to get any significant answers as to what happened before I die. I came to accept that a long time ago."

"Well I won't accept that," griped Angel. "I came here to bring back the origin story of thirty-nine boys and girls. You can't tell me you'll never know."

"Somebody nuked my brain and you all blossomed out of the fallout; a whole race of humans born from continuous fear," droned Dawn, staring off into space. "How's that for an origin story?"

"You can't just give up," groaned Angel, unsatisfied. "Why don't you call up Trillum? I can get her in touch with my club. We can get her work out there. There's tons of us and we're all over the country."

"I want a new life that's finally under my control," replied Dawn with a sudden rise in confidence. "The more Lium looks for answers, the more of her time they've taken away. And now, you're saying they should take away your precious years too?" Dawn stood up from her chair and grabbed her jar. "No."

167

"What do I tell the club, then?" sneered Angel. "That our existence hinges upon forces we can never understand?"

"Isn't that the case for everyone," smirked Dawn as she walked back to her room. She called out over her shoulder, "Just tell them not to follow in their mother's footsteps. Live free. Travel the world. And don't have children."

Profile: Mago Schlecter

Americans are kind of obsessed with BBQ and, as culture has changed over the years, so has the aesthetic of the BBQ pit. The drive-thru BBQ of the 60's was followed by the open field BBQs of the late 70s; which was then usurped by BBQ bar & nightclubs in the 80s and 90s. Then came the wide-spread construction of family-friendly chain BBQ in the ever-so-plastic early 2000's. Nowadays we're dealing with sheen BBQ futurism where your food is served by young men with Grecian physiques coated in tattoos that match the recycled metal wall art.

So then what is the next big step in BBQ's evolution? While the outlandish designs of today were a direct rebellion against the depersonalization of 2000s McBBQ, the rebellion of tomorrow may be a stance against the outlandishness and a return to basics. But with a twist; this time with a celebration of the marginalized cultures from which BBQ originated.

Caribbean barbacoa restaurants have begun to spring up in the more youthful parts of the South, and they cook their meats in a style reminiscent of countries like Barbados, Haiti, and Jamaica. Customers have been slow to ditch the bearded and brightly-colored, social-media savvy competition and try these down-to-earth traditional options; but hipster BBQ has absolutely noticed the knock in their sales. Their pre-opening lines have gotten smaller; their Twitter followers are plateauing; and their regulars are MIA off trying something new.

This shift in power caught the attention of numerous foodie publications, and so they each scouted out their own small example of the much larger phenomenon. *Chomped* did an interview with Chef Leo Abelman in the same room as his rival, Chef Abisai Alleyne; *Skillet Squad* did a blindfold taste test comparing the sides of several Austin establishments; and food reviewer and podcast personality Mago Schlecter was sent by *Feud for Thought* to document the ongoing debacle between newcomer Linford Jamaican BBQ and the combined forces of the Flavorful 5; which are, for the uninitiated, Amarillo's top five spots for BBQ.

Mago and *Feud for Thought* were a little late to the scene, they were distracted by the international chicken war between Korea and the Commonwealth of Kentucky. They were sullenly expecting their episode to be a rehash of the same points as their competitors. But lucky for them, the recent disappearance of Linford's manager Fitzroy Lewis had shaken things up since the initial media wave.

"The man was collapsing inwards from the sudden popularity," recalled Waldo Miller, owner of Bullet Claw BBQ, just one of the Flavorful 5. "Back when we first introduced Saccharine-Saffron dry rub, the overwhelming influx of customers led me to long episodes of binge drinking and hard drug use. I'm sure something similar happened to Fitzroy."

"Bombaclaat!" snarled Linford Lewis, Linford's co-owner and Fitzroy's brother. "They stole away Fitzroy on his smoke break and cooked him alive."

"Who did?" questioned Mago with a look of shock.

"It's a conspiracy," replied Linford. "It's one of the Flavorful 5. Maybe all of 'em!"

"But why?" asked Mago.

"They thought taking out the manager would take out the competition. They thought wrong, though. We're still going strong, even in mourning."

170

Mago was immediately intrigued with the possibility for obscure immersion journalism. He decided to pursue the opportunity presented to him in order to spice things up. Mago decided to bring Linford's strange accusation back to the Flavorful 5 to observe their reactions. Oddly enough, it did not seem to come as a shock to them.

"He thinks all native Texans are cannibals," replied Waldo, "and it comes from unflattering caricatures."

"Texas Chainsaw Massacre, Devil's Rejects, and The Hills Have Eyes," detailed Linford. "All of them are based on true accounts."

"The latter is particularly ignorant," rebutted Waldo. "The Hills Have Eyes took place in Southern California. That's the exact opposite of Texas."

"There's hard physical evidence," further pursued Linford. "We've seen blood and organs going out in their garbage,"

"We butcher live cows behind the kitchen to assure the freshest meat," explained line cook Van West of M.O.L. Meats, another of the Flavorful 5.

"Well I've got spies too, and look at what they photographed in M.O.L.'s break room." Linford slid a photo of a calendar sheet in front of Mago. "They got a detailed timeline of when each of my personnel is taking their smoke breaks. Is that just coincidence?"

Waldo laughed when Mago showed him the photograph. "Those are their smoke breaks; you got me there. But that's not for murder, that's for strategic counterattacks. When their staff are down a man, we overstaff and increase our production to appear better managed."

171

"Bullshit! What kind of sense does that make?" Linford was getting frustrated, he could tell he wasn't making a believer out of Mago. "I can get you indisputable evidence, if that's what it takes to convince you."

Mago nodded. "I mean I'm not law enforcement. Or a jury. But if convincing me is important to you, then yeah, I'd like to see more…"

"Then let's check your stomach for DNA."

"My stomach?" Mago looked confused. "I thought they were the cannibals?"

"No. They're just the chefs. They fed him to you!" Linford prodded Mago's pectoral with his thick finger. "They're mocking me. Trying to beat my BBQ with meat from my own family."

"You just sound paranoid," replied Mago.

Linford shook his head. "Fitzroy was a slacker behind the scenes. There wasn't nearly enough pressure to break him."

Mago suddenly felt a weird pressure in his abdomen, like he was about to vomit. Linford quickly handed him a waste basket. "I'm sorry," apologized Linford. "I added a little something to your food to get the evidence."

Linford had slipped ipecac into Mago's sauce when Mago sampled Linford's wings for the review. Mago angrily spewed out all the samples he'd taken that day into the trash can provided to him. He was then left with a difficult choice. He'd just been poisoned by the owner of a restaurant, a serious offense, and one punishable by law. But in true immersion journalism fashion, instead of suing Linford for food tampering,

172

Mago decided to take the story arc to its fitting conclusion and get the ending he needed: A DNA analysis of his bile.

"It was actually positive for his brother's tissue," sighed Mago with a tired look. "Forgive my nonchalance, but it doesn't really prove anything. I mean for a second I thought Linford was right, but then I realized Linford himself could have slipped me a piece of his brother. He already slipped me drugs in my wings, what's stopping him from adding a few skin flakes."

Mago handed his bile sample and its positive results over to the FBI to do further examination of all the restaurants. In the end, all six of them had to shut down for over three months as a thorough investigation scoured every last corner of their properties. The sales lost during that time nearly put them all out of business, and worst of all, no one was ever convicted.

"Maybe his brother was a slacker and he serves him better 'dead'," suggested Mago. "More likely he's just hiding. Helping to frame the Flavorful 5."

"I have no reason to frame the Flavorful 5. I was winning," argued Linford. "There's a missing person and men with criminal records working over there. And people want to say it's me. Well, I'll leave it like this; my brother was a batty hole, but I'd trade anything for another day working beside him. He didn't lift a finger. But he made me laugh and, for that, I loved him."

From what I've heard, journalist jobs are a dime a dozen and so you tend to just take whatever jobs you can get. Mago became a food blogger, but what he really wanted was to write opinion pieces on xenophobia. He wanted to cover the tension growing in America, the Xinjiang re-education camps, the racial bias of Wikipedia, and Apartheid denial. The story he did in Amarillo

173

was the closest he's ever come to writing something that actually interests him.

Mago was happy to share with us some of his assignments from his creative writing courses back at Northwestern. I chose the best of the bunch, which apparently only earned him an 82/100. "Ring the Belles". He probably earned all his points for choosing to write a historical fiction, then lost the tip because it's also a hardcore slasher.

Ring the Belles

When her father and her servants had fallen asleep for the night, Beatrice Battle snuck out of her estate. She tiptoed barefoot to the front door, but once she stepped onto the porch, she slipped on a pair of dainty cream-colored boots. They matched well with her ruffled chartreuse gown and the large amber ribbon wrapped around her waist. She was dressed to impress a young man she'd become quite smitten with.

This boy, Forbes Murphy, was waiting patiently for Bea with the rest of his family. They were all drinking and dancing around a bonfire in celebration of Samhain, the Irish harvest festival. They were in the woods right outside of Alexandria, Virginia, only a short thirty minute stroll from the Battle family's plantation. Bea crossed through the streets of the city to get there. The roads were nearly empty; most folk were inside keeping shelter from the brisk Autumn air.

When Bea arrived, Forbes was playing a game of snap apple with his cousins. Once he heard Bea's cheers joining the crowd, he quickly tore off his blindfold and locked eyes with her. He quit the game and embraced Bea tightly in his arms. He was so glad to see her. He wasn't sure she'd show up. Bea had to keep their meetings a secret, so there was always a chance she'd have to bail.

Forbes led Bea over to a nearby stump where the two of them could talk. Bea mentioned she felt famished, so Forbes brought her a meal of cider and cake. He sat beside her laughing and telling stories as he watched her happily indulge. At one point, Bea's fork hit something hard stuffed into the center of her dessert. She looked confused.

175

"It's just part of a traditional barmbrack cake," explained Forbes. "We put in little trinkets to predict your future. If it's a coin, you'll be rich. If it's a ring, you'll soon find love."

Bea reached down into the frosting and pulled out a small bone. It looked avian, like something from a pheasant or a small hen.

"Weird," chuckled Forbes. "That must have somehow fallen in when we were making tonight's stew." Forbes plucked the bone out from between Bea's fingers and tossed it over his shoulder. He then planted a kiss on Bea's lips. He could taste the cake's spices on her tongue. "Forget magic pastries, we should be making our own destiny."

Bea blushed. She pulled back her lips and motioned for Forbes to follow her away from the festivities and go deeper into the forest. Once there, she hiked up her dress, revealing an undergarment that looked like a cage. It was a hoop skirt made to give a single petticoat the same volume of several layered garments without all the weight and heat. She undid its hold around her waist and the cage collapsed into a flat circle around her feet. She then threw her chest against a nearby tree and invited Forbes to lay against her. Forbes accepted the proposal with feverish haste.

By the time the couple had stopped their frolicking in the forest, most of the festivities had died down. The youngest Murphys had finished carving their pumpkins and were all worn out. Their parents decided it was time to sober up and take the children back home. The rest of the party was soon to disband.

"Please, it's late," said Forbes to his lover. "Allow me to carry you home…"

Bea laughed and shook her head. "You're sweet, but my feet work just fine."

"Then just take my arm, we'll go hand in hand."

Still Bea refused. "You can't come with me. I have to walk through town…"

"So?"

"I'm sorry, Forbes. A lady of my class can't be seen with an Irishman," she said with a sullen glance. "It could get you hurt."

"Then I won't be seen," said Forbes with a sly smile. He grabbed a Samhain mask left behind by one of the kids and slid it over his head. It was a cheap costume, a flour bag with a face drawn on it. A winding streak of coal made the nose and eyebrows. Rosey cheeks were drawn using crushed beets and a mouth hole was cut between them. Two more holes were made for the eyes.

Bea snickered and looked at Forbes strangely. "Am I really worth all the risk?"

Forbes nodded and planted a kiss on Bea's cheek through the hole in the mask. Bea grabbed Forbes' wrist and led them forward into town. The streets were even more barren than when she'd first arrived. It was so quiet, in fact, the two could make out a faint chirping noise following close behind them. Bea turned to face their stalker only to burst out into laughter. It was just a young chorus frog, somehow displaced from his bog and moving aimlessly throughout the city.

Forbes kneeled down and scooped up the little creature in his palms. He gave it a stroke on the back and held it up between their faces. "What a handsome gentleman," said Forbes with a smile. "He's out for a midnight stroll."

"He's looking for a slimy green molly," jested Bea. She reached up and gave the little frog a pet between his eyes. The frog croaked. Then suddenly, he flipped up into the air as the hand cradling him was swatted away. A large steel instrument had collided with the side of Forbes' head, which sent him to the ground.

Bea stared at the tool that had now displaced Forbes in front of her eyes. It was a tamper: A long pole with a square panel at the end of it. It was normally used to flatten the soil on a farm. But in this case, it was used more like a mallet. Its frontal face had been twisted intentionally as to collide the sharp corner of its square with the skin in front of Forbes' ear.

Bea stared at the blood dripping off the tamper's corner. She tried to focus her eyes on the man behind the tool, but before she could manage, the plate on the end came hurtling forward. It collided with her face and sent her quickly to the ground right beside her lover.

When Bea regained consciousness, she thought she saw Forbes standing in front of her. But quickly, she realized the body didn't match her lover's. It was taller and stronger, with unfamiliar clothes. A dirty blue button up, leather gloves, and brown slacks with suspenders. Her attacker was just wearing Forbes' Samhain mask. Forbes' body was nowhere to be seen.

Bea tried to scream, but it was futile. In fact, she could barely even breathe. There was a rope tied tightly around her neck. A thin wisp of air flowing in and out of her nose kept her conscious. As the man stepped away from the front of her vision, he revealed the backdrop behind him. She recognized the white farmhouse in the distance with the noticeably rounded roof. She was in the fields behind the Achord's property, a rival plantation on the other side of town.

Her eyes focused on a light in the topmost window of the farmhouse. They locked on that glimmer and stayed there as her head was lifted off the ground. The last thing she heard was the zipping noise of a rope sliding against bark.

178

Bea wasn't discovered until the next morning when Georgia Achord, the matriarch of the family, left her home at sunrise in order to eat her morning's sausages and cornbread under the shade of her favorite tree; a beautiful goldenchain imported from England and planted atop the hill overlooking their grainfield. When she first saw the body swinging from its highest branch, she thought it was just a Samhain prank by some young, rowdy Irishmen trying to scare the rich. Upon closer inspection however, she realized her once posh decor had been reduced to a hangman's tree. She gasped and dropped her meal on the hill. The sausages rolled all the way down to the bottom.

The first to be called to the scene were, of course, Bea's parents: Elvis and Leora. Bea also had three sisters and two baby brothers, but they'd all been forbidden to see the body. Leora thought it would warp their minds.

"Where the fuck were the nightwatch?!" shouted Elvis to the local constable. "Why the Hell weren't they there to protect her?"

"Half the nightwatch are Irish… they were all off celebrating the harvest."

"Then how about the slave patrol?" cried out Leora. "You're telling me they saw nothing?"

The constable shrugged. "You think a slave might be responsible?"

"Our daughter's been lynched!" screamed Leora. "The killer beat the mick with a tamper. He could have done the same to Beatrice, but he chose to use the noose. It's intentional… it's a symbol! A reversal of roles. The slaver's daughter hung from a tree by a buck."

179

"Maybe it's internal," suggested Georgia. She'd stuck around to comfort Leora after discovering the body. "Hoyt's always snuffing out talk of rebellion amongst our boys. Perhaps you need to do the same."

Elvis shook his head with disbelief. "It's not like that with my slaves."

Georgia gave Elvis a strange look. "Naive man…"

Elvis shrugged. "We have mutual respect."

Georgia snickered. "What, you think your slaves are your friends? That they'd stick around without the chains around their ankles?"

Elvis frowned. He looked embarrassed.

"If they talk with you, you go easier on them. If they laugh at your jokes, you give them more food. It's all just survival, Elvis. You can't possibly trust them."

Elvis gave a frustrated snort, then stomped away off of the Achord's property. He left Leora standing there by herself. She turned to Georgia and warned her. "You have a girl just about the same age. Please keep her safe."

"I doubt she'd be next," replied Georgia. "Unlike your daughter, she spends her nights safely in bed."

Leora's mouth hung open. She looked offended.

"I didn't mean it that way. You know I'd never speak ill of the dead!" said Georgia, breathlessly. "Our Ivy is just a little less social than your Bea. She spends all her time buried in her books."

180

Leora stomped off. The implication that her daughter was a hussy was subtle, but it couldn't go unacknowledged. She couldn't stand the thought of anyone pinning Bea's demise on herself. She was only sixteen. She was just doing what sixteen-year-olds do.

"I'm sure there's some word of who is responsible." Upon returning home, Elvis had gone up to his appointed overseer, an older slave named Luge. He was begging him for insider information. "It's your job to be my eyes and ears."

"Mr. Battle, I am your eyes and ears. In the fields. But I don't even sleep in the same quarters as fieldhands. I don't know if they sneak out at night. Your best bet is to check under their beds, see what they're hiding."

"Fine then, but I'm not stepping in there without support. You will come with me," demanded Elvis. He took them to the slave's cabin, a few meters East of his manor. A small shack constructed from uneven wood. There were no windows, a crass door in the front, and a stone chimney on its side.

It was after sundown and their duties were finished, so the occupants were all packed inside. It was a dozen slaves crammed together on top of one another. They were all trying to get close to the fire lit in the hearth. Upon seeing Luge step inside, they all scowled. Then they saw Elvis, and they all feigned a smile.

"Everybody up! Hands raised!" shouted Luge. The slaves all did as they were commanded. Luge blocked the door as Elvis stepped around the slaves, frozen-still, some of them shaking. The furniture wasn't very elaborate, so searching the premises was easy. He simply tore up the hay stacks they used for bedding and kicked over the barrels they used for stools. He didn't find any weapons or masks or rope, but Elvis did find necklaces stashed beneath their pillows. The same type, constructed from the same materials, over and over. The string was made from collected horse hair, and there was a glass shard in the center with a symbol cut into its front plane. It was a P with an X carved over its center.

Having jewelry was a minor offense that Elvis took lightly and even tolerated to some degree. But seeing as each necklace seemed to have the same significance, he refused to leave till he got some clarification as to what exactly these pendants were.

"Your daughter read to the kids from the Bible," said a slave shivering in the corner. "She taught us prayers and symbols to protect us from evil. That one there wards off the undead."

Elvis stared around the room as he rubbed his thumb along the dulled edge of the glass shard. The eyes of these slaves were filled with fear, not guilt. Elvis walked up to the slave who spoke. "What undead are you hiding from?"

"It's the ghost of Grafton," cried out a little girl closer to the fireplace. "He killed Beatrice..."

"Grafton," sneered Elvis. "The ravager? He raped two women. So we rightfully hung him."

"He raped them both at once?" snickered Luge. "With one riding atop his face?"

Elvis gave Luge a look of disdain. "We rightfully hung him."

Luge stepped back towards the opening to the cabin. He averted his eyes and looked down at his shoes.

Elvis shook his head and tucked the talisman down into his pants' pocket. He asked the slaves to hand him a couple more. "You can always make more, I won't stop you," he promised. He just needed one for his wife. And five for his kids.

182

As the slaves gathered around their master to hand over their jewelry, the ones closest to the fire quickly gasped and leapt out of their seats. Everyone turned to face the hearth where a cloud of smoke was now beginning to rise.

"What's that now?" called out Elvis.

The little girl from earlier stuck her head into the fireplace and examined the smoldering kindling. The flame had been put out by a large ball of ice. "Hail," shouted the little girl, "big as an onion!" Suddenly the rattle of more ice pellets began to roar from the top of the chimney.

"Everybody outdoors now!" shouted Luge, flinging open the cabin door. He covered his brow with his hand and looked up into the sky. The once orange dusk had become suddenly clouded. "I need men to round up the cattle. Get them inside. Women and children shoo in the chickens!"

A hailstorm in Virginia never comes expectedly; but it was especially strange to see it this late in the year. For many of the slaves, this was the first hailstorm they'd ever seen, so the situation caused them to panic. As they led the animals into protection, they cringed as the ice lashed at their skin. Welts raised from the impact. Blood was drawn. The children cried out, and the women shrieked.

Back at the Achord manor, all these noises had disrupted the eldest daughter, Ivy Achord, as she attempted to read her newly purchased novel. It was Melmoth the Wanderer. She'd gotten only three pages deep when the storm began and her house erupted with noise. Loud banging footsteps echoed off the walls as her father ran door to door enlisting the help of every offspring and house slave. When he came to Ivy's door, she snapped. "I'm not stepping foot outside!"

183

"We need someone to cover the asters!" shouted her father, Hoyt.

Ivy pointed to her book, then pointed to the slave dusting the sides of her armoire. "Just have Ruth do it," she sneered.

Ruth laid her feather duster on an end table, then stared at Hoyt awaiting instructions.

"I guess..." Hoyt sighed, "I guess she'll do just as well."

In a matter of minutes, all the manor had been cleared out except for Ivy. She was relieved to hear no more running around. The noise had been reduced to the roll of ice pellets pelting her roof. She found this racket to be rather relaxing actually. It helped to drown out the screams of the slaves working outside.

It also helped to cover up the tiny squeak as a stranger walked right through the front door into a house now left unguarded. The rumble masked each step he took, first through the foyer, then up the steps, and finally down the hall.

The intruder had swapped out his tamper for an asparagus knife. It was lightweight and good for picking locks. The latter wasn't as necessary as the killer had predicted. Neither the front door, nor the door to her room had any resistance.

Her face buried in her book, Ivy didn't see her door slowly open. And masked by the hailstorm, she didn't hear the killer's footsteps as he marched up to her bed. She finally looked up when the top half of the killer's head appeared above the top edge of her page. The flour bag mask looked more bleak than ever. Facial oil left a brown stain down its center, and the beat-colored cheeks had smeared.

Ivy screamed. She screamed louder and longer than most ears are used to encountering. But even then, there wasn't any

184

reaction to the screeches. They penetrated the sound of the hail, and they reached the ears of Ivy's family; but the family just figured they were hearing the screams of their slaves, still crying out in pain from pellets bruising their thinly veiled flesh. Their rag-like clothing offered little protection.

Eventually the killer got his hand around Ivy's mouth, silencing her. She tried to bite, but she couldn't penetrate the attacker's leather gloves. With his free hand, he reached over to the armoire beside her bed and he pulled open the drawers. He lifted out a periwinkle ball gown and a white handkerchief. He stuffed the dress under his right arm and stuffed the small cloth down the girl's throat. He then lifted the girl with his free hand and carried her down the hall. He swiftly got her down the stairs of the manor and right out the same front door he came in. Still busy with rounding up the animals, none of Ivy's family saw the couple leave. But Ruth did, she was at the front of the house, stuffing a Lady in Black under a tin can for protection. She looked up from her gardening at the peculiar shape moving fast in her peripheral. Then she looked down at the weals growing atop her hands and forearms. She huffed, then got back to work.

Ivy was shoved through corners, alleys, and empty streets, cleared by the fierce storm. Ivy was eventually tossed over a fence into the Chinese garden built into the back lawn of Alexandria's top tobacco moguls, the Whitfields. Ivy's back was shoved against what looked like a tree in the garden's southernmost corner; it was actually a vine, wisteria, trained into a tree-like shape. It had bright blue flowers blossoming on its "branches".

Ivy started to cry, but the tears were short lived. They were dried clean as the killer shoved Ivy's ballgown over her head. The porous fabric quickly absorbed the tears as it passed over her eyes and cheeks.

The killer pulled out a string of rope wrapped around his chest. He pulled the full length out from the collar of his shirt. He then tied it tightly around Ivy's neck and tossed the other side over the wisteria.

Ivy thought back to a short story that ended in an execution. She was too panicked to remember the name of the volume, but she recalled the feelings described. The book was wildly inaccurate. There was no numbness building in her neck, or a great sleep clouding her mind's eye; there was just pain, shocking pain drilling into the top of her spine. She prayed the choking would end her life before her back snapped in half.

Ivy's body wasn't discovered at all like Bea's. The residence in which Ivy was hung was actually temporarily unoccupied. The Whitfields had left for a vacation at Folly Beach in South Carolina where the weather was still warm and inviting. Ivy's body was therefore discovered by a slave named Oscar who tended the Whitfields' garden while they were away.

Oscar's only concern was whether the body being in his work area would implicate him. Without any knowledge of the previous murder, Oscar was sure the Antebellum atmosphere would point their fingers at him. So Oscar just left. He had no choice. No one would believe him. So he stole some food from the garden and some supplies from the manor, packed it tight in a bindle, and headed North, sweating bullets every stretch along the way.

With Oscar gone, the body began to rot as the garden's vast collection of macrofauna feasted on its flesh.

The garden was finally checked out about four days later when the Achords finally accepted the constable's theory that the killer may have struck again. They noticed Ivy's blue dress was missing, and so following the killer's previous murder, they

186

searched the town for a blue flowering tree. Thus, they went to the only one in Alexandria.

When the Achords entered the Whitfield's garden, the sight of their daughter's head hanging over its detached body made Georgia faint. Her husband, Hoyt, quickly caught her body mid-air. "Somebody call a doctor!" screamed Hoyt.

"I'm fairly certain your daughter's dead," replied the constable.

"It's for my wife!"

"I'll take care of her," shouted Elvis. He'd come as soon as he heard another girl had been found just like his daughter. He was hoping there'd be more clues left behind, but that wasn't the case. Given the time between murder and discovery, there was far less reliable evidence than before.

Elvis carried the petite body of Georgia Achord to a nearby doctor working in the back of their most prominent pharmacy. The doctor was out at a house call when they arrived, so the pharmacist helped Elvis lie Georgia on a bed in the doctor's room. There, Elvis waited beside Georgia until help could arrive.

Georgia would open her eyes intermittently just to hiss faintly. "they're... savages."

Elvis sighed. He pulled out his charm necklace stolen from the slaves. He stuck it in the pocket sticking out from under Georgia's petticoat. "You and I are in the same boat now. Our daughters were taken by the same monster. I can hardly call it a man."

"sick... savages."

"A slave couldn't move like it does. In and out of our houses. Passing through the streets without any attention. It sneaks like it can pass through solid walls."

"..."

"A ghost, perhaps."

Georgia pounded her fist on the wall beside her. "It's deranged coons, you blunderbuss!"

Elvis gasped for air. Georgia's sudden awakening shocked and frightened him. "But what coon moves so swiftly, Georgia?" He asked between breaths. "Where could it live freely amongst us?"

"It's not working alone," she snarled. "Someone among us is aiding the perpetrator. Lending it its hiding place. An abolitionist among us."

Elvis shook his head. "But this is the south."

"Not the deep south," replied Georgia. "We've had Quakers pass through in just the last month. Handing out pamphlets and preaching on doorsteps. We're being targeted, they think they can change us."

"They aren't abolitionists. It's beyond the work of reasonable men."

"But ghosts?" questioned Georgia. "What miraculous death cursed us with a ghost?"

"The hanging of young Grafton."

"Grafton is as mundane as any other hanging. If a ghost rose for every nigger slain with distaste, the streets would be crowded with souls."

188

"Perhaps." Elvis frowned. He hadn't considered that fact.

"What would make Grafton at all unique to the public atrocities that occurred every other-"

The door suddenly opened. The doctor stepped in. "I see the patient is feeling somewhat better?"

At the site of the doctor, Georgia abruptly cut off her words. She dropped her head back onto the bed sheets and slammed her eyes shut. She transitioned back into her wilted state. She returned to the periodic whimpers about savages stealing her girl.

With Georgia in good care, Elvis thought it was inappropriate to stay any longer. He did his part as a human being, but it was her husband's place to comfort her any further. Elvis left the pharmacy and made his way back to his home.

Upon returning to his acres, he saw smoke rising from the fireplace inside the slaves' quarters. An odd site for the early hour. He then heard the sounds of lashing followed by loud muffled screams. They were emanating through the walls of the slaves' cabin.

Elvis hurried inside the cabin and immediately encountered his wife, Leora, standing with a whip slung over her shoulder. She stood in front of a crowd of cowering slaves protecting their heads and faces with their arms. Leora had a furious expression as she threw the end of her whip haphazardly into the crowd. She was translating all the remorse from her daughter's death into every blow.

Elvis looked into the fireplace and saw the slaves' protective jewelry caught up in the flames.

"You didn't need to destroy those," sighed Elvis. "I gave them permission."

"I didn't. They did," sneered Leora. "This isn't about the necklaces."

"Then why are you beating them?" shouted Elvis.

Leora pointed to the cabin's entrance. "Check above the door frame."

Elvis stepped outside and saw the rusty, brown stripe hanging overhead. It blended in so well with the wood he missed it on the way in. "Is that old blood?"

Leora panted furiously. "It's from Prissy. They killed her about an hour ago..."

"Myrtle's son?" shouted Elvis. Myrtle was their prize-winning sheep. She'd recently been bred and gave birth to three healthy lambs. Prissy was the fattest of the three, a would-be champion. And now, she was gone. "...savages," grumbled Elvis under his breath.

"Please," begged a young mother near the front of the slaves. "We're trying to protect our own children. Surely you understand that."

"By killing our precious livestock?"

"It's from your book," pleaded the woman. "The Bible tells us to."

Elvis raised an eyebrow. He pulled the whip out of his wife's hand and asked her to leave.

"But... Prissy?" frowned Leora.

190

Elvis shook his head. He pointed to the door. Leora followed directions and left. Once he was left alone he sat the whip down and took a seat beside the roaring fireplace. He stared into the flames and eyed the glass pieces left behind as the threading turned to ashes.

"Your charms can't offer you the same protection as my lamb?" questioned Elvis. He peered into the crowd with a stern look on his face. "What's changed?"

"It's not a ghost," called out the mother near the front.

Elvis nodded. "Is it better? Or worse?"

"Depends who you're asking."

"Then what is it, now?" said Elvis. There was a tinge of annoyance in his voice.

The mother turned over her shoulder and stared into the crowd. There was an uneasy look on everyone's face. She wasn't sure how her master would respond. But the odds weren't well. She swallowed hard and spit it out. "A plague."

"A disease?"

The woman shook her head. "A Biblical plague."

Elvis snorted, then let out a little snicker. He then turned his head to the cabin door. He looked up at the top border, then turned back to the crowd. He was putting it all together. He chuckled. "My daughter taught you about Moses?"

"It's exciting, so it's easy to remember."

"And it reminds you of... now?"

191

The mother nodded. She looked back at the other slaves. They nodded in agreement. "The hail storm yesterday. And the firstborns dying."

"Anything else?"

"Locusts on the crops."

Elvis smiled. "They're just grasshoppers."

"Frogs in our beds. And the sheds. And the fields."

"It's the South! We've got swamps and bogs. And so we've got plenty of frogs."

The mother shook her head. She sat in silence for a moment with a look of assurance. Then she spoke, "Well we think this is serious. Otherwise, we wouldn't have risked death taking your lamb."

"I suppose you wouldn't..." sighed Elvis. He pointed to the door frame. "So then the whole town does this? And what... it goes away?"

The slaves all looked at each other. The woman in front shook her head with a sullen look. "That wasn't good enough in the Bible."

Elvis thought back to the story of Moses. He recalled that there was only one way to stop the plagues.

A week later, the Whitfields returned from their vacation. They were immediately surrounded by concerned neighbors, shrieking at them to protect their daughter. Last time the killer hung a body in someone's backyard, it was that family he

192

attacked next. Therefore, if the pattern was consistent, the Whitfields were next.

Rayford Whitfield asked the constable what would be the best thing to do to protect his daughter May.

"Give her a gun," suggested the constable.

"I only got one gun," griped Rayford, "and it's best not to trust it in the hands of a lady."

"Then make sure you never leave her side," replied the constable. "May doesn't go anywhere anymore without you."

"Impossible! I got a farm to run, officer. I can't follow her around. You follow her."

"I got my own job, sir."

"Nobody needs to follow anybody," called out Elvis. He and Hoyt Achord had come to make sure Whitfield took this all seriously. Neither of them wanted a third little girl buried. "After doing some thinking, I think there's a rather obvious way to keep the killer away from your family."

Rayford looked interested. He smiled. "What is it?"

"You just…" Elvis took a deep breath and prepared himself for ridicule, "free your slaves."

Rayford frowned and patted Elvis on the shoulder with a look of sympathy. "Oh Elvis. How are you holding up?"

Elvis shoved the man's hand off his back. "I'm fine. Just fine. Now listen here, I'm being serious."

"Slaves?" laughed Hoyt. "Now what's any of this got to do with slaves?"

"We're all slave owners," answered Elvis. "I think that's why they target us."

"They don't target us," sneered Hoyt. "They target our daughters."

"Our first born daughters…" Elvis shrugged. "Might I remind you who else had their first borns taken away."

Hoyt and Rayford both looked disturbed by the suggestion.

"But we're not pharaohs," huffed Hoyt. "We're Christians!"

Rayford rolled his eyes. "Regardless… does anyone have a suggestion that won't bankrupt me."

Hoyt shoved Elvis aside and made his own suggestion. "We know how the killer works, he always stuffs his victim in a pretty dress before he kills her… take that away and he can't operate."

"Take those away?" pondered Elvis. "That dress is the icon of the South. You're saying you'd rather take that away than even consider freeing a slave or two?"

Hoyt cocked his head to the side. "Oh Elvis, if you're so concerned with preserving Southern tradition, then how about we avoid cutting out its very foundation."

Elvis squinted and gave a bitter expression.

Rayford nodded. "Agreed. It'll be much cheaper to burn a dress than gut an entire social class."

Rayford immediately charged into his home and ran up the stairs. He sternly asked his daughter to leave the room so that he might make certain alterations to her wardrobe selection. He found a pink spring dress with a floppy long-brimmed hat. It was precisely what the killer sought. Rayford plucked the items from his daughter's closet and ran them downstairs. He then went door to door, encouraging all the other fathers in Alexandria to do the same.

"Unless you want a girl to die, you'll throw her dresses in the fire."

A new bonfire had formed in the woods outside of Alexandria; this one burned bright yellow as the pile of linens in its center condensed into a smoldering black mound. The wiring from matching parasols stuck out on top. Farmers from all over Alexandria joined in emptying whole dressers and drawers into the flame. It had enough fuel to last the night.

For a good fifteen days, it all seemed like it was over. No attack was ever attempted on the Whitfields or their daughter. But Elvis remained unconvinced.

"It's not over," repeated Elvis, again and again. One morning he said it to Luge as he poured a mound of dried up grasshoppers out of his boot. Again and again, the plagues made themselves present. The eldest boy caught staph. The youngest caught lice. And the cows howled all night from a swarm of horseflies fixated to their flesh.

Luge shook his head. "There's nothing to worry about. The slaves daydream this all up while their minds wander during work. It's all the product of a powerful imagination."

Elvis directed Luge's attention to the patches of red bumps spreading along the sides of his cattle. "If you refuse to let them go and continue to hold them back, the hand of the Lord will

195

bring a terrible plague on your livestock in the field," quoted Elvis.

"It's bite marks. From the bugs," groaned Luge.

Elvis frowned and shook his head. He looked into his cow's eyes and saw signs of fever. Red marks. Tiredness. He stared down at the pasture under her hooves. A small pile of vomit had spread across the grass between her legs.

Stockmen all across Alexandria were seeing similar signs in their goats, sheep, horses, and steer. This included folks just passing through. One traveling salesman coming all the way from Connecticut got caught up in the madness; his oxen slowly worsened and worsened the further he drew to the town's center. At the midway, his oxen dropped.

Angered, the salesmen got out of his conestoga, walked up to his fallen bull and grabbed hold of its horns. He shook the beast's head and yanked him upwards back onto his feet. The bull cried out with a low, sad gurgle. He fell back down to the dirt.

"Come on, Augustus!" shouted the salesmen. He then tried the other ox; slapping at its face and shoving it with his shoulder. "Move it, Almond!"

"Stubborn cow?" A soft, gruff voice sounded from over the salesman's shoulder. He dropped his frustration and put on a nice smile to accept what was expectedly a stranger coming to his aide. The salesman couldn't refuse some good ol' Southern hospitality. He spun around on his heel and held out his hand for a greeting.

When his eyes first adjusted to the figure's face, the salesmen wasn't sure what he was looking at. A distorted face drawn onto a dirty sack. He looked at the stranger's hands, they weren't willing to shake and greet. They were full.

196

The stranger's arms swung forward and lunged the square end of a tamper into the salesman's gut. He fell to the ground and toppled over. All the air had left his lungs. He struggled to breathe, heaving and vomiting right beside his bulls doing very much the same thing.

When the salesmen came-to, his bulls were completely dead and all his goods were gone. He reported his robbery to the local constable who wanted to know precisely what was so valuable in the salesmen's cart that was worth stealing.

"Well I'm a silk salesman from Manchester, trying to find a market in the South," he explained. "So it's all very pricey merchandise."

"But can you be specific? What exactly am I looking out for?" probed the constable.

"There's embroidered napkins. Tons of doilies. A night gown. Some gloves. And six or so dresses."

"Dresses?" repeated the constable. "Dresses… oh my word."

The constable apologized to the salesmen for his sudden departure, but an urgent matter had come up and the life of a young girl, and perhaps many more, was at stake.

The constable rode his horse across town to be as quick as possible. He got off at the Whitfield's farmhouse and rushed through the front door. The house slaves working inside screamed in horror. The constable begged them to quiet down and point to the nearest parent available. The constable was directed to Mr. Whitfield, standing outside where his wisteria, tarnished of all joy, was now removed. A small colorless sapling sat in its place.

"Rayford, please! Where is your daughter?"

"Swimming with her friends?"

"But where?"

"Holmes Run... why?"

"How far? You've got to get us there now!"

"What's happened?" snarled Rayford. He grabbed the constable's arms tightly. "What's gone wrong?"

As the constable explained the inevitability that trade would return ornate dresses to their widely accessible town, May Whitfield and her four friends swam playfully in a local stream. While her friends wore flabby brown swimming dresses with matching caps, May wore nothing but bloomers and a corset, trying to look impressive for the two boys joining them in their afternoon dip.

May would occasionally dive under the surface of the water to reemerge with her costume clinging tightly to her skin. But as the water poured from her eyes and she could see things clearly, the boy in front of her was full-on sprinting out of the water and onto dry land. She stared at him mystified till the water around her neck began to feel oddly warm and oily. She looked down and saw that the river around her was turning blood red.

Panicked, she spun around and directed her gaze towards the bridge crossing the river at her back. There she saw the second boy wriggling in a strange man's arm. The man had reached down from the low-hanging bridge and locked the boy's chin under his left arm. With his right hand, he drew an asparagus knife over the young man's chest, letting the blood run-off into the stream.

May locked eyes with the stranger through his hideous mask. He let go of the boy and let the body fall back under the water. May took off, dashing out of the water and hurrying away from the bridge, into the woods.

As she darted forward, she regretted wearing such a skimpy bathing suit. It would have been nice to have sleeves as the branches around her whipped at her arms and shoulders and lacerated her skin.

Two minutes into her run, May took a second to catch her breath. She was already tired from treading water all day; a difficult feat for the untrained swimmers of the time period. She put her hands on her knees and breathed deep. On the exhale, she let out a loud holler as a pair of hands wrapped around her ankles and flipped her onto her stomach. The stranger whipped her body like a sandy beach towel, knocking her head against the hard, stoney ground. May went completely silent as she was dragged through the leaves.

Meanwhile, Rayford and the constable arrived at the watering hole to find the teenagers missing, all except for a miserable looking male with lacerations cut across his chest. He was putting pressure on the wound, slumped against a tree.

"We're too late," frowned the constable.

"No we're not," growled Rayford. "Quick. Take me back to the salesmen!"

The two darted off back towards the center of town where the salesmen still sat beside the now bloated bodies of his dead oxen. Upon seeing the constable, the salesmen perked up. "Did you find my things?"

"What color were the dresses?" screamed Rayford, leaping off his horse and getting right up in the salesman's face.

199

"Who are you?" questioned the salesmen, stepping away from the disgruntled father.

"You have to remember!" shouted Rayford. He shook the salesman's sides violently.

"Piggy!" called out the salesmen with a frightened expression. "The designer called it piggy. Something to suit the Southerners' tastes. Bright, pale pink."

Rayford nodded. He let the salesmen go and got right back on his horse. "Constable, what is the punishment for defacing a tree?"

The constable shrugged. "I'd probably charge you for the damages. But nothing corporal."

Rayford kicked the sides of his horse and began his route back home, where he grabbed the nearest axe. He then took off to scout out each of the biggest, richest estates in town. He thoroughly scanned their horticulture and spotted a bright pink dogwood growing in the corner of the Campbell's hedge-maze. Rayford made short work of it with his axe before anyone could spot him. He then went two estates further and saw a pair of flowering cherries sandwiching the entrance to a gazebo. Rayford cut them down in just six strong swings. Rayford then went more south and found a slave lying in the shade under a redbud. Rayford swung his axe in the poor boy's face, chasing him far off of the property, before turning the redbud into a grey stump.

By sundown, Rayford had desecrated enough gardens to enrage a small mob, now formed in the center of town, surrounding the constable.

"You have to do something!" they called out. "The man's gone mad. He's demolishing our property. Ruining years of our hard work." It was actually their slaves who raised the saplings up into their current glory, but I digress. The crowd wanted proper payment for their discarded trees. And they wanted to see Rayford Whitfield thrown into a madhouse.

"A madhouse?" sneered Rayford, appearing at the edge of the crowd on horseback. "Who's mad? I was just rescuing my daughter." He threw his daughter on the ground in front of the crowd and shouted. "I found her ditched along the side of the road. There was no place to hang her thanks to my actions… the killer gave up and set her free."

The audience began to gasp and scream. "But you still can't just… massacre our things. These things have a cost you know."

"But she's alive!" cried out Rayford. "She's alive because I took away every piggy pink plant in this town. And we shouldn't stop there." Rayford held his axe up high. "We'll never truly rid this town of dresses, not as long as seamstresses plague our fair nation. But the killer can't hang our girls if there's no colorful trees left to suit his sick interests. Every flowering tree needs to go. Starting tonight."

Elvis, standing near the center of the crowd, shoved himself up to the front, where he took to Rayford's side. He helped Rayford's daughter off the ground. She was soaking wet and shivering cold. Elvis looked up at Rayford and shook his head. "Listen to yourself. You want to drain this town of every last drop of color. And you think yourself the more reasonable of us two?"

"He can find dresses, Elvis. Any color. Any cloth. But without the trees, he can't do the last step."

201

"But the ornate trees. And the big puffy dresses. Getting rid of all this color. It's taking away the Southern identity! Isn't that worth more than just a couple of slaves?"

Rayford put on a manic grin. He cackled. "Mr. Battle. These slaves are our Southern identity. I think they're truly the only color this town needs."

Elvis shook his head. "You can't be serious." He looked around at all the nodding heads in the crowd. They were actually considering Rayford's plan. "You can't all be serious?"

But they were. Under the bright full moon, all the farmers in Alexandria took their axes and saws and tore into their most fluorescent flora, discarding the fallen foliage into the woods where it could safely decompose and foster the dull colorless sand pines and sweet birch that grew wild. By the next morning, the town looked as though it had been raided by a new inquisition. It was chastised of anything brilliant.

Elvis sat on his porch and failed to participate. Nobody cared; as Elvis's daughter had already passed, his trees would never be used again. The morning after, Elvis popped open a bottle of whiskey and asked Luge to disregard his usual responsibilities and join him on his front porch. He poured them each a highball of bourbon lemonade and put all his frustrations on Luge's shoulders.

"Did I deserve to have my daughter taken from me?"

Luge had his drink up to his lips when the question arose. He took large gulps to buy some time. The alcohol hit him quicker than he expected. He tried to strum up an acceptable response, but he hesitated.

"I mean it never occurred to me that maybe I might be the bad guy. Not until I saw my whole town take such ignorant steps to avoid our obvious destiny," grumbled Elvis. "But now it's driving me mad. And so it must be driving you mad all the time! For years! For all the time I've known you!"

"Elvis… you don't drive me mad."

"But I see the light. Whether this town sidesteps its fate or not, I know what we were intended to do. And that's an act of God. I made God send a monster after our little girls. I'm the bad guy in the Bible. I'm the sinner. I can barely live with myself right now."

"...what are you saying?"

"I'm saying that... that…" Elvis broke down into tears. "That maybe if this town did the right thing, my daughter's death wouldn't be in vain. Maybe it'd be worth it to teach us all a lesson, but instead, she died so that a town could add serious regulations to its floriculture. That's pathetic."

Luge looked down into his drink. He brought it up to his lips and sipped.

Elvis sat down his glass and put his hands behind his head. He laid back in his rocking chair and wondered. "What if Pharoah hadn't gone back on his promise to free the slaves?" asked Elvis. "Would we still remember him as the bad guy? And more importantly… would God have brought back his child?"

Luge frowned. He picked up the bottle of whiskey between them and added two more shots to Elvis' glass.

The town of Alexandria would never free their slaves. Not the Whitfields or the Achords. Or even the Battles. Lincoln would have to do it for them on June 19, 1865. But I'm sure you already knew that.

Due to the lack of bright and colorful trees, the murders ceased and the firstborns lived on. It seemed as though the curse was lifted, and for a hundred years or so it stayed that way. But what was truly occurring was a dormancy of darkness, mitigated by the curse's loopholes but never truly diminished. The curse would pass on generation to generation all the way up to the modern era where the ancestors of the Whitfields and the Battles found themselves crossing once again. This time through a happy marriage.

"I think that dress looks great on you," said Charlotte Epps, co-owner and head stylist at Epps Bridal Shop & Flowers. "It really accentuates your hips."

Wynona Whitfield, bride-to-be, peered at herself in the mirror. She ran her fingers down the sides of the white mermaid-style dress sloping down her frame. She heaved a short frustrated sigh. "I don't think we want the same things. I don't care about how good my ass looks."

Charlotte, a young black woman, took that comment to be slightly offensive. She squinted her eyes and tried to hide a full-on look of disdain. "I'll fetch you something else…" she murmured. She then disappeared into a backroom.

When she came back, she had a new dress in her hands that could take any definition out of a woman's ass. The entire bottom of the dress was a massive conical structure covered in waves of ruffles. "It's a throwback dress," she explained. "Vintage Southern Belle."

Wynona's face lit up at the sight of it. There was something inside her that immediately reacted to it. It felt like a sense of deep separation had finally been lifted. Wynona slipped on the gown and embraced her body, the dimensions were all just right. Nothing needed fixing. She bought it as it was.

204

Wynona's dress matched perfectly with the rest of her wedding's aesthetics. They were getting married inside a cute red barn they rented from the groom's distant uncle. All the glasses were mason jars. The chairs were old wooden stools. The decor was all antiques. The groomsmen were all to wear white shirts with overalls. And the bridesmaids would be wearing cornflower dresses and cowgirl boots.

The night before the wedding, the groom-to-be, Teddy Battle, sat with his best man, Beau, at a bar in West End. The two of them sat and reminisced about their bachelor's party during the past weekend. Teddy had a great time, but apparently his groomsmen were less than impressed. They all woke up the next morning with a strange rash around their pelvis, irritated skin surrounding shiny white carbuncles.

"I've got it. Duke's got it. Grady's got it, " said Beau. "We must have picked it up from that chick we ran a train on."

Teddy cringed. "Maybe you shouldn't be doing that."

"Nah. That's like the third time it's happened. It's not us. It's the girl. We shoulda' known better. Girls that look like that carry hella' diseases."

"Girls that look like what?"

"Strippers."

Teddy shrugged. "I think she said she was a teacher."

"But she dressed like a stripper. Cheetah print? A wig?"

"That's just..." Teddy sighed and rubbed at the back of his neck. "Some girls just don't like their natural hair."

Beau shrugged. "Then just use a straightener."

Teddy rolled his eyes. "Your not gonna be fucking scratching yourself during the ceremony are you?"

Beau laughed. "No. But I can only speak for myself."

Teddy cringed. He was worried about tomorrow. Lately, everything seemed to be working against his wedding day. First the weather reports for tomorrow turn sour. Then his uncle's cattle all get BVD and the place apparently wreaks. Now his groomsmen have questionable hygiene. What else could go wrong?

Suddenly, the lights at the bar went out. The bar went into sonic chaos as bartenders tripped, customers collided, and the easily-startled screamed for attention.

"What's the deal?" called out a faceless voice above all the shouting. "You forget to pay the bills?"

Suddenly a beam of light poured in as the front door opened up. One of the bar's owners peered outside. "Looks like power's out all over town."

"I know what you're thinking," came the voice of Beau in Teddy's ear, "but I don't want you to stress. The wedding's outside. In broad daylight."

"But the reception's at night…"

"Then we'll light torches. You want this wedding to be rustic, right?" Teddy didn't reply. Beau could tell he was getting frustrated. He reached out through the dark and patted Teddy on the back. "There's nothing that could happen between now and your wedding that we can't find a fix for."

Across town, Wynona was in a similar state of distress as her fiancé. She was trying to ease her wedding nerves by watching a few of her favorite romantic comedies: Sixteen Candles and Breakfast at Tiffany's. Both films she often described as "flawless".

Without anything left to distract her, Wynona's anxieties were getting the best of her. She figured she could continue watching her films on a portable device, but her personal computer was dead. She'd left it unplugged on sleep mode. She had a second laptop used for work, but that was in her car. She figured it might be worth the trip downstairs.

Wynona hopped out of her apartment and stared up to the top of the highrise. Every floor was dark. So were the neighboring buildings. It was extremely eerie. There didn't seem to be anyone on the street.

She walked to her parking space in a lot she rented down the street. She found her white Ford Aerostar in the corner and clicked twice on her key fob. Beep. Beep.

Crash! A large black panel smashed through the front door window from the inside. It collided with Wynona's face and sent her to the ground. She fell in and out of consciousness. She heard her car starting. She felt her body get lifted off the ground and shoved in the front seat. She turned to her right and saw darkened houses in a part of town called North Ridge-Rosemont. She turned to her left and saw a man with a bag over his head struggling to keep control of the car.

They suddenly braked in the middle of the street. They were parked at the entrance to a narrow cul-de-sac with three houses around the circumference. The stranger opened the passenger-side door and grabbed onto Wynona. She reached over and caught him by surprise, attempting to slash her nails across his eyes. Instead, she simply tore off his mask.

She was expecting some sort of scarred monstrosity. Or a lumping deformity. Not something so bright and beautiful. Tight blonde curls and Adam-esque features. It was breathtaking. She couldn't understand why such an angelic figure would stay concealed.

The face behind the mask smiled. "He has not forgotten you," said the stranger. His hands quickly latched onto the back of Wynona's head. They pushed her skull down onto his raised knee. Everything went dark.

The next day, an officer would say the same phrase into the telephone over a dozen times, as he made it his personal responsibility to call up every member of the wedding party and deliver the bad news. He knew the parents nor the groom would have the energy. "I'm afraid there's been a terrible accident. The bride-to-be… and the stress of the wedding…"

A sweet bay magnolia blew in the breeze as the coming storm approached. In its branches teetered the body of Wynona, adorned in her wedding dress. She swung back and forth in the breeze like a wedding bell. Her limp legs kicked at the mouth of her skirt like a clapper. There was an eerie absence of noise.

When Teddy arrived, people stared suspiciously at him. He wasn't weeping. Or breaking down. It wasn't like him to hold back whatever horrifying emotions he should be experiencing. But he just couldn't manage to push out a single tear. He was too distracted by the unfamiliar faces backed off away from the rest of the crowd.

It was the Buchanans. They owned the yard where Wynona had been killed. It was their tree that had been desecrated. There was a husband and a much younger wife. Two young sons and an older daughter. She looked about sixteen.

Teddy couldn't fathom why, but he wanted to scream at them. He wanted to tell them to run far away and never let their daughter out of their sight. Miraculously, Teddy knew this was only the beginning, and for some reason, he felt obligated to stop it.

But little did Teddy know that the opportunity to stop it had passed long ago.

Profile: Casius Crown

Midwest Furfest is the world's largest furry convention, taking place in Rosemont, Illinois. Casius Crown has attended the festival annually since 2010, going in plain clothes as compared to the extravagant outfits of the rest of the crowd. Costumes weren't his thing, instead he always paid for a booth where he'd show off and sell his Conte portraits of canine characters. They were usually dogs; dobermans and pitbulls he'd anthropomorphize into contrasting nerdy personalities. But for Furfest 2013 his drawings were different. This time, he had wolves on display.

It was a coded message. The wolf's pupils were drawn to look like a pair of black stars, signaling the attention of a specific set of dark web recruiters attending the convention. One of the recruiters approached, dressed in a plaid suit with a pair of black dog ears pinned in his hair. He eyed Casius's drawing and frowned. "I'm afraid that species hasn't been available since 2011. Pick another."

He'd originally chosen Ethiopian. He liked the red fur. He settled on a Himalayan. At least it shared a similarly sharp face.

The recruiter gave him a note with a time and a place. 8PM-8:15PM. The Pavilion. Room 403. Filled with excitement, Casius closed down his stand early and waited patiently in the Pavilion's lobby till the proper hour came. He then ran up the steps, found the door, and knocked softly three times.

The door opened, just a sliver. A hand shot through the opening and latched onto Casius's shoulder. It pulled him inside.

The hand was attached to a young girl, early-twenties, same as Casius. She was wearing an argyle dress and more dog ears. Casius smiled at her. She did not smile back.

Casius was pulled forward into the apartment and placed on a dingy black couch covered in long animal hair. He waited in the living room until the bedroom door opened up, then he was hurried inside.

Casius could see the recruiter from earlier standing next to a wolf with yellowish-white fur, chained by its neck to the bedpost. The recruiter knelt down and beckoned Casius to come forward. He pulled Casius's arm up to the wolf's snout, then quickly and carefully removed the animal's muzzle. At first it just snarled and sniffed Casius's meat. Then it clapped its jaws twice before latching on tightly to Casius's wrist. Casius tried to scream, but his wailing was muffled by a hand over his mouth. "Sssshhh..." said the girl in argyle. They gave the wolf a second to really sink its teeth in, then the recruiter stuck a needle in the wolf's neck and knocked it out cold.

Casius stared at his bite wound. It looked bad, but if everything went as planned, he should heal up after the next full moon. Casius paid the woman in argyle six grand, savings he'd earned since he graduated high school, then he left with a smile on his face.

The first full moon was only a week away. Every day till then, Casius felt stranger and stranger. His wrist had swollen and yellowed. He started breaking out into cold sweats, and he caught himself panting from time to time. He knew this was his transformation slowly approaching.

He prepared for the big day and started eating tons of protein to support the tissue growth that would surely be coming. He ate a steak for breakfast, lunch, and dinner. Sometimes he'd add a fourth one for dessert. He then bought an XXL Impact ® dog crate and found a pet sitter who was okay with exotic animals. He paid this man an extra hundred for his services if he agreed to watch him through the odd hours of midnight till morning.

When the night finally came, Casius crawled into his oversized cage and brought with him a stack of ten raw, unfrozen ribeyes. He shut the cage's door, reached through the bars, and locked it up tight. He then curled up into a ball and waited for the fuzz to start to grow over his body.

Right around midnight, he felt a tingling sensation in his wrist and his body starting to go numb. His breathing became rapid and his head felt dizzy. He let the clammy feeling on his skin consume him all over, then he let out a final gasp for air before completely blacking out.

Three hours later, Casius found himself reawakening. But instead of the tight confines of a cage, he was lying comfortably in a hospital bed. There were machines hooked up to his mouth to help him breathe. Casius was confused; he was worried his restraints weren't enough. Perhaps he'd escaped. Perhaps he'd hurt somebody and they hurt him back.

That's when a familiar face appeared above his eyes. He only recognized it from the profile picture online. It was the pet sitter.

"I found you in your pet's cage, barely breathing," said the sitter. "You've got pneumonia. You almost died, man, I saved your life... can I get double pay for that?"

The doctor appeared beside the sitter and asked him to leave the room.

"It's MRSA," explained the doctor. "It looks like you got bit by your pet and didn't get it treated... the infection spread to your lungs and blood. We gave you a transfusion about an hour ago. You seem to be getting better."

212

Casius frowned. This was not the curse he was promised. He felt like a fool.

"The authorities want to have a word with you when you're feeling better," continued the doctor. Casius's heart began to flutter.

"It seems in your confusion you freed your dog and stepped into his cage. It could be out there spreading its disease to the strays. We've got to find it."

Casius nodded.

"Next time you take in some street dog, make sure you take it to a vet. We almost lost you today."

This was Casius's second attempt at becoming a monster and it would certainly not be his last. He first tried becoming a vampire back when he was a teenager. He found a Facebook group offering the curse to new members, but the curse turned out to just be a "lifestyle". They bite you but it doesn't really do anything. They just give you an all-black costume afterwards and encourage you to start adding pig's blood to your diet.

Casius was into paranormal romance. A once niche story genre that's grown into a million dollar industry with the popularity of Twilight, Dark Lover, and Halfway to the Grave. Casius felt he was spoiled by these books. The love between two ordinary people bored him at this point. He needed curses tying him to a theoretical lover through their shared abnormality.

Casius felt bitter when the vampires weren't being serious. But those were just kids playing pretend, these "werewolves" were actual scammers and it filled Casius with dread. Every time one possibility fell through, Casius realized he'd have to go to even shadier extents to reach the real thing. He couldn't use Facebook

213

groups. And, apparently, he couldn't even use the dark web. He needed to meet real, real criminals. He figured the best place for that was jail, or in his case, community service.

In an act of vengeance, Casius blew the lid off his scammers' operation. In return for his cooperation, he dodged any animal abuse charges. They stuck him with aiding and abetting a kennel without a license. He just had to spend a couple hours each day picking up trash off the side of I-90. Here, Casius would meet a man named Adriel Begay.

Adriel Begay was doing community service for petty theft in Des Plaines. A tattoo on his left shoulder caught Casius's imagination, and almost instantaneously they became friends. It was a distorted face without any lips, skin held tight against its skull, and its teeth were long and chipped.

"The wendigo. It's Native legend," said Adriel. "My father showed me one as a kid, if you believe it."

Casius nodded. He wanted to know more. How did it come to be?

"You've got to be starving, in the wilderness, on the brink of death. You resort to cannibalism. You grow fifteen feet tall and you become gaunt and hairless. It's not sexy. You don't want this."

Casius assured the man. He did. "It's gotta be a little creepy. That's what makes it so taboo. You ever see Shape of Water?"

Adriel laughed. "A girl falls in love with a fish. That's a lot less creepy than what you want to be."

"But can you make it happen? Like let's not talk about it if you can't even do it."

214

Adriel nodded. "I can get you the meat," promised Adriel. "It's pretty easy."

"How is it easy?"

"I come from a bad part of town. There's bodies hidden everywhere. All I gotta do is wait till I find a fresh one. Then I shave off a few slivers."

"It can't just be a few slivers. We got to do this exactly. It's got to be enough to bring me back from the brink of starvation. It's got to be in the woods. And just to be safe, the victim's gotta be Native. And I got to use a Native recipe to eat it."

"A Native recipe?" Adriel snickered. "Yeah, yeah. We can do that. But that's a lot of specifics. And all that work calls for a little extra pay."

Casius shrugged. "Just name your price."

Casius's virtual wallet was emptied into Adriel's account. Adriel immediately held up his end of the transaction and found a body discarded in a local drain pipe. He decided to cook up something easy, something that he could brew in a crock-pot while still being "Native".

"It's tripe soup, thickened with brains."

Casius popped off the top and inhaled deeply. "It smells too good to be guts and brains."

"I spiced it right."

"It probably helps that I'm so hungry…" sighed Casius, putting a palm to his stomach. He'd fasted for three days in preparation. They both now stood in the middle of the Sand Ridge State

Forest. Casius was as excited as he was exhausted. He needed fuel.

"How do I know it's really human?" said Casius staring into the broth. "Could be beef..."

Adriel rolled his eyes, then pulled out something from his pocket. He grabbed it by its end and hung it by a thread in front of Casius's face.

"Does that look like a cow's eye?"

"Oh shit!" cringed Casius. He would have vomited if there was anything left inside him. He held down his stomach acid and asked Adriel to put the organ away.

"You asked me, man..."

Casius took a moment to calm his nerves, then he reached the thermos of soup up to his lips. He sucked on it briefly, then shut his eyes. "Oddly satisfying... that's probably a good sign."

Adriel nodded.

"How long will this take to kick in?"

Adriel shrugged. "Could be just a week. Could be much longer. Magic's tricky."

Casius started chugging the soup down to the last drop. "Then there really isn't much else I can do till it happens. I got to keep myself away from the general public, so when I change, no one gets hurt."

"Then it's for the best that I leave," suggested Adriel.

Casius agreed.

216

While Adriel ran off, Casius set up a campsite with warm sleeping arrangements and Tupperware full of the tripe soup. He figured he'd wait it out in the wild until his transformation was complete. Over a matter of mere days, the first signs of change had become apparent. The muscles in his extremities began to sting as though they were extending and mutating. He trembled with every move he made, as though a savage rage was building inside him.

As he reached a full week, the laughing started. It was maniacal and evil. He had no control over it, it just consumed his mind. He began to lose track of where he was. He'd wander farther and farther away from his campground. Each time he left, it became exponentially harder to find his way back. Eventually, he just stopped trying and accepted his place amongst the wildlife.

Unfortunately, cut off from society, there would be no witness to help him this time. As disease once again riddled Casius's body, he would die all alone in the center of the forest.

Casius's remains would be found by hikers, six weeks later. The cause of death would only be determined after a detailed autopsy analyzed the contents of his skull. Inside they found signs of transmissible spongiform encephalopathy: A neurological disorder transmitted through eating infected brain matter.

Casius's final hours are speculative and based mostly on Adriel's account of the events. Adriel was tracked down soon after Casius's body was found. The money transfer between their accounts tied the two together.

Adriel was charged with negligent manslaughter, as it could not be proved he purposely poisoned Casius. Adriel had no means of determining whether the brains he found were infected.

217

Adriel's community service has been upgraded to a five year prison sentence.

Casius's writings have been published on numerous public forums like AO3 and Commaful. His unpublished works were left to his family, a very loving mother and father, who read through all of their child's stories after his death. When I asked if I could share one of Cassius's stories for my collection they were happy to lend me "Zooland", their favorite of the bunch.

I agree with his parents in that "Zooland" captures Casius's interest in transformation best. It was written some time during his werewolf interest and seems to suggest it was more than just romance he sought with his bestial form. I believe deep down Casius thought he had to become a monster externally to reflect the id he saw within himself.

Zooland

Michael Kent and his daughter, Cheryl, had driven non-stop from their old home in Burlington to their new house in Lake Fuchane, Maine. It was a tiny mountain town on the northern tip of the Appalachian trail. Michael was happy to get his daughter away from the city to a more intimate community. They disassembled their furniture and fit as much as they could in a single rented U-Haul. When they arrived at six in the morning, the sun's glow through the pine trees gave them a warm introduction to the neighborhood.

"That's where you'll be studying," said Michael, pointing to a school tucked into a clearing. This one building houses their whole K-12. The community was small, and so would be the classes. "And that's where I'll be spending the weekend," he laughed, pointing to the only bar in town. It was on the same road as the school, Hourwood Street. Same as the post office, the three restaurants, the coffee shop, the gym, and the ice rink. It was all right there next to each other and within walking distance of the adjacent housing.

Michael and Cheryl's new house was at the bottom of the mountain. It was a timber-framed, one-story cottage. No basement, three bedrooms, one bathroom. It was a cheap little thing, an affordable option for a low-income family. Before they moved, Michael did auto repair. He could make a fine living, but there's stiff competition. He was confident his skill would be more specialized in a rural area. But that wasn't the most important reason for becoming more isolated.

After parking their van on the street out front, Michael quickly hurried to his daughter's car door and opened it for her. He offered her some support while she made the big step down from the interior.

"Dad, you don't... you don't got to."

"Nonsense!" he exclaimed. "We can't be too careful." Michael made sure his daughter stepped down on the ground softly, then instructed her to wait just a few minutes while he set up her bed. That way she could get some rest after such a long car ride.

Cheryl followed behind her father as he brought his toolbox and the parts to her bedframe inside. Cheryl wanted to help her dad put it all together, but he warned her it could be arduous.

"You're doing too much," argued Cheryl. "I'm not letting you put this whole house together by yourself."

Michael set down his wrench and stood up from beneath the bed frame. He reached out and touched his daughter's stomach through her sweatshirt.

"You're not gonna feel anything," laughed Cheryl. "I'm only in the first trimester. So please let me help around here while I can still fit through the doors."

Michael rolled his eyes. "Fine... there's plenty of boxes to unpack. Go decorate the living room. Just don't touch any furniture."

Cheryl followed orders and walked outside to the van. She tried to pick out something lightweight and found a box full of wall art. She carried it into their living room and began to cover up any strange marks on the old wall paper. There was a particularly noticeable grey square between the windows facing the backyard. The former owner used to have something hanging there.

Cheryl picked out a large family portrait that could cover the area. She nailed it into the wall and stepped back to see if it was centered. As she stared, she noticed something odd fluttering outside of one of the back windows. She hurried out into the backyard and looked up into the trees. There was a sandy yellow beach towel hung on a low branch. It flapped loudly in the breeze.

"Dad, how much of the land out back is ours?" she called into the house.

Her father shrugged. "Just the first three hundred feet, really. But I mean, we're not in the type of place that cares too much. We can play around back there and no one's gonna make too much of a fuss."

Cheryl looked deep into the forest sloping upwards behind their house. Her eyes slowly ascended, scanning the trees all the way up to the top of the mountain. The whole way there she saw more towels scattered throughout the canopy. They were all different sizes and colors. Some were pearl. Some were pink. Some had flowers. Some had cartoons.

Cheryl began to worry. She looked up at the clear sky overhead then quickly ran back into the house. "Dad!" she called out. "How bad does the weather get out here?"

Her father couldn't answer. "I didn't really look that up to be honest with you…"

"There's linens blown everywhere..." griped Cheryl. "If the wind gets this bad… that's actually dangerous."

Michael sighed. "It's the wilderness, sweetie. It's not dangerous. It's just challenging. A lot less challenging than the city, I'll guarantee you that much."

221

"Oh don't go blaming the city, Dad," huffed Cheryl. "It was Billy, not Burlington, that drove us away."

William Malrose, or Billy as Cheryl calls him, is the father of Cheryl's coming child. Billy was born with a dark side that he hides well from even his own parents. Cheryl's seen it peek through however, particularly when he threatened her with infanticide if she didn't agree to an abortion. "They won't know it's me," he hissed at her. "You'll just wake up with it scooped out between your ankles."

"We can't let the city off the hook entirely," griped Michael. "They wouldn't give you a restraining order or police protection because they chose the word of a Malrose over a Kent."

Michael let out his frustration with a series of loud whacks that set in the last piece of Cheryl's bed frame. Michael and Cheryl carried in the mattress together and folded up some sheets and blankets on top. The once dismal space was beginning to look a lot like a sixteen-year-old's bedroom.

"Need any help, neighbor?" A young man, Cheryl's age, led a small pack of locals up to the Kent's new front lawn. These folks were all smiling and waving. The young man extended his hand to Michael. "I'm Andre."

Micheal shook the boy's hand and pointed to the crowd. "You're all up so early. Did I wake you with all my hammering?"

"Oh no!" A short, portly woman appeared at Andre's side. Her name was Sue. "We're just all a little excited to see a newcomer. News traveled fast that you were coming today."

"It's a small town," continued Andre. "There's no avoiding each other, so we wanted to see if you're just as Jane described."

"Jane?" questioned Micheal. "The lady who sold me this place? She talks about me?"

"Well we asked about you," replied Andre.

"She said only good things!" swooned Sue. "We really respect a parent of your quality around here. A real protector."

"So she talked about... my daughter? That was barely her business to begin with." Micheal looked over the portly woman and saw several of the men in the party grabbing boxes out of the back of his van. "Now wait just a second! You don't know where those belong..."

"Well then show us!" said one of the men with a dark blue hat and a cheery disposition. "I'm Paul and this is Blake. Between the three of us, I'm sure we can get this all moved-in before sundown."

"Come on, dad. Let them help," said Cheryl, putting her palm on Micheal's shoulder. "Especially if you won't let me."

Micheal smiled. "Okay. I'll ease up."

The rest of the day went by like a breeze. Paul and Blake helped Micheal with the heavy lifting, while Sue and Andre helped Cheryl decorate. As a team, they worked pretty well. A good sign that the Kents would fit in easily with the rest of the friendly faces in Lake Fuchane.

After everyone left for dinner, Micheal finished the last of the moving by himself. All that was left was to build his own bed frame, just in time for a good night's sleep. Having done the more intensive labor, Michael was excited to finally pass out. He was hoping to get a good night's sleep so he could be more bright and cheery when they met the rest of the town the following morning, but unfortunately his daughter wouldn't let that happen.

Micheal was particularly groggy when his daughter jostled him awake only an hour into his shut eye.

"Deers…" was the only thing he'd heard her say. He asked her to stop and held his ears under his pillow. Cheryl grabbed her father's shoulder and shook him lightly. He groaned aggravatingly and tossed his pillow aside, revealing his face.

"What," grumbled Michael.

"There's deers," whispered Cheryl. "There's deers outside my window."

"Uhm, okay?" sneered Michael. "Cher, this ain't the city anymore. There's some real wildlife out there. Just try to ignore it, so I can get some rest."

"I'm trying," she pleaded. "But it keeps tapping on my window every time I look away from it."

"It must be… mating season," chuckled Michael, finding the energy to peel his face up off his mattress. "I guess that… I'll go scare him away, okay?"

Michael slowly rose out of bed and trudged begrudgingly to the family room. He didn't have time this afternoon to mount his rifle, so it sat in a box against the wall. He lifted it up and checked to see if it was loaded.

He then walked the gun over to his daughter's bedroom and prepared to prod the barrel at the deer, but, as he walked into the room, he was shocked out of his half-sleep by a surprise at the window. There were now three deer staring through the glass. There were two does and one buck, they had their snouts

224

side by side and pressed against the glass. Their breathing caused a large ring of fog to dilate in and out.

"I bet people in this town eat venison," scoffed Michael, cocking his gun. "We could sell enough steaks from these three to pay off the house!" Michael dashed out of Cheryl's bedroom and out the front door to the house. He barged outside onto his front porch and took a kneeling stance on the wooden planks. He rested the end of his barrel on the guardrail and aimed at the nearest doe.

Suddenly, a brown blur blocked the path of his scope. He raised his head from the sight and saw a fourth deer had arrived and stepped into his aim. It was a massive elk that kept its eyes locked on Michael's as it walked up to him boldly. It stepped up to the guard rail, then reared up onto its hind legs, making a low whining noise like a donkey.

"Woah there!" stuttered Michael, confused by the animal's behavior. He dismounted his gun and turned back towards the front door. That's when he saw another two deer on the opposite side of the porch. Michael turned to his front yard and saw between eight and ten more. They were everywhere and they had completely surrounded his porch.

"Dad!" called Cheryl through her bedroom window. "Should I get help?"

"Don't go anywhere!" commanded Michael. "Stay inside and lock the door!" Cheryl followed her father's instructions and made sure the house was completely sealed. She then returned to her bedroom window and continued to watch. The deer were closing in on her father.

"Get out of here!" he shrieked as he fired a warning shot above their heads. It had no effect.

225

Suddenly, two bucks jumped over the railings on either side of Michael. He fired at one and only nicked its antler. The other one came up behind him and bit down onto the collar of his shirt. Michael was pulled to the ground and lost his gun. It was carried away by a nearby doe, while three more deer ascended onto the patio and bit onto Michael's pant legs. Together they lifted Michael a foot off the ground and began carrying him out into his front yard.

"No! Let go!" shouted Michael, yanking against their hold. They refused to set him free until he was out from under the shade of his porch and completely basked in the moonlight overhead. At this point, the deer all released Michael at once. They stepped back and watched him in a crowded circle.

Michael hadn't felt any pain while being pulled along by the deer, but now that he was free, his skin had begun to burn. It felt like the glow of the moon was cooking him alive. His face was pink and sweating. He felt drunk and suddenly stupid. Like he couldn't remember his own name. He forgot how to walk. And how to speak. His knowledge was being boiled down to the bare essentials.

His hair follicles began to enter rapid mitosis and quickly his entire body was covered in fur. At the sight of its silver pigment, several deer began to run away. But those that remained hopeful, watched eagerly.

Michael continued to change, growing claws and fangs. His torso began to widen. Michael had grown too large for his clothes and had shredded them to bits. At this point, his long, lupine tail was revealed, making his final form lamentingly clear. But it was too late now for the remaining deer to escape.

Cheryl had lost sight of her father long ago, but she was certain he was still alive in the center of the deer. But when a sudden howl sent the herd scrambling, her father seemed to have been

226

replaced with a snarling beast. It was a bright-grey wolf. He had two does struggling in his grasp. One's back leg was caught in his teeth; another's chest was pinned under his paw.

The wolf chomped down hard, breaking the leg of the victim in its mouth. It then bit onto the neck of the deer trapped under its feet and beheaded it with a twist and a tear. It then got to work feeding on their meat, before running away into the woods behind the house.

In his wolf form, Michael was filled with pure id. All his desires and impulses were streaming through his animal brain. With each kill he finished off, he felt a sudden rush of catharsis that left him only wanting more. He didn't attack any humans. That wasn't a part of his appetite. All he wanted was the taste of venison, till the moonlight finally dimmed and the sun finally arose.

Michael woke up very confused and very naked in a part of the woods he did not recognize. He couldn't tell if he was far from town or not, since he'd only moved in yesterday. He began to wander around the forest unsure which direction to go in, and his splitting headache didn't help.

Micheal wasn't sure what had happened that night, but he understood some of the basic details. He was attacked by a herd of deer. He fought back. He clearly survived, but in the process, somehow lost his clothes. After a bit of aimless travel, he realized he wasn't the only one stripped.

Micheal couldn't believe it. He recognized another nudist, scampering about between a few nearby trees. It was that boy. Andre. He had a white towel wrapped around his waist. His face looked bleak and defeated.

"Andre!" shouted Micheal. "Yo, kid!"

"Keep your distance, man!" shouted Andre. He looked offended by Michael's presence. "I don't want anything to do with you right now."

"Hey... hey wait!" called Michael as Andre hurried away. "Wait, were you attacked by those deer, too?"

Andre shook his head and refused to make eye contact. "No," he sniffled. "Just a wolf." He sped up into a sprint and quickly hurried away behind a thick patch of bushes.

Michael couldn't figure out what was going on. He couldn't tell if he was even close to home. He decided to follow the path Andre took, but immediately regretted it. The way the sun shone through the trees made it hard to see what was in front of him. And with no dirt road, Michael was worried he was just wandering farther and farther from home.

He just kept moving forward, shielding his weak spot with his one hand and moving flora out of the way with his other. Michael saw a few more nude denizens along his way. He recognized them from Andre's introduction but he couldn't remember their names. Michael called out to them, but as soon as they saw him they ran off before he could ask them for directions.

After about a half-hour of searching, Michael felt exhausted. His whole body was covered in sweat that dripped into fresh scratches and stung him. Micheal dropped down to the forest floor and sighed in frustration. But just as all hope seemed to be lost, a new face suddenly appeared to Michael's side.

"You look lost neighbor," said a handsome young man. He looked about twenty. His hair was notably blonde, shimmering in the sunlight. He had a well-toned chest and wore a pink bath towel covering everything below the waist. The young man smiled, "Do you know where you are?"

Michael shook his head. He was relieved to get some help and allowed the young man to pull him off the ground. The young man led Michael over to a nearby tree and reached up to a branch close to the ground. He plucked a towel off of its leaves and coiled it over Michael's privates. "Feel free to use the towels. We leave em' hanging around for this very reason."

"What's your name?" asked Micheal.

"Jonas," said the boy.

"What happened to us, Jonas?" begged Michael.

The boy pointed to a puff of smoke in the distance rising into the air near the horizon. "That's Spike's Bowling Alley. See, you were never far from home!" gleed the boy. "How about we get some wings and we can talk about it?"

"We should get some clothes on first," suggested Michael, but the boy insisted it didn't matter.

"We won't be the only ones like this," laughed the boy. "Long as we got a towel on, it's not weird. All that shapeshifting leaves people with an appetite. People don't waste any time filling the hole it leaves."

When they walked inside, the place smelled like a weird mixture of soft pretzels, hot oil, and old shoes. It wasn't the most appetizing atmosphere, but the boy was correct, Michael found himself suddenly starving now that the panic of being lost had faded away.

They sat down at a table near the front entrance beside a window.

"Gentleman," said a glum looking lady in a half-tucked t-shirt sporting the alley's logo. It looked like she'd just changed clothes. "Are you ready to ord-"

"Don't even," smirked Jonas, blocking her with his hand. "Just get me Charlie, please."

The waitress gave him a cold glare, then turned to Michael. She then sighed angrily and walked off into the kitchen behind the counter.

Jonas turned to me. "I don't like being rude, but she'll spit on our food."

"How come?" asked Michael.

"We're wolves. And she's a deer. They hate us. Particularly you, at least for the moment," explained Jonas. "But Charlie's a wolf like us. He's the fry cook, here. He'll serve us directly."

"Hey, hey!" shouted Charlie. A tall boy in an apron and a hair net came prancing out to their table. "How's the new guy feel?"

"Oh the deer didn't tell him shit before last night," snickered Jonas. "I need to fill him in on everything."

"Oh, really?" exclaimed Charlie. "Well Michael just be happy you ended up on the winning team."

"So everyone in town transforms?" asked Michael.

Jonas nodded. "Yeah, it's a curse caused by a science experiment gone terribly wrong. It releases our ids every night. For some that id takes the form of a deer. Deep down these folk are balls of insecurity and self pity."

"They're victims by their own allowance," Charlie chimed in.

"And deep down we wolves are… well we're confident and we get what we want."

"We're vicious and ambitious," said Charlie. "It's just our nature. If someone's standing in our way, we're more likely to bump him off."

"So then they wanted me here to add a new deer to their team?" asked Micheal.

"No, no," interjected Jonas. "They want a third type of id. It's rarer than rare."

"It's the bear!" shouted Charlie. Michael noticed the more excited Jonas and Charlie got, the more people seemed to disperse to tables further away from their seats.

"The bear is supposed to be a guardian of sorts to the deer," nodded Jonas. "His id is a protector complex. A white knight. His character is completely selfless."

Michael thought back to the strange personality test the town's realtor had given him. She said it was to find him the perfect home to match, but some of the details it queried were a little too in depth. He figured it asked for any possible arrests as a means of weeding out sickos. In a way, it was.

"I'm flattered, I guess," said Michael. "Personality tests never really accurately depict me. I'm too borderline this and that. I guess, in truth, I'm a little bit more type A than type B, then?" asked Michael.

"It's more like, you're a little more sadist than masochist," said Charlie with a grin. "More predator than prey."

"No, it can't be that…"

"Oh come on, I mean, why are you really here with your daughter?" pressed Charlie.

"Don't gross him out, Charlie, he's still new to this," snapped Jonas.

"He's not Yogi after all, so it can't just be to protect her," shrugged Charlie. "He may not even realize it, which is the sad part, but the wolf doesn't lie…"

"Are you implying that I just want my daughter all to myself?"

Charlie nodded. "…deep down we all have strange desires winking from our subconscious."

Michael stood up and headed for the exit.

"Michael wait!" called out Jonas. "We haven't even gotten our food."

Luckily for Michael, everything was so densely populated that it only took him a short, angry stroll to get back to his house from the bowling alley. He threw open the front door and yelled for his daughter.

"Dad!" cried out Cheryl, from behind her bedroom door. She quickly unlocked it and embraced her father. "God, I thought something terrible happened to you."

"It was terrible," said Michael. "I turned into a wolf."

"Like a werewolf?"

"It's actually more like a Myers-Briggs with animal totems," he said with a stern gaze. He patted his daughter's shoulder. "Pack up a backpack with the essentials, we're leaving now."

232

"What?"

"I'm serious. I'll hire a moving company to pick up the rest. I'll dip into my savings if we have to. But we don't want to get sucked into this town's bullshit. It's like a furry caste system."

Cheryl nodded with a look of shock. "I, uh, alright. I trust you. But you owe me some details when we reach the highway."

Cheryl grabbed a toothbrush, her chargers, her laptop, her cell phone, and some snacks. She packed the rest of the space with clothes. Michael packed nearly identically. Once they were both finished, Cheryl threw herself into their van while Michael hurried after.

He was stopped half-way across his front lawn by none other than Andre. He was fully clothed and letting begrudging sighs roll out of his mouth. "We've got to talk, Michael. Stop what you're doing for a second."

"No need to run us out of town," sneered Michael. "We're leaving on our own accord. That's one less wolf for you to deal with."

"Look, I'd love to see you disappear, which is why you've got to trust me here," replied Andre, "You can't leave… or you'll die."

Michael stood still for a moment and faced Andre. "Why not let the wolf die then?"

"We deer are sickeningly pro-life."

Michael rolled his eyes. "What happens if I leave? Do I explode?"

Andre pointed up into the sky. There were very little clouds overhead and the atmosphere sort of blurred the coloration as though a heavy blanket of ozone was right over their heads. "There's a gas that hangs over our town. The moonlight filters through that gas up there and causes anyone it touches to transform. Once your body transforms for the first time, it needs to bask in the moonlight every 24-hours, like a drug. Otherwise, you get sick. A fever like nothing you've ever experienced before. You burn up and you die."

Michael looked pissed. He suddenly felt trapped and his body immediately found blame. He clenched his fist and walked firmly up to Andre.

Andre stepped back. He raised his hand. "Don't waste time like that," said Andre "Listen. Your daughter is still free to go. I insist you give her the keys-"

"She doesn't have her license…"

"Then drive her yourself, drive as far away as possible, check her into a hotel, and make it back here by sundown," suggested Andre.

"Why can't I just hide her in my house?"

"You're pretty naive for a wolf. Don't you know your own kind?" said Andre with a sneer. "There's a new wolf in town, which means there'll soon be less deer. They'll replace that prey with any options available. Your daughter's gonna get dragged out of that house sooner or later."

"There's a psychopathic boyfriend after her… would you leave your sixteen-year-old daughter to fend for herself?"

"To be honest, I was hoping you could separate yourself from her for a bit. It's a shame you seem to have to have her so close,"

234

said Andre with a judgmental glance. "You know people in this town have seen Lolita… we know what it looks like."

"Oh God," Michael looked disgusted. "Rumors spread fast in small towns… look that's not true."

"Your inner-thoughts say otherwise."

"I don't know who makes the rules, but they got me wrong."

"Dr. Skadi makes the rules. She made the gas," said Andre, matter-of-factly.

"Is Skadi here in town?"

Andre nodded. "She's in the big property at the top of the mountain."

"Does she see guests?"

Andre smiled. "Not always. But she'll talk to you."

Michael got in his car with his daughter, but he explained to her that they wouldn't be leaving. Instead, they were headed for the top of the hill. Here, the doctor's house was obvious. Its luxury clashed with the mundane buildings beneath it. Two stories. Two wings. A bright white minimalist exterior, with whole walls made from reinforced glass.

When Michael knocked on the door he expected to be greeted by some hip forty-something dressed in thick-rimmed glasses and a sari. But instead, it was a small child who answered the door. "Yes?" he said with a big grin. "Are you here for an- for an appointment?"

"No," said Michael bluntly. "Go get your mom."

The boy's smile faded away. He nodded fast, then hurried off. Michael waited in the doorway for the boy's mother to appear. She was still not what he expected. Although he got the glasses right.

"Is this Michael?" said a long face covered in brown fur. "You're the guy who took the Huntsons' house. Shame what happened to them."

"You knew I was coming?"

"No. I just know there's a Michael new in town and I haven't seen your face before, so you must be that Michael. And the girl in the car is Cheryl? Does she want to come in, too?"

Michael nodded. He beckoned for Cheryl to come join him. She slipped into the nice house and took a seat on a leaden-blue couch. She smiled and played with the doctor's two boys, while Michael and Dr. Skadi talked in the kitchen.

"You're not fully human," said Michael, pointing out the obvious.

Skadi's body was trapped somewhere between a human and a wolf. Her mouth came to a slight point, and was filled with razor sharp teeth. Her nose was black and shiny. Her ears remained mostly human, except for the layer of fur overtop of them. This fur covered every last inch of her skin.

"I hope my figure isn't too alarming."

"It's just unexpected," replied Michael. "Are you like this at all hours?"

Skadi nodded. "In order to get to this point, you have to remove the barrier between your id and your public persona. It's quite a rare accomplishment. But once you succeed, you no longer need to feed on the moonlight."

"So you can leave?" questioned Michael. "Then why on Earth do you stay?"

"I owe the people in this town their escape. It's my work that caused this curse," replied Skadi. "I have enough money and connections to see the world's leading therapists. That's what got me to this point. These people don't have those resources, so I stay here and try my best with them. I'm a trained therapist, as well as an experimental psychiatrist. But it's a struggle, most of the people in this town don't keep their appointments. The ones that do are desperate to leave here, but that doesn't mean they are desperate to make the change that requires. Most are still too insecure to open up to me."

"Who makes more appointments, wolves or deer?" asked Michael.

"Wolves for sure. The deer are shy, while the wolves are in a constant battle to expand their territory."

"That still doesn't sound like me… I'm just not this ambitious creature that your gas insists. Could it be defective?"

Skadi shook her head. "It's carefully formulated. And well tested."

"Maybe, I could admit to some anger issues. I bottle up a lot of stuff. But these rumors that I want to feel up my daughter are just absurd."

"Who says these rumors?"

"The fry cook at the bowling alley."

237

"Charlie?" snickered Skadi. "That's the pot calling the kettle black. I have good reason to believe Charlie raped somebody when he was a teenager. He might have raped again if it wasn't for this town. It satisfies his id in a completely legal way. So no need to act out."

"This can't be legal…"

"It's animals killing animals," shrugged Skadi. "No one's breaking the law. And the bodies don't change back once they're dead. A deer dies a deer. Besides, the deer have tried their damnedest to get justice. The government shuts down all their social media, all their cries for help."

"Why?"

"Who do you think released my gas? Certainly, not me," scoffed Skadi. "The government wanted to experiment on people. And now they're doing a fine job at covering it up. And before you ask, there are tons of ways this transformation can better Uncle Sam. They could use it to test any operative or asset for their true intentions. If they're a deer, we can trust their word. If they're a wolf, let's think twice. And let's not forget they could pour this solution all over a rival country and just let them eat each other."

Michael nodded. "I believe you. And if that's the case, I might be comfortable taking sessions with you myself. If you'll have me?"

"What do you think this is right now?" said Skadi with a smile. "Introducing ourselves and building trust are how I prefer to start with my patients. Only then do we dive into what I see as their… vulnerable spot."

"Do you know about Billy?"

Skadi nodded. "Because of that survey you took, everyone here knows about Billy. But I know a little bit more. I did some digging on the internet. And I think I've already found some evidence related to your lupinity."

Michael shrugged. "I hate Billy. But does that make me a predator?"

"It might, depending on just how much you hate him. Running away from Billy sounds like something a deer would do. So we know you aren't running, are you?"

"I'm here, aren't I?"

"But why here specifically? You could have stayed in Vermont. But Vermont doesn't have castle doctrine, does it? By no sheer coincidence, Maine does."

Michael nodded. "I'll admit, I'm well aware of that."

"Fair enough. And alone, I would call that cautious, not predatory. But Michael, what's with all the breadcrumbs you've left behind?" asked Skadi, pulling out her cell phone. She showed Michael his own Facebook page where he left a few details online as to his whereabouts. "That's your address. It's in a public place."

"I thought that part of Facebook was private," said Michael with a shrug.

"No, no," said Skadi. "You're not some grandpa helpless with new age technology, you left a big clue online. And that's not the only one. You left your current address to your old home's new residents, so they could forward any calls."

"I told them not to give it to Billy."

"And you're too stupid to think Billy would just lie about his name?" questioned Skadi. "You may not be aware of it Michael, but to me, it seems as though you want him to find you out here."

"You think I've laid a trap?"

"I mean, back in Vermont that boy is well-off and well-protected. You can't shoot a rich boy in his hometown. But you lure him out here and his intentions become undeniable. No one around here would take his side over yours. No one will question why you shot him dead. He traveled miles away to hurt your daughter."

Michael laid back in his seat and crossed his arms. "So what? I admit to that and I can leave this town. Well, then fuck it: Hell yes I intended to kill the boy when I moved out here. Hell yes, hell yes, hell yes."

Skadi gave Michael a smug look. "That's a lot like planning a murder. You're setting up a scenario to legally kill a minor."

Michael sighed. "It sounds awful when you put it that way, but fine. Maybe I watched too many revenge movies in the 80s. It's clearly turned me into a psycho. I admit. Now when do I grow that full body beard of yours?"

"I mean, we've made progress. You've accepted you can be a wolf. But I never transformed till I reached the root of it all. And I doubt it's just 80s movies," explained Skadi. "Your willingness to change should help the process, but we still need more time together. Perhaps we can expedite the process with another session tomorrow?"

"I'm scared to spend another night here," said Michael. "I've been told that the wolves could try to pull Cheryl into all this."

"Psychologists limit their sessions, because the mind needs time to process what we talked about. You need at least one night's sleep before we go on," explained Skadi. "Go out tonight. Be a wolf. Do what you have to. And I'll look after your daughter. No one comes after me or my kids because that would cut off their only hope of leaving. Cheryl can spend the night in my guest room. She can pay me back by babysitting my kids. They seem to get along."

Skadi and Michael turned around and saw Cheryl playing a game with the two brothers where they each held a card. They were all smiling and laughing, keeping their cards hidden, holding them close to their chests.

Michael drove home leaving his daughter behind. He spent the rest of the day packing their things back in the van, until sundown came around. Then, he stripped his clothes off so they wouldn't tear again and stepped outside onto his front lawn.

As soon as the moonlight touched his bare flesh, it was like leaping into a warm bath. Michael's head was suddenly flooded with dopamine. He charged forward and followed the smell of food into the downtown area. Once he was there, he started stalking up and down Hourwood Street, howling at the moon and sniffing out deer hiding behind the shops.

Michael saw a small deer struggling to get out of the dumpster where it was hiding. Two adults were biting onto its budding antlers, trying to offer help by yanking downwards on its head. Once the adults saw Michael, they let go and sped off, leaving the young one to fend off the wolf all on their own. In his human state, Michael would have been disgusted by this choice in poor parenting. But in the wolf state, he felt nothing but joy as he closed in on what was essentially fish in a barrel.

When Michael awoke the following morning, his memory would be a fuzzy mix of low growling sounds and terrified bleats. Deep down, Michael hoped that he hadn't hurt anybody. He touched

241

his stomach to feel if he was full of flesh. His gut felt empty, full of only gas and hunger pangs.

"That's no way to tell," explained Charlie with a sneer. The two had woken up in the same clearing this time. They must have been hunting as a pack. "The wolf state uses up all that we eat in a single night. There isn't anything left when we wake up as humans. It's a small town, we'll notice if someone's gone before the end of today."

"But you can't tell which one of us did the deed?"

"Sometimes you can… for example, we got this pile of loose dirt sitting here right between us." Charlie stood up off the ground and walked over to the dust pile. He cleared it off with his hand and reached down inside the uncovered ditch. He pulled out a deer's skull. "Yep, it seems we shared a meal together before we changed back. No clue who took him out though. And there's no way to tell. But then again, why bother asking?"

Michael used a tree at his back to pick himself up. His whole body felt sore and tired. He shook his head. "I'd like to know if I took someone's life. Don't most people?"

Charlie pointed up at the sky. "Any lives lost are not our fault. It's the gas."

"That's a little apathetic."

Charlie shook his head. "It's tough empathizing with animals."

"Then maybe you could use a shrink," suggested Michael. He pointed up to the top of the mountain. "Have you spoken with Skadi?"

Charlie snickered and rolled his eyes. "Yes. I know Skadi. I visit on occasion. I'm guessing you two have been recently acquainted?"

Michael nodded. "She's already beginning to crack me. She's quite thoughtful."

Charlie sighed. "She's charming. She's a wolf after all. But she's dangerous. Just like us."

"What do you mean by dangerous…" questioned Michael. "I left my daughter there last night…"

"Oh you big, naive child…" snickered Charlie. "I guess no one told you. She's a damned pervert. Why would you keep her around your kid?"

"A pervert?" scoffed Michael. "What do you-"

"Why do you think she's a wolf? And now that she's 'enlightened', she's out about it and acts like she's completely proud of herself for it."

Michael shook for a brief moment. First it was shock, then it was horror. He didn't bother grabbing a towel. He ran in the buff as fast as he could towards the smoke rising in the distance. Once he reached Hourwood Street, he made a hard left and sprinted towards his home. He threw on some pants, got in his vehicle, and drove back up the hill.

Bang. Bang. Bang. Michael gave a few knocks out of decency, but when no one answered within ten seconds, he just grabbed the door handle and let himself in. Skadi's older child was standing in the entry's hallway. It looked as though they were about to answer the door. He now stood in shock at the bizarre intrusion. "Mr. Kent, you look effed up."

243

Michael stormed past the child and found Dr. Skadi skyping with somebody in her home office. When she saw Michael's pink face, she apologized to the man on the other end of the line and hung up. She turned to Michael with a look of concern. "I wasn't expecting you…"

"You're a damn sexual deviant."

"Pardon me?"

"Charlie tells me I left my daughter with a proud pervert."

"Ugh," sighed Skadi, rolling her eyes. "He's referring to me being gay."

"Is he now?" snarled Michael with disbelief.

"Yes. I had to come to terms with it in order to begin my transformation. I was getting uncomfortably close with all the married wives in this town. Subconciously, I was trying to fuck them. I had to accept that."

"Where's Cheryl?"

"I'm right here, Dad," called out his daughter, smoothly descending the stairs. She'd heard her father's disgruntled voice and got curious.

"Romeo and Remmy, shut your ears for a minute!" called out Skadi. "Cheryl, did we fuck?"

"Uh… what?"

"Your father needs to know we didn't fuck each other last night."

"No… we didn't fuck," huffed Cheryl. "What the fuck, dad?"

244

"I'm having a hard time understanding what it means to be a wolf is all," said Michael with a grim expression. "So forgive me for getting paranoid."

"Don't apologize, this is good. This feeling is good. I want you to hang on to that feeling," directed Skadi. "This feeling could lead us to the route of your homicidal rage towards Billy. Tell me, before Billy, when's the first time you felt like this?"

"Well," Michael rubbed nervously on the back of his neck, "I guess it's when Cheryl got pregnant."

"Further back. Before that."

"When I found out she was having sex!"

"Even further. Come on," pressed Skadi. "We are close, Michael, close to unlocking what could be the key to you escaping this awful place."

"I don't know," said Michael with an uncomfortable scowl. "Or maybe I do. And I just don't wanna say."

"Might it have something to do with your daughter's sexual abuse as a toddler?"

"W-what? How did you-?"

"I told her dad," called out Cheryl. "We did a session with just us two last night…"

"You feel responsible for her abuse, don't you Michael?" questioned Skadi. "You let your brother babysit. You trusted him and it cost you your daughter's innocence."

"Fuck," whispered Michael. "What do you want me to do with that? Just admit that it happened? Or admit that I'm wrong blaming myself? Or I don't blame myself enough?"

"You can accept some responsibility, any good parent would. But what we need to establish today is why you can't talk about it with her," said Skadi, pointing at Cheryl.

"Oh god, cause who would want to?" winced Michael. "No one wants to talk about sex with their daughter. And molestation is just... horrifying. I'd rather hope she forgot about the incident."

"I haven't," sighed Cheryl. "I've been just patiently waiting for you to bring it up."

"Hear that. She hasn't, Michael," said Skadi. "So maybe now would be a good time, more than ever, for you two to get this out in the open."

"Well what does she want to know?"

Skadi shook her head. And pointed towards Cheryl.

"Oh sorry." Michael turned to face his daughter; he found it hard to look her in the eye. "What do you want to know?"

"Was he punished?"

"Yeah," said Michael with a nod. "I told the cops. He was arrested. Spent two years in jail. He's on a public list of offenders."

"Is he miserable?"

"He lost communication with me. And I was his best friend in the whole world. So yeah, he's miserable."

"Could he ever find me?"

"I've filed a restraining order on your behalf. If he ever comes within 200 yards of you…"

"But can he find me?"

Michael nodded. "He can…. and so can Billy."

Cheryl nodded. "I know that. Skadi told me." Cheryl stood up and walked over to her father. She spread her arms and tightly hugged him. "It's okay you're a little violent, dad. I know it just means you care."

Suddenly, Cheryl felt a strange scratchy feeling rubbing against her skin. She pulled away to see her father's hair had grown downwards to cover up his entire body. "Oh dad," said Cheryl with a frown. "You look kind of gross. We can leave, but how the Hell are you gonna live like this."

"Don't be rude," snapped Skadi. "He'll do what I do when I leave town. Just say you have trichosis."

Skadi had tons more advice to give to Michael. They sat down with both their families included and talked about the many differences between a wolf-man and a man-man. The physical features were just the start of it. Skadi talked about the urges she sometimes feels to act on her impulses, and the little voice in her head that tells her to indulge. She talked about the caution she puts into her every move, wolf-men are incredibly strong when compared to the standard.

Their conversation carried on through dinner. Michael was introduced to a proper wolf-man's diet. It had to be high in fat and protein and low in carbs. Michael was enjoying his delicious leg of lamb, a Skadi family specialty, when their supper was suddenly interrupted by four knocks at the door. Romeo, the older of Skadi's boys, got up out of his seat and politely answered. "Are you here to see my mom?"

"Michael," replied a familiar voice. "We're here to see Michael."

The pair was Charlie and Jonas. They had umbrellas unfolded over their heads to shade them from the moonlight.

"Cheryl, stay close to Dr. Skadi," called out Michael. He turned to face the would-be wolves. "What do you two want?"

"Help," said Jonas.

"It's not our fault," said Charlie.

"What could possibly have two big bad wolves so scared?" snickered Michael.

"A cat," said Jonas. "A big cat."

"There was a newbie who rolled into town today, asking for your daughter's whereabouts. He told them he was there to rescue Cheryl from her creepy father," explained Charlie. "With all the rumors going around, the deer believed him."

"Oh god. Billy." Michael cracked his knuckles. "I travel all this way and people still take the word of a Malrose over a Kent."

Jonas spoke up. "They acted chummy with him till sundown, then pushed him into the moonlight, desperate to finally get their bear."

"But they got a cat?" questioned Michael.

Jonas nodded with a grim expression. "A panther. It's a whole different type of predator."

248

"What's the difference?" asked Michael.

"It's their attitude and their motivation," said Dr. Skadi, stepping forward. "Their id is a dark and basic concept. While wolves kill when they're hungry. Panthers just kill for fun."

"We came here to recruit you. Maybe we can take him out all together. But I see... it's not your problem anymore is it." Jonas scanned Michael's new body up and down.

"It's not," said Cheryl in her father's ear. "We can leave and Billy will be trapped here for the rest of his life. Sounds good to me."

"No, honey," said Michael in a soft voice. "I need to take care of this."

"But it's too dangerous."

"I didn't make all this progress," said Michael, pointing at his hairy form, "just to go back to ignoring my feelings. This is my nature and I've come to accept it. I want to kill Billy. And while he's a panther, I'd say it's never been more legal."

Michael walked with the two visitors to their car. They drove to the bottom of the mountain, then entered into their animal forms. The wolves seemed to have an interesting attraction to Michael's wolf-man visage. They began to follow him around like an alpha.

Michael got down onto his hands and feet and crept low to the ground in between his wolven allies. He tried to keep them from being distracted by the various deer watching them from afar. These deer were curious as to why they weren't being chased. Little did they know, their real enemy was hiding in the tree right above them.

Baaa! Baaaaaa! Ba! A deer cried out in agony somewhere on the south end of town. These calls were followed by cracking noises and a soft purr that could only be heard by the wolves' enhanced canine hearing. Michael hurried them forward in the direction of the noise, all the way to the school yard. Here the wolves began sniffing the air, trying to make out the scent of feline musk, but before they could pinpoint the panther's location, it let out a greeting.

A hissing noise caught their attention. They turned to see a dead deer carcass sliding off the school's slanted roof. It clanged on the piping around the top edge, then landed with a loud thud on the grass.

Charlie and Jonas broke with the pack and sprinted up to the fallen deer. Their animal instinct kicked in and they began digging into the fresh meat. Meanwhile, Michael stared from afar, fighting the pangs building in his stomach from watching them eat.

Suddenly Michael called out. "Guys, no! It's a trick!" But it was too late. The panther snuck up behind Charlie while he was distracted with his dinner and pounced onto his back. The panther's teeth slowly sunk into Charlie's neck. His eyes went wide and he started to whimper. Then everything went silent.

The panther opened its lips and Charlie slid out onto the ground. Jonas had quickly run off, leaving Michael all by himself. The panther stared at Michael for a second. It seemed like Billy recognized him, even with the layers of animalism covering them both.

There was enough distance between them that Michael had the choice to run. He chose to stay. As the panther slowly closed in on him, Michael crouched down low and accepted the running blow with his arms outstretched. He gripped tightly to the panther's neck muscles as it sank its claws into his back.

In his semi-lupine form, Michael's strength was doubled from his usual limits. He could feel the cat's windpipes coming to a close as he pressed harder and harder. That's when the panther removed its claws from his back with a painful swipe. It then placed them onto Michael's chest. It pressed down on Michael's lungs, making it hard for him to breathe just as well. They were both suffocating each other simultaneously.

Michael threw his head upwards and smashed his head into the panther's nose. He repeated the blow over and over until splashes of blood scattered over his forehead. He was nearly about to lose consciousness from lack of air, so Michael shoved his shoulders forward and threw the cat off of him. It fell to the ground a few feet in front of him; it just laid there and gasped for air.

Michael crawled over to the fallen predator and pressed his nose against its pelt. He smelled its flesh and raw emotion filled his mind. Michael's whole body reacted to the opportunity presented to him. The hairs on his back grew out and stood on end. His eyes changed to a bright yellow and his teeth narrowed to sharp pin-like points. He couldn't fight the urge.

Michael's tongue licked Billy's furry neck hairs. He could taste the metallic flavor of the bruising he left. His stomach growled. He bit down hard. Black blood guzzled into his mouth as the panther's pounding heat forced it hard and fast out of the wound. The panther couldn't calm down. Michael pulled out and swallowed a large chunk of Billy's splenius.

Nothing had tasted so satisfying in all his life. It replaced his fondest memories. The best t-bone he'd ever had in a steakhouse in Houston. His first taste of Coca-Cola as a five-year-old boy. That time he gave oral to his high school crush. Dunkaroos. Everything before it turned to bitter mush.

The next morning, the whole town of Lake Fuchane gathered around the school yard. The population was halved due to the panther's assault. Andre was missing. So was Sue. So were Paul and Blake. Those that remained included Cheryl, Dr. Skadi, and her kids. They all stared at the skeleton picked bare, lying in Michael's arms like a lover. The fluff around his mouth was drenched in thick, black slime.

"Dad?" called out Cheryl. "Can we go home?"

Profile: Bonny Bride

It was the summer of 1986 and Bonny Bride had just put together a rebellious group of ex-debutants to form her soon-to-be hit rock band, Ouroboros. They had serious talent and a unique sound, but the only thing holding them back were demographics and expectations. Ouroboros was an all-female band operating in a male-dominated rock scene. If they were going to be taken seriously by the scouting A&R execs, they were going to need a bit of a stage gimmick to capture their attention. When they were invited to play 86's Limpkin, a rock festival showcasing South Beach's up-and-coming talent, Bonny Bride took it upon herself to come up with the perfect visual representation of what they were about.

"We're Ouroboros, so my first thought is that we got to do something with snakes," explained Bonny. "We tried wearing snake-skin jackets and shoes, but that just made us look like girls playing dress up. Then I thought, let's throw live snakes at the crowd, but that's not original enough; Moray did the same stunt with a bunch of eels just last year. So then, I'm out of ideas, I'm feeling like a failure; and then our keyboardist stands up, this young girl Cassie Grey, only sixteen at the time, and she says, 'Bonnie, an Ouroboros is constantly eating itself... we've got to eat ourselves!'"

Recorded cases of auto-cannibalism have arisen from desperate situations where there is no other food source available except eating oneself. In these strange circumstances, practitioners tend to start by devouring their outer extremities starting with the

253

fingers. Then, they work their way down the arms and legs until there's nothing left but stumps. If by then still no change has come to their predicament, they'll start to gnaw away at their faces, chopping off their noses, and ears, maybe even their own tongue. Then, if they still have the will to survive, they will resort to genital mutilation, followed by shearing off pieces of their abdomen.

None of this seemed ideal for the members of Ouroboros, who all very much enjoyed having ten fingers and toes, and preferred to keep their pretty faces intact. But they knew if they could find some part of themselves to consume, there was no doubting how hardcore they truly were. Their show would automatically become legendary. So they did their research and discovered a list of internal organs that one could live without. The most common , and least life-changing, to have removed was the appendix.

"We're all young girls. I mean real young. Besides Mary, we all grew up with a silver spoon out in Hialeah. None of us knew how to get a black market surgery in Tijuana. Our best option was to get our appendix removed legitimately and the easiest way to do that was to give ourselves appendicitis."

Appendicitis can be caused by worms or cancer, but these weren't options the band members were comfortable exploring. They were too risky, and overall, there was a much simpler option: the most common cause of appendicitis, an appendicolith or "appendix stone". It's a calcified fecal deposit that gets stuck in your appendix and they're not hard to create. All the girls needed to do was get themselves as constipated as possible.

To plug themselves up, they all took copious amounts of iron pills, courtesy of their anemic guitarist. The idea worked a tad too well, however, and all of them were quickly rushed to the hospital due to severe abdominal pain. Here, four of the five

254

girls had their appendices removed, while the remaining member had a portion of their liver lobbed off. The iron toxicity had accidentally poisoned the drummer's internal organs. But she persevered, and in the end, still got something she could eat.

"Jamie was the last one of us to leave the hospital and that was just a day before Limpkin. The doctors didn't want us going on stage, of course, but we assured them there'd be no drugs or partying afterward, we just wanted to put on a good show."

The girls kept their promise, and after they played their first song "Kave Baby", their stage crew brought out their jars and the ladies explained what was inside. They then poured out the formaldehyde and popped their organs in their mouths. They each popped open a can of Wild Cherry Pepsi and washed the slippery little blobs down their throats. Bonny claims that her appendix mixed with the soda ended up tasting like a candied shrimp.

Bonny is very well known for her music, but she also dabbles in all sorts of creative mediums. She's hosted several art galleries for her still-life paintings. She's directed her own music videos as well as videos for her tour mates Bon Ostrich and The Opal Clothes Band. She's also a kick-ass writer with a series of children's books published by HarperCollins called "Bandmates".

Bonny didn't have any adult fiction at the time I reached out to her, so she was kind enough to expand her work just for the sake of this collection. I kid you not, it only took her three days to get back to me with a complete work, and it's honestly one of my favorites in the collection.

Bonny wrote "Glee-Maiden" as a means to vent about her problems entering the music industry. She had talent, but she felt like some of the larger powers were afraid to see her on-stage in fear that she would bring irreversible change to the world of music. "Glee-Maiden" seems to be her vengeance against the patriarchy and their numerous attempts to assassinate her character.

Glee-Maiden

The art of clowning has always been a celebration of manic episodes. When manic, the performers are without boundaries, making them bizarre and entertaining; two key features for a traditionally successful clown. But that same manic energy has the potential to be dangerous if and when it spirals out of control. The manic mind can show a blatant disregard for the safety of others. At this point, the manic state advances into aggressive hedonism and episodic violence. With this in mind, it's no surprise that the art of clowning would give birth to a dark deviation: commedia omicida, referred to in the States as killer clowning.

Killer clowning has existed tangentially to its source material since clowning's earliest development in France and England. The earliest known example, Mr. Punch, real name Pietro Giomond, committed a horrific prolicide while dressed up as an English jester in 1662. Mr. Punch maniacally ground up his own baby into sausage and fed it to his unfaithful wife as a "practical joke". His wife sought revenge, and so he beat her to death with a slapstick routine. He then continued his rampage and beat the three constables that attempted to arrest him, the lawyer that attempted to defend him, the priest that attempted to console him, and the hunter that inevitably put him down.

Two hundred years later and clowning would expand into the United States where it would experience a significant rise in popularity alongside the Golden Age of Circus. By no coincidence, isolated incidents similar to the Mr. Punch model began to become more frequent. A hitman in the 1940s Newark underground bleached his face white and sliced up several prominent members of the DeCavalcante crime family with nail bombs hidden in jack-in-the-box toys. In 1957, hobo clown

Robert Grey lured several children into his shanty town in the sewers of Bangor, Maine. He then poisoned the children with tainted candy and fed them to his collection of retired circus chihuahuas.

Much like how American capitalism turned clowning into a business, killer clowning also mutated during its exposure to the American psyche. It gained a competitive edge some time around the 1960's when copycat killers of Robert Grey began to popup, seeking to gain his level of notoriety. These sociopaths thought Robert had an enticing strategy to get high kill counts: dress as something trustworthy and target weak, vulnerable children. They each tried to outdo each other's kill counts, claiming their victims' bodies with specific markers: playing cards, face paint, red balloons.

John Wayne Gacy, aka Pogo the Clown, changed the landscape again in the 1970's when his kill count exceeded that of any other killer clown before him. The issue, however, was that a lot of his rivals called his work "cheap and humorless", critiquing his less-than-unique style of attack. Pogo was able to accumulate so many kills because he didn't even dress in his clown outfit while murdering. He just strangled and raped any teenage boy that came to his door, while just happening to work as a clown on the side.

His competitors believed his record of 33 victims should therefore be discounted, and that new rules be put in place to make sure that killer clown kills are both creative and/or clown-related. Luckily, Pogo's controversial reign just happened to coincide with the rise of commercially available handheld video cameras. Pogo truly separated a serial killer in a clown suit from a true killer clown; all murders thereon would have to be videotaped and scored by a group of killer clown experts called Ringmasters.

The Ringmasters differ regionally, but they always consist of that region's top three consistently high scoring killer clowns. In Green Country, these top three consisted of Peter Pallor, Brisket, and Oleg Popov Jr. They'd received hundreds of entries in the mail over the past two months and threw out any of them with a mean rating below 3. On the last day of July, all the clowns in Green Country gathered for their bimonthly meeting at an old training camp for acrobats left to dilapidate in the woods of Edmond, Oklahoma. The clowns used the rises on either end of the rig to hold up a large white sheet on which they could project their films. The clowns all sat in nine rows of double-wide bleachers. Oftentimes, the crowd would be too many, and as the seats reached capacity any latecomers would be forced to stand.

This was the case of young Jessie L'Belle, who struggled to reach the front of the throng. Her film was up next and she wanted to see it again, even though she'd already panned through each still-frame half a dozen times. If anything, she probably just wanted to put the rest of the crowd behind her, so she didn't have to watch their reactions till the very end.

The film before it was by Gary-Bot. His schtick was dressing up like one of those street-performer robots, slathered in silver paint, with a kazoo in his mouth to make the noises. On screen, he pretended to "malfunction" and crushed a guy's neck with his bare hands all while making a noise with his kazoo that sounded like a compactor slowly flattening a car.

The first judge to speak was Peter Pallor, a devilishly clever white-face, who pointed out the deep flaws with Gary's choice in theme. Robot artists are slow in their movements and so killing and capturing a moving target would be far more difficult if not impossible. Gary got lucky, but with that luck came something truly fascinating. 4.5

Then Brisket, the killer rodeo clown, broke out in uncontrollable laughter. He was impressed with Gary-Bot's physical commitment, doing extensive hand muscle training in order to squeeze the bones to the point of breaking. 4.2

Oleg Popov Jr. never thought too hard about his scores. He let his feelings do most of the calculations. He rarely gave any sort of explanation and this time was no exception. 4.1

This was Gary's second time on the video monitor and the time beforehand his average was 0.2 higher. Jessie watched as the group of clowns in front of her turned to face Gary-Bot. They patted his back and forced him to keep cheery. While they were all distracted, Jessie shoved forward and squeezed her way to the front of the crowd.

The audience went quiet as her clip began to play. An unsuspecting mother left her room at the Hotel Vinita to obtain some cigarettes from a nearby Kum & Go. Her boyfriend wasn't able to make the trip, so looking after her child was her sole responsibility. She took the baby with her, cradling him in her arms tightly as she traversed the dark streets of micropolitan Oklahoma.

Two blocks away from the hotel, Jessie stepped out from an alleyway, sporting a deceptive smile and a bright green glow-in-the-dark balloon animal. A basic four legged structure with randomized proportions. It could be whatever the kid wanted it to be.

"Look Liam, it's your favorite!" said the mother with glee. "She's got a pony for you."

Jessie inched the balloon closer and closer to the mother, till she finally took her hand off her baby and reached forward. With the baby loosely balanced in one arm, Jessie snatched the infant up and took a few steps back; leaving the mother with the balloon

260

and a shocked expression on her face. The mother took a second, then laughed. "I appreciate the thought, but I think I left my camera in the car," said the mother. "I'm gonna have to ask for him back…"

Jessie smiled with her mouth wide open. She then began tossing the baby up into the air. First just a few inches, then a few feet.

"Stop that!"

Jessie started pulling eggs from her pockets. She began juggling the groceries along with the baby in a large arc over her head. But as she added more and more eggs, Jessie started to make a funny face, as though she were losing control of the act. "Wowowo!" cried out Jessie. She squinted her eyes like she was having trouble seeing. She wobbled her legs like she couldn't sustain the baby's weight. Jessie grabbed at the air too late and one of the eggs came hurtling downward. It cracked on the pavement behind her back.

The splat was followed by the mother's shrill screams. Another egg dropped, this one cracked on Jessie's forehead. It dripped down into her eyes. "Whoops," she jested. Blinded, she continued to juggle but staggered. She took a large step back, purposely stepping on the broken egg behind her heel. She made herself slip and fell onto her back.

The mother screamed in horror as gravity took hold of her infant child. Jessie quickly kicked up her legs and turned the bottoms of her feet toward the sky. She caught the baby softly with the bottom of her giant shoe. She kicked the baby back up in the air, then caught him with the other sole. She began passing the baby back and forth between the two feet.

The mother started crying out for help. Jessie knew her time for fun was coming to an end. She decided to wrap up the performance by yeeting the small child back into the mother's arms.

The mother stopped her screaming and fell silent. She quickly threw open the quilt wrapped around the child and inspected her boy for a head injury. She was surprised to see a child-sized surgical mask put on the boy's lips. The mother's eyes squinted in confusion.

Jessie then reached out with a bobby pin and popped the green balloon still resting in the mother's hand. A glowing green smoke quickly dispersed. Jessie sped off, leaving the mother to pass out on the ground as the toxic vapors boiled her lungs.

The clip ended there.

Back in the crowd, Jessie gulped. It was very abnormal for the audience to cheer for any clip, and yet the silence felt personal for some reason. She was able to block the crowd's faces from view, but the judges sat at a table in front of the bleachers; their heads were clearly visible. Peter Pallor nodded warmly. Brisket whispered to his right. Oleg Popov Jr. shook his head.

"A flesh tone base. White patches on the mouth and eyes. She's an Auguste clown," called out Peter Pallor. "It's difficult to tie that theme into horror. The Auguste is known for being the clumsy fool, which I didn't realize could be so horrifying. But what's scarier than a baby in the hands of a fool. I like what I see. 4.0."

Jessie nodded. An admirable score. A little less than she was expecting, but it was nothing to get discouraged over. She held her breath and eagerly awaited Brisket's thoughts. He wasn't laughing like the last act. This time he looked more serious.

"I would have liked to see the infant die, if I'm being honest. It seems to me like she dropped the whole narrative she so

262

carefully crafted. But I got to say... that juggling did take a lot of athletic prowess. You practiced and it shows. 4.2!"

Jessie wiped her brow. She couldn't believe it. It was her first time on the screen and she was about to pass the 4.0 mark. Only one judge was left to laud her.

Unexpectedly, Popov lifted his chin and opened his mouth. "Ne strashno," he sighed. He cleared his throat. "Not. Scary." He held up his scorecard. 3.0

Popov's silence was so rarely broken that a faint whisper of chatter trickled throughout the crowd. Their surprise was only wound up further as Jessie broke the usual code and spoke up for herself.

"What's not scary about a baby dying?" called out Jessie.

Popov shook his head. He wasn't going to say anything else.

"Put yourself in the lady's shoes. It's scary! It's really scary!"

Popov sighed again. He leaned forward with his eyes shut condescendingly. "That is scary. You're not scary."

"Miss, we usually don't allow this much rebuttal, if any," called out Peter Pallor.

"Oh yeah? And what's your deal then? A 4.0? You sounded like you hated Gary-Bot's and you gave him half a point more."

Peter Pallor looked offended. His mouth hung agape. "I'll have you know: Points were redacted because of your inability to choose an original theme. Gary's robot routine has never been attempted before. But while challenging, you're far from the first Auguste killer clown I've ever seen. A young Louis Seagram comes to mind."

263

"Louis was a hack…"

"Go have a tantrum somewhere else!" shouted Brisket.

"Brisket please… I'm handling it," called out Peter.

"Get your emotions in check!" snarled Brisket. "And let us get on with the next film!"

Immediately after her breakdown, Jessie fled the scene and immediately contacted one of her deepest connections: a clown named Miss Creant. The two of them decided to share dinner at a Braum's where Jessie relayed every line of dialogue spoken. Missy wasn't there herself to witness it. She wasn't invited. Missy wasn't like Jessie in most ways, which is how Jessie preferred her relationships. While Jessie was a killer clown, Miss Creant was a clown prostitute.

"Get your emotions in check?" Missy mocked Brisket's words with a sarcastic tone. "You know, at least in my profession the men are much more blunt. If they mean it, they'll just say it: Shut up, bitch!"

"They're trying to keep professional," replied Jessie. "The irony is they're sort of right. I was losing my nerve… Brisket nor Pallor deserved any sort of criticism. It's fucking Popov that scorned me."

"Trust me babe, killing babies is plenty scary to us outsiders," said Missy. "Maybe he's just jaded from seeing too much. He clearly doesn't know what scary is anymore."

"Oh he does. But it's a very limited perspective." Jessie took a bite out of her burger and a sip from her shake. She spoke with half of her mouth still busy chewing. "Men like Popov *smack* think you have to have a dick to be scary. Because *crunch* let's

264

face it *crunch* it always adds that little creepy insinuation… *smack* is this clown going to rape me?"

"That's a cheap scare man."

Jessie nodded.

"You know it is possible for women though. To be scary like that. I've acted out fantasies for my clients. I sneak in. Pin them down. All we need to do is get you a strap-on. I got one that should match your getup perfectly."

Miss Creant's matching dildo was no coincidence. The two had first met shopping at the same costume store, in the same aisle, eyeing the same prop. The candy-blue wig that they both wore on their scalps. Oddly enough, Jessie's look and Missy's look were very similar despite the two opposing objectives. It seems the same things that creep people out turn others on.

"I'm not stooping to their level. I'm trying to prove a point with the way I do things."

"What do you mean?" asked Missy, crumpling up her garbage into a tight yellow ball.

"There's a whole new generation of killer clowns. Minority groups are teaming up, trying to get some fresh ideas into the Ringmasters. We've disqualified old scores in the past. My idea is to clear the slate even further. A mass reorganization as to what counts as killer clowning. I'm taking the sexual aspect completely out of it. That should be left to your people."

"Ooo," Missy smiled. "I never knew you were a revolutionary. That's inspiring… but now how do you go about it with the Russian in your way?"

"I can impress the other two. I'll max out my score in spite of Popov's tampering. As much as I can. I just need something even better than last time."

With her last film being only a 3.9, it wasn't worth keeping around for a highlight reel. Instead, Jessie decided it was better used cashing it in for favors. She could reinvest it into her next kill.

There was market demand for "rainbow snuff" the street-name for the VHS tapes immortalizing killer clown killings. These tapes were passed around between collectors for top-dollar, but Jessie could supply these same collectors with fresh tapes straight from the source. And she didn't charge any numerical amount. She just needed to trade for some supplies.

One of her town's biggest collectors was, by no coincidence, once the wealthiest men in Vinita. The Chief of Medicine at Saint Francis Hospital, Dr. Nelson Beck. Jessie always arrives posing as a performer for the cancer kids, then sneaks her away into the on-call room at the designated hour and minute. Here, she ejected a dusty copy of Hold-Up from the VCR and shoved in her latest tape for Nelson's viewing pleasure.

Nelson shut off the lights and held his face up close to the glow of the Magnavox. "You're a thinking man's clown, you know that?" said Nelson with a wide grin. "I like that you play games with your prey. It's hypnotic."

Jessie stood beside the mini-fridge with her arms crossed. Compliments meant nothing coming from Nelson; fans aren't critics. There's no reward, not even satisfaction coming from a fan.

Last time they did the trade, Nelson had lent Jessie some radon from the radiology department. He always requests she not tell him how she plans to use his supplies in her act. Nelson likes the thrill of the surprise. When the balloon popped and the mother fainted, Nelson made a loud clap with his hands and tittered.

"I'd like to see a lot more like this…"

"It's doable," said Jessie from her corner. She walked forward and pulled the doctor away from the screen. "All I need this time is some valuable information."

"Privileged information?" said Nelson with a serious gaze.

"It won't come back to you," promised Jessie.

Nelson rubbed his chin. He sat down at his computer and logged in. "You can guarantee that?"

"Just give me the names of patients from a single doctor," suggested Jessie. She came up behind Nelson and watched him open up their database. "It'll look like he's the leak."

Dr. Nelson sorted his patients by their primary care physician. He then filtered only those under Dr. Quale. "What's the identifier?" he asked.

"Who gets Flublok?" replied Jessie.

"Why- no wait," Nelson held his tongue. "Don't tell me. I like to let my mind… ruminate."

Later that week, Jessie found herself meeting her closest ally in the world of clowning. Not so much a friend, but a mutual revolutionary. Hopfrog, the killer jester, has been a killer clown as long as Jessie has. As a little person, Hopfrog believes his community should be more than just props for the other clowns, but full-on killers themselves. Hopfrog believes the current Ringmasters are exceptionally ableist. He and Jessie recognized each other's liberal intentions early on in their careers and agreed to help each other out: Hopfrog and Jessie film each other's kills.

Hopfrog's short stature allowed him to easily hide while he shot from afar. On the day of her latest kill, Jessie had Hopfrog sit in the car and record through the windows of the Clanton Cafe. Hopfrog was in his civilian clothes, so he just looked like a guy playing on his phone. The eye of the phone's camera was fixed on an old man of his seventies, Wyatt Wilson, eating his breakfast in a ray of sunshine.

Wyatt's meal consisted of bacon, sausage, hash browns, and toast. One would expect an egg with this type of combo plate, but Wyatt substituted his for the extra meat. Wyatt couldn't have eggs. he was ovo-intolerant; the same reason why Wyatt always got the Flublok shot during flu season. It didn't contain any albumin.

Jessie came rushing into the diner claiming to be there to sing old Mr. Wilson a birthday song on behalf of his grandkids. She shoved herself into the booth across from Wyatt's. She slowly raised her arm. Wyatt looked up from his meal, sausage grease dripping from his mustache. His lip quivered as he eyed the pie resting in the palm of Jessie's hand.

"Oh," huffed Wyatt. "No thank you."

Jessie lifted the pie onto her fingertips. She felt the cool metal pie tin; within its volume was a quiche filled to the brim with savory custard. The type mixed from whole milk, cheddar cheese, and lots and lots of fresh brown eggs.

It was a classic clown attack. She pushed her arm forward and really shoved it in hard. The tin crunched and Wyatt's nose penetrated all the way through. The pie's innards expanded over Wyatt's face. The filling spread over his eyes and into his mouth. Unaware of what he was allowing into his body, Wyatt gasped, releasing the custard into his throat. Slowly, the surprise faded and he became painfully aware of the taste in his mouth. Wyatt tried to cry out, but it was already too late. His esophagus had swollen shut and within moments he was rolling around on the diner's tile floor unable to breathe.

Jessie slipped out of the restaurant through a door in the back of the kitchen. She got in the car with Hopfrog and the two rolled out to their next destination. Jessie had a whole list of similarly allergic patients, and a dozen more homemade pies in her trunk. Jessie wasn't just making a one-shot, this was going to be a massacre.

Jessie hurled a quiche down a tube slide at the park and struck a teenager smoking weed on the inside. He rolled out the bottom lifeless, his eyes red and full of tears.

Jessie pulled up beside an orange convertible and launched a pie at the woman behind the wheel. The woman panicked and crashed her car into the corner of a brick pizzeria.

Jessie let out a sharp whistle from the rooftop of an office building just as a young executive stepped outside. The man looked up and saw the quiche falling quickly onto his face. His suitcase dropped and popped open, spreading papers along the sidewalk. The man died on a thin layer of his daily work load.

After each kill, the audience at the old trapeze grounds cheered louder and louder. Without a doubt, Jessie's newest work made it to the next live screening. This time Jessie had gotten to the grounds far before anyone else. She sat beside Hopfrog and his little person friends in a group lined up on the top row of the bleachers. With each laugh she got, Hopfrog patted Jessie at the bottom of her back and smiled up at her, but Jessie couldn't smile herself. She just stared with a straight expression on her face. Fans meant nothing to her. Her fellow killer clowns were all the same. The only three that mattered hadn't spoken yet, and so, there was nothing to get excited about.

Jessie's film ended with a nice outro of every victim's inflated features covered in custard, flipping from image to image to the beat of "Rockin' Pneumonia and the Boogie Woogie Flu". As the music faded out, Peter Pallor opened up his mouth, but remained silent as one last round of cheering grew out of the audience. Once it was finished, he could finally speak his mind.

"An impressive sophomore effort. Another clever demonstration of the Auguste theme and the dangers of foolishness. Disregarding a person's allergies before throwing a pie in their face," Peter Pallor looked directly into the audience and smiled at Jessie. "Ms. L'belle, I hoped to see a better reaction to criticism from you this time. But, I'm afraid I won't get the opportunity, cause I doubt you'll argue with a 4.9."

Jessie shook her fist in the air as the crowd exploded into cheers. Pallor motioned for the audience to quiet down, but the excitement in the air was overflowing. Brisket, losing his patience, fired his Ruger over his head, bringing everyone to a respectable silence.

"Now, I often recommend homemade props as a means of dazzling me. The fact that you cooked these yourself, shows heart. My one wish is that maybe you went with strawberry rhubarb over a quiche. Just cause, I don't know, is a quiche actually a pie?" Brisket shrugged his thick shoulders and gave a small smirk. "Regardless, this is easily a 4.5."

Another round of cheering. This one shorter than the last. Everyone in the audience was as eager to hear from the last judge as Jessie was. This was Popov. And Popov's face was as deflated as ever. A muscular condition caused by a wild yorsh bender that hasn't ceased since he hit puberty.

270

"Rockin' Pneumonia and the Boogie Woogie Flu…" Popov sighed, then he smiled. "ICP and Slipknot have always been a little too on the nose, ya prav?"

Jessie's mouth hung open just an inch. She breathed small, soundless wisps of air.

"I like originality… 4.1"

The moment the score was clear Jessie almost considered jumping out of the stands and racing off to the bars for a celebratory drink. But she stopped herself and held onto her seat. She thought it'd be rude to leave the event so early, even after such a big win. Especially since her comrade Hopfrog had his first clip ever up on the big screen. It was a fire eating act that ended with the victim in a ball of flames. Jessie didn't find it particularly original when they filmed it, but of course this wouldn't be the first time she and the judges didn't share the same opinion.

By the time midnight rolled around, the final film finished up and the audience began to disperse. Most clowns left for home, they were tired and had a long drive ahead of them. Other clowns went off to drink to their big wins, while others got started on their next kills to try and compensate for their big losses. The judges themselves usually split a plate of hot wings at the nearby Pickles Pub, where they'd catch up with each other like a trio of old friends. But one of the three had to skip out this evening. Popov had other plans. Plans very far away.

Oleg Popov Jr. was the bastard child of renown circus artist Oleg Popov. At least, that's what his mother had always told him. She may not be reliable however, this is the same woman who sexually abused him for most of his childhood. The ensuing insanity mixed with Popov's natural born talents, creating a drunken, juggling monstrosity.

Despite his alcoholism, Popov had a lucrative double life as a top salesman at Chiodos Used Auto when he took off his makeup. So it wasn't hard for him to afford a last minute ticket from JLN to BGR. Once in Bangor, he hopped in a taxi to the Graham Building and slipped under the nearest manhole cover. Underground, he made his way into a particularly large tunnel that carried the city's gray water to a waste treatment facility in the neighboring municipality. At the midway, a relic of killer clowning's prestigious past persisted in the sludge. His birth name was Robert Grey, but his clowning name was He.

He was a hobo clown with a ragged beard surrounding a bright white frown. His suit was mangled and his top hat was crushed. Over his shoulder he always carried a bindle of hypodermic needles. The sharp points stuck out through the fabric of the bag.

He had many acolytes hidden throughout the States, working to assure the old guard still maintained some control over the way things ultimately progressed in the killer clowning community. Popov was his eyes and ears in northern Oklahoma.

"She's good. She's very good," relayed Popov. "She could easily take my place in a couple of years."

"Is she reformist?" hissed He. He sat in a partially submerged lawn chair laying against the side of the pipe. His fingers tapped anxiously against the plastic arm rests.

"No sex with our victims. No killing minors. Illegitimizing records. Yours included."

"The Apocalypse," cringed He. He snorted angrily, then picked up a wet rod from beneath his chair. It was a child's arm, slowly decaying in the rancid water. He threw it over his shoulder. He's collection of rabid chihuahuas came tunneling out of the smaller pipes hanging above. They descended upon the limb, growling and fighting one another over the moldy sinew.

272

Popov nodded. "I can't continue to hold her back. I've rated her highly to draw away any suspicion. You can strike when ready."

He pushed himself up onto his feet. Dark, black water dripped from the seat of his polka-dotted pants. "I've given you my blessing. You don't need me to do the deed. We're all perfectly capable of murder..."

"Well it needs to be poetic," said Popov. "Extremists need to know it's her ideas that got her killed. So I figured... Jessie L'bell. It's clearly based on Jezebel. And the Jezebel found herself eaten... by dogs."

"Fine then. You just take them with you."

This wasn't the first time the old guard had "influenced" killer clown culture from beneath the surface. A killer mime out in Miles County was advocating for more gay representation. He was found stripped naked in a hotel room and drained of all his blood from a gash in his genitals. Then there was that greenhorn out in Naples trying to normalize rubber clown masks over the traditional makeup. His body was found floating in the Everglades, with his face shaved off and placed in his cold, dead hands.

On the day of Jessie's demise, she wasn't even dressed in her usual clothes. She was in civilian gear, more specifically a McDonald's uniform, working her shift as a day manager. Their McDonald's was a particularly unique model that hovered like a bridge over I-44. It attracted significant attention from truckers and travelers at all hours of the day. And yet on a Tuesday morning, 9AM, the crowd lulled just enough to allot some time to take out the trash. Jessie Bellerose, Jessie's name at work, liked to take the responsibility to show egalitarianism between her and her underlings.

Jessie clenched her nose and lifted the lid to her dumpster, expecting the stench of discarded pickles and overcooked fries to raise up into her nostrils. She was surprised to see the dumpster completely empty. She reached down for the trash bag she dragged behind her, but it was gone too. She spun around.

There was Popov. Standing there with the trash bag in one hand and a laundry bag in the other. The laundry bag was shaking and howling.

Jessie's first thought was preserving her secret life. She motioned for Popov to leave. "I'm not in costume, you know the rules!" she snarled. Popov sighed. He kicked Jessie in the chest, knocking her backward inside of the emptied dumpster. He then untied his laundry bag and poured the contents inside. Three ravenous man-eating dogs.

These chihuahuas were trained. They knew where to bite to cause the most harm. The oldest of the three, Dippo, dug into the carotids in her neck. The largest of the three, Bippo, crammed its face into her armpit and went for her axillary. The final one, a puppy named Cheezo trained specifically for torture, went straight for her eyes.

"Is this Hell?" The blood loss from the attack quickly turned severe and Jessie's body ejected its soul. "Where am I?"

The afterlife around Jessie was nothing like Hell nor Heaven were described. There were flames but they were purple, yellow, and green, and there were clouds but they were red, orange, and blue. The world was a kaleidoscopic hurricane, swirling inwards towards a bubbling center a mile out. Out of this center rose a beam of bright white light. Jessie stepped forward, she could feel oscillating warmth and frost blasting over her ankles. She trudged slowly, bewildered at the rainbows constantly shifting around her.

274

This was Manea. It's not killer clown heaven nor killer clown hell. It's not a moral plane. It's just the eye of the whirlpool for any and all who harness the power of manic episodes. Manea's guardians, the Larrys, quickly rose from the cosmic steam and stopped Jessie in her path, acting as a solid wall built in front of her.

"Stop, maiden!" said the Larry on the left, Larry Palms, a killer clown with sharp yellow fangs, red diamonds on his eyes, and thick green gloves covering his claws. "There's a place for you in death, but it is not here."

"What is this place?" called out Jessie. Her voice echoed in the vast atmosphere.

"All the manic energy in the universe flows through here before it funnels back to its source," said Larry Mo, the fattest of the Larrys with a chubby blue face. "This is Manea, the beginning and the end."

"Are you here to guide me?"

"No," said Larry Pigeon, the ugliest of the three, with a giant horn protruding from the top of his head. It was striped and colored, like a party hat. "We're blocking your way."

"Why?" begged Jessie. Every bone in her body wanted her to go into the pit in the center of the flames. It felt right. It felt like completion. "Let me have my peace."

"Sometimes manic energy takes on a form that no longer needs to be recycled," explained Larry Mo, rubbing at his fat chin.

"What's that mean?" cried out Jessie.

"You're not welcome here any longer," snarled Larry Palms, for the second time.

275

"Sometimes it helps to dissipate our overall presence in the universe if a portion has gone irreversibly sour," explained Larry Mo. "It's time to skim off the old withered tissue."

"I'm... withered tissue?"

All three Larrys nodded at once. "You tried bringing order."

"I just wanted things to be more... respectable. I wanted to class things up is all!"

"By imposing rules. Violence doesn't need rules."

Jessie disobeyed the barriers before her and tried to move past them, but the Larrys emitted a psychic force like a strong gale. They blew her backwards off of her feet. She fell onto her back, writhing in pain in the exotic flames. "If I'm not allowed here, then where do I belong?"

"Hell," said Larry Pigeon. "They're always happy to have our rejects."

The claw of a giant black langoustine reached through the flames and latched onto Jessie's shoulder. Slowly, it began pulling her backwards away from the Larrys. The three of them grinned while their eyebrows tilted devilishly.

The claw tightened its grip and a searing pain enveloped the right half of Jessie's body. She could feel the spines lining the insides of the clasp tearing into her flesh. She couldn't fight the massive pull of the monster any longer. She was being torn backwards, her feet dangling in the air. But before she was dragged fully into the oblivion, a shooting pain entered her chest.

276

The whole world around her began to shake and flash. Suddenly, it all vanished. In place of the fluorescent flames was a plain, white room with machines placed around its circumference. They all looked mundane and earthly. There was a man standing by her side. His clothes weren't vibrant and his teeth were incuriously dull.

"She's waking up," said a familiar voice. It was that of Dr. Beck. He was hovering overhead dressed in a white coat over a blonde button up. Beck smiled wide. "You may notice some slight discomfort over your left eye."

Jessie reached her hand up and felt the bandages covering up the left side of her face.

"The nerve was completely severed and the eye was consumed by your perpetrator."

While feeling the bandages, Jessie passed over her bare skin and suddenly remembered she wasn't wearing any of her makeup. She tried to keep her identity secret. "I was… I was attacked by coyotes… small coyotes… you know what, they were baby coyotes."

"Yeah no, I'm pretty sure they were chihuahuas… circus chihuahuas I'm guessing; if that really is you, Jessie?"

Jessie hesitated to come clean. She wasn't sure if anyone should know her two identities were one in the same. Beck was pretty loyal. And he had just saved her life. She sighed. "Yes, I suppose it's me."

Dr. Beck rolled his eyes. "Well of course it's you, I can recognize you without the makeup. I've only watched your videos every Sunday night for the past two years."

The obsession made Jessie feel awkward. She winced and made a nervous smile.

"Trust me," said Dr. Beck. "It's a good thing I know you. You wouldn't get this level of care otherwise. You don't even have insurance. I doubt you would have lived in anyone else's hands. I was determined. Determined not to lose my favorite character on my favorite show."

Jessie cringed once again.

"Is it normal for clowns to be offing each other?" questioned Beck. "I know it may be presumptuous, but this type of murder is the shit a killer clown would do. Did they know who they were hitting?"

Jessie nodded. She thought back to Popov standing there with the bag of dogs. Then she remembered her dream in Manea where the Larrys spiritually excommunicated her. "I think it's safe to assume certain levels of my organization don't like my politics."

"Internal affairs. Fascinating," said Beck with a look of interest. "Do they think you're dead?"

Jessie shrugged. "Can you make it seem that way?"

"For your latest tape… I can make a couple cops want to tell a few lies."

Jessie agreed. She surrendered a copy of her egg tart massacre.

Over the next week and a half, Jessie regained her strength in the hospital while the rest of the world assumed her death. During this period of recovery, she had a lot of time to think about the attack. Enough to notice a tiny little detail that meant more and more the more she thought on it. At first, it was a mystery, how

278

did Popov even know she had any radical ideas? He could have just assumed she did because she was a woman. Or perhaps, one of the only two people she ever shared those thoughts with was playing both sides.

With Jessie "dead", Hopfrog got a new videographer, Whimper, a fellow little person with a clown-baby theme. His partner in crime got caught by SAMHSA and locked up in an asylum, so he too needed a new partner to film with.

Hopfrog was filming Whimper's most popular trick where he hides in a stroller and waits for a passerby to think he's an abandoned child. When they pull back the stroller's canopy, Whimper leaps upward and cuts them with a serrated rattle. It was really only ever a 4.0 act; too fast, low tension, uninspired weapon; but Whimper kept repeating it hoping that with the right victim's reaction, the Ringmasters would find the genius in his work.

Hopfrog started up a big, plastic silver Panasonic Omnimovie and directed his lens at the stroller, hidden across the street. The stroller sat in broad daylight for five minutes, till someone other than Whimper finally stepped into the frame.

Bang! Bang! Bang! Three sparks lit in the corner of the shot. Three streams of blood squirted from the side of the cradle. It tilted after the first, then the third bullet pulled it down onto its side. Whimper's body rolled out onto the ground.

Hopfrog pulled his eye away from the viewfinder, then dropped the camera. It cracked as it hit the concrete. Across the street, Jessie was standing with her arm outstretched. She redirected her gun and turned to face Hopfrog. "Don't run," she said. "I'm not going to shoot."

Hopfrog froze as instructed. "Jessie?" he said with a smile. "You're alive!"

279

Jessie charged up to Hopfrog with a look of disgust. She pistol-whipped the man so hard he flew into the window of the drug store behind him, shattering the glass. Hopfrog lost consciousness.

When the little jester came to, he was strapped to a gurney in an empty ward. This wing of the hospital was brand new and still under construction. Soundproof partitions were placed all around the sector so the machines wouldn't wake or disturb the sick and elderly patients. Construction was off on Saturdays and Sundays, so Jessie and Hopfrog had the room to themselves.

Miss Creant was there, too. She filmed in the corner. Jessie needed her own replacement. It was considered taboo to have an outsider record, but none of this was kosher to begin with.

"Make peace with me now," snarled Jessie. "You won't get another chance."

"I thought you said you wouldn't kill me?"

"I said I wouldn't shoot you."

Jessie pulled out an old soda siphon with a copper top and a green glass bottom. She popped a cartridge of CO_2 into the charge holder, and shook up the potion inside. She then held the nozzle up to Hopfrog's lips and fired.

"*Beh*. It tastes. *Peh-peh*. Like batteries."

"It's lithium. Three thousand milligrams. First it's gonna take away all your mania. And then it will turn your kidneys to stone."

"You're fucking crazy."

280

"You won't be soon." Jessie shoved the nozzle up Hopfrog's nostril this time. She held the other side closed with her thumb and fired. Water spewed from Hopfrog's sinuses and sprayed off the bottom of his mouth. Jessie's plan was that if there really was some grand nirvana for manic cases, Hopfrog would be denied just like her. She figured she could cleanse his spirit of anything interesting with the right amount of meds.

"What do you want to know?!" cried Hopfrog as he spit out the bitter foam. It tasted like Beverly.

"Everything involving you and my death," droned Jessie. "Why did you tell Popov about my… aspirations?"

"He's on our side."

"Liar." Jessie shot another blast into Hopfrog's nose.

"He's the liar! He said… he said he's this new-aged Yabloko-type."

"If it's all so innocent, then why did he reward you for information on me?"

"That's not… what happened."

"So it's just a coincidence. The night before I'm killed, you place high enough to make it to the big screen. Your Poe allusions suddenly become 'unique and unexpected'… two generous words coming from… which judge?"

"He didn't tell me you'd die."

"Well you didn't seem surprised when I did… how long have you had that replacement waiting?"

Hopfrog went silent. He looked up at Jessie and frowned.

281

Jessie suspired long choppy breaths. "They pit us against each other, so they can pick us off one by one. If you want to represent a cause, you can't fall for tricks like that. You've been reduced to a pawn..." Jessie sighed. "...a prop." Jessie shoved the nozzle in Hopfrog's mouth. He gagged as he tasted his mucus on the tip. Jessie fired the stream down Hopfrog's throat till the bottle completely emptied. She gave little breaks for him to breath, so he wouldn't drown before he OD'd.

Miss Creant filmed a nice close-up of Hopfrog's face as the concoction burst from the sides of his mouth. She backed up and filmed his body as he entered into tremors. The drugs were frying his nervous system. Eventually his bowels let loose and Missy got a nice shot of that. She'd done scat porn before, so she wasn't afraid to get close and intimate with the filth. When the footage was edited to perfection, Jessie mailed it out through the usual channels, assuring the Ringmasters would come across it while analyzing their entries.

"We got to warn everybody," groaned Brisket, holding his hat over his quivering heart as he watched the graphic clown-on-clown violence. "It looks like we've got another Edwin."

Edwin Troma was a killer clown at the end of the 1980s best remembered for his controversial rise and fall in the Panhandle. Edwin's main trick was squeezing the big red nose of a fellow killer clown which would, through some unexplained magic trick, blow the clown's brains out the back of their head. Most theories allude to some hidden pistol up his sleeve, but that's besides the point. Killing fellow killer clowns wasn't illicit at the time as it hadn't been done before, but Edwin thought it added flavor. There was nothing more hilarious then watching the face of the hunter becoming the hunted after he'd jump out from behind some corner and honk his victim's last honk.

Edwin was stopped when a new law was passed disqualifying any videos that used a fellow killer clown as the victim. Edwin proceeded to seek horrible vengeance and bombed the Panhandle's former screening location at the Jean Pellerin Opera house, taking over a dozen lives along with himself.

"We've got to cancel our next screening," cautioned Brisket. "She's flying off the rails. That midget was her friend. Who knows what she has planned for the rest of us?"

"It's not the same," said Peter Pallor, motioning for Brisket to calm himself. "Ms. L'Belle wouldn't resort to an Edwin. It's not her style. She's a poet."

"A clown is a poet…" scoffed Popov. "This is a competition. We are all desperate for atten-"

"Her eye," interrupted Peter. "Her eye is missing." Peter pointed to the monitor, laying his fingertip over the bandages on Jessie's face. "A missing eye seems to suggest she's recently survived some incident intent on taking her life."

Popov swallowed the rest of his words. He remained silent.

"This tape isn't meant to be judged at all. This isn't meant for all of us. Just one."

Popov and Brisket turned their heads toward Peter. They both stared intently.

"My guess is Popov."

Popov sneered. "Why Popov?"

"'Cause Popov gave her a three," answered Peter. He turned to face Popov and smiled. "Of course, it seems to me that there's been something much more violent going on between you, judging by her scars. An altercation, perhaps?"

Popov shook his head.

"Well, assuming you know what this is about, it seems to me the message is clear," said Peter, nodding at the television set. "You once referred to young Jessie as 'not. scary.' I believe this footage was sent to you to test that statement. Do you still think she's not scary, Oleg?"

"Da," affirmed Popov.

"Then don't run."

Popov wouldn't run, but he couldn't remain still. He needed to track down Jessie's location before she could sneak up on him or she'd easily have the advantage. All he had to go off of was the strange scenery shown in her submission video, but none of it looked familiar. Popov decided a lure might be appropriate.

Popov had been working on an old Good Humor ice cream truck sold to his dealership a few years back. He left most of its dilapidation as is, but updated the sound system. He gutted the music box and inserted a couple of PA speakers that could blast the song of his choice. He set it to a creepy Russian birthday song "Ya Igrayu Na Garmoshke".

"Pust' begut neuklyuzhe, Peshekhody pa luzham, A vada - pa asfal'tu rekoi…" Popov slowed the lyrics down to half-speed in order to create a menacing vibe. A down-pitched accordion creaked in the background. "I neyasno prokhozhim, V etot den' nepogozhii, Pochemu ya veselyi takoi…"

Driving through the streets of Vinita at midnight, Popov's music awoke the tenants of any building he passed. All were too afraid to approach the vehicle, however, frightened by what kind of treats this ice cream truck was offering. The streets remained empty for Popov, until he passed the hospital. That's when Jessie finally stepped out into the path of his headlights.

Popov hit the breaks and slowed to a halt. He lowered the volume on his music down to a crackling whisper. "Get in," heaved Popov. He reached over and opened the passenger side door.

Jessie sighed and accepted his invitation. She hopped into the seat and shut the door. The ice cream truck continued to drive.

"So…" droned Popov. "Talk to me…"

"About what?"

"You want to… 'brighten up' our games?" pondered Popov. "Tell me about it."

"Are you considering a change of heart?" questioned Jessie.

"I just want to appear open-minded. But no, I doubt you'll swing me."

"I guess I just thought, what's the point of rape in our field? It's not surprising anymore… it's a fucking cliche. And all it does is paint us as perverts instead of murderers. Perverts are erased from history, but murderers have fucking fan clubs. They get TV series made about them."

"We don't want TV," groaned Popov. "We're not supposed to be celebrities. We're supposed to be nightmares. Our unpopularity should be refined. Your generation cares too much for notoriety. You're willing to sacrifice tradition for it."

"Killing minors is a terrible tradition. It makes us look weak, picking on children. All our acts look one-hundred percent better on an adult. It's not so one-sided. There's risk involved. And, half the time, the adults deserve a little punishment. Kids are too fucking innocent."

"We kill kids to frighten their parents. Until you find something that rattles them more, that can't change."

Jessie laughed. "Then clearly we're not being scary enough."

Popov nodded. "Maybe we're not." He stopped the car. They were in the backwoods where they screened their films. Popov got out of the car first, Jessie followed after. Popov popped his trunk and pulled out something heavy, he dropped it in Jessie's hands. It was a unicycle. A nice one. A Pashley 1994 Muni with a leather saddle and a bright blue titanium frame.

"We're gonna fight on the trapeze," explained Popov. He pulled out another unicycle; this one was for him. It was a different model with a giraffe seat, extra tall for comic effect. He then pulled out two knives and handed one to Jessie. "It's both of us in our element, one on one, the playing field completely even. The winner is truly the next wave of killer clowning."

"You're serious?"

"No. I'm a clown," sneered Popov. "None of this should be too serious… or it wouldn't make sense."

Jessie nodded. "Fair enough."

"Do you want music?"

"What kind of music?"

"t.A.T.u.?"

Jessie shrugged. "Is this because you think I'm a lesbian?"

286

Popov shook his head. "It's just good. And it's Russian."

"All the things she said, all the things she said, running through my head, running through my head, running through my head." The music blared through the horns of the ice cream truck as Jessie and Popov climbed their respective ends of the trapeze.

Jessie reached the top of her post and balanced herself atop her unicycle. The two would cycle along the top of the movie screen hung between the posts. This border was a tad bit thicker and just as taut as the usual rope that hung across a traditional trapeze. Jessie looked across the distance between her and Popov. He seemed to be struggling to balance on his exaggerated ride. But eventually, he stood up tall, and looked prepared to fight. He brandished his knife, then shoved his feet against his pedals. He came rolling down the edge of the screen.

Jessie's heart raced. She pulled out her knife and rushed to balance atop her vehicle. She found her place, then charged forward.

The two met in the middle. They both slowed down when they came within inches of each other, then started swinging. Jessie aimed upwards. Popov aimed downwards. Their blades nicked each other's knuckles and wrists, but there were no critical hits for the first five minutes.

As his mid-section began to tire out, Popov began to wobble in his seat. He felt how top heavy the design of his unicycle truly was. Any lean at all could send the seat swinging downward like a lever. And so Popov took a moment to straighten his back. Jessie took advantage and jabbed him under his rib.

Popov sneered in pain. He threw caution to the wind and swatted back angrily. Slik. The blade struck the top of Jessie's forehead, sending her wig to the ground below. The flesh-tone fishnet beneath it still held tightly to her skull. The elastic around the rim absorbed the blood beading up on her forehead and turned black.

Jessie screeched and raised her blade high over her head, blocking a series of hard strikes from above. She leapt off her unicycle and rose into the air. When she came down she plunged the blade deep into Popov's shoulder. Popov's checkered hat flew off his head. His body came tumbling after.

Miraculously, Jessie stood up tall and immediately gained her footing on Popov' taller cycle. She held herself in place, then breathed a sigh of relief. She looked down and saw Popov's crumpled frame at the bottom of the movie screen.

It took Jessie ten minutes or so to bike back over to one of the poles at the sides and climb back down. When she reached Popov, she saw the bones protruding through his major organs. Popov was nearing his end.

"Priblizitel'no…" he coughed.

Jessie closed her eyes and perspired. "I don't know what that means."

"Sozhaleyu. Ya ne umru, govorya po-angliyski." Popov refused to speak English with his dying breath.

"There's these clowns on the other side," said Jessie, taking a knee beside Popov's head. "I wouldn't worry about the afterlife, they're going to love you."

"Angely?"

"Yeah, yeah, angels. I need you to relay a message to them, okay? Cause I'm not planning on visiting them till after a long, fruitful career as a Ringmaster. I want them to watch me

288

carefully, okay? Tell them this, please. Tell them I'm going to change everyone so that they're just like me. And when no one's killing kids, and no one's raping victims, and everyone thinks those things are cringey and weird, just like me, they're not gonna have any manic energy left to recycle."

Popov gave a little nod then shut his eyes.

"Tell them times have changed here on Earth. And it's about time they change at every level."

Popov smiled. "Chto izmenilos'?" Then he turned his head and stared off into the distance.

Profile: Sandeyu Yamamoto

Children have adorable habits that may take a little extra work to appease, but parents do it anyways because that's their job and it feels good to get those extra smiles. A lot of these habits involve their diet, as children are some of the most picky eaters. It's not their fault, it's an evolutionary reflex made to keep them from being poisoned by strange, unfamiliar sustenance; e.g. food made in a way that's not how their parents make it.

I personally would not eat a PB&J made by anyone else but my mother. She knew to leave the crusts on and the jelly thin. The more peanut butter, the better. Anything else was unacceptable. For other kids, they may only eat their fruit sliced in a certain shape; or their sloppy joes prepared with Heinz brand ketchup; or their cereal drenched in *whole* milk.

A similar behavior could be found in Sandeyu Yamamoto, a young girl, four years old, who lived with her mother in Nagoya, Japan. Sandeyu's mother, Tombo Yamamoto, was a renowned itamae, or sushi chef, and she would create unique school lunches for her daughter that were of the same quality as her cooking at work.

Because of this, Sandeyu expected her bento boxes in a very specific design. Tombo would make her daughter's sushi into three adorable characters. She'd make a salmon roll on one side that looked like a tiger. Then, she'd make a tuna roll on the other side that looked like a snow monkey. Between the two faces, she'd make a heart out of eggs.

It represented a story. A little bedtime tale Tombo would tell to Sandeyu. The little monkey was left behind as a baby, and the

290

momma tiger adopted and raised it. And despite their many differences, they went on awesome adventures together.

Much like the tiger and the monkey, Tombo and Sandeyu went on their own journeys throughout the world. Tombo liked to meet other chefs with a large presence on social media, and she took her daughter wherever she went. Sometimes it was Europe, sometimes the United States, but nothing seemed more exciting than when they were set to meet a chef in the Republic of Madagascar. He had his restaurant in the capital city of Antananarivo, and he turned the local ingredients into Michelin star-worthy dishes. Tombo was excited to learn his techniques with cocoa. Sandeyu was just excited to meet the exotic animals; especially the lemurs.

Unfortunately, neither dream would be actualized and it's not entirely clear why. What we know is that their captain lost control of their flight and attempted an emergency landing when passing over the center of the Indian Ocean. The flight recorder was not recovered, so the cause of the turbulence is unknown. Sandeyu remembered hearing a blaring noise coming from the cockpit right before they entered into a nosedive.

Luckily, the captain was able to signal his coordinates to authorities before crashing, but it would be quite some time before the survivors could be reached. There were only three of them: Sandeyu, Tombo, and a third passenger, Juro Suzuki. All three had swam from the wreckage of their plane to a nearby desert island, an atoll with no fruit on its trees and no fish in its lagoon. There was no obvious food to sustain them; at least not at first.

Sandeyu claims that her mother hadn't killed Juro in front of her. After the third day on the island, she just woke up to her mother trying to feed her raw meat. The body was hidden somewhere Sandeyu wouldn't see it. She didn't put together where the meat was coming from as a child. But now, she realizes it was pieces of Juro.

"I wouldn't eat them, at first," she recalled. "Even without the knowledge of where it was coming from, I was a picky eater. Everything was nasty if it wasn't served the way my mother usually made it."

Lucky for Sandeyu, her mother was there and she realized just how she could get her daughter to eat Juro. All it needed was the right artistic touch.

The monkey was easy. She substituted the pink tuna with some muscle tissue from Juro's arms. She'd planned to use fat for the white fur instead of rice, but she was surprised to see Juro's lipids were closer to yellow. She instead settled on using his sclera.

Recreating the tiger face was a little more tricky, as the common understanding of the human body paints most organs red, brown, or white. This meant finding something orange proved to be a challenge; but after a little bit of exploring Tombo was able to find a good amount of bright orange tissue clinging to the sides of the intestines. This was the oft-ignored mesentery. She tore it off and formed it into the proper shape for a tiger's face. Then she used some black tissue she found deep in Juro's lungs for the eyes and stripes. She was lucky Juro was a heavy smoker.

All that was left was the heart, which Tombo usually made from omelet bordered by spicy seaweed. This is where that yellowed fat finally came in handy, and for the green trim, she peeled apart Juro's gall bladder and flattened it out with some rock until it was a thin band.

"I was starving, so I didn't acknowledge the taste," explained Sandeyu. "The aesthetics were all I cared about, and it did its job."

292

During their grueling three week stay on the island, Juro's body parts were separated and reassembled into pandas, piggies, Totoro, and duckies with sailor hats. Virtually anything that could remotely resemble one of Sandeyu's favorite meals. Slowly but surely, Juro was picked clean, down to the bone, only a day before their rescue ship would finally find them.

Juro's head was found to be flattened, which made it quite obvious he did not die of starvation. Tombo was quick to admit she'd made a mistake. She stubbornly stuck to a defense of temporary insanity. She was sentenced to spend the rest of her life in a mental ward. Sandeyu used to visit when she was younger, but now, twenty-six years old, she prefers not to speak with her mother.

"I used to feel gratitude, but when you're just a child you only think about life and death as pretty black and white. Now, I'm not so sure what my mother did was moral. Juro had his own kids, now they don't have a father. In the end, my mother killed a man and fed his body parts to a minor. Saying it out loud, it doesn't feel nearly as noble as it once seemed to me."

Since Sandeyu turned eighteen, agents and publishers have been pressuring her into starting a literary tour de force all about her experiences on the island. Sandeyu, however, has refused to write any non-fictional accounts of the events. She's instead been trying to get these same literary circles to help her develop her fantasy writings. She's yet to find one that will do so without first giving them the rights to her life story.

Sandeyu often uses fantasy to escape the drama in her life, particularly the tension between her and her mother's half of the family. Sandeyu describes them as "the type of people to easily cave into savagery when times get tough". Sandeyu is convinced

293

that if her mother hadn't acted out on the island, her poor self-control would have manifested in some other way right within the confines of their home. Mental illness rules amongst her maternal relatives, and she fears that she too has inherited this poor reaction to stress.

I like Sandeyu's story "Antiquing" because, unlike her other fantasy, it doesn't run from her fears, instead it meditates on them. Sandeyu's stand-in, Reina, is twisted up in a family dynamic that could be arguably worse than Sandeyu's. I believe that if Reina can find the answers she needs to deal with her dilemma, then there is obvious hope for Sandeyu.

Antiquing

Reina Kumogami is a genetic crossroads where two diseased lineages have met to create an adolescent enigma.

Reina has inherited a predisposition to cancer from her mother's side of the family. Li-Fraumeni syndrome did nothing to her mother, her grandmother, or her great grandmother, but its dormancy ended with Reina. She was diagnosed with an inoperable brain tumor on her sixteenth birthday. She now has six months to live.

From her father's side, she inherited an equally terrible curse. Her father's family has a genetic predisposition to haunting. Doctors say it's because of a unique form of OCD. They tend to obsess and have a hard time letting things go. For the last three generations, every deceased family member has haunted a piece of furniture or personal item they were particularly involved with. These possessed items are stored in an old house in the country built by the first Kumogamis to immigrate to the States; it's in a ranch just west of Ogden, Utah.

"My dear sweet, Rei Rei," said the mirror, hanging in the center of the living room's accent wall. "How could the world be so cruel?"

While the rest of the ranch house was plain white, the wall facing the front door was a beautiful sky blue. Reina helped paint it when she was just a little girl. It was a gift for her family stuck in the house all day. She used to visit with her parents two or three times a month when she was younger. Now, her parents only visit on holidays. Reina, on the other hand, has been visiting every day. She's been trying to get a feel for what it might be like living with these people for the rest of eternity.

"It's all that Korean from your mother's side," continued the mirror. An image of her Grandaunt Kyoko appeared in the reflection. "It's the smog they have there. It turns them into mutants."

Reina realized that in order to endure the company of her elders she would either have to learn to ignore their prejudice or she could experiment with confronting it directly. Their antiquated minds might just need an update from a millennial with enough patience to teach.

"Japan and America have their fair share of pollution as well," replied Reina. She stared into Kyoko's eyes. "My LFS only made me more susceptible to a tumor. The lump itself probably started right here with a breath of that sweet Salt Lake ozone."

Kyoko smiled weakly and stared away. She wasn't comfortable speaking poorly about her own home state. She had the largest ego of her family, obsessing over her own reflection to the extent of being banished to a mirror for the whole of her afterlife. Luckily, she wasn't representative of the rest of the family residing in the house.

"Who cares about the cause and effect? There's nothing we can do to stop it now. What we need to focus on is giving you the best remaining days of your life," called out a Tiffany lamp sitting on a sideboard against one of the blank walls. This was Haru, Kyoko's brother and Reina's grandfather. If Kyoko was the embodiment of senility's ignorance, Haru was the embodiment of all the things the elderly did best: unconditional generosity. "Now I want to see that inheritance of yours going to something fun. You didn't spend it all on school supplies, did you?"

296

"No, jiji," said Reina with a soft laugh. "Just a laptop and some new clothes. I've got plenty left over."

"Then get a ticket to Tokyo and catch a train to Hakone. See where *my* grandparents were raised," suggested Haru. With every word he spoke the bulb beneath his shade did a little flicker, projecting the colors of the stained glass across the room. Little blotches of pale pink flashed in Reina's eyes as her grandfather began to ramble on and on about his own trip to Hakone in his twenties. "We'd hop onto a ferry at Lake Ashi and we'd eat with the captain, and your grandmother wouldn't touch the tempura unless it was done exactly right... your father was only a boy but he loved to see the shrines, he has this eye for detail just like I did and I'm sure you do too... first they piece together the wood chips into spades and stars, then they slice off the top layer into a sheet as thin as paper... there's butterfly koi, showa koi, asagi koi, tancho koi..."

Long winded babble was perhaps another weakness Reina would have to adapt to. Surprisingly, this was far more worrisome than any of her grandaunt's nationalism. When people speak aimlessly and endlessly, the mind of an OCD person tends to feel under-stimulated and therefore begins to wander. And when it wanders, it's rarely to good places. They tend to focus on things that scare them, and they're often things far out of their control. Phobias, regrets, and religious guilt ruminate in their mind till the speaker's droning finally comes to an end and something more interesting graces their ears.

During her grandfather's monologue, Reina found herself obsessing about the concept of eternity; being trapped in an everyday object till time itself comes to an end; being unable to move your arms and legs ever again; being unable to smile ever again; being unable to cover your ears and drown out the incessant sounds of geriatrics. Reina started thinking of all the ways she could have prevented her death from happening to begin with; all of it was unrealistic hindsight. If only she stopped herself from smoking that cigarette in sixth grade. If only she got a brain scan years earlier. If only she didn't blame those headaches and vomit spells on her period. If only she ate more fatty fish. If only she drank more green tea.

"I need to go." Reina cut off her grandfather as he'd just begun ranking Hakone's train stations by the quality of their food.

Her grandfather's tale stopped mid-sentence, as did his annoying flickering. Reina rubbed her eyes and stood up. She began walking towards the front door.

"Wait!" called out her grandfather. "Do me a favor before you leave?"

Reina already knew what he was going to ask. She turned around and walked back over to her grandfather's lamp. She reached beneath the lampshade and pulled the steel-beaded cord four times. *Click. Click. Click. Click.*

Haru gave a sigh of relief. "Thank you."

Reina's grandfather used to make those four clicks every night before bed. Being possessed objects, they don't need to sleep anymore, so it's no longer a necessity; but when given the opportunity, Haru still loves to hear those clicks. OCD can be oddly rewarding that way. Though it binds you to fulfilling arbitrary needs, it gives the mundane an almost drug-like quality.

As Reina got in her mom's car and drove down the driveway she saw Mormons dressed in their white shirts and little black ties down on the ground, praying at the edge of their ranch's property line. Reina honked loudly as she passed them by, disturbing their silence. They looked up at her car. Reina flipped them off and sneered.

The Mormons had always had this weird thing against their ranch house. They believe it's filled with unholy entities, the type that can only be cleansed with the proper showing of faith. They're outside the Kumogami Ranch day and night, seven days a week. Their level of obsession almost mirrors that of the Kumogamis themselves.

"So what do *I* tend to obsess over?" asked Reina to her immediate family. They were all sitting at a deli just down the street from their apartment back in Salt Lake City. It was Reina, her brother Aran, and her mother and father, Kyo and Ryo.

"Honestly, you kind of have this weird fixation on men's teeth," said her mother. "You dumped that poor boy Beckett because you said his molars felt like coral."

"I'm not talking about boys," clarified Reina. "I'm talking about an object, a personal belonging, something that I'm always fiddling around with."

"How about some context?" suggested her father. "Are we talking about what you might inhabit after you've passed?"

Reina nodded. "Like a mirror or a lamp."

"Chabo," said her parents in unison.

"My rooster plushie?" exclaimed Reina. "I haven't played with him in years..."

"Four years to be exact," said her mother. "You turned thirteen, then begged me to find him a good home."

"If the object you haunt is based on the object you obsessed over the most in your lifetime," explained her father, "that toy's been integral to you for 75% of your existence."

299

"Oh my god," bemoaned Reina. "I don't want to be an evil doll..."

"Chicken Chuckie," laughed Reina's brother.

"That's fucking awful," whined Reina. "Please, there's got to be something else we're forgetting."

"Why does it matter?" asked her mother. "It's all the same experience. Is the life of a doll any more or less exciting than that of a sofa or a foot stool? It all just lays there."

"We just need to get you something cool and have you spend every waking minute with it until you die," suggested her brother. "Let's go buy you a gun!"

"I don't want to be a gun, Aran," groaned Reina, pinching her nose between her fingers, "Whatever I inhabit people are gonna assume I was obsessed about, and only a serial killer would eat, sleep, and bathe beside their gun. Same goes for knives and swords."

"It's just our family," interjected her father. "I don't think you need to worry about them judging you based on what you get."

"It *might* just be our family," replied Reina. "I haven't decided yet."

"Decided?" questioned her father. "I didn't know there was a choice..."

Reina's mother glared at her husband angrily.

"No-no! I'm not saying she doesn't have the right to choose... I'm just saying, I was unaware she was thinking of other options..." clarified her father. "No one keeps me in the loop."

"I'm worried I might get bored," explained Reina. "Besides talking, what do these people even do for fun?"

"Alone from night to night you'll find me, Too weak to break the chains that bind me, I need no shackles to remind me, I'm just a prisoner of love..." All the items in the living room of Kumogami Ranch were singing along with the song as the hits of Perry Como emanated from the radio sitting on the stool against the accent wall. As they sang, the room sort of came alive. The rocking chair swiveled. The urn slowly turned. The broom bounced on its bristles. *"For one command I stand and wait now, From one who's master of my fate now, I can't escape for it's too late now, I'm just a prisoner of love..."*

As the song faded out and finally came to an end, Reina forced a smile and gave a modest round of applause. Reina had done Disney sing-alongs numerous times since she was old enough to talk, so she wasn't going to judge her relatives for choosing such a wholesome pastime. She did, however, take issue with the song selection. She figured that people who lived forever would eventually have to update their music taste or else the same old songs were bound to get stale. Apparently, she was wrong.

She went up to the radio, it was her Great Uncle Toho. She asked him how he chooses what songs to play.

"Oh, I can play any song I remember," explained Toho, "and I remember only the best of the best. Real crooners."

"If I play new songs for you, couldn't you memorize them too?" asked Reina.

"I'm an old man," laughed Tomo. "All the brain cells built for learning have long gone away. All I got left are my memories."

"Brain cells?" exclaimed Reina; she rolled her eyes. "There's no brain left at all. You're a Bakelite box full of wires and coils. Nothing's stopping you from giving it a try."

Toho huffed.

Reina took the hint and backed off. She decided to talk with someone a tad younger. Besides her grandfather, the youngest person in the room was her first cousin, twice removed, Hisa. Hisa was placed on the top shelf beside the front door. She took the form of a ceramic urn.

When Reina got close, she could make out the cracks in Hisa's side. The entire left portion of the vase had been shattered, then reassembled. A fresh coating of black paint barely masked the damage. Inside the urn was what remained of Hisa's daughter; whatever ashes could be recovered after the urn had toppled.

"So you all like stories and songs, huh? Then, why not get a tv?" suggested Reina to her dear cousin.

Hisa answered sweetly. "Most of us don't have any eyes, dear! We would have to rely entirely on Kyoko to explain the images to us, and she's much too self-involved to show such compassion."

"Couldn't you just listen to it at least?"

"Well we also don't have hands, sweetie," sighed Hisa. "We'd be stuck on a single channel till someone living showed up to change it for us. There's no single channel we can all agree on like that."

"What about games?" pondered Reina.

"Oh we have games!" exclaimed Hisa. "You ever play Yamanote Line?"

"Like the drinking game?" replied Reina. "But none of you can drink?"

"There's other ways to repay failure…" said Hisa, slyly. "Here, I'll choose a topic. Toho, start the beat."

Great Uncle Toho spat out a smooth jazz beat with a cymbal and a snare that volleyed back and forth.

"Alright everyone," called out Hisa. "Universities in Utah!"

"U of U!"

"Bringham Young!"

"Utah State!"

"Dixie!"

"Weber!"

The game had come full circle and Kyoko had to give her second answer. She wasn't expecting it would get this far. She had nothing to say. Her beat passed by and her opportunity closed. The music stopped and everyone went quiet.

"What happens now?" questioned Reina.

"Kyoko's fair game," explained Hisa. "We can now hurl any insults we want at her."

"Selfish!" called out Haru.

"Narcissist!" called out Tomo.

"Childless!"

303

"Unlovable!"

"Piss-drinker!"

"Ignore the last one," called out Hisa. "They're supposed to be insults specific to the loser. Your Cousin Noa just isn't very good at this game..."

Upon receiving her barrage, Kyoko played along. She winced and swallowed as though she was taking down a hard shot. Then she opened her eyes wide and exhaled loudly. "Smooth."

"Alright, Reina, you're playing along with us this time. Do you get the gist of it?" asked Hisa.

"I mean, yes," answered Reina hesitantly, "I'm just worried about how I'll handle the criticism..."

"Then don't lose!" laughed Kyoko from her mirror. "Next category: root vegetables." The music started up again.

"Radish!"

"Potato!"

"Yam!"

It was Reina's turn. She panicked at first, but the threat of insult compelled her to take a quick guess. "Garlic?"

Kyoko nodded. Garlic counts.

"Parsnips!"

"Beets!"

It circled back to Hisa. The beat passed by and she didn't say a word. She was going to say beets before it got stolen. She couldn't think of another one that fast.

Hisa had lost. The music stopped yet again. Several players took deep breaths so they could howl their slights with ferocity.

"Deviant!"

"Closet-case!"

"Rug-muncher!"

Reina looked over at Hisa. Her urn was twisting side to side as though she were squirming in her seat.

"Guys this seems kind of fucked…" said Reina.

"Self-destructive!"

"Suicidal!"

"You'll never see your baby again!"

"Oh my god, stop it!" exploded Reina. The insults came to a sudden halt and the decor suddenly fell still. "I understand you all must think you're pretty jaded, but this can't be any less harmful to you. Can't you just play a game without verbally abusing each other?"

"Huh," laughed Kyoko, "and I was worried we'd look like the boring ones."

The whole room erupted into laughter. Reina stood up with a look of shock. She kept looking over her shoulder at Hisa to see if she was okay. "They really laid into you," she said with a frown. "You can't take that shit."

"Yeah, yeah. It's just a game, dear," said Hisa, forcing out a weak laugh. "Try to lighten up a bit."

Reina departed without giving her grandfather his usual clicks. He, nor any of these sadists, deserved any sort of satisfaction.

When Reina got home, her parents were cooking dinner together. Her father was pan-searing some coconut shrimp, while her mother added toppings to their baked potatoes.

"So how were your grandparents?" called out Reina's mother as she sprinkled cheddar cheese on top of a spud.

Reina stared off into space. The day's events were a lot to process. She hoped that maybe her parents could help fill in some blanks.

"Mom, Dad... what actually happened to Cousin Hisa?"

Reina's mother finished mixing chives into the sour cream, then looked up at Reina.

"I guess, more specifically, what happened to her daughter?"

Reina's mother cleared her throat, gathering her father's attention. "I think *you've* got to tell this story."

Reina's father took his pan off the burner then turned to his wife. He nodded and signaled for her to leave. Reina's father was used to explaining the madness that was his half of the family. He liked to give his wife a break from all the drama whenever possible.

Reina's father sat down at the kitchen table. Reina did the same.

"Well honey, Rebecca, her daughter, went to school with me, and she was about your age when she passed away. She had an asthma attack in her sleep. Your cousin blamed herself for losing her."

Reina crossed her arms on her placemat. "Why's that?"

"Well, Rebecca was adopted, so she didn't have our family's abhorrence to filth. Because of this, Hisa considered her to be a relatively unclean house guest. Not that she didn't love her all the same, but she constantly doused her bedroom with all sorts of cleaning agents; her secret blend being ammonia and lye. Now no doctor would admit to it, but one might assume the chemicals weren't good for poor Rebecca's lungs..."

"There's no way it's all her fault..." interjected Reina.

"She doesn't see it that way," sighed her father. "Now, while everyone else in her bloodline gets to see their children after they die, because of the adoption, Hisa is the only person truly separated from her daughter. Hisa is crushed and spends the rest of her life glued to that urn. She shines it three times a day till the day she dies. The whole time she's alive she tries her hardest to get rid of her OCD, so that there's a chance she, instead, ends up in Heaven with her daughter. She tries Prozac, Anafranil, Busprione, but none of it works, none of it helps. She dies with her daughter's ashes in her arms. The pot immediately springs to life."

Reina stared at her father intently. "So then... how does the pot break?"

Her father's face suddenly turned to guilt. His eyes slid downwards. His shoulders slouched. "Fast forward three years, and there's this Christmas party at the ranch. Hisa was a close friend of mine, so I spent the majority of the time trying to cheer her up. She's reliving every Christmas she had with Rebecca. She starts getting emotional, and then, she tells me to pick her up and smash her to the floor." Reina's father placed a hand on his face. "I was young and bold, and drunk on egg sake, so when she asked me I was easily convinced. She told me I wouldn't be killing her. She's already dead."

"It's okay, dad. You clearly thought it might help her escape."

Her father nodded. "It did nothing like that. It only filled her with unfathomable pain as her body divided into a hundred tiny little pieces. This pain would last for months as I reassembled her bit by bit in my garage." Her father uncovered his face. "Does she seem better at all to you?"

Reina shrugged. "It's hard to get a read on her. Everyone acts sort of phony in that house."

"Well I think she's excited to have your company," replied her father. "A young woman to converse with; you remind her of Rebecca."

"I'm not sure if I like that."

"You'd be doing her a great honor."

"Dad..."

"I'm just saying. There's more to consider than you may realize. I want you to understand how moving-in might help them. You mean so much to them."

Reina nodded. "They like to see family. Perhaps they wouldn't feel like they have to trap them there in death, if their family just visited once in a while while they're still alive..."

Her father stood up out of his chair. He gave no response. He walked over to the shrimp and put them back on the burner.

"If the sight of them depresses you, just tell me the truth."

Her father shook his head. "I assure you, it's not that." He dashed garlic over the pan. "There just needs to be healthy separation between the dead and the living, dear. There are aspects of their afterlives the living simply cannot comprehend."

"If you rearrange us, we will repay you with our eternal wisdom!" Back at the ranch, Noa, another first cousin twice-removed, called out to Reina. Noa took the form of a shag rug in front of the room's second entrance leading into the kitchen area. "I've been around quite a long time, young lady, and I can teach you forbidden knowledge."

"Like...?"

"I can teach you how to make a bong out of a Barbie doll."

"I'm going to need something better than that."

"Oh come on!" called out a broom in the corner. It was Great Aunt Tanaka, Noa's mother. "I feel kind of claustrophobic where I am now. I've got a killer pot-brownie recipe I'll give you in return."

"Why do you all assume I want to know about weed? Weed's a pretty easy system to figure out," griped Reina. "How about some life advice to make my impending doom less frightening?"

"Well... that would be to smoke more weed, dear," called out Tanaka. "I don't think any one of us here died sober."

Reina rolled her eyes and picked up the broom. She left Tanaka lying on the ground on top of her son. "Could you stand me up straight please?"

Reina tried but the broom kept teetering over. "It's not working. If you want to be standing, I'll need to lay you in the corner."

"Here, there's a little loop of string attached to the end of my handle. Just take Kyoko off the wall and hang me on the free nail."

"No!" sneered Kyoko. "I like where I am."

"Here, sweetie," called out Hisa. "You can wedge her over here between the floor and the bottom shelf. She might be kind of angled, but it's pretty close."

Reina did as she was told.

"Now, put me closer to the blue wall!" called out Noa. "I want to be near everyone else."

"I'll switch spots with you," suggested Great Grandpa Taro, Haru and Kyoko's father. He took the form of a puffy, leather armchair. "I could use some space."

"I can try to move you, but your chair's kind of heavy..." cautioned Reina.

"It's all volume. No mass."

"I'm weak!" argued Reina. "I'm taking chemo pills!"

"Come on," said Taro. "Nothing's stopping you from giving it a try..."

Reina begrudgingly obliged and walked over to the chair. She laid her back on the accent wall, then placed her heels on the back of the chair; she kicked outwards, trying to push it forward. She managed to move it a few feet. As it scraped along the floor, a loud scraping noise echoed through the house.

310

"Keep going!" shouted Taro. "You've got it started…"

Reina was out of breath. She repositioned herself behind the chair and leaned her full body weight against it. It nudged forward another few inches. She was making progress, but it was going slowly. She felt sweat building up on her face. Her stomach felt queasy.

"Sounds like you could use some help!" came a chipper voice off in the distance. Reina heard footsteps stomping up the stairs from the basement beneath them. The stranger wandered through the kitchen and appeared at the entrance to the living room.

Reina looked up and was surprised to see another person among the living. He was a tall man with anglo-saxon features; auburn hair and round eyes. He was about her parents' age and dressed nicely, like he was going to church.

Reina snarled. He looked like one of the Mormons. She figured they finally grew the balls to trespass.

"What were you doing down there?" asked Reina. She picked up Aunt Tanaka and swung her bristles at the robber's head.

The man looked confused. He raised his hands and covered his face.

"Reina, stop!" called out Haru. "Stop! Stop! It's not an intruder… that's your cousin."

"My cousin?" questioned Reina. "Then why didn't he say so?"

"You might be my cousin, I wouldn't know," said the stranger. He dropped his hands and gave a shy smile. "I've never met any of my *living* relatives."

311

Reina sat down the broom and cocked her head. "Why's that now?"

The stranger looked around at all the furniture in the living room. His mouth hung slightly ajar. He sighed. "I think it would be better if you asked them." He looked awkward, as though all the furniture was staring at him. "I should probably just go..." He kept walking forward and sped past Reina. He dashed through the front door and disappeared into an Uber that pulled up out front.

"What was he doing here?" probed Reina.

"He's like you," answered Haru. "He's visiting relatives."

"But you're up here?"

"...and they're down there," said Haru, sullenly.

"There's more of you... in the basement?"

The room fell silent.

"It's for their own comfort, dear," interjected Kyoko. "Don't worry. They're not alone."

"We tolerated your cousin for years," explained Haru. "We weren't going to isolate him. That's cruelty. We instead waited till someone could go with him. That's when your other cousin joined us, and we couldn't bear to be around him either."

"You banished people?" sneered Reina. "But you kept Kyoko around?"

Kyoko shrugged with a smirk.

312

"Kyoko's a lot, but she's no traitor. She's kept her honor despite all her flaws," continued Haru. "Cousin Hiroto and cousin Yutaka have made unforgivable life choices."

"It's all about who we fucked," chuckled Hiroto. "I assure you, despite how bad they make us sound, we never hurt anyone. That boy you saw was simply my son. They don't like him cause of his mother."

"Is it because she's white?" asked Reina.

Hiroto, taking the form of a shamisen, nodded by tilting his tuning pegs forward and backward. "There's more to it though... she's also a Mormon."

"That's pretty significant," said Reina with surprise. "Did you convert?"

"Oh absolutely. I'm still a firm believer in the teachings of Joseph Smith," explained Hiroto. "I was converted long before I met Dinah though. We met on tour. We were both in Christian rock bands. We were Special Intelligence. They were Order 44."

"...but why?" questioned Reina. "We're Shinto. Shinto's cool as fuck."

"Sorry?" laughed Hiroto. "I just didn't feel like our family was ever that spiritual because the curse kind of ruined any hope of an afterlife. The Mormons however, promised that if I worshiped God their way, I'd have a chance at Heaven as opposed to being stuck in a cold, lifeless heirloom."

"...they were wrong, though?"

"I'm still hopeful," replied Hiroto confidently. "I think this might just be a final test of faith. As long as I stay in the light of

313

God, I should attain exaltation between ten and a hundred years from now."

"Huh," huffed Reina. She turned to Yutaka. He was a kiseru, a Japanese pipe. "So then, what did *you* bang to bring dishonor to the name Kumogami?"

"Oh… a lot of people." Yutaka's voice was slow and nasally. "I've been to a lot of places, darling, with a lot of women. I've spread my seed far and wide since I was old enough to ride a plane."

"You couldn't wear a condom?"

"You forget little things when you're high on shabu," replied Yutaka, matter-of-factly. "That's meth, darling."

"Right…" Reina sat down on the bottom step of the staircase. She thought it through. "So you've got like ten or twenty kids out there without a father who are going to die and be terribly confused when they end up stuffed in their favorite coffee mug for an eternity."

"I'll admit, at first I couldn't care less, but I've sobered up with old age," said Yutaka. "Hiroto's kids have been helping me track down my offspring. I'm making sure they know what they've inherited. But to be honest, none of them seem interested in traveling across the world to live in a farmhouse in Utah. Not now at least, but they'll learn."

"What do you mean they'll learn?"

Yutaka's pipe tilted and rolled onto its side. "I tried to ruff it when I first transferred bodies. I figured I'd lucked out, I ended up in something quite portable. I figured the life of a pipe might be worth witnessing. Passed around by interesting people from drug dens in Paris to parties in Berlin. But that optimism fades

314

the first time you're left alone. It turns out human products, even something beautiful like an ornate pipe, still end up washed up and stuck on the shore. Forgotten."

"What shore?"

"A pawn shop in Brooklyn."

"Oh my god…"

"I was there for five years. I begged customers to buy me but it just made things worse. Nobody comes to a pawn shop to adopt a basehead," explained Yutaka. "I tried keeping quiet, but the owner had me priced ridiculously. I pleaded for him to lower the value, but he wouldn't budge. It took five years, five long years before someone finally paid the man and took me home. It was a sweet little hippie, I begged her to send me to the ranch house and I was lucky she obliged."

"Jesus…" exclaimed Reina. "Is it really that bad out there?"

Yutaka rolled back upright. "Let's just say there's risks involved. Nobody takes good care of their stuff forever. I'm just lucky I didn't wind up in the trash."

Reina peered down at the floor.

"I think I've decided to stay." When Reina got home that evening, she joined her parents and her brother for a special dinner shared with their grandmother. She was her father's mother, once married to Haru.

"You want to stay in the ranch house?" questioned her mother. She glared angrily at her husband. "What did your father say to you?"

315

"No, no. He didn't pressure me. I've reached this conclusion all on my own," explained Reina. "The afterlife is a scary place. I don't want to do it alone. I need people I can rely on."

Reina's father smiled.

Reina's mother nodded warmly.

Her brother didn't react.

Her grandmother looked horrified.

"Baka! You're just going to let her move into a nuthouse!" screamed her grandmother. "For God sake, Kyo, set your daughter straight."

"She has a good point," said Reina's father. "Her family won't abandon her."

"But you know as well as I do that place is no place for a little girl." Reina's grandma turned to face her. "Why do you think I never visit there, sweetie? Not even for Haru..."

"Grandpa? I don't know?" replied Reina. "I figured you moved on. Marriage is *till death do us part*. You were free to go."

"Our marriage was rock solid. I would have loved to keep seeing him. *He* was the one that moved on."

"Mother, stop!" shouted Kyo. "Don't go spreading rumors."

"It wasn't rumors till your baby got sick," sneered Reina's grandmother. "Now you're just in denial."

Reina's father's face fell flat. He stared down at his plate with a lifeless glance. "It's still the safe choice."

316

"She at least deserves to know the truth." Reina's grandmother stared intently at Reina. "You've got to see them when they think you're not watching."

"What?" said Reina with a look of shock.

"Leave now! Catch them in the act," growled Reina's grandmother. "Go in through the back and just listen... you need to hear what really goes on!"

Reina skipped out on dinner and grabbed her car. She immediately hit the road and made it back to the ranch in about forty minutes. She took her grandma's advice and wandered around to the backyard. She took a moment just to stare at the eerie setup behind the house. Seven graves in a straight row, perfectly aligned. The name Hotei was carved into the center stone. This was the man who built the house.

Reina turned away and walked up the back steps. She made each move slowly, reducing any noise to quiet taps and creaks. She was worried they'd hear even these minor sounds, but the racket inside drowned out any of her turbulence.

"And then what are you gonna do to me?" shouted a seductive voice across the living room. Reina immediately recognized it as Kyoko's.

"First I'm going to take off your girdle with my teeth." Reina's jaw dropped. It was Noa's voice. "Then I'm going to shove your face against the mirror and have my way with you..."

"I can see you behind me," moaned Kyoko. "You look so heated. Your face is flushed. Your chest is shimmering."

"You're squeezing me so tight!" growled Noa. "I think I'm close!"

317

"Don't finish just yet," called out Kyoko. "I want you to pin me down on the shag rug."

"Oh yeah?"

"Oh yeah!"

"My fucking ears!" cried out Reina. "Please stop, stop!"

She ran out into the center of the living room. She startled all of her relatives. Their respective objects shook like an earthquake had struck.

"Reina!" gasped her Cousin Hisa. "Why are you snooping around at this hour?"

"You've interrupted the show," sneered her Great Aunt Tanaka.

"Tanaka that's your son! Why don't you care?" screeched Reina.

"He's a grown man, he can do what he wants to."

"But with Kyoko? That's his cousin…"

"Options are limited," sighed Kyoko. "We get each other, we're born in the same generation."

Reina gave Kyoko a look of disgust. "Where's your class?"

"Oh what did you think?" snarled Kyoko. "That we just lost our sex drive when we lost our privates?"

"Do you all do this?" probed Reina.

Nobody spoke up.

"Go on and tell me!" shouted Reina.

318

"What's the big deal?" questioned Noa, with a tinge of irritability. "We aren't really doing anything. We're just saying words."

"You don't talk like that to someone you're related to."

"Our bodies are all glass, plaster, and wood. There are no genes left to relate us together," replied Noa. "We're practically personalities floating in jars."

"That can't be the way you see each other; a bunch of personalities trapped in storage. If it is, then you're saying you're not family." Tears built up in Reina's eyes. "And if you're not my family, I don't think there's any reason for me to keep coming here."

Reina looked at her grandfather Haru. She imagined what he did with Kyoko, or Tanaka, or even cousin Hisa. Reina cringed and ran out of the room. She ran through the backdoor and slammed it closed behind her. She felt tears rolling down her face and she sat down on the steps.

Reina just sat there sobbing. All her worries came flooding into her head. She saw herself as the chicken doll, trying to make it on her own. She's tossed into a Toys for Tots box. None of the kids want her because she's a creepy abomination. She finds herself abandoned in a landfill. The walls of trash crash down on her head. She can't see anything. Everything's dark.

"It's gotten bad, hasn't it?" A low booming voice suddenly sounded behind Reina's back. She turned around and was shocked to see the door was still closed.

"God?" whimpered Reina.

"No. Just Grandpa."

"Which Grandpa?"

"Grandpa Hotei…" said the voice. "Let me think for a second. I'm old." The voice paused. "I think I'm your *Great Great* Grandpa. I'm your Grandpa's Grandpa."

"…you're the one who built the house?"

"That would be me."

"My God," Reina dried her tears and looked up towards the roof. "Why don't you ever speak?"

"I've been here longer than any of you. I've spoken more than enough for two lifetimes. I just like to listen."

"But you break your silence, now?"

"I have to. This is my fault. I started all this," explained Hotei. "A long time ago I asked that my family keep me company in this long, dreary afterlife. Ever since, the tradition has prospered, but the results are not what I expected. I had a dream of a massive family fully connected with their history. Something magical. Where you could see your family evolve right before your very eyes from humble farmers, to doctors and lawyers, to CEOs. But I was wrong Reina... do you know why people prune their trees?"

Reina shook her head.

"It prevents disease. I'm afraid our family tree is now deeply infected. There's only one cure."

"You're not gonna tell me to chop it down are you?"

Hotei let out a long exhale. All the shingles on the roof shook. "You certainly must do something."

"Well I won't be having any kids, I suppose that could put an end to the curse. I think you might have some trouble stopping the Mormon boy from doing that though," answered Reina.

"Then kill your cousin. End the bloodline!"

Reina couldn't tell if he was serious. She squinted at first, then cracked a smile. "That's a horrible idea," scoffed Reina. "You gotta be joking."

"You kill him and it ends like you said. It doesn't matter who you kill, you're dying anyways.

"I don't know what it was like in your day, but no one just ends bloodlines like that anymore. This isn't Feudal Japan. It's the Northwest."

"Then burn down the house… with everyone inside!"

Reina shook her head and rolled her eyes. "No! That's ridiculous. You're being ridiculous."

"Our ashes will scatter across the world. We'll never stop moving. We'll never grow bored. Traveling by air, earth, and sea."

"Somebody already tried to take themselves apart," said Reina, sharply. "You'll be left in unfathomable pain!"

"…it's worth it."

Reina breathed deeply, then shook her head. She got up off the back steps and walked out into the yard. She stood at Hotei's headstone and shook her head. "You fucking lost it, man. The people inside there have been around half as long as you and *they* certainly lost it. They word-fuck their own family. I think it's safe to say you're at least twice as batshit as that."

"...coward."

Reina nodded. "I have a brain tumor Hotei... I'm allowed to be scared." Reina walked away from the tombstone and walked to the edge of the property. When she reached the Mormons that prayed over her front lawn, she waved to them and smiled, then got in her car. She went back home to Salt Lake City and would never return.

"I'll share with you my infinite wisdom, if you drag me over the other side of the room," said Noa.

"That's not necessary," replied the caretaker. "I'll be happy to move you wherever you'd like." The caretaker reached under Noa and grabbed him by his corners. She pulled him over to the side of the room so his mother could hear him better.

Reina had used the money her Grandfather Haru left her to buy a caretaker for three hours a day, five days a week, for the next ten months. It wasn't perfect, but she figured it might become a new family tradition to funnel their inheritances into affording the help, special help paid an extra special salary to tend to extra special people.

Reina herself became her worst nightmare, eventually inhabiting her stuffed chicken. A chicken she'd leave to her brother in her will.

Reina decided she would put her trust in her family after all; just in her own way. She had herself stuffed in the main pocket of her brother's backpack. Her head and arms stuck out through the top. The two of them were going off on an adventure together.

Reina spent her piece of her grandfather's inheritance on the caretaker, but Aran still had his piece of the pie. Just enough to afford a single plane ticket to Tokyo. Reina didn't need one. Tickets are free for stuffed animals.

"If you get tired of me, promise me you won't toss me out."

Aran smiled. "The 60's had Talky Tina. The 80's had Chuckie. 2010's had Annabelle. Haunted dolls aren't ever going out of style," he said. "I think it's cool to have my own."

Reina couldn't smile, but a warm feeling filled her all the same.

Profile: Joss Iger

In the fall of 1982, eight weeks into her pregnancy, Sandie Iger received an ultrasound by Dr. Oswald Jones and his accompanying sonographer. Dr. Jones first made note of the obvious, pointing to the space separating two grey masses in the middle of the screen. "Twins," he confirmed. He then pointed out that both babies were perfectly healthy. They were growing in the uterus and not the Fallopian tube. They had a normal heartbeat, no cysts or fibroids, and no outward abnormalities that would suggest risk for miscarriage. Every detail had the doctor optimistic.

The pregnancy remained healthy until the second ultrasound early-on in the second trimester. There wasn't as much space between ultrasounds as originally planned; a significant depression befell Sandie, and Dr. Jones worried it might cause complications. Depressed mothers are susceptible to underweight babies and premature births. Sandie promised her mood swings hadn't caused her to take up smoking or drinking again. The baby's weight was well within average: 1.5 ounces. The doctor seemed satisfied.

"What about the other one?" asked Sandie. "How big's his brother?"

Dr. Jones shrugged with a melancholy glance. The second baby had no weight. The second baby had ceased to exist. "No need to panic," assured Dr. Jones. "It's not as strange as it sounds."

Vanishing Twin Syndrome is common enough that there's a name for it and an acronym. VTS, in fact, is theorized to occur in one in eight pregnancies, most of which go completely unknown due to the frequency mothers receive ultrasounds. Now VTS usually occurs within the first trimester, so Sandie's case is slightly unique in that it seemed to occur in the second. But Dr. Jones believes the difference is negligible and that VTS is really the only logical theory

However, if you ask Sandie herself, she says there's a second way it could have disappeared. "Joss ate his brother," explained Sandie; Joss being the surviving fetus of the initial twins. "It was the first documented case of intrauterine cannibalism in humans."

"No," grumbled Dr. Jones. "No, it's not. Her theory is a manifestation of her paranoia. Intrauterine cannibalism isn't possible in mammals."

Dr. Jones believed Sandie suffered PTSD from a traumatic episode that triggered her depression during her pregnancy. Sandie's husband, the father of Joss, was arrested for serial murder.

"I love him but there's animal in him," explained Sandie through sullen eyes.

"I made sure Sandie's therapist was well aware of these thoughts," explained Dr. Jones. "I was worried she thought Joss was defective and would mistreat him. Social workers have kept a close eye on that family since Joss was born but... for the best... nothing abnormal ever happened between mother and son. Whether or not she thought of her son as a cannibal, she treated him very well. He grew up to do good things."

—-

Joss was born in 1983. It's been 37 years since then and I'm happy to say Joss is a functioning adult. Despite his dreary beginnings, he's chosen a career path with a lot of levity.

Joss is a stand-up comedian with a dark sense of humor. He has an interesting routine where he mocks his father's arrest after only three kills as "amateur hour". He also talks a lot about eating his brother.

"It's the perfect crime because it's not a crime at all," jokes Joss. "According to the left, I'm not a murderer 'cause neither one of us was technically alive yet."

Because of Joss's occupation, he submitted one of the only stories that fits under the major category of comedy: "Six Os". Unsurprisingly, this story deals heavily with precarious procreation, inspired deeply by the darkness associated with his own conception. Sexual health will only remain a macabre topic solely for the way he came into the world.

Six O's

I had sex three times in college, which I imagine is below average. Though I guess, compared to the zero times I had sex in high school, it could be considered an achievement. But I know I could have done it way more if I had used the soft-reset between secondary school and university a lot more wisely. Most kids used this fresh start to shed the molds their parents pressed them into and assume a more naturalistic character. I, however, dove further into the bullshit.

For one thing, I wouldn't shut up about my major. It was petroleum engineering, and I liked bringing it up because everyone knew a petroleum engineer would be making a six-figure salary straight out of college. I wanted to seem impressive, but I actually came across as a bit of a joyless square who only talks about his academics. It also didn't really sit well with a lot of the environmentally-minded hippies at UT Austin. They weren't really enthusiastic about me profiting off of using up all our earth's precious natural resources.

I also liked to dress a certain way that I would say lacked a lot of creativity; which is a shame because I think I'm a pretty imaginative person. But I stuck to polos and chinos in the hot months, and button-downs and khakis in the winter. I wasn't ugly, but I was far from original.

Of the three girls who did decide to have sex with me, one girl was as fake and terrible as me; one girl claimed she could see through to the real me; and a third girl openly admitted she was "attracted to sociopaths".

When I got out of college, I moved to Houston to work for a start-up that does reservoir design. I considered this a second

327

chance in order to make the transition right this time. I threw out all my preppy clothes and stopped caring about fitting into a certain class of twenty-somethings. I decided to go to a thrift store and buy cheap t-shirts with references to movies and hobbies I actually liked. I found out that when you wear your interests on your person, it looks to strangers as though you want to start a conversation about them. Henceforth, making you more inviting.

"Marmite," said the girl sitting across from me on the METRORail. She was reading the logo printed on my shirt. "Have you actually tried marmite?"

I nodded. It wasn't really an interest per se, but marmite was an oddity that existed in my kitchen cabinets since I was a child. I considered it a unique quality, and so I bought the shirt even though it was a size too small. "I put it on grilled cheese."

The girl nodded. "I put it on popcorn."

This may not be enough in common to tie two people together for life, but it was just enough to sleep together. We held conversation before and after our sex, and this time I made sure to neglect mentioning my career. I talked about my anxieties instead; mainly about moving to a new town. She liked what she heard and she was happy to show me around; she took me to a breakfast spot in the morning that bakes fresh cinnamon raisin bagels. I thanked her and we parted ways.

Just a month after moving, my number of partners had suddenly quadrupled. A v-neck with a reference to my succulent collection won the heart of a guitarist at a honkey-tonk. A tank top worked twice in the same night on two different girls with the same adolescent interest in SimCity. But the real big hit was the shirt I had with a cute cartoon of a chubby, little pika on it. It's my favorite animal and it turns out I'm not alone.

"Back in Albuquerque they'd eat the weeds out of our backyard."

"My dad kept one as a pet. Not like illegally. He had a sanctuary."

"They're such good little poofs."

"They're such cute little boofs."

"Is that a fat mouse?"

The last girl actually hadn't heard of pikas, but regardless, the conversation got rolling because of the shirt. Or maybe it was just the confidence I felt wearing the shirt. Either way the outfit change led to a personality change, which in turn led to a change in my sexual activity. In other words, I was finally myself and I was loving it.

But it seemed that with an increase in partners I also increased my likelihood of genital infection. And being relatively new to frequent intercourse, I hadn't been the best at using protection. I never picked up a habit of carrying condoms around. And by the time I realized that might be a smart thing to subscribe to on Amazon Prime, two months in Houston had already gone by.

I remember the day I first spotted the abnormality. I was changing in a friend's bathroom after a pool party and noticed the tip of my dick was looking darker than usual. Mine was usually pastel pink, but now it seemed to be a pansy purple. At first I thought it might have just been a trick of the light; after all, I was staring down at myself in an unfamiliar room with some of the brightest LED bulbs I'd ever seen. But when I reassessed back at home, everything still seemed discolored.

"Mountain Bible College Syndrome," explained the doctor. "Or just MBC."

329

I immediately Googled it on my phone. MBC was named after a small Christian college in Kentucky, where the first major outbreak was recorded. Rampant sexual denial helped it spread like wildfire, leading to county-wide sterility.

"There's a really low chance of contraction," the doctor said with a nod. "500 cases yearly. Only ever recorded in the US and Canada."

I breathed in deeply and tried to slow my heart. I was panicking. "Am I sterile?"

"No. Not exactly," replied the doctor. "It's a mitochondrial disorder, to which we have no known treatments available. You're lucky though, most mitochondrial disorders affect vital organs and motor function leading to death and paralysis; but MBC only affects two muscles, the bulbospongiosus and ischiocavernosus."

"Those are where?"

"Your penis, Brexon."

"Oh…"

"They're the muscles that allow you to ejaculate."

"Oh?" I considered what he was saying. It took a second for it to sink in. "Does that mean I can't… cum anymore?"

"Not necessarily," said the doctor, taking a seat beside me. His expression looked grim. "Have you had any sex since the discoloration."

"No, but I was planning on having some tonight."

"Girlfriend?"

"No, I'm just on a hot streak."

"Well there are some things you might want to consider first…"

I nodded and locked eyes with the doctor. I listened intently.

"Since you haven't had sex since the discoloration, then we can predict based on case studies that you have enough ATP in storage to afford you six orgasms. But your muscles down there are no longer replacing any of the ATP that's lost. So when you reach six… that's it."

I cupped my hands over my nose and mouth. "I'm an idiot," I exclaimed. "This is my fault."

"It's in no way your fault," assured the doctor. He patted me on the shoulder. "It's too complicated to pin on anyone. Girls tend to get it and not realize it because many have problems orgasming to begin with. They don't notice that they're gone. Whoever gave it to you thought she was perfectly healthy."

"Do I need to figure out who it was?"

The doctor shook his head. "We need to focus on you. There are some things you're not going to want to hear, but I have to recommend we do… we've got to freeze a couple of those orgasms."

"What for?" I snapped.

"…in case you ever want kids."

"Can't I just make sure I have one in me when I meet the girl I wanna marry?"

331

"Well, exactly how old are you?"

"23."

"Then, realistically, I don't think you'll last that long."

I felt insulted. "What's that supposed to mean?"

"Look, you're a fine looking dude in a city with some very attractive women… I don't think it's gonna take you long to use up those six. Hell, I'd give it only a year."

"So you just want me to freeze a load cause you don't trust me?"

"A load? I'm afraid I'll need three."

"But I'd only want one kid?"

"It's three per kid."

"So you want me to give up half?" At the age of 23, I hadn't given much thought to kids. This would count as my first major investment towards them. I tried to think rationally, but this was a big decision and my anxiety wasn't helping. What if my future wife wanted kids and I couldn't supply them? Would she leave me? There's always adoption, but what if I wanted my kids to be like me. What if my wife wanted our kids to be like us. What's more important? My kids having my genes, or a couple of extra orgasms. "I might do it."

"I'm not forcing you…"

"I've been putting out a lot lately. I just don't know if I trust myself."

"Listen, let's space them out, that way you can cherish them," suggested the doctor. "How about once a week for the next three weeks? I doubt you'll use them all up by then. Unless you get a girlfriend… if you get a girlfriend, please call me."

I didn't end up getting a girlfriend. I was, in fact, in no mood to date. I was kind of in a state of panic for the next couple of months. In this time frame, I had to make some quick and painful transitions. One, I gave up on wearing my fun shirts, they added too much temptation to my life. I didn't go back to polos however, I just stuck with blank cotton crew-necks you can buy in bulk at Walmart. I paired them with mesh gym shorts. These were the most asexual garments I could think of. I immediately noticed a lot less people striking up conversations with me. I started to just blend into the background.

The next big transition I had to make was giving up porn. I couldn't watch it anymore or I'd risk the temptation to shoot one off to some meaningless images. I didn't know yet how exactly I wanted to spend these orgasms, but I was certain they'd be spent on real people.

Giving up masturbation actually ended up freeing up some time before bed. And after work. And sometimes after breakfast. The point is I had extra time to fill and, considering I no longer expressed myself through clothing, I thought expressing myself through a hobby could lighten things up a bit. I went with turning my succulents into a vertical garden on my balcony.

"It's so wonderfully verdant." As soon as my true colors showed through, a new girl appeared in my life. Her name was Soline. She lived two apartments over. She was sipping a Mad Dog margarita on her balcony when she saw me wedging cacti into my trellis. She immediately abandoned her beverage to knock on my door and see my work.

"I might do this with my orchids," she said, brushing the back of her hand against the spines of my prickly pear.

I could tell where this was going and I was concerned. I hadn't considered sex since I fell into my deep depression, but it might just be what I need to snap out of it. After all, there was no saying I needed to cum during sex. People fake it all the time. I just wondered if I'd get any of that sweet, sweet stress release from the act if I didn't finish.

"I can't tell if you're enjoying this," commented Soline as she rode me. "You look kind of distracted."

It turns out having sex while worrying about controlling your orgasms is actually a very stressful experience, especially when your partner was setting the pace. I flipped our position and got on top of her, hoping that with me in control of the strokes I'd feel more comfortable. But any time I felt any good sensation, I just got more nervous that a climax would sneak up on me. I realized how impossible this was going to be to enjoy, so I decided to call it quits early.

I pumped really hard for thirty-seconds all while making a ridiculous amount of noise with my breathing. I then stopped, wiped the sweat off my face, and curled up intimately against Soline. I gave her a kiss on the cheek as if to say "finished".

"Uh… can you help me get off too?" she asked, followed by a small laugh.

"Uh, sure," I said with a shrug. "Can I just use my fingers?"

"No…" she replied with a look of confusion. "I'd just do it myself then."

"Sounds like a plan." I got up out of bed and began sliding my clothes back on. Soline looked pissed. She got off of my bed and grabbed her underwear off my floor. She didn't bother putting it on. She stuffed it into a ball and covered her top. She ran out my

334

door and made the quick trek to her own apartment while half-naked.

Me and Soline never spoke again. I didn't feel too bad about it; after all I needed to experiment with the concept of having sex again and there was undoubtedly going to be some awkwardness. I considered maybe trying again with a different girl, but this time using a different type of condom with a numbing agent inside it. They sell those so couples can last longer. But then I realized, at that point, I wouldn't be getting any stimulation at all during sex. I suppose I could enjoy the fact that my partner was enjoying it, but in that case I'd really have to like the person for that to matter to me.

Till the day I'd meet this special girl, I decided to abstain from having sex at all. There were some exceptions, however; exceptions where I'd be willing to sacrifice an orgasm. They were rare circumstances: sex with multiple girls at once, sex with a celebrity, and sex with a crush from my childhood.

These conditions seemed like they would take years to meet and, had I let my condition keep me indoors, it probably would have. However, after speaking with a therapist, I came to the conclusion that not all social activities had to come with the possibility of meeting someone for sex. You can just participate in a community garden for the sole purpose of making friends and flexing your green thumb.

This is where I'd meet Devon and Hess, who would become my go-to friends for drinking on the weekends. We'd go out to bars and talk about our weeks at work. Then Devon would diverge from the pack and do some flirting, while me and Hess played arcade games or did some karaoke.

"I thought that was you on stage," said a familiar voice as I stepped away from the microphone. I'd just done a throaty rendition of Cher's "Believe". "I can barely recognize you. You dress differently."

"Kind of boring?" I asked.

The lady nodded.

Upon closer inspection, I recognized her face and I placed a name. It was Nichole. We went to the same high school. There was never any romantic tension; it was all feverish animosity. We tirelessly competed to be the most interesting person in our high school, constantly updating our styles in an "I'm different" arms race. At one point my hair color was shifting faster than an RGB keyboard and I ran out of places to stick a ring. I guess one could argue that our competition had a certain passion in it, but she was never the girl I dreamed of taking to the prom. It was close to a childhood crush, but not near enough to make me feel completely comfortable wasting an orgasm. That is, assuming she even wanted to have sex.

"I hope this isn't too forward, but I'm looking for someone to fuck my face."

She was certainly putting out some strong signals. I had to hold back however, a childhood rival just isn't the same as a childhood crush. However, soon fate would bring more to the table.

An older woman suddenly appeared over Nichole's shoulder. She looked less than amused. "You want to get going soon," she yelled in Nichole's ear. "There's literally no one here I'd like to see naked."

"Maybe you should get going. I think your friend needs you."

"Oh that's not my friend, it's my agent," explained Nichole.

"So... you're a singer?"

"Oh, no," Nichole looked up at the stage and shrugged. "The karaoke night's just coincidental. I'm an actress. I couldn't sing to save my life."

"How big of an actress?"

"I have an IMDb page."

I Googled her name, right there in front of her. I was disappointed with what I saw. There were acting credits, she wasn't lying, but there were no theatrical releases, it was all straight-to-streaming.

"Christmas with the Kranks 2: Party in Peru," I read sullenly. "I had no idea it merited a sequel."

Nichole nodded with a smile.

"Are you two going to go at it or what?" called out Nichole's agent. She bit down on the edge of a plastic martini glass. "I could probably just get myself off to you two. As long as he faces away from me."

"What's that now?" I asked.

"She's a voyeur," sighed Nichole with an eye roll. "She likes to watch couples do it, but she won't participate."

"Ew," sneered the agent. "That wouldn't be very classy."

At that point I realized I had a tough decision to make. This situation didn't meet any one of my parameters perfectly, and yet it slightly touched on all three. It would be a sort-of threesome, with a maybe celebrity, who used to be my childhood meh. I had no reason to rush things and I had plenty of time to achieve one of my goals in their perfect state. And yet, I realized there was a chance that this opportunity may never come again and I'd look back on this loss with regret.

"I'm in."

It had been four months since my last orgasm. I remembered them lasting longer. The amount of semen I unloaded into the condom almost burst the reservoir. It would have been impressive to see it fly, but I'm not raw-dogging anyone with a venereal disease. I wouldn't wish this curse on anybody.

At this point, three of my six orgasms had gone to my doctor and the fourth had now gone to a mediocre quasi-threeway. I say mediocre because it turns out Nichole has really gotten over her need to appear unique. She fucks like a diagram in a Sex Ed class. No twists. No surprises. Also, the agent watching us made things super awkward. She didn't touch herself or seem amused by us fucking at all. She just sits in this steel chair cross-legged and looks as though someone is forcing her to watch her grandparents make whoopie.

With two orgasms left, I changed my conditions, convincing myself that I wouldn't waste another load on a woman unless she was the woman I loved. To some extent, I stuck to my principles.

The next time I'd orgasm was a year later. At this point I was going out for drinks with Devon and Hess at least four nights of every week. It was a bond I never had with female friends in the past. I think our friendship might have crystallized easier once they knew I had so many rules about sex. There was never any doubt that I was in it for the laughs, not the fucking. It helped build trust in two girls who had both been prospected by their male friends in the past.

It was different having female friends, they talked about men as much as my guy friends talked about women. But they're far more vulgar.

"So he wanted me to stimulate his prostate, which is fine and all, I've done it before," explained Hess, "but I ended up sticking six fingers up his ass."

"Like a whole fist… then a pinkie?" asked Devon.

Hess shook her head. "Like three fingers each hand. He was very specific."

"You ever ask for anything like that, y'know, when you could?" asked Devon, staring at me.

"No. I never had enough sex to get that jaded."

"It has nothing to do with being jaded!" argued Devon. "It's a whole other feeling. Deep and sensual. You really should feel it before you run out of opportunities."

"Well… if I'm going to do it, I'm not gonna half-ass it, so to speak," I explained. "I should try it to its ultimate extent, to make sure I get the most out of it. So, not just a finger. I'm thinking a dildo. Maybe a buttplug."

"Well Brexon, why not a dick?" suggested Devon. I waited for her snicker, but she seemed dead serious.

"A dick?" I exclaimed.

"Yeah!" replied Hess. "I mean sometimes we talk about men… and you talk too."

"Oh…" I felt embarrassed; kind of misunderstood. "I'm just trying to feel included. I mean, if my guy friends talk about a

339

girl, I might not actually be that interested in that girl, but I talk about her too so as to not be rude. I want to do the same for you two."

"But you mention things… things only someone might notice if they had real experience analyzing a man for… y'know… sexual purposes."

"Like when?"

Devon smiled. "You called John Livick's forearm a masterpiece in texture mapping."

I shrugged. "The tops like a field of wheat. The bottom's like a map of the Rio Grande."

"Details like that… it just makes me wonder. Are you sure you're not gay?"

"I mean I like sex with women."

"Then maybe you're bi!" called out Devon.

"What if it turns out you like sex with men more?" asked Hess. "I mean you have two orgasms left. What if you waste them on girls, when you were always meant to spend them on boys?"

"I guess I could use one to…" I dropped my sentence and sighed from the frustration. "Is now really the time to experiment though?"

"You should know which one you prefer before you run out completely. It's gonna be hard enough to find somebody to marry without ever being able to orgasm for them. If you can add men to that list, it might help your chances…"

"That's kind of negative, Devon," sneered Hess.

340

Devon shrugged. "I'm just saying, men don't care if their partner cums. Not nearly as much as women. Life would be far easier for our dear friend Brexon..."

Finding a man could be as easy as letting Devon and Hess drag me to a gay bar, but I didn't want it to be that easy. I wanted to dilate our plans; make it last. I wanted to prolong the end of my sex life as much as I could, so I waited for a sign.

"Ope!" I yelped. "Damn, that's stuck inside their pretty good." Six weeks ago I added a separate section dedicated entirely to succulents in the northwest corner of the community garden. I was so used to little soft whiskers I could pet without gardening gloves because that's all I like to plant. So when I saw someone add their own succulents to my mix I was so excited I did my usual pet and ended up with a massive prickle shoved into my thumbprint.

"You just touch other people's plants without asking?" said a voice behind me.

I turned and saw a handsome man in his 40's with long blonde hair approaching me. I immediately noticed Dr. Wright on his t-shirt and knew he was special.

"Do you regret what you've done?" he asked me with a stern face.

I tried pulling out one of the spines and it wouldn't budge. I felt my flesh tearing, and I hissed with my teeth clenched. I looked at the man and nodded.

He broke into a warm smile. "This is a cholla cactus," he explained. "The spines are barbed, so you can't just yank them out." He reached into his pocket and pulled out a hair comb with thick teeth. He grabbed my hand. I blushed a little. He placed

341

the teeth of the comb against the heel of my hand, then coyishly pushed it upwards toward my fingertips. When it passed over the point of insertion, the tip of the thorn popped right out. "You see. The trick is delicacy."

In case you haven't read the story of Androcles & the Lion, it's a parable about the reciprocation of mercy. A runaway slave pulls a thorn out of a lion's paw and in return the lion spares the slave's life when he's condemned to death by wild animals some time later. Similarly, I also showed the 40-year-old man with the long blonde hair, Thane, my mercy. I showed it to him, he ate it, and then he stuck his dick in it.

"I'm gonna pass…" I explained to Devon. I called her as soon as it ended.

"It hurt?"

"No it felt great," I replied, "It was stronger. I felt it everywhere. It radiated. And the length was huge. Easily twenty-five seconds, maybe even half a minute. But the whole time he's fucking me, I've got my eyes closed, and I'm imagining he's a woman."

"So your last one should be with a lady then?" asked Devon. "Like a trans lady? Or is she just wearing a strap-on."

"It doesn't matter," I tried to explain. "I realize that maximizing the pleasure is never going to be as fulfilling as just having the right partner."

Devon went silent, then she sighed in frustration. "I think spending it on someone you love is a huge mistake and I think you should reconsider," said Devon, suddenly serious.

I squinted my eyes. I didn't know what she was getting at. "It's the mature decision."

342

"It's a selfish decision. Right now it's only your problem, but if you start dating someone seriously, suddenly it's both your problem," countered Devon. "You've got to both worry about when you're going to use it. Cause let's face facts, when you get to the point of intimacy you're talking about, you're both using it."

I tried to consider what she was saying. "You're saying it's selfish to share my final orgasm with my future wife."

"Empty the clip before you start dating, Brexon," warned Devon. "Or I guarantee you, it'll cause you far more stress than it's worth."

I heeded her warning throughout my remaining months in Houston. And every time we went out she gave me a refresher, inching me closer and closer to doing it without the love. But before she got what she wanted, something pulled me away from her.

After a year-and-a-half of good work in Houston, my boss Arjun pulled me into his office to deliver the bad news. "The Beaumont well is all dried up. They no longer need our input."

"Ask them for another well to work on," I begged.

"We promised them ten good years of shale production. They got seven."

"That's not far off."

"It's not good enough. They moved on and they're not recommending us." Arjun sighed, then smiled at me. "Good news is, I'm recommending you."

"For what?"

"Hydrogeology. Water's the new oil," said Arjun with a confident smile. "I'm moving to a new company and I'd like to bring you with me. We'll be building reliable water options for rural communities."

"...right here in Houston?"

Arjun's smile dropped. His face strained. "No..."

Strang, Nebraska. I was going to be living in a town with less than a thousand people.

"Let's not panic, here, Brexon," replied Hess. "There's other pipelines in Texas..."

"None that will pay this well," I explained. "160K at 25 years old."

"When you came to Houston, you chose to stop caring so much about a salary. Where's that Brexon?" countered Hess.

"I chose to stop talking about my salary. No one said I stopped caring."

Hess lowered her chin and stared down at the table.

"Let him go," huffed Devon with a moue of disappointment, "but good luck finding a Nebraskan who can sympathize with something as delicate and complicated as a lifelong STD."

"Yeah no, I've got HIV," explained Liam, a beautiful physical therapist I met on my third day in Strang. "Got it from a boy at the Kool-Aid Days festival. We should go next year."

I met Liam the same way I met plenty of girls back in Houston. I brought back the funky t-shirts, but this time with a twist. I

344

wanted a long-term relationship, so I wasn't going to be shy about my most controversial feature. I decided to wear my MBC on my chest like an advertisement. I ordered a custom t-shirt with our awareness ribbon, pansy purple of course, and the tagline "One shot left."

Liam saw me at the gym and was intrigued about what corner of pathology my ribbon represented and whether or not it was I or a loved one infected. Once I shared the concept of my STD; she felt confident in sharing her own.

"I mean, technically, I have unlimited orgasms, but it sure doesn't feel like that," explained Liam. "I think that every STD limits your sex life in one way or another. There's no avoiding some new inhibitions. For me, I used to sleep with everyone in this town. Now it's one person and they also got HIV. They show up on my doorstep maybe once, twice a month. Before this disease, my average was five lays a week."

"Are they just afraid to get the disease?"

Liam nodded. "But I take my ART, so my levels are too low to pass on. Combine that with basic protection and no one should be uncomfortable with fucking me. But let's face it, I'm the girl with AIDS, and whether or not they think they'll get it, that title just doesn't turn people on."

I shook my head. "I disagree. I'm ready to fucking do this."

Liam looked at me with surprise. She smiled. She was going to say something, then she stopped. She itched the back of her neck nervously, then looked inside the women's locker room at the gym. "It's empty..." she said with a sneaky grin.

The first couple of months in our relationship, we got creative so that I didn't feel so nervous about accidentally busting a load. We did activities that didn't directly involve my crotch. There

345

are so many different types of oral, so that lasted a while. And then we started using toys, including a strap-on; which I should mention does come in a specific size that fits over the male anatomy. It's sort of like an athletic cup with a dick growing out of it. I didn't think this was invented yet so I was delightfully surprised.

I only started using my real dick again when we reached about half a year. At this point, I'd built up enough confidence with Liam that I decided to give edging a try; where I build up the sensation in my dick right before orgasm, then suddenly stop. That lasted us a good three months, over which we shared some of the most intimate moments of my life. I'd say my first time "making love" was with her, which was extra special considering, if you think about it, it never ended for me. This is why it pains me so much when, one night, she broke my trust.

"What was that?" I lamented in the dark. Things had gotten out of hand and I distanced myself from her. I sat at the side of the bed playing with the sweat on my chest hairs.

"What was what?" She sounded clueless.

"I told you to stop," I explained, sully, "but you just kept riding me."

"I wanted to see how far we could push it," she quickly responded.

"Well that's kind of careless," I fussed. "What if I went off?"

"So what?" she shrugged.

My mouth gaped in disbelief. I shook my head angrily.

"I mean I thought we were at 'so what'…" she sneered.

I started to get frustrated with all the coded lingo. "Define 'so what'!"

"So what if you cum, you're doing it with the love of your life…"

"…but if we can control it…"

"You do love me don't you?"

"Yes, I love you!" I huffed. "But that doesn't mean… I don't want to save this for a special day."

"Today was special…" shrugged Liam, "you took me out to dinner. I had a nice time."

"But I need it to be like the night of my proposal," I suggested. "Or what about the night of our wedding?"

"Ew no!" exclaimed Liam. "God, you're gonna make it so corny! Like I'm deflowering you in some weird ritual. I don't want to plan this out so much. I want to share an organic moment with you."

"This wasn't organic. This was selfish."

"Selfish?" cried out Liam. "What do you mean?"

I kept quiet. I shook my head, then I said softly, "I take it back."

"No really?" pressed Liam. "Do you think I'd try to steal it from you? Like it's some priceless treasure I can just run away with."

"Like I said, I take it back…" I sighed. "I just want to make sure you understand, I'm waiting for the right time."

Liam shook her head. "No Brexon, I'm afraid… you're still waiting for the right person." She grabbed my bed sheets and

347

dried her eyes. She got changed and left. I didn't go chasing after her. I wasn't feeling well. I was confused.

Things got more messy with every passing night. Sex became an awkward chore. The whole time I knew I couldn't pleasure her. I knew she wanted me to cum and I couldn't give her that. At the same time, she couldn't pleasure me. She knew I was paranoid about her 'stealing' the last of my vigor. Nobody was satisfied and it became impossible for us to enjoy our time together.

For brief stints, I would lean toward just using it up just to get it over with so we could go back to the way things were. But Liam couldn't do it, she thought it felt forced, like we were sweeping a larger issue under the rug. In a way, we were, but I was perfectly fine doing it if it meant enjoying the love of my life again.

"I don't know what to do," I cried into the phone. I'd called Hess looking for some advice from the opposite sex. "I feel trapped between a rock and a hard place."

"Oh I know this seems like a lot right now, but I'm sure you'll - wait, I'm talking to him - you can wait your turn!" Suddenly, I heard the phone fumbling around. Then, a new voice came over the line. It was far less sweet and far more steely.

"Brexon, we need to talk…" It was Devon. I didn't want to talk to Devon. I didn't want to admit that she was right. "Look, you don't have to admit I was right."

I was all ears.

"You were a good friend and I just want to see you in the perfect relationship," she continued. "Please listen… are you listening?"

I sighed. "Yes. Go on. Tell me."

"Porn, Brexon," suggested Devon. "Porn. Any porn. Your favorite porn."

"Devon, no," I groaned.

"Just get rid of it! I don't need to remind you how much it's already screwed with you. Just get rid of it and you get on with the rest of your life... with the rest of your relationship!"

"But if I don't use it on her, I'll feel like I'm betraying her."

"Sure. Good point," replied Devon, "but there's a way around that.."

The day of my last orgasm was a Sunday, a holy day. Liam left the apartment around noon to help her mother pick up groceries. I stayed behind and prepared the ceremony. It began with me stripping down to my socks. I was going to be releasing a lot of fluids and I didn't want them to get all over my clothes. My socks were already white, so that didn't matter as much.

I then had to choose between using my phone or my computer. I went with my phone only because I already had a whole cache of naughty pictures saved on there.

There was then the choice of position. I know some guys prefer sitting up while they do it, as that's how they learned to do it while sitting at their family's desktop, but I'm used to doing it before sleeping. I decided to just lie down on my couch; I'd just made the bed and I didn't feel like making it again.

Once I was comfortable, I started touching myself. I had one hand on my phone, flipping through the images with my thumb. The other hand was stroking. First tenderly and slow, like petting my plants. Then hard and fast like pulling out the weeds.

I took a quick break to get my mind off of gardening. It was a trick I used to do while Liam rode on top of me to distract my mind and keep myself from cumming. But this time was different.

Suddenly the friction in my hand grew into such a mighty heat that it felt like the real thing. I shut my eyes and saw little blue and green circles dilating wider and wider till they disappeared from sight. The contractions, my final contractions, grew closer and closer together. I felt the warm buzz glowing in the core of my dick. It got stronger and stronger till I couldn't hold it back.

It felt like a warm slug had just hopped on my face. I aimed my streams upward so that they'd land on my chest, but the first few were too powerful and they made it past my neck. After the first three, the force weakened and they fell beneath my tits. I felt the more watery blasts lose stick and start to flow into my navel.

I just sat there for a moment and let the oxytocin rest in my head. As long as I didn't move a muscle the feeling just stayed there, a bright white star floating behind my eyes. I didn't want it to end, but in case Liam brought her mother home with her, I needed to clean up and make it look like it never happened.

I stood up and gravity pulled all the slime downwards. I quickly ran to get some paper towels before any of it fell to the floor. Half a roll later and the job was done. I was dry; with little patches of dried mucus and towel fibers left behind on my belly. I put my clothes back on and waited for Liam to come home.

At dinner that night I told her the truth about what I'd done. "I recorded it all," I explained to her. I pulled out a video on my phone, a split shot with my screen shared at the bottom and my reactions shown on top. She could see me touch myself as I scrolled through the nudes.

"They're pictures of me?" she said inquisitively.

350

"They're pictures of you!" I replied excitedly. I'd used the folder of Liam's nudes hidden in a fake calculator app; pictures she's been sending me since the start of our relationship.

I played the video up the point where I finished. A stream of white foam hit the camera in the last still-frame.

Liam took the phone out of my hands and watched it again. "I suppose this is… unexpected."

"And you wanted it to be unexpected!" I said, looking proud of myself.

"And it's also me…"

"And you wanted it to be you!"

Liam nodded, but her face still looked sullen. "But did you get what you needed out of it?"

I nodded. "I wanted it to be you too, babe." I said with a grin.

With my ATP used up, I was immediately curious as to what my dick could still do. Feeling a strain lifted from our relationship, myself and Liam went straight to testing it out.

"It just!" she exhaled. "It just keeps going!" It turns out, with no ability to cum, my dick just stays hard forever; meaning Liam can enjoy herself for much longer than before. She didn't need to stop or slow down to give me time to cool off, so as soon as she felt the waves crashing she was really able to dive in. I may have been out of climaxes, but she now had more than enough for the two of us.

As we got older, we would eventually get married and try having kids. As long as Liam took her ART, there was no risk of

351

our child getting her disease. Unfortunately, none of my three sperm samples connected with her eggs. So, we ended up adopting anyway.

Every now and then I make a new acquaintance who tries to pity me for my condition. They look at me like I'm a eunuch. They pat my back and look deep into my eyes. "Are you really okay?" they ask, trying to draw out some secretly suicidal subconscious. "Could there ever be a cure?"

I shrugged. It wasn't something I dwelled on. Sometimes I did think it'd be funny if there was one, and they filmed one of those videos like they do when they give deaf people those hearing aids. I come out of the bathroom after masturbating for the first time in twenty years and everyone just starts clapping and cheering.

I'm not going to argue that anything is better than an orgasm, but when you're denied orgasms for so long, you do forget what they're like and so you question it. Is this brownie batter better than an orgasm? Is this fat joint better than sex? Sometimes, I can convince myself they are. And so, it's not a bad life.

Epilogue

A vegan is surprised by the life of a vegetarian. The vegetarian spends their Sunday mornings eating eggs at old diners and their Summer nights eating ice cream from trucks. They feel sophisticated pairing their wines with the perfect cheeses. They have a reliance on animals that vegans need not feel tethered by.

A vegetarian is surprised by the life of a carnivore. The carnivore celebrates his business success with a comically large steak served from a five-star restaurant. They eat sushi on vacation. They have fond memories of their mother's roast on Christian holidays. They rely on the murder of animals in order to feel warmth and victory.

An omnivore is not surprised by the life of the vegan, or the vegetarian, or the carnivore. They can pick and choose from all of their experiences. They test all of their emotions in various different combinations. They can rely on plants to feed them, or animals, alive or dead.

The omnivore is only surprised by the life of a cannibal. Human flesh is the one limit to the omnivore's plate. As we've seen, the cannibal is wracked with guilt for what they've consumed; far more than any fast-fooder can feel for a mere cow or chicken. Arsenio and Joss have to live in constant fear that some dark-half inside them will break out and devour the innocent. Cannibals like Sandeyu and Mago didn't even kill the men they ate, yet they are now tied to that murder solely for having feasted on its spoils.

Cannibals feel otherwise unattainable highs as well. Bonny Bride struck a Faustian bargain for fame and stardom. Greige Wagner defeated infertility. Cassius Crown made literal magic happen.

353

These people have experienced police investigations, secret organizations, and spiritual confirmations. The life of a cannibal cannot be mundane because the mundane do not cannibalize. When faced with a hard decision, the mundane choose to starve on the island. They choose to follow gods blindly. They choose to go childless and fameless. They let witches steal their souls and they leave their romantic fantasies to the imagination.

We should read from cannibals because there is so much to take from cannibals. But can we copy their boldness without eating each other?

Made in the USA
Middletown, DE
12 August 2024